The Academy

ALSO BY ELIN HILDERBRAND

The Beach Club
Nantucket Nights
Summer People
The Blue Bistro
The Love Season
Barefoot
A Summer Affair
The Castaways
The Island
Silver Girl
Summerland
Beautiful Day
The Matchmaker
Winter Street
The Rumor
Winter Stroll

Here's to Us
Winter Storms
The Identicals
Winter Solstice
The Perfect Couple
Winter in Paradise
Summer of '69
What Happens in Paradise
28 Summers
Troubles in Paradise
Golden Girl
The Hotel Nantucket
The Five-Star Weekend
Swan Song
The Blue Book

The Academy

Elin Hilderbrand and
Shelby Cunningham

Little, Brown and Company
New York   Boston   London

The characters and events in this book are fictitious. Any similarity to real persons, living or dead, is coincidental and not intended by the authors.

Copyright © 2025 by Elin Hilderbrand and Shelby Cunningham

Hachette Book Group supports the right to free expression and the value of copyright. The purpose of copyright is to encourage writers and artists to produce the creative works that enrich our culture.

The scanning, uploading, and distribution of this book without permission is a theft of the authors' intellectual property. If you would like permission to use material from the book (other than for review purposes), please contact permissions@hbgusa.com. Thank you for your support of the authors' rights.

Little, Brown and Company
Hachette Book Group
1290 Avenue of the Americas, New York, NY 10104
littlebrown.com

First Edition: September 2025
Published simultaneously in the UK by Quercus

Little, Brown and Company is a division of Hachette Book Group, Inc. The Little, Brown name and logo are trademarks of Hachette Book Group, Inc.

The publisher is not responsible for websites (or their content) that are not owned by the publisher.

The Hachette Speakers Bureau provides a wide range of authors for speaking events. To find out more, go to hachettespeakersbureau.com or email hachettespeakers@hbgusa.com.

Little, Brown and Company books may be purchased in bulk for business, educational, or promotional use. For information, please contact your local bookseller or the Hachette Book Group Special Markets Department at special.markets@hbgusa.com.

ISBN 9780316567855 (hardcover) / 9780316580779 (large print) / 9780316596176 (signed edition) / 9780316596183 (B&N signed edition) / 9780316597838 (international)
LCCN 2025930866

Printing 1, 2025

LSC-H

Printed in the United States of America

*For our beloved mother/grandmother
Dr. Sally Hilderbrand,
lifelong educator.
Thank you for blazing the trail as a strong, independent woman.*

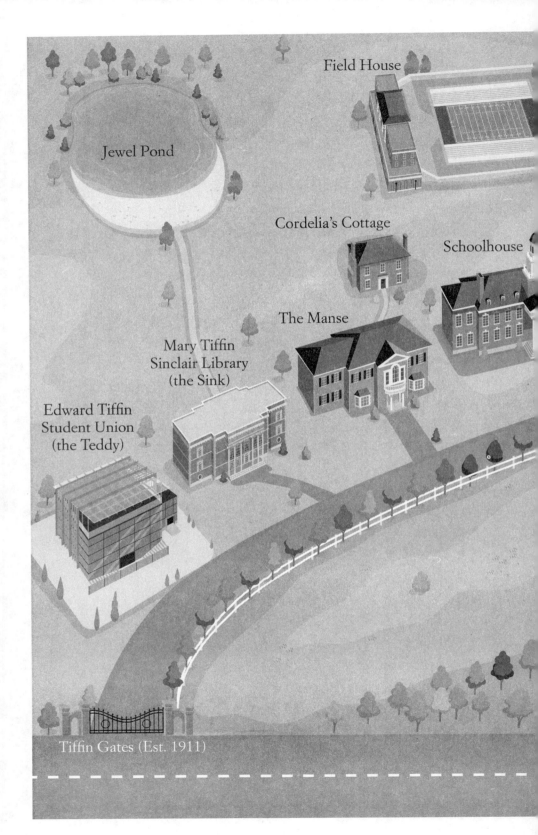

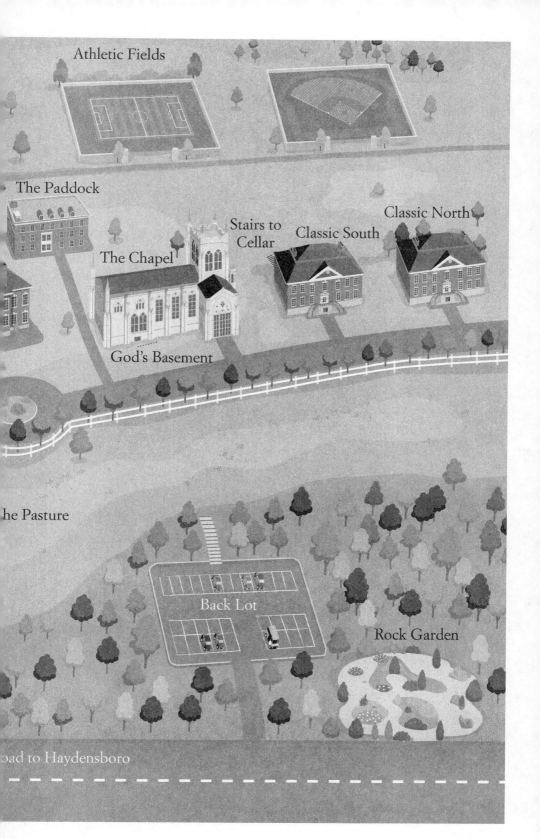

Who's Who at Tiffin Academy

The Administration

President, Board of Directors: Jesse Eastman
Head of School: Audre Robinson
Director of Tiffin Admissions: Cordelia Spooner
Head of Security: Michael James
Head Chef: Harrison "Haz" Flanders
School Chaplain: Laura Rae Splaine
College Counselor: Honey Vandermeid
Athletic Director: Coach Pete Bosworth

The Faculty

Simone Bergeron (History)
Felipe Chuy (Music and Theater Director)
Roy Ewanick (Math)
Alejandro Perez (Spanish)
Rhode Rivera (English)
Kent Wully (Science)
Ruth Wully (English)

The Students

Notable Fifth-Formers

Webber "Dub" Austin
Davi Banerjee
Tilly Benbow
Andrew "East" Eastman
Charlotte "Charley" Hicks
Olivia Hudezech-Tottingknaffer
Madison J. (Floor Prefect)
Willow Levy
Hakeem Pryce
Royce Stringfellow
Taylor Wilson
In Memoriam: Cinnamon Peters

Notable Sixth-Formers

Teague Baldwin
Lisa Kim (Head Prefect)
Ravenna Rapsicoli (Editor, *'Bred Bulletin*)
Annabelle Tuckerman

September

1. Move-In Day

At nine a.m. on Tuesday, September 2, just as the chapel bells are heralding the start of a new school year, the first vehicles proceed onto the campus of Tiffin Academy. Every student for the past 114 years has traveled the same route: through the wrought-iron gates, down the Pasture lined with shade maples and white horse fencing, past the "Teddy" (the Edward Tiffin Student Union) and the "Sink" (the Mary Tiffin Sinclair Library), around the circle in front of the Schoolhouse, and along the stretch of freshly mowed athletic fields to the dormitories—Classic North (boys) and Classic South (girls).

Monogrammed duffel bags, mini fridges, field hockey sticks, guitar cases, snowshoes, beanbag chairs, cross-country skis, wireless speakers, makeup mirrors, LED strip lights, extra-long twin sheet sets, skateboards, scooters, a Frank Ocean poster. Audre Robinson—who is in her sixth year as Head of School—helps unload exactly one item from each vehicle. In her first year as Head, she wore a raspberry linen sheath and stacked heels and stood atop the Schoolhouse steps waving to the processional of cars as though she were some kind of royalty. This was how the Heads of School who preceded Audre—all of them white men—comported themselves on Move-In Day. But Audre found it made her feel silly and uncomfortable, not to mention lonely, and so in year two, she donned a pair of mom jeans and a hunter-green Tiffin Thoroughbreds T-shirt (available from the school store for $17.95) and greeted each student and their parent(s) or guardian(s) with a smile, a handshake or (for the returning students she favored) a hug, and the ceremonial unloading assistance.

Audre thinks of each new school year as a blank composition book, a fresh box of sharpened pencils—but this reveals her age. To these kids, it's...what? An empty Google doc, the cursor blinking at the top of a laptop screen?

Audre is also thinking, *Nothing bad has happened...yet.* For example, no one has appeared at Audre's residence between breakfast and Chapel to say that the door to 111 South is jammed and Cinnamon Peters isn't responding to either knocks or FaceTimes.

She's always the first one up, Cinnamon's best friend, Davi Banerjee, said on that fateful day last spring. It was Davi, the queen bee of her class, who was dispatched to the Residence to alert Audre because the head of security, Mr. James, didn't come on duty until ten. *I think something's wrong.*

Something was, in fact, wrong. Hideously, tragically wrong.

Audre shivers despite the heat of the day—early September is still full summer; the temperature is nearing eighty even at this early hour—and she forces a smile for the next car, a Hyundai Sonata with Georgia plates, a rental. Audre sees a woman with a graying ponytail wearing a GO 'BREDS T-shirt in the driver's seat, and on the passenger side, a boy hunched over his knees. *That's what happens,* Audre thinks, *when you accordion a six-foot-four frame into a midsize sedan.*

It's Webber "Dub" Austin, the Thoroughbreds' starting quarterback. He unfolds himself from the car, removes his massive headphones, and rolls his sunglasses up into his bushy hair, which has gotten a few shades lighter over the summer. He has tan lines on his face where his sunglasses rest. *What does Dub do for a summer job?* Audre wonders. *Park ranger? Ranch hand?* The hair will be shaved off by tomorrow. In his cowboy accent, Dub says, "Mornin', Ms. Robinson."

"Dub," Audre says, and she rounds the car to give the boy a hug.

By the end of the month, Audre will know every student by name, though she occasionally gets tripped up by all the Madisons and Olivias. She tries not to have favorites—but she feels extra protective of this year's fifth-form. They've been through a lot.

The mother climbs out. The students have a joke where they call one another's mothers "Karen," but Dub's mother is actually named Karen, Karen Austin. She's the single mom of four boys, of whom Dub is number three; he's attending on a full scholarship (athletic, though in his case, need-based as well). Dub's oldest brother played football at Colorado State; the second brother is a wide receiver at CU Boulder. Then there's Dub. But the real star is apparently the youngest brother, who is starting quarterback as a freshman for their high school back in Durango.

Audre doesn't usually retain this much information about the students' families—especially those who never donate—but she has had an earful on the Austin family from Coach Pete Bosworth.

Audre gives Karen a hug as well, and Karen says in her ear, "How're you doing?"

Audre has anticipated being asked this question several times today, and so she's formulated an answer that she hopes strikes the right tone. (What *is* the right tone when a student has died by suicide on your watch, but you have 239 other kids in your care who deserve a top-notch educational experience?)

"We're all still hurting," Audre says. "But optimistic about the year ahead."

Karen releases Audre and says with watering eyes, "Good for you."

"How's Dub handling it?" Audre asks in a whisper, though it's doubtful he'll hear her. He's been out of the car for mere seconds and is already being swarmed by Olivia P., Madison R., and Olivia H-T.

Karen stares at the car key she's gripping in her hand. "You know, he's my sensitive one." Then she snaps back into her no-nonsense boy-mom persona and calls out, "Hey, Romeo, help me get this shit out of the car, please."

Audre opens the Sonata's back door. Sticking out of a gaping duffel bag is a framed picture of Dub and Cinnamon Peters last Halloween—they went as Travis Kelce and Taylor Swift—with Dub's hand placed chastely on Cinnamon's upper back. All the other students considered them #couplegoals. They weren't gross, they didn't make out in public, you never heard rumors about them "joining the Harkness Society" (having sex on the Harkness tables) or sneaking down to God's Basement below the chapel, though they were always together, deep in conversation, laughing. Cinnamon cheered from the sidelines with her face painted green and gold when Dub played football. Dub sat in the front row on the opening night of the high school musical, a bouquet of convenience store roses on his lap. Cinnamon was Sandy in *Grease*.

At the memorial service in the chapel, Dub called Cinnamon a "friend of his heart." Not a dry eye, of course.

Audre leaves the duffel bag where it is and grabs a bulk-size box of protein bars from the trunk instead. Her cell phone buzzes in the back pocket of her jeans, but she has to wait for a break between cars before she can check it.

It's a text from Jesse Eastman, known to all, including Audre's phone, as "Big East," the president of Tiffin's board of directors.
Have you seen the rankings yet?

Ugh, Audre thinks.

Before coming to Tiffin, Audre served as Head at an all-girls day school in New Orleans. She didn't know a national ranking of boarding schools even existed, much less how important the rankings in *America Today* were to the board, the alumni, and the parents.

When Audre took over as Head of School, Tiffin was a study in mediocrity, the gentleman's C of boarding schools. Its heyday was long past; the whole place felt like a once-grand hotel desperately in need of a renovation. But alas, there was no money for improvements—they were barely getting by on their operating budget and the teachers hadn't had a raise in four years. Tiffin's ranking in *America Today* (released annually the day after Labor Day) reflected their complacency: They usually appeared somewhere in the lowest tenth of the top fifty—numbers forty-six through forty-nine—and this probably only as a nod to their esteemed past.

But three years ago, Audre—and Cordelia Spooner, head of admissions—met with New York real estate magnate Jesse Eastman about his son, Andrew. Andrew had a "nontraditional" background, which was a euphemism for having been kicked out of two New York City private schools and barely hanging on at a third. Together, Audre and Mrs. Spooner agreed they'd take a chance on admitting Andrew Eastman the following year—and, as tacitly promised, an *enormous* endowment from Jesse Eastman followed.

They've since been able to elevate the entire Tiffin experience—and better rankings in *America Today* have ensued. Two years ago, they rose to number twenty-four (breaking the top twenty-five was a cause for jubilant celebration), and then last year they appeared at number nineteen (and popped the champagne after breaking the top twenty!).

There are even greater expectations for this year, though Audre tries to keep a clear perspective about the rankings. Nobody knows the algorithm, so what does it really *mean*? Old Bennington and Northmeadow—both members of the Independent Schools of New England Coalition, to which Tiffin also belongs—have been ranked numbers one and two respectively since Audre has been at Tiffin. Other perennial achievers are the Phillipses (Exeter and Andover) as well as the Saints (Paul, Mark, Andrew).

It's been rumored that *America Today* dispatches reporters who pose as prospective parents. They take tours and attend admissions information sessions. They ask current students probing questions. Cordelia Spooner is always on the lookout.

Audre won't lie: She's nervous about their ranking this year, especially after what happened in the spring. If Tiffin falls out of the top twenty-five, everyone will blame her and her alone. Just the previous evening, Audre wondered if a dramatic-enough plunge might cause her to lose her job. She shooed the thought away as preposterous, though as a businessman Jesse Eastman is only used to growth, to success. *We have to be ranked nineteen or higher,* Audre thinks, *or there will be hell to pay.*

To Big East's question, Audre replies casually: Not yet. Surely he has an assistant at his zillion-dollar company whose sole duty this morning is to hit refresh on the *America Today* website. He'll know before she does.

When Audre takes a sustaining breath, she smells freshly cut grass and the aroma of bacon (both real and vegan) wafting over from the Paddock. Tiffin's chef is a burly, tattooed gentleman named Harrison "Haz" Flanders, whom Big East hired away from his private club in New York two years earlier. The food in the Paddock — once the subject of a thousand memes — is now so fresh and delicious that nearly the entire Tiffin community has put on the freshman fifteen, Audre included. Chef's specialties are fried chicken and waffles, homemade focaccia, a new salad bar sourced with heirloom vegetables from a local farm. Haz requested a pizza oven (which Big East promptly donated), and now, every Friday at lunch, Audre can look forward to the "rustica" — bubbling mozzarella and smoky pancetta topped with a handful of lightly dressed arugula. Haz also took the edge off Mondays by instituting Burger Night: charbroiled Angus beef with an array of toppings and sauces, followed by an hour at the new Piano Bar in the Teddy, where Mr. Chuy, the music teacher, takes requests and all the kids sing their preppy little hearts out.

Audre starts to hum "Tiny Dancer" as another car pulls up — a shiny black Escalade with tinted back windows and a uniformed driver.

Here's Davi.

Davi hops out of the back seat wearing an enormous pair of sunglasses; white low-waisted, flared jeans; and a crocheted, off-the-shoulder crop top. Her bare midriff is a glaring violation of the Tiffin dress code (forbidden: page 8 of *The Bridle*, Tiffin's Rules of Conduct), but Audre is too shocked by Davi's new look to comment about the top (or lack thereof). Davi has cut off most of her shiny dark hair, which used to reach down past her derriere. It's been replaced by a bob.

She gives Audre a tight hug. "Ms. Robbie," she murmurs. Davi is the only student in six years brave enough to give Audre a nickname, and Audre has to admit, she's fond of it. "Thank god I'm back."

This, Audre thinks, is why she loves her job.

Davi Banerjee, whose parents started the fashion label OOO (Out of Office), is an international influencer. She has 1.3 million devoted Instagram and TikTok followers from twenty-seven countries, and she has more than thirty corporate sponsors. She lives in London with her parents, though Audre has seen, from checking Davi's social media accounts, that she spent most of her summer at her family home in Tuscany, followed by a quick trip to Ibiza with her glamorous European friends.

Audre likes to believe that Davi is universally loved at Tiffin, though the more accurate term might be "revered." Davi rules the social landscape mostly benevolently, though Audre is aware that the other girls spend a lot of precious energy currying favor with her; there's fierce competition to be included in her inner circle. The one person who was exempt from all this was Cinnamon Peters, Davi's best friend since day one at Tiffin.

In the aftermath of Cinnamon's death, Davi organized a

candlelight vigil, directed donations to a reliable mental health organization, and then went dark on social media. There were times in the days following Cinnamon's death when Audre thought the school might have fallen apart were it not for Davi.

"Welcome back," Audre says. "You'll need to change your top before All-School Meeting."

"Yes, I know, I know," Davi says. Her English accent always makes Audre think of chintz and clotted cream. "I promised I'd post myself wearing it...This is the style Akoia Swim named for me." Davi holds her phone up over her head, wraps an arm around Audre's shoulders, and snaps a photo of the two of them with the mullioned windows of Classic South behind them.

Will 1.3 million people now see Audre in her mom jeans? No, she thinks. She isn't cool enough for Davi's Instagram, and for this she's grateful.

"Has the new girl arrived yet?" Davi asks.

There are a number of "new" girls this year—thirty third-formers (freshmen), seven fourth-formers (sophomores)—but they're not who Davi is asking about. Davi is asking about the only new student entering as a fifth-former (junior): Charlotte Hicks from Towson, Maryland, the girl who will be living in 111 South, formerly Cinnamon Peters's room.

"Not yet," Audre says. She heads to the back of the Escalade, where Davi's driver is unloading plastic bins, labeled by designer. Audre reaches for the Hatch alarm clock, new in its box. She feels maternal about Davi. The poor girl flew from London by herself and will be moved into 103 South by a complete stranger. As far as Audre knows, there's only one other student arriving without a parent.

But Audre needn't worry about Davi. Within seconds, she's surrounded by her squad, all of them exclaiming about her hair, her top. *You look so cute!* Phones are brandished, selfies snapped.

This is as good a time as any, Audre thinks, to step away.

Growing up in New Orleans, Audre had heard of "intuitive"

women who were rumored to practice voodoo and have connections to the supernatural. Audre, the daughter of two Tulane professors, viewed this as just another part of New Orleans culture, like jazz and jambalaya. However, Audre herself experiences a fingernails-down-the-proverbial-chalkboard chill from time to time. This "Feeling" has turned out to be prescient: It's a warning that a threat to Audre's peace of mind is imminent.

She has the Feeling now. It could be due to the impending news of the rankings, but on a hunch Audre decides to check the Back Lot.

The Back Lot is where the staff parks, where deliveries are dropped off—and where Mr. James sneaks slugs from his flask of whiskey in his garage office.

As Audre stands at the top of the stairs that lead down to the lot, she sees a black GMC pickup pulling in. Audre hears strains of "Many Men" by 50 Cent pumping out the window; it's so loud she feels it in her tooth fillings.

The truck pulls into its usual spot, the music cuts, the driver gets out. He grew a couple inches over the summer, Audre notes, and his dark hair flops over his aviator sunglasses like he's a character from *Top Gun*. He's wearing Oliver Cabell sneakers, athletic shorts, and a vintage baseball jersey. When he spies Audre, he lifts a hand in greeting.

"Welcome back, Andrew," Audre whispers to herself. She's the only person at Tiffin who calls him by his given name; everyone else calls him East. Andrew Eastman, son of Jesse Eastman, is the only student who's allowed a car, the only student who's allowed to use the service entrance, the only student granted the freedom to do a lot of things. Audre sometimes thinks the question isn't *if* East will get kicked out of Tiffin but *when*—though bringing any kind of disciplinary action against East would be an existential threat to the school.

If East goes, the money goes—and the bright, prosperous future of Tiffin goes. For this reason, Audre has turned a blind eye to his vaping (forbidden: page 2 of *The Bridle*) as well as his barely passing (and by "barely passing," Audre means failing) grades in English and history.

As Audre waves back, she sends East a silent message: *Don't do anything this year I can't forgive. Please.*

Stationed in front of Classic North is Rhode Rivera, the person Audre hired to replace Doc Bellamy, the fossilized English teacher who rarely gave a grade above B and never smiled (he'd retired in the spring after forty-two years, hallelujah). Audre had desperately wanted to hire a woman, preferably a woman of color, but Rhode interviewed well and said many promising things. He'd been a student at Tiffin himself twenty-some years ago. Doc Bellamy had been his English teacher, "both inspiring...and intimidating." Indeed, a check of Rhode's transcripts showed that he'd received one of the rare A's Bellamy had granted during his tenure. Rhode went on to college at Wesleyan and pursued an MFA at the University of Michigan. He'd also published two novels. (Audre hadn't heard of them but had looked up reviews of both books: not bad.)

What had sealed the deal for Rhode's hiring was his plan to overhaul the English curriculum. He would revamp the reading list, making sure it was current and inclusive.

Before being hired, Rhode had been living in Astoria, working as an adjunct professor at Queens College. It was an urban life, he said, and he was ready for a change.

He looks chipper in his green polo shirt (school-issued, with a racehorse embroidered on the chest) and khaki shorts. (He's wearing Skechers and white ankle socks; the kids will be merciless.) Most teachers loathe Move-In Day—they consider it glorified manual labor—so it's no surprise that the only two faculty members Audre could corral are new: Rhode and one of the history teachers, Simone Bergeron, a recent graduate of McGill in Montreal. Rhode and Simone seem to have developed a rapport. Rhode is regaling Simone with the high jinks of his own boarding school days, something about a ferret one of his floormates in Classic North was keeping in a cage under his desk, very much in violation of school rules (forbidden: page 3 of *The Bridle*, "pets," listed just below "firearms").

"Our prefect noticed the smell," Rhode says. "But he thought it was Townie's socks."

Simone's laugh is like a bell. She gathers her braids into a bun on top of her head and ties a silk scarf around it in a way that seems very elegant and French. "You had a classmate named *Townie*?"

"Nickname," Rhode says. "Because he grew up in Haydensboro, the closest town to campus. His parents owned a bar called the Alibi."

"Is it still there?" Simone asks. "I was wondering if there were any fun places around."

"If by 'fun,' you mean 'gritty and depressing,' then yes," Rhode says. "I'll take you there sometime."

"I'd love that!"

Internally, Audre groans. She encourages camaraderie among the faculty, but she has never had two new single teachers before and would have no idea what to say or do if a...romance were to blossom. Will she have to worry about this? Furthermore, Audre likes to pop into the Alibi herself from time to time. It's gritty but not necessarily depressing — a string of colored Christmas lights hangs over the bar year-round, and the jukebox features songs ranging from Motown to One Direction. Jefferson the bartender keeps a bottle of Finlandia vodka in the freezer expressly for Audre. One or two icy shots followed by a glass of cheap chardonnay, and Audre can forget all about Tiffin for a while. The last thing she wants to do is bump into a couple of teachers on a field trip.

The chapel bells ring to signal ten o'clock, and Audre's phone buzzes again. She's about to check it—it's Big East, she's certain—when she sees a car approach. Audre gets the Feeling again. It's a silver panel van, nothing remarkable about it, and yet somehow Audre *knows:* This is the girl she's been waiting for. This is Charley Hicks.

Charley's admission to Tiffin was...unusual. Her application had arrived on May 23, either tragically late or comically early. A quick check revealed the former: Charlotte Emily Hicks was a sophomore at her public school, applying for admission that very September. Tiffin didn't generally admit students as fifth-formers, though there were exceptions. Such as when Tiffin had an unexpected opening.

Cinnamon Peters had died eleven days earlier.

"This is uncanny, right?" Cordelia Spooner, head of admissions, had said to Audre in a stage whisper. "It's almost like"—she cast her eyes up toward the ceiling rosette in Audre's office—"divine intervention."

Mmmmmm. Audre had thought this might be stretching things a bit. Was Cordelia intimating that some kind of greater power had sent them Charley Hicks of Towson, Maryland?

"Is she Tiffin caliber?" Audre asked. They certainly weren't going to admit someone just because they happened to have an opening for a fifth-form girl.

"Top one percent," Cordelia said. "Otherwise I wouldn't have brought this to you. Her GPA is above a four point oh, she's taken only honors classes, her PSAT scores were nearly perfect. Her English teacher wrote a glowing letter saying she had never had a student who loved reading as much as Charley. Always reading, apparently. My only concern is that she might be too...*brainy* for Tiffin."

Cordelia was right to be concerned: Very cerebral kids didn't tend to do well at the school, which was aggressively social. The Head of

School before Audre used to brag that they were cultivating Tiffin students to be sought-after guests at cocktail parties, though Audre sometimes worried they were raising the next generation of douchebags. "Any extracurriculars?" Audre had asked.

"Editor of the literary magazine," Cordelia said.

Tiffin didn't have a literary magazine; Doc Bellamy had tried to start one many times, but not a single student signed up.

"Sports?"

"No."

The girl will have to acquaint herself with a field hockey stick, Audre thought. "Anything else of note?"

"The letter from her guidance counselor said she was top of her class, a lock for valedictorian. But he also mentioned her mental toughness. Apparently her father died suddenly last fall—he was an attorney with a big firm in Baltimore—but Charley kept her grades up."

The father dying probably explained why the application was so late. "Attorney with a big firm" had piqued Audre's interest. "Is she seeking financial aid?"

"No," Cordelia said. "Full tuition."

Tiffin wasn't need-blind, and so it had been this revelation that tipped the scales in Charley Hicks's favor. Admitting Charley also prevented 111 South from sitting empty. Audre had feared the other girls would light candles (forbidden: page 11 of *The Bridle*) at séances where they might try to contact Cinnamon's spirit.

"Should we offer her the spot?" Cordelia had asked.

"Let's," Audre said.

The side of the silver panel van says, HICKS LANDSCAPING & GARDEN SUPPLY—TOWSON, OWINGS MILLS, ELLICOTT CITY. The woman who climbs out of the driver's side—Charley's mother, presumably—has a suntan, a dark ponytail, and feet in rubber clogs.

Audre recognizes the expression on the mother's face; she sees it multiple times every Move-In Day: dread, sadness, fear.

"I'm Audre Robinson, Head of School," she says. "Welcome to Tiffin Academy."

"Fran Hicks," the woman says, shaking Audre's hand. "For the record, I'm one thousand percent against this."

Ah, okay, Audre thinks. She can never be sure who in the family is "driving the bus" on the decision to go to boarding school—but Audre much prefers it when it's student-motivated.

"Charley will receive a blue-chip education," Audre says. "Better than she would at most universities." She extends a Vanna White arm to showcase the students around them laughing, chatting, playing cornhole. From an open window in Classic North, strains of Luke Combs's "Beer Never Broke My Heart" float down. (That would be Dub's room; no one else listens to country music.) "Besides that, she's going to have a wonderful time."

Charley climbs out of the passenger side, and Audre takes stock of her new student. Her first thought is, *Have we made a terrible mistake?* Charley is tall and lanky with sallow skin. Her light brown hair is in two braids; glasses perch on the end of her nose. She wears a kelly-green Lacoste polo, a khaki skirt in a length Audre can only describe as "awkward," and a belt embroidered with whales. On her feet are boat shoes; Audre hasn't seen a pair up close in decades.

It looks like she stepped right out of *The Official Preppy Handbook;* if it were 1984, she would fit right in. But forty years have passed. Now the girls all wear Reformation, Golden Goose, and— for those who can afford it—Davi's parents' label, OOO. Audre wonders if Charley watched some old movies—*Love Story,* perhaps, or *Dead Poets Society*—and thought this was what the kids would be wearing?

Oh dear. Mr. Rivera's Skechers are a minor problem compared to what they have here.

The Academy

But then Audre chastises herself. The girl is fine, it doesn't matter what she's wearing; this school could use someone who doesn't conform.

Charley steps forward to shake Audre's hand but doesn't smile. "Thank you for admitting me, even though my application was so late." Her eyes flick to her mother. "There were extenuating circumstances."

Audre's phone buzzes again. "Let me help you unload," she says. Fran Hicks slides open the side of the van, releasing the pleasant scent of cedar mulch. There are stacked bags of it, along with peat moss, a gas can, a Weedwacker, and a cast-iron planter that must weigh several hundred pounds.

There's also a plastic bin filled with plants. Charley reaches for one that looks like a small palm tree.

"Are you bringing that in?" Audre asks.

"Yes," Charley says. "Plants are allowed, right?"

Audre tries to think. *The Bridle* specifically says no pets—not even a goldfish in a bowl—but does it mention plants? Audre regards the bin. Are *all* those plants coming inside?

She recalls a student who once nurtured a succulent garden she'd received as a Christmas gift.

Fran Hicks seems to note the ambivalence on Audre's face. "They aren't pot plants," she says. "I told Charley to leave those at home."

Audre laughs. The Hickses have a sense of humor, a good sign. "Yes," she says. "Plants are allowed."

Behind the ferns, topiary, and a leggy philodendron, Audre spies at least a half-dozen milk crates overflowing with...books.

She blinks. Does she recall a student ever bringing *books* to school? It's rather like bringing sand to the beach. Audre lifts a milk crate so that she can peruse the titles: *The Plot* by Jean Hanff Korelitz, *Nightbitch* by Rachel Yoder, *Homegoing* by Yaa Gyasi. All books Audre would read herself if she could find the time.

When Fran Hicks opens the back doors to the van, Audre sees *more* milk crates. More books! Penguin Classics, Vintage Contemporaries, a tattered copy of the Cheever stories. There's one crate dedicated to poetry: Edna St. Vincent Millay, Anne Sexton, Nikki Giovanni.

Audre is impressed — and a little intimidated. If old Doc Bellamy knew how to use a cell phone, she might be tempted to text him now at his cabin in the woods, up in Robert Frost country. We have a genuine reader!

Audre leads the way to 111 South. Technically, it's Simone Bergeron's job to show new girls to their rooms, but Audre wants to do this herself. She swings the door open. The room is clean, orderly, unremarkable: extra-long twin bed, desk, dresser. However, Audre can't help seeing it as it was on the morning of May 12: Cinnamon Peters splayed across her bed, her skin gray, her mouth open (though eyes, blessedly, closed). On the floor: her acoustic guitar (flipped upside down), her laptop (closed), an empty sandwich bag that had held a cache of pills, half a glass of water. Cinnamon had left a note on her desk that said simply, *I'm sorry,* tucked under a vase of wildflowers that Dub Austin had picked for her from the Pasture.

"Here we are!" Audre says brightly. She's waiting for either Charley or her mother to protest — *a girl died in this room!* — but they simply set Charley's plants and books down and leave to get another load.

Audre stays with Charley and Fran Hicks until it's time for Fran to depart. Other distractions vie for Audre's attention: Her phone is buzzing away, she's getting a headache from the sun, and she's famished. Chef Haz is making blueberry pancakes this morning, but there's no time for Audre to eat; she still has to review her speech for the All-School Meeting at noon. The speech will be followed by a cookout on the beach at Jewel Pond, and the kids will all go swimming. It's Move-In Day tradition.

But for now, Audre reminds herself to be present with the Hickses.

"Be sure to log into the Parent Portal on the website," Audre says to Fran. "Please reach out if you have any questions or concerns." She and Fran shake hands again, Fran slides the doors to the van shut, and Audre steps back so Fran and Charley can have some space to say their goodbyes.

Fran goes in for a hug, her eyes teary, but Charley pushes her away with both hands. Fran stumbles backward in her clogs.

"You're not allowed to cry," Charley says. "This is all your fault."

"I love you, Charley," Fran says. "I'll see you at Thanksgiving."

Charley spins in her Top-Siders and storms into Classic South.

Audre has seen a lot of partings in her six-year tenure, but never one quite like this.

Fran wipes under her eyes. "She hates me."

Audre isn't sure how to respond. She's tempted to normalize it by saying, *It's the age* or *She's pushing you away to mask her ambivalence about separating from you.* But Audre doesn't have time to delve into the teenage psyche, so she simply smiles as kindly as she can. "Safe trip home," she says.

Audre hurries around the back of the chapel with a quick peek through the lower-level windows into God's Basement (surely no one is hooking up down there yet, though now would be the perfect time, while everyone else is occupied), past the Schoolhouse—the cupolaed Georgian brick building where all academic classes are held—and into the Manse, which is home to the admissions office, the administrative offices, and Audre's residence. Her phone is positively ablaze, but she won't check it until she's upstairs in her beautifully appointed suite of rooms. The original house, once the home of Edward "Teddy" Tiffin, who raised thoroughbreds for the races in Saratoga on these acres, has been (thanks to Big East) completely restored to its original grandeur: crown moldings, ceiling rosettes, chandeliers. A sweeping grand staircase in the front entry leads up to Audre's personal rooms, including a library where sensitive conversations can take place. Audre goes into the library now, cranks the air-conditioning, and settles on the Victorian fainting couch. Edward Tiffin's grandfather clock ticks away the seconds in a manner that Audre has always found comforting. The bay window in this room affords the best view of Jewel Pond, a deep, clear kettle pond that reflects the sky like a mirror. The pond has a crescent of golden sand beach, trucked in from Cape Cod. Audre had bemoaned the installation of a sandy beach as a prime example of Big East's impractical showboating, though she has to admit, the beach at Jewel Pond is now the most popular stop on the campus tour, and it's a vast improvement over the muddy grass bank that used to serve as the "beach."

Audre takes a deep breath. She loves this school and adores her job. This is frightening for her to admit since she might be only moments away from being fired.

There's no doubt in her mind that the rankings are out.

With great trepidation, she touches the screen of her phone. If they've fallen out of the top twenty-five — or, god forbid, the top fifty (this isn't possible, is it?) — Audre will devote all her time and energy to rebuilding, just like a sports franchise that finds itself in last place in its division. As long as Big East gives her the chance.

There are three missed calls from him. *Oof,* she thinks. A call is bad. *Three calls,* unheard-of.

There are three texts from Big East as well.

Call me.

CALL ME PLEASE.

I'm standing by, Audre.

Audre should go check the rankings on the computer in her office, but she's too anxious to move. Her hands are shaking, her gut is twisting.

She types "America Today" in the search bar. There's no need to navigate the site because a banner announces: New Rankings — Best Boarding Schools.

Here goes, Audre thinks, and she clicks the link.

For a second, she doesn't understand what she's seeing. What... *is* this? She scrolls to the bottom of the screen, scrolls back up. All the other schools are more or less where they're supposed to be.

Just not Tiffin.

Audre's phone rings. Big East.

"Hello?" she says. "Jesse?"

"Audre," he says.

A little before noon, Audre stands at the altar of the chapel, her favorite building on campus. The chapel was built in 1911 when Edward Tiffin's daughter, Mary Tiffin Sinclair, inherited the horse farm and decided to found a coed Episcopalian boarding school. The chapel is Perpendicular Gothic Revival, most notable from the outside for its soaring tower. Inside, it's one long barrel vault with a slightly raised altar and magnificent stained glass windows. The student pews are carved from dark walnut and face each other over the tiled center aisle. The kneelers were needlepointed by a crew of devoted student mothers. Most feature equestrian subjects — horses, jockeys, saddles, riding rings — rather than religious ones. A visiting minister once famously quipped, "Why not just add a racetrack, an odds board, and a bookie office while you're at it?" But their chaplain, Laura Rae Splaine, is the kind of pastor who believes god is everywhere and with everyone, even the bookies.

All-School Meeting is one of many time-honored traditions at Tiffin. It's part ceremonial (Laura Rae begins with a prayer and ends with a blessing), part administrative. It's the green flag at the start of the race, the gun at a track meet, the official start to the school year.

Audre's hands have stilled, though her insides are queasy. She hasn't eaten; she spent the time after her phone call with Big East rewriting her speech.

She watches as the students file in, taking seats according to class. The sixth-formers all look smug and a little bored, and Audre can't blame them. The only thing the sixth-form students care about is getting into college; once they're admitted to SMU or Trinity, they party their asses off. Annabelle Tuckerman wears a T-shirt that says NO SLEEP TIL PRINCETON, which is in violation of Chapel dress code, but Audre is too distracted to send her back to South to change. Lisa Kim is Head Prefect this year, and she'll address the students as well—but Audre's attention remains on the fifth-form students. She sees Dub enter with his teammates, then Davi in a cloud of Madisons and Olivias.

Audre worries that no one has told Charley Hicks about All-School Meeting. Did Simone Bergeron mention it? Did she shepherd all the girls out of Classic South? By the time Audre finally spies the green polo and khaki skirt, the fifth-form class pews have filled up, so Charley has to sit in the back, where folding chairs are lined up in rows facing the altar. This seating is very undesirable: It's overflow, for latecomers—and Charley is all alone.

Oh no, Audre thinks. *This won't do.* Audre searches for Cordelia Spooner—she's seasoned enough to step in and remedy this—but then Audre sees Andrew Eastman lope in. Shockingly, he's removed his baseball jersey and put on a collared shirt. Is he turning over a new leaf, then? Will he be following the rules this year? He scans the fifth-form pews and, despite a bunch of people waving him over, insisting they'll squeeze him in, he takes the seat next to Charley.

The Academy

Audre watches him introduce himself. The two shake hands, and East whispers something in Charley's ear that makes her smile.

Audre can't believe it, but in that moment, she's grateful Andrew Eastman exists.

Laura Rae rises to deliver the opening prayer—Audre barely hears it, though she does automatically say "Amen"—and then it's her turn to take the podium.

"Welcome to a new school year, Tiffin students," she says. She pauses just long enough to watch everyone's eyes glaze over. Whispering begins; a few phones appear (forbidden at Chapel: Appendix A of *The Bridle*), and Cordelia Spooner requisitions one. The kids don't care what Audre has to say; they're waiting her out.

Audre's eyes land on Charley Hicks, the only student who seems to be listening attentively.

"This morning, *America Today*'s rankings for the best boarding schools in the country were released. I am thrilled"—*and utterly stunned*—"to tell you that Tiffin Academy has been ranked...number two, right behind Old Bennington." She pauses dramatically. "You are attending the *number two boarding school in the country.*"

There's a split second of complete silence. Audre can practically hear the kids thinking, *Is this a joke, a prank, a mistake? Number twenty-two, or possibly number twelve, makes sense—but number two?*

Audre says in a louder, more confident tone, "Tiffin has jumped from number nineteen to number two."

The chapel erupts in cheers. It's bedlam—kids are up out of their seats, hugging, screaming, jumping up and down. Davi whips her phone out of her Staud Bean Bag clutch and films the celebration.

At a certain point in the future, Audre will think back on this moment—when their ascent to the top of the list had seemed like good news.

2. Tiffin Talks: The Rankings

Being ranked *number two* consumes our group chats and private stories, not because anyone actually *cares* (notable exceptions: our parents, who feel like their tuition dollars have increased in value, and sixth-former Annabelle Tuckerman, who believes this is somehow gonna help her get into Princeton) but because it feels as if the metaphorical dark cloud that has been hanging over camp since Cinnamon Peters died just let in a stream of sunlight.

At the Move-In Day cookout by Jewel Pond, we form a pyramid in the sand. Dub Austin anchors the bottom, Davi is smack in the middle, and Willow Levy, who weighs less than ninety pounds, climbs up top. Our Spanish teacher, Señor Perez, asks everyone in the pyramid to hold up two fingers indicating *numero dos*. He gets one decent pic before the whole thing collapses.

We have chicken fights in the water—Dub and Madison R. versus Taylor and Hakeem. Lisa Kim glides out to the center of the pond on the paddleboard she bought in Maui, where she did a "summer service project" (eye roll emoji). A JBL speaker blasts rap music, but Ms. Robinson doesn't balk at the explicit lyrics and she doesn't make Davi change out of her cheeky bikini bottoms, even though they violate dress code.

The sixth-formers among us are old enough to remember when the Move-In Day cookout meant frozen hamburger patties and bags of generic-brand potato chips. But this year, Chef Haz serves beef brisket that he's been smoking for days. There are rainbows of grilled vegetable skewers, homemade potato salad and broccoli slaw, and fluffy cheddar-chive biscuits. Instead of store-bought sheet cake, there are blackberry hand pies and rocky road brownies.

As Dub Austin drenches his brisket with Chef's secret-recipe BBQ sauce, he says, "Number two is kind of like losing the Super Bowl."

"That's so negative," Taylor Wilson says. "Number two is *crazy*. We beat *Northmeadow*."

Most of us agree with Taylor: It *is* crazy. Tiffin ahead of not only all the brainiacs at Northmeadow but also Choate, Groton, Hotchkiss, and Deerfield? Seriously?

Everyone notices when East shows up (late, obviously; rules and schedules don't apply to him). The past two years, he came to the cookout high as a kite, but today he seems clear-eyed. He strips off his T-shirt and charges into the water.

The new girl, Charley Hicks, is sitting alone in the grass behind the beach. She's wearing the same clothes she arrived in—a green polo, like something a fourth grade boy would wear for school pictures, a khaki skirt that hits below the knee, and boat shoes. Her belt has *whales* on it. And that's when we wonder if Charley Hicks is trying to be *ironic*. (Mrs. Wully tried to teach irony back in third-form, but most of us still don't understand it.) Does Charley Hicks not have a bathing suit, a cute cover-up, or a sundress if she doesn't want to swim? She's sitting on a patchwork quilt that looks like it came straight out of a Conestoga wagon, and she's reading a book called *The Night Circus*.

We've heard that Charley Hicks is here to challenge Royce Stringfellow for valedictorian. (This would actually be great; Royce is a dick about his grades, and we're like, *Bruh, who cares, wouldn't you rather get laid?*) But even Royce is out in the water today, trying to impress Tilly Benbow with his dance moves.

What is up with Charley Hicks, reading all by herself? Is she super weird, or is she...intriguing? We've seen this storyline on

Nickelodeon—a new girl shows up and doesn't fit in. Should one of us say hello? We were all new once.

"Want to go over?" Olivia H-T asks Davi Banerjee.

"Not yet," Davi says. "We can't overwhelm her."

"She doesn't seem overwhelmed," Olivia H-T says. "It's like she barely notices we're here."

"She notices, trust me," Davi says. "She's observing us just like we're observing her."

Ohhhh okay. Olivia H-T gets it. Davi is like a naturalist with a new species of wild animal. Or is Charley the naturalist?

Just as Olivia H-T is about to offer Davi her brownie—Davi eats like a long-haul trucker and never gains an ounce—an astonishing thing happens. East emerges from the pond, shaking water from his dark hair in a way that makes every girl swoon (except for Davi; she thinks East is a douche canoe, but Olivia H-T suspects this is because East is the only student at Tiffin who gets more attention than Davi herself). He strides across the beach to the grass, where he plops down on the quilt next to Charley Hicks.

Olivia H-T gasps, but Davi says, "Oh god, he's *so* predictable."

Predictable? Olivia H-T thinks. *What about the hottest (and richest) guy at school sitting next to the freak show is predictable?* Olivia H-T fears she'll spend the whole school year one step behind Davi.

"How so?" Olivia H-T asks.

"She's supposed to be smart."

Ah yes, Olivia H-T thinks. *East will charm Charley Hicks, then get her to tutor him in English and write all his papers. Charley will be unable to resist because...well, because he's East.*

Over on the quilt, Charley shows East her book. He studies the cover, flips through the pages, then sets it down, leans back on his elbows, and says something that makes Charley laugh.

"Oh god," Davi groans. "She's falling for it."

Charley kicks off her ghastly shoes, stands up, and untucks her shirt.

Hello? Olivia H-T thinks. *What is* happening *here?* She checks to see if any of the adults are watching this. Ms. Robinson is talking to Mrs. Spooner and Señor Perez. The new English teacher, Mr. Rivera (he has a dad bod but is otherwise kind of hot), and the new history teacher, Miss Bergeron (who looks so young she could pass for a student), are sitting in beach chairs with their feet in the water, but they're deep in conversation and don't notice anything but each other.

Olivia H-T is both surprised and relieved to see that Charley is wearing a bikini under her clothes—and she has a figure: teacup breasts, a cute ass. She folds her clothes, takes off her glasses, and follows East into the water, where the two of them start to... *race* across the pond.

"Holy shit," Davi says. "She can really swim."

Charley's freestyle stroke is so strong and clean that she keeps pace with East. (None of us realized East could swim like that, but he's our school's answer to James Bond: He has all kinds of hidden talents that he whips out when they're useful.) The cinematic ending to this little vignette would be Charley *beating* East in the race—those of us in the water start to cheer as East and Charley make their way back—but when they reach the middle of the pond, East pulls away and wins by two or three lengths.

Charley emerges from the water with a shy smile, her braids hanging down her back like two wet ropes. East offers her a towel from his backpack. Charley dries her face, wraps the towel around herself, and follows East over to the grill, where they pick up plates and dig in.

"He's using her," Davi says.

Davi is probably right, Olivia H-T thinks. *What other explanation is there?*

On Saturday, we play our first home football game against the Excelsior School, which can't even be considered a rival because they're too good: Their record of beating us is 114 years old. Sports at Tiffin have never been about winning, but rather about spirit and sportsmanship. (This is a nice way of saying that most of our teams suck.) We dress up in green and gold, paint our faces, and cheer when either team does something good. The score is 17–14 — Excelsior is, of course, ahead, there's less than a minute on the clock, but we have the ball and are driving for the end zone. Dub Austin sinks back in the pocket, and just as he's about to be steamrolled by the Excelsior left tackle, he chucks a pass to Hakeem Pryce, who catches it and charges into the end zone.

When the final whistle blows, we storm the field. The offensive line hoists Dub and Hakeem into the air.

We are gracious hosts; this has been instilled in us by Ms. Robinson and the faculty. We congratulate the Excelsior team. "Good game, good game!" We invite the Excelsior fans over to the food trucks that line the Pasture. *Does anyone want carnitas?*

At Sunday's church service, Chaplain Laura Rae praises us for our "resilience" (she doesn't mention Cinnamon Peters, but she doesn't need to) and encourages us to be careful and thoughtful — indeed, *intentional* — in all things.

"Our ranking at number two and the unexpected win on the football field may lead us to believe that Tiffin has entered a golden era," she says. "But in my experience, quality is never the result of dumb luck. Quality comes from hard work, time, and energy."

Laura Rae has a way of telling us what to do without telling us what to do: We sit up a little straighter and remove our phones from their hiding places within the Book of Common Prayer.

When the new week begins, we get to class on time, come prepared, listen attentively. The boys' shirts are tucked in, ties tied (Windsor knots are big this year; Teague Baldwin—who's frankly the only sixth-form boy worth emulating—shared an instructional YouTube video with the boys on his floor), and the girls' skirt hems fall below their extended fingertips. There have been no disciplinary infractions since the start of school. Has this ever happened before?

Monday is the first Burger Night and Piano Bar, a tradition started by Chef Haz. We choose Swiss or cheddar, crispy bacon or slices of beefsteak tomato, homemade pickles, special sauce or just plain ketchup, brioche bun or lettuce wrap. After dinner at the Paddock, some of us hurry over to the Teddy to get milkshakes from the Grille while our music teacher, Mr. Chuy, waits at the baby grand, ready to take requests. Last year, Piano Bar was attended by mostly choir and theater kids—Cinnamon Peters always took the seat next to Mr. Chuy on the bench—but then word spread about how much fun it was. Mr. Chuy plays old songs like "Rich Girl," or "Santeria," but sometimes he surprises us. He ends the first Piano Bar of the year with "Love Story" by Taylor Swift. The girls go nuts (and not just the girls, to be honest).

Dub Austin is wrong: We didn't lose the Super Bowl. The ranking in *America Today* has raised us up, literally and figuratively. There's something in the atmosphere now that suggests a world of endless possibilities.

3. The Alibi

Tiffin Paddock Dinner Service

Wednesday, September 10

Selection of homemade breads and rolls
with parsley-lemon compound butter

SALAD BAR
Tonight's additions: roasted candy-striped beets,
rosemary-bacon pecans, creamy maple dressing

SOUP OF THE DAY
Summer squash bisque

ENTRÉES
Roasted chicken with lemon-wine pan sauce, mussels
in tomato-shallot broth, mushroom and goat cheese
ravioli with mint pesto

SIDES
Crispy frites, sautéed spinach with garlic

DESSERTS
Apple crisp with amaretto whipped cream,
German chocolate cupcakes

Rhode Rivera has heard the saying *Those who can, do; those who can't, teach,* but he pays it no mind. Didn't the pandemic prove that along with first responders and everyone in the medical profession, teachers are our nation's heroes? He's *lucky* to have secured this job: The salary is adequate, the benefits package is solid, it includes room and board, the setting is aesthetically pleasing, the work is meaningful. Rhode imagines becoming the kind of teacher the kids will remember even after they head out into the world to do great things.

But there's a small part of Rhode that worries his new situation is pathetic. He's not only teaching high school, he's teaching at his own high school. It's as though his life is a game of Chutes and Ladders and he's just slid down the longest chute, landing him back at Square One. When he was a student sitting in the front row of his English classroom (Schoolhouse 108, which hasn't changed), listening to Doc Bellamy expound on Stephen Crane's *The Red Badge of Courage,* he dreamed of heading out into the world to do great things. If someone had told him that, more than twenty years down the line, he would become the next Doc Bellamy, he would have told that person to fuck off.

How did he get here?

This past May, Rhode received the *Thoroughbred Tribune,* a biannual newsletter meant to keep alumni abreast of all Tiffin news, and to solicit donations. As Rhode barely had enough money to keep himself afloat, he only ever gave the *Tribune* a cursory glance, checking the back pages where notable achievements of alumni were listed by class. Any news from the Class of 2003? Oh sure—marriages, babies, political appointments, scientific discoveries, IPOs, gallery openings, promotions to chief of surgery. Back in 2017, Rhode himself had submitted an announcement: His first novel, *The Prince of Little Twelfth,* was being published by Stonecastle. Rhode's novel was met with good reviews, and Rhode was hailed as the newest member of the New York literati. He was invited to do a signing at McNally Jackson, Terry Gross interviewed him for NPR's *Fresh Air,* and *New York* magazine ran a back-page profile asking him to name his favorite downtown hangouts as though he were the second coming of Norman Mailer.

Sales of *The Prince of Little Twelfth* were respectable enough that Rhode was offered a contract for a second novel entitled *The Writers,* about a group of students at a famous Midwestern graduate fiction workshop, all of whom want to birth the Great American Novel. Rhode expected *The Writers* to be even bigger than *Little Twelfth.* But *The Writers* was published in early 2020, just as the pandemic hit. Rhode's in-person tour pivoted to a series of virtual events that only a handful of people attended. He tried to get his book noticed by Bookstagram, but he was immediately castigated because his female characters "lacked authenticity."

Sales of *The Writers* didn't earn out Rhode's advance. In fact, the disappointing results — it wasn't a *flop,* but maybe it was — led Rhode to face some tough professional and financial realities.

He took a job as an adjunct professor at Queens College and moved from his one-bedroom on East Eighty-Second Street in Manhattan, which he could no longer afford, to a studio in Astoria, Queens. All was not lost because he started dating a woman named Lace Ann, who lived in his building. Lace Ann was an artisanal baker — her specialty was savory stuffed croissants — and when they met in the elevator, Lace Ann had a smudge of flour on her nose. It was like something straight out of a Hallmark movie. They were together nearly three years — Rhode teaching and starting a third novel half a dozen times, to no avail, and Lace Ann trying to start her own bakery.

Lace Ann found an investor — a tech bro named Miller with an aggressive handshake and a talent for mentioning that he graduated from Yale in every conversation—who backed her with enough seed money that she could open a stylish storefront on the hottest block of Ludlow Street. She called the place Atelier 2A, and with the help of New York's key influencers, there was a line down the block. The line then *became* the story—Atelier 2A routinely sold out of stuffed croissants by ten a.m.—and soon after, Williams Sonoma called. They wanted to feature Atelier 2A's croissants in their catalog.

Does Rhode need to explain how this story played out? Lace Ann became "overwhelmed" by her success, she was the city's new darling, she got the invites and the write-ups. She told Rhode that they should "take a break" while she "adjusted to her new normal." Part of this "new normal" was Lace Ann dating her investor, Yale-alumnus-Miller.

The job offer from Tiffin was a godsend.

There was also a certain pleasure on Move-In Day when Rhode received a text from Lace Ann. Wow! Tiffin ranked #2! Congratulations! A flurry of colored balloons floated up Rhode's screen.

Now, a week and a half into the semester, Rhode has to manage the brass tacks of his new life. He spent the first week of school on Getting-to-Know-You exercises, doing a read-and-response to Anne Sexton's poem "The Kiss," and tackling Herman Melville's short story "Bartleby, the Scrivener," which missed the mark with most of the kids. Rhode wanted to dive right into Jonathan Escoffery's collection of connected stories and talk about race and identity, but his reading list had yet to be approved. What? How? Audre Robinson—the first woman and the first person of color to ever serve as Tiffin's Head—had made it clear that she appreciated Rhode's enthusiasm for creating a reading list that reflected the diversity of the country.

But on Friday afternoon, just as classes ended for the day and students were striding across the impossibly green, manicured grounds on their way to football, soccer, or field hockey practice, Rhode received an email from Audre entitled Reading List.

After much discussion...blah blah blah...it's been determined...blah blah blah...you will need to retain certain texts from Dr. Bellamy's syllabus, including the following...

"They're making me teach Emerson and Thoreau!" Rhode says to Simone Bergeron. It's Friday evening and they're sitting at the bar at the Alibi in nearby Haydensboro. Although they have a half day of class tomorrow, they were granted permission to leave campus because the following night is First Dance and both Rhode and Simone have been enlisted to chaperone. Even with permission, sitting at a bar, especially a dive like this, feels illicit. The lights are low, the air redolent of cigarette smoke like it's 1999, and Simone has fed the jukebox ten quarters for ten plays. Her first three songs were by Fleetwood Mac, Metallica, and Chappell Roan, which is proof that not only is Simone beautiful but she has that elusive thing called range.

This is strictly an outing between "colleagues" who need to decompress. Even with the extraordinary news of the number two ranking and everyone subsequently on their best behavior, life at Tiffin is...a lot.

"Those old white men?" Simone says.

"It gets worse," Rhode says. "I have to teach *The Crucible.*"

Simone drops her forehead to the bar and, in the process, nearly topples her glass of sparkling wine. When they took their seats, Simone cheerfully ordered champagne from the grizzled bartender, who shook his head and said, "Nup."

Simone said, "But we're celebrating. We just survived our first full week of teaching at Tiffin."

The bartender, Jefferson, sighed, then said, "Let me check the back." He reappeared with a dusty, room-temperature bottle of something called Pour Deux, a rosé sparkling wine, and Simone squealed her delight while Jefferson poured two glasses, one for her and one (unfortunately) for Rhode, who quickly ordered a Budweiser as well.

"*The Crucible*," Simone says now. "*Mon Dieu,* I hated that play. It never made sense to me. I know it was Miller's response to McCarthyism..."

"It's turgid," Rhode says. "The kids will resent me for making them read it. But Audre said it's nonnegotiable. So now I can't teach the Escoffery stories, though I might assign them as supplemental reading for anyone who's interested."

"I didn't think we were allowed to give extra credit," Simone says.

"It wouldn't be extra credit," Rhode says. "Just additional reading for anyone who wants to know what I would have assigned, were it not for the board of directors' archaic mandates."

"You really think any kid is going to do additional reading just *because*?"

"I have one kid who will," Rhode says. "Charley Hicks. She's the kind of student I dreamed about when I took this job." Rhode realizes there's nothing worse than a teacher with a pet, so he has tamped down his enthusiasm about Charley. She's new this year, just like he is, and she's the first student in recent memory to enter Tiffin as a junior. After class lets out each day, Charley lingers just to talk about books. On her Getting-to-Know-You sheet, she wrote that her full name was Charlotte Emily Hicks, she was named for the Brontë sisters, and she wanted to work in publishing at an imprint like Little, Brown or Scribner. Rhode couldn't help but comment: *That is so cool! Publishing needs someone like you!*

"Charley Hicks is a problem for me," Simone says. "I'm the dorm parent on her floor. She refused to come to any of my ice-breaking activities, and she hasn't made a single friend. Her door is always closed." Simone throws back what's left of her Pour Deux and helps herself to more from the bottle on the bar. In Montreal, even the cheap champagne is good, but this stuff tastes like pink pickle juice. Simone is catching a nice buzz, however, which is all that matters. The social isolation of Charley Hicks—her refusal to even *smile* at any of her floormates—worries Simone. She's planning on going to Audre Robinson with her concerns if the situation doesn't improve. She's relieved to hear that Charley has, at least, bonded with Rhode.

"Charley isn't like the other kids, that's for sure," Rhode says. Tiffin in 2025 is a hell of a lot more diverse than it was in 2003 when Rhode graduated, but in other ways, it's more homogeneous. The girls all wear belted miniskirts with their Veja sneakers; they all smell the same and have the same vocal inflections; they all constantly (and incorrectly) use the word "literally." Their confidence is dizzying.

Charley is an entirely different species. Her wardrobe is "preppy"— she wears polos and oxfords, A-line madras skirts, battered boat shoes, collared dresses that would not have been out of place at a 1962 Junior League luncheon. She either wears her hair in two Pippi Longstocking braids or pushes it off her face with a grosgrain headband; she wears horn-rimmed glasses. He can tell just from the expression on her face and the way she carries herself that she knows she doesn't fit in...and doesn't seem to give a flying fuck. Rhode isn't sure that he's ever met an "old soul" before, but if it means someone who presents as ten to fifteen years older and wiser than her actual age, Charley is the first.

"She doesn't seem bothered by her isolation, is the thing," Simone says.

"Then you shouldn't be bothered by it," Rhode says. "So, what about you? Do you have any students who stand out?"

Simone tips champagne back in her mouth. Ohhhhhh yes, she does. But she doesn't want to talk about it.

Simone empties the remainder of the bottle of Pour Deux into her glass. "This stuff is *merde*," she says to Rhode. Yet she flags Jefferson, who is at the other end of the bar talking to a beefy guy covered in tattoos. Does the guy look familiar, or is Rhode imagining things?

"Do you have another bottle of this?" Simone asks.

Jefferson chuckles. He's either mellowing as the night wears on or succumbing to Simone's charms. "There's a whole damn case from an engagement party that was canceled during the pandemic. I'll give you the next bottle for free."

Simone raises triumphant fists over her head. Rhode can't help noticing as her vintage Montreal Expos T-shirt pulls free from the top of her jeans, exposing a strip of flesh at her waist.

Rhode peers down the bar, sees the guy with the tattoos checking out Simone as well, and feels a surge of protectiveness that verges on the territorial. Simone is the only woman in the place — and tonight, she's with him.

The guy with the tattoos at the end of the bar is Harrison "Haz" Flanders, Tiffin's chef. Haz recognizes the man and woman drinking champagne as Tiffin faculty, though he doesn't know their names, and he figures they won't recognize him out of his white jacket.

Harrison arrived at Tiffin two years ago — and he has two years to go until he's reinstated as head chef at the Dewberry Club on East Seventy-Third Street.

We need time for the scandal to fade, Jesse Eastman told Haz. *In the meantime, I have another gig for you.*

Haz was forced to take a "leave of absence" from the Dewberry Club because he'd been caught using club funds—money allocated to Haz's budget for the ladies' luncheons and dinner dances—to pay off his gambling debts.

Big East was the Dewberry board member who dealt with HR issues, and while he could have easily fired Haz on the spot, he had a different idea. Big East was sending his son to a boarding school in northwest Massachusetts, and it just so happened the school badly needed a chef. The phrase "northwest Massachusetts" was only slightly more palatable to Haz than "boarding school." Haz was being shipped off to the middle of bucolic fucking nowhere to work in a *cafeteria*?

Haz almost said no, but he feared that if he turned Big East down, the Club would press charges. At the very least, Haz would be blackballed across the five boroughs and would end up overseeing banquets at a Marriott somewhere along the New Jersey Turnpike.

And so, to Tiffin he came, but his salary is less than half of what he made at Balthazar his first year out of the Culinary Institute in Hyde Park.

When he complained about the pay, Big East said, *You have free housing and free food. Your salary will cover gas and beer. What else do you need?*

Haz needs a break. He's suffered a string of betting losses that have caused him to max out two credit cards. He used to be a regular at Harrah's in Atlantic City, playing poker and blackjack, but then he decided to save himself the trip and downloaded the FanDuel and DraftKings apps and started betting on sports. He once laid down five grand on a second-division soccer game in Brazil when he knew nothing about either of the teams—and he won big. He needs another score like that so he can pay off his cards and get ahead enough to put a down payment on a new truck. That's all he wants. After that, he'll stop gambling for good.

Paltry paycheck aside, Haz likes his job at Tiffin. He takes great satisfaction in elevating "school food." The moment Chef replaced the white chunks of iceberg in the salad bar with tender organic butter lettuce and crisp baby romaine, he became a hero. Audre Robinson, the Head of School, invites him out to the dining room every Sunday after brunch service to accept a standing ovation. Burger Night has become legendary, and so have the wood-fired pizzas he serves for lunch every Friday. He's learned the kids' tastes, their preferences. Cinnamon Peters loved his eggs Florentine; it breaks Haz's heart just thinking about it.

Haz nurses his Jim Beam as he eavesdrops on the two teachers. The dude, he learns, is also a transplant from New York City; he was some kind of writer but now teaches English. The chick is from Montreal; she teaches history. She's young — closer in age to the students than to either Haz or the English teacher — and at the moment, she's also very drunk. Haz watches her finish the second bottle of sparkling wine by herself. She's talking too loudly, slurring her words. "I want the kids to respect me, but I also want them to like me. I know it's wrong, but I want to be their favorite."

The dude says, "I think we should probably be heading back."

The chick throws her arm around his neck, leans into him, and says, "Let's have one more bottle, but you have to drink some this time. It's called 'Pour Deux,' which means 'For…'"

"Not a good idea," the dude says. He sets three twenties on the bar, then stands. The chick lists so far left in her seat, Haz fears she's going to topple over. "Whoa, okay, Simone, upsy-daisy." The dude helps Simone get up, but the weight of her throws him off-balance. He's not a big guy, and so Haz moves in for the assist.

He strides over, saying, "Need help getting her out to the car?"

The dude glances up — "No, thanks, man. I got it" — but Simone's knees buckle, and it's obvious he hasn't got it. Haz props Simone up on one side while the English teacher holds her up on the other. Her feet slip out from under her like she's on skates, but somehow they make it out to the parking lot, where a dinged-up red RAV4 is the only vehicle other than Haz's piece-of-shit Ford Ranger.

"This you?" Haz asks.

"Hers. But I'm driving, obviously."

Haz leads Simone to the passenger side and gets her buckled in. Her head drops forward like a wilting flower.

When Haz closes the door, he regards the English teacher over the top of the car. "I'm Harrison, the chef from school."

"*That's* why you look familiar!" The English teacher's expression brightens, and he comes around to pump Haz's hand. "I feel like I'm meeting a celebrity right now. My name is Rhode, as in Rhode Island. Rhode Rivera. Man, that chicken with the lemon pan sauce..."

Haz shrugs. "It was just chicken..."

"And what about the mussels? How did you get fresh mussels?"

"I had them shipped overnight from Point Judith," Haz says.

"You're a genius, man. I know I speak for the whole school when I say we are goddamned lucky to have you. How'd you end up at *Tiffin*?"

"Long story," Haz says. He looks through the window at Simone. "And you'd better get her back."

"Yeah," Rhode says. "For the record, we were just blowing off steam. This wasn't a date or anything. I wouldn't want you to get the wrong idea."

"None of my business," Haz says, holding up his palms.

"If you could not mention that you saw us? Or that Simone got so...blotto? We're both new this year."

Haz nearly says, *How much is it worth to you?* But he isn't desperate enough to extort his colleagues. Not yet, anyway.

"Your secret is safe with me," Haz says.

The Academy

Friday night, Charley has finished her problem sets for trig and is deciding whether to read ahead in history or finish *The Night Circus* when her phone dings with a text.

It's Beatrix, her best friend from home. Wyd.

Studying, Charley answers. Friday is a school night.

Saturday classes went into the "con" column when Charley was deciding whether or not to go to boarding school, though secretly it appealed to her. She would go to school seven days if she could.

Have you made any friends? Beatrix asks.

Charley responds: Nope.

Three dots rise, then vanish. On the one hand, Charley knows, Beatrix will be relieved that she hasn't been replaced; Charley and Beatrix have been friends since before memory. But on the other hand, Beatrix will feel guilty. What happened with Beatrix at Charley's house made Charley's decision for her. She couldn't stay at home with her mother and Joey.

Have you seen Davi Banerjee? Beatrix asks.

Yes, Charley says. She lives on my floor.

Again, three dots rise, then disappear. Charley and Beatrix have long been staunchly anti-influencer, but Charley knows that Beatrix is fascinated by Davi Banerjee. Charley and Beatrix worked side by side all summer at the Towson Hot Bagels off York Road, and Beatrix spent two hundred dollars of her paycheck on a denim bustier by Out of Office, which everyone knows is the label started by Davi's parents.

Is she a bitch? Beatrix asks.

We haven't spoken, Charley says. However, Charley has noticed Davi watching her, then turning and whispering to her minions. They're making fun of Charley's clothes—but guess who doesn't give a fuck?

Charley spent over a thousand dollars of her own THB paychecks on Poshmark buying a vintage Brooks Brothers navy blazer, a boiled wool Tyrolean jacket from The Eagle's Eye, a Pappagallo belt with scallop-shell buckles. After Charley's father died the previous fall, Charley raided the shelves of his home office and came away with his yearbooks from St. George's School in Rhode Island, as well as a dog-eared copy of *The Official Preppy Handbook*. Charley recognized a future version of herself among the penny loafers and striped rugby shirts.

Davi could slut it up all she wanted. Charley was going Fair Isle.

What about the boys? Beatrix asks.

Now it's Charley's turn to type, then delete. She thinks about what happened on Move-In Day—the hottest guy she had ever seen in her life plunked down next to Charley during Chapel, introducing himself as Andrew Eastman, just call him East. Then, East sought Charley out at the cookout by the lake (which Charley was planning to skip before she learned it was mandatory). East asked to see her book, and she showed it to him, wondering if he might also be *literary*. (Was the world outside of Baltimore County filled with super-hot guys who read?)

Not this one. When Charley offered to lend him *The Night Circus* after she was finished with it, he said, "That's all right, I already have a book." It was a joke, but not.

So they wouldn't bond over Erin Morgenstern or Emily St. John Mandel or Sally Rooney, but East was able to persuade Charley to race him across the lake. All the lessons at York Manor Swim Club paid off; for a few shining moments, Charley was starring in a rom-com.

As they stood in line to get their lunch, East said, "I almost let you win, but I sensed that would have pissed you off."

"You sensed right," Charley said. "I hate being patronized."

"You held your own," East said. When he handed Charley the spoon for the potato salad, their fingers brushed. "Which kind of turned me on."

Charley had been struck dumb by this. It was only later, when she was back in her room, that the right response came to her: *You're that easy?* But in the moment, she had made a squeaking noise and scurried back to her quilt.

The next day, East turned up in Charley's history class. He chose the seat beside hers, but his eyes were glassed over and she was pretty sure she smelled weed. This was unsurprising, but a disappointment nevertheless.

Nothing to report on that front, Charley writes, which feels a bit disingenuous. Since fifth grade, Charley and Beatrix have shared every interaction with every boy they've spoken to or even looked at. Beatrix would gobble up these stories about East... but she would also make too much of them. Charley realizes that, at least in this, her mother was correct: Beatrix tends to blow things out of proportion.

But when it came to what happened with Joey, Charley believes her.

I miss you, Beatrix writes. Everyone at school misses you.

Charley's social life in Towson included movies at the Cinemark, trips to Owings Mills Mall, parties in people's finished basements, where Charley would drink exactly one White Claw (she could only tolerate the grapefruit flavor) and then spend the rest of the night babysitting Beatrix, making sure she didn't do an impromptu pole dance or disappear upstairs with one of the assholes from the lacrosse team.

If Charley's being honest, she sort of prefers reading by herself in this room on a floor where nobody's sure what to make of her. She has escaped the shackles of her former existence: her father's death, her mother and Joey, and yes, Beatrix.

I miss you too, Charley says.

4. GRWM

"She's still in her room," Olivia H-T says.

It's time, Davi thinks. She'd hoped Charley Hicks would approach her—wave, say hello, smile at her in the bathroom mirror—but it's been quite a while and she has remained *occult* ("beyond the range of ordinary knowledge; mysterious"). Davi hunts for the First Dance dress she packed before her mother (in an attempt to make amends for the hellscape their home life had become) presented her with an Out of Office custom creation—neon purple, bedazzled with Swarovski crystals, cut with diamond-shaped holes. Although Davi hates her mother (hates both of her parents, if she's being honest), she can't *not* wear the dress.

Davi remembers First Dance as a third-former when the whole grade wore tie-dye and they gathered in the common room to crop their shirts with safety scissors in an attempt to elevate the look (aka make them as slutty as possible). Davi feels a sudden rush of *altruism* ("the practice of selfless concern"): She wants to give Charley a good First Dance experience. She rummages through the basket of costumes that lives on the floor of her closet.

"Aha!" Davi says. She pulls out a neon-yellow-and-pink piece of nylon fabric punctured with holes, something considered a "dress" by only the fifth-form girls at Tiffin. She marches down the hallway, preparing to enter Room 111, which she hasn't done since Cinnamon died. Usually she would burst in unannounced, but Davi's mind travels back to the morning of May 12.

She'd snapped Cinnamon the night before and Cinnamon had left her on read, which was sort of weird, but when Davi tiptoed down the hall after lights-out and pressed her ear against Cinnamon's door, she heard faint guitar chords. Cinnamon was playing herself to sleep, something she did when she was anxious. Fine, Davi wouldn't bother her. In the morning, Davi texted as usual to see what Cinnamon's day was like. They were both doing community service as an afternoon activity, but they had recently gotten back their PSAT scores and Davi's verbal score was *abysmal* ("extremely bad; appalling")—so now, Davi adds to a list of potential testing words with definitions in the notes app of her phone.

Davi was planning on switching out of community service so she could take an online SAT prep course. She was hoping Cinnamon would join her, even though Cinnamon's score was far superior to Davi's.

There was no answer to her text. Davi went to the bathroom, but Cinnamon wasn't at the sink as usual. Also sort of weird; the girl was programmed like a robot.

When Davi got out of the shower and completed her skin care routine—her followers had been begging for another getting ready video but TBH, Davi was growing sick of her followers—she padded back down the hall in the new fluffy pink slippers that Gucci sent her and, once in her room, checked her phone. No text back. Davi considered going down to knock on Cinnamon's door, but instead she FaceTimed. No answer.

Davi texted: Girl pick up.

She got dressed and filmed a GRWM video for TikTok, though she was half-hearted about it. She grabbed her backpack thinking she and Cinnamon would snag the Booth for breakfast since they were early. It was Monday, which meant sausage and biscuits, and tonight was Burger Night and Piano Bar, which Cinnamon loved. That would cheer her up.

There was no answer when she knocked, and when Davi pressed her ear to the door, she heard nothing. "Cin?" she said. "I'm coming in?"

The door was locked. But no, not possible, the doors in the dorms didn't lock, which meant what? Cinnamon had jammed it?

"Cinnamon!" Davi shouted.

There was no response. She turned around. Olivia H-T was standing in the hallway. "Call Mr. James," Davi said.

"Ew, no," Olivia H-T said.

Mr. James was the one who patrolled the Schoolhouse and God's Basement for kids having sex, and everyone thought he got off on it. He'd once leered at Tilly Benbow's boobs, apparently. Davi liked Mr. James — he drove Davi to class in his Gator when she slipped on the ice and sprained her ankle in winter of third-form.

"Fine," Davi said. "I'll go get Ms. Robbie."

Davi's throat constricts as she remembers how Ms. Robinson and Mr. James forced open Cinnamon's door. Davi was hovering and Ms. Robbie shouted at her, *Stand back, stay in the hallway!* And then she heard Ms. Robinson cry out.

Davi takes a deep breath. She's here at Room 111 on a mission for good. Charley is probably having an outfit crisis, and Davi will be her savior. Davi knocks.

"What," Charley says.

Davi opens the door to find Charley sitting at her desk reading *The Talented Mr. Ripley*. Davi blinks; she uses her desk solely for filming makeup videos. She automatically goes to plop down on what she can only think of as "Cinnamon's bed" when she notices a tower of milk crates stacked into bookshelves and a whole corner of the room that looks like a greenhouse. There must be a dozen houseplants. A copper watering can sits on top of Charley's mini fridge.

Cute? Davi thinks. *Or weird?*

"Sorry to bother!" Davi says. "Everyone's getting ready for the dance, and I figured you might not have the right dress since this is your first year, so I brought you one."

Charley doesn't look up from her book. *Rude,* Davi thinks.

"Each class has its own outfit for First Dance," Davi says. "Fifth-form girls wear...these." She stares down at the neon mess in her hands.

Charley finally raises her eyes and grimaces. "That looks like one of the stress balls I used to beg my mom for at Five Below," she says.

Davi smiles. "In London, we'd get them at Home Bargains. You're right, they do have a certain...*semblance.* You're quite clever, aren't you?"

Charley blinks.

"Well, anyway, here you go. It'll fit, I think."

"Thanks," Charley says. "But I'm reading tonight."

"What?" Davi says.

"I'm not going to the dance," she says.

"You can't miss First Dance," Davi says.

Charley turns back to her book.

Davi knows she can wear this girl down, though why does she want to? Charley is *such* a freak, maybe the biggest freak to attend Tiffin in Davi's tenure. But there's a challenge to it (and if Davi were honest, she would admit to being a little bored socially). She would love to post the transformation of Charley Hicks on her TikTok— from weird to normal in a few short weeks. Viral, for sure.

But...she only has thirty minutes left to get ready, and she hasn't even started her body glitter. She leaves the dress draped across the bed; it really is hideous, but who is Davi to argue with Tiffin tradition?

"The dance starts at nine. It'll be fun, I promise," Davi says. She takes a beat. "Even East goes." This is a flat-out lie. East never goes to First Dance.

Charley doesn't move, but Davi notices a slight change in her facial expression at the mention of East's name and rolls her eyes.

"Why did you come here?" Davi says. The words sound *belligerent* ("hostile and aggressive"), but Davi is genuinely curious. Rumor has it this chick was a lock for valedictorian at her high school back in Maryland.

Charley gives Davi a decent stare down, and Davi feels a grudging respect. "There were some things at home I wanted to get away from," Charley says.

Well, Davi thinks, she and Charley have *that* in common. "Fair enough. Have a good night."

Davi opens the door and hears A Boogie blasting on the JBL speaker, everyone singing along. When Davi pops into the bathroom, Olivia H-T turns down "My Shit" and everyone crowds around, waiting for the tea.

"She's not going," Davi says.

"What?" Olivia H-T exclaims. "She does realize who you are, right? She should be grateful you're taking an interest."

Davi shrugs. Olivia H-T is a suck-up, and Davi is weary of suck-ups (which are basically every one of her friends).

"She's reading," Davi says. Charley Hicks will probably get a perfect verbal score on her SAT, and for one crazy second, Davi entertains the idea of staying home and studying herself. Haha! Is she losing it? She turns the music up. She would like everyone else to back off and find their own pathetic weirdo to save.

As the girls sing lyrics into the mirror, Davi runs a hand through her bob. She misses her long hair; next to her, Tilly Benbow throws up an effortless messy bun. Olivia H-T blends out her contour and takes a selfie.

Davi sighs. She longs for Cinnamon.

5. Admissions

You'd like to apply for a spot in the Tiffin Academy Class of 2030? Cordelia Spooner murmurs at her reflection in the bathroom mirror as she fastens her turquoise statement necklace before heading over to the Teddy for First Dance. *Hahahaha! You and everyone else in the country!*

The phone in the admissions office has been ringing nonstop, every single interview slot for the first semester is filled, and don't get Cordelia started on how robust the numbers for group tours have been this week. Tiffin offers an information session every weekday at ten, followed by a campus tour. A very busy week in past years would see groups of three, maybe four students per session, each with a parent or two. But yesterday there was even a group that totaled thirty-one people—twelve prospective students and nineteen parents. Annabelle Tuckerman had given the tour. She wasn't Cordelia's first choice, but Cordelia was desperate and Annabelle was eager to add one more piece of flair to her already gaudy application to Princeton.

The best tour guide Cordelia Spooner has seen in her twenty-two-year tenure was Cinnamon Peters. Cinnamon made a wonderful first impression—her dancer's posture, her musical voice, her long auburn hair—and, of course, her unusual and yet fitting first name. Nobody could sell Tiffin to prospective students the way Cinnamon could.

Cordelia blinks back tears. Cinnamon was beloved on campus by students and teachers alike. Her death *makes no sense.* But then, other people are mysteries. Cordelia Spooner understands this better than anyone.

After the thirty-one-person tour had dispersed, Cordelia had sent a text to Honey Vandermeid, the college counselor. America Today has made my life a special hell.

Honey texted back: Oh Cord, how about a little gratitude?

Of course Honey was right and Cordelia felt bad for complaining. The previous school year had ended with tragedy and heartbreak. If the media had learned that a student committed suicide in Classic South, Tiffin's application numbers would have plummeted. But Audre Robinson did a superlative job of preserving the privacy of the Peters family and the school alike. She handled the situation with care, dignity, and above all discretion.

America Today bestowing Tiffin with the number two ranking this year—above Northmeadow! Above Milton!—has provided exactly the boost they all needed. Even if the reason how/why is a bit perplexing. Even if Cordelia Spooner's workload will double (and maybe triple).

The night of First Dance has always been Cordelia's favorite. She strolls from her one-bedroom cottage behind the Manse over to the Teddy, enjoying the still-balmy late summer air. She overhears giggling, singing, happy chatter. The Tiffin football team won again yesterday, this time on the road, thanks to another spectacular pass from Dub Austin to Hakeem Pryce. A two-game winning streak might be the longest in Cordelia's tenure. Cordelia chuckles about this as she enters the Teddy.

The Edward Tiffin Student Union, known as the Teddy, was

constructed in the late '90s, thanks to a donation from Edward Tiffin's great-great-grandson "Teddy Five," who was an original pioneer in Silicon Valley at the start of the internet boom. The Teddy features soaring, open spaces, reclaimed-wood floors, and massive plate-glass windows that offer views across Tiffin's resplendent acreage. The Teddy had "work done" two years ago when Jesse Eastman joined the board of directors. He suggested turning the auditorium—once only used for Friday assembly and the school musical—into a three-hundred-seat theater with a retractable movie screen and Dolby surround sound. He also renovated the grill, added an "e," and modeled the new Grille on an English pub—with leather booths, burled wood tables, and brass pendant lighting. The Lower Level, which used to house a few Ping-Pong tables, became a proper arcade, a place very popular with the third-form boys.

The one spot Big East didn't dare change was the Egg, where school dances are held. The Egg is a large oval ballroom with a domed, illuminated ceiling that looks like, well, an egg.

At First Dance, the girls dress according to class. The third-form wear tie-dye, the fourth-form wear metallic, the fifth-form wear neon, and the sixth-form wear black. How did this start? And why do only the girls do this while the boys from every class wear black? Cordelia believes the matching dates back to the dawn of Instagram and Snapchat. And why only the girls? Maybe because the school—and the world at large—remains stubbornly gender-biased. Boys are judged for what they do. Girls are judged for how they look doing it.

Tonight, the Egg has been transformed into a nightclub. Green and gold laser lights crisscross the dance floor, and a disco ball spins. At one narrow, curved end of the Egg, a DJ named Radio (ironic?) is spinning tunes (Rihanna's "Please Don't Stop the Music";

the songs will get more explicit from here). At the other end of the Egg is the mocktail bar, where students can procure either a frozen piña colada or a strawberry daiquiri with a chocolate rim. The mocktail bar is, of course, controversial. The idea was proposed a number of years ago but was shot down by the former Head of School Chester Dell (who was a notorious killjoy). He didn't understand why the students couldn't just drink punch like Tiffin students had been doing since time immemorial. Audre Robinson was the one who finally okayed the mocktails. Did she find it unsettling that the kids were mimicking adult behavior, hoisting their daiquiris for a toast? A little bit, yes, but she wanted to pick her battles, and mocktails weren't among them.

Cordelia makes a beeline for the buffet. There's a charcuterie board complete with salami roses and a seeded cracker river. There are pigs in a blanket and deviled eggs. Cordelia contemplates inhaling the entire tray of pigs in a blanket, but then she spies Honey Vandermeid at the entrance, where students are checking in. "Checking in" means looking an adult in the eye and stating your first and last name. Are your eyes red and bleary? Are you slurring your words? If yes, then you may be subjected to a pat-down. (It goes without saying that kids hide nips of Tito's and Captain Morgan in their clutch purses and tube socks and then slip them into the mocktails.) The students have been told that the chaperones keep a Breathalyzer on hand; they don't, but the rumor has served as a useful deterrent. Cordelia has seen plenty of kids arrive at First Dance completely wasted—a fourth-former named Jonas Brim once threw up at Cordelia's feet; a girl named Lily Corning fell in her platform heels and broke her ankle. Neither child had been Honor Boarded because the school preferred to save Honor Board—the panel composed of five students and three faculty who decide upon consequences for disciplinary infractions—for more serious offenses such as cheating, stealing, and sneaking out.

"How goes it?" Cordelia asks. Honey looks beautiful tonight in a gauzy ivory dress that shows off her toned, tanned arms. Each day this summer, Honey swam twenty lengths of Jewel Pond, then lay out on the beach to dry off in the sun. Cordelia would often meet her there with a picnic and a chilled bottle of rosé. The rest of the staff and faculty left Tiffin for the summer while Cordelia and Honey "held down the fort." They spent mornings in the office dealing with administrative issues, then took the afternoons off. It was a luxury, having the whole campus to themselves. The only other person who stayed on was Mr. James, a Tiffin legend—he's the custodian, handyman, security. He's quirky—and a drunk—but he alone knows where all the bodies are buried, so Cordelia likes to keep on his good side.

Cordelia Spooner and Honey Vandermeid have been conducting a clandestine love affair ever since they bumped into each other unexpectedly at the Alibi the Christmas break before last. Cordelia had always found Honey attractive—her blond hair, her athletic build, her elegant style—and she intuited that Honey might be gay, if way out of Cordelia's league. Honey was eleven years younger—forty-six to Cordelia's fifty-seven—and a good deal less matronly. (Cordelia wore her hair sensibly short, and she favored embroidered sweaters, voluminous blouses, and Eileen Fisher schmatas meant to camouflage her shelflike bosom and the muffin top she could not seem to lose.) But that evening at the Alibi, as the bartender, Jefferson, refilled their glasses, they gossiped about Tiffin students and staff (except for Audre; they both adored Audre), and they laughed until they fell into each other. The night ended with them making out in the back seat of Honey's Jeep Cherokee.

The relationship with Honey has changed Cordelia's entire experience at Tiffin. The solitariness (indeed, loneliness) of Cordelia's out-of-school life has vanished. She now has a friend who is also a lover.

When Cordelia caresses Honey's elbow, Honey yanks her arm away as though she's been burned, and—almost too late—Cordelia sees that Simone Bergeron is just on the other side of Honey, holding a clipboard.

"It's been mostly third- and fourth-formers," Simone says. Simone is wearing a cocktail dress spangled with purple paillettes that is so short, it wouldn't pass dress code.

Hmmmm, Cordelia thinks. If Simone were a student, Cordelia would send her back to the dorms to change. Did Honey say anything to her? Maybe suggest adding a cardigan or putting on flat shoes so her legs don't seem quite so long?

The school year has just begun, but Simone Bergeron has already garnered a fair amount of attention from the students. Part of it is her age—Simone has just turned twenty-four; she graduated from McGill only two years earlier. Between graduating and getting the job at Tiffin, Simone worked as a barista at Le Brûloir in Montreal. Simone's mother is Quebecois, her father from Mali; they spoke both English and French at home. Simone had, in fact, applied to be the French teacher, but what was (desperately) needed was history, and Simone agreed to give it a shot. She was apparently as eager to take the job as Audre was to fill it.

"The fifth- and sixth-formers won't show up until nine," Cordelia says. "They like to make an entrance."

"Nine?" Simone says. "What time does the dance usually end? I was out late last night with Rhode Rivera. He took me to the Alibi, and I was overserved. I was hoping to meet my pillow by ten o'clock tonight."

"That's not going to happen," Cordelia says. "We need to be vigilant tonight, constantly monitoring who comes and goes. The kids will sneak off to the Schoolhouse, or to God's Basement. One of us should do the rounds in about an hour." She would like to suggest that Simone be the one to do the rounds so Cordelia and Honey can have some time alone, but Simone is wearing those impractical heels.

"Why would the kids go to the *Schoolhouse*?" Simone asks.

"To join the Harkness Society," Honey says. "That's what the kids call it when they have sex on the Harkness tables."

"It's a prestige thing," Cordelia says.

A look of distaste crosses Simone's face. "I teach at a Harkness table," she says. "And where is God's Basement?"

Is the woman daft? Cordelia wonders. Has no one filled her in on the very basics of Tiffin legend and lore? "The basement of the chapel," Cordelia says. "There are couches and chairs down there. Years ago it served as a reception area — before we had all this." She indicates the walls of the Teddy around them.

"The kids have sex in the *chapel*?" Simone says.

"The Harkness Society is a bigger coup," Honey says. "God's Basement is second choice."

"Although well-used," Cordelia says. "There are stains all over the furniture."

Simone bows her head and sways on her feet. She hands the clipboard to Honey. "I need to use the ladies' room." She hurries away.

Now Cordelia feels free to touch Honey's back. She and Honey have never had sex on a Harkness table, but they've stolen moments in God's Basement.

"Simone is a hot mess," Cordelia says. "Hungover. And that dress is disgraceful."

"Oh, lighten up, Cord, she's young," Honey says.

"All the more reason why she should be setting a better example. I'm sure you've noticed the boys ogle her…"

"The boys aren't the only ones," Honey says. "She might have the most fantastic legs I've ever seen."

Cordelia clears her throat. Is Honey trying to make her jealous?

"And the girls are dazzled by her as well. She needs to understand that she's a role model and not act in a manner unbecoming."

"You sound a hundred and fourteen years old," Honey says. She stiffens under Cordelia's touch. "Hands to yourself, please. We're in public."

"No one's here," Cordelia says. There's a group of third-form girls in a cluster on the dance floor, all playing with their hair, singing along to "Saving Up" by Dom Dolla. The new English teacher, Rhode Rivera, is lingering by the mocktail bar. He glances up at Cordelia and Honey, but he'll think the touch platonic.

"Cord," Honey says.

"What's *up* with you?" Cordelia asks. She can't keep the longing out of her voice. When school resumed, the romance and reverie of their summer came to an abrupt end; Honey became busy and distracted. Cordelia realizes that Honey has sixty sixth-formers to place in college, some of whom have very high and possibly unrealistic expectations (Annabelle Tuckerman comes to mind). But Cordelia also worries that Honey is tiring of her, and of their arrangement. Honey hasn't spent the night in Cordelia's cottage since Move-In Day.

"Nothing is up," Honey says in a voice so tight with irritation that Cordelia knows she's lying.

Cordelia tries not to panic. Has Honey become infatuated with Simone Bergeron? There's no time to ask because a gaggle of fourth-formers in their skintight metallic pink-and-blue skirts and silver bandeau tops approach the entrance checkpoint. The poor fourth-form — or sophomores, as they're known elsewhere — are probably the most overlooked class at Tiffin. They aren't upperclassmen, nor are they ingenues like the third-form. Cordelia smiles at the girls, though she can't recall a single one by name, and how is that possible when she would have interviewed at least some of them?

She feels relief when, behind the fourth-formers, she sees Hakeem Pryce and his girlfriend, Taylor Wilson, and with them (of course), Dub Austin. Hakeem raises a hand. "Yo, Mrs. Spooner, Ms. Vandermeid, Happy First Dance!"

Cordelia can't help but beam. Even twenty-two years in, she feels proud to be acknowledged by the students.

"Hakeem!" she says. "Taylor! Dub! Welcome!"

Honey, who now has the clipboard, squares her beautiful shoulders. "State your name, please," she says to Hakeem.

Lighten up, Honey, Cordelia thinks. Hakeem and Dub don't drink or do drugs. Not only do they care too much about their bodies, Hakeem aspires to play football in the Ivy League and Dub is a scholarship student and knows any infraction puts him at risk of being sent home to Durango. Taylor Wilson is also a good kid—her mother, Kathy, sits on the board of directors—though Taylor's eyes are suspiciously bright, her cheeks rosy. She's wearing the dress chosen (for what reason Cordelia cannot fathom) by the fifth-form: a neon tube with contrasting neon mesh overtop. The overall effect is that of a garish laundry basket.

"Taylor Wilson," she says to Honey, making eye contact and flashing her dazzling smile.

Does Honey see a glimmer of contraband in Taylor's demeanor? Taylor likely took a shot of Tito's from the "water bottle" she keeps in her mini fridge. Can Cordelia blame her? She'd love a glass of buttery chardonnay herself.

"Have fun," Honey says, admitting all three kids to the Egg.

With the arrival of the upperclassmen, First Dance officially begins.

Simone locks herself in the end stall of the girls' bathroom and throws up the banana she ate at lunch. When it comes to upset stomachs, Simone's mother, a pediatrician, swears by BRAT—bananas, rice, applesauce, toast. But ew, banana was an unappealing choice. What even *is* a banana but a rubbery, phallic-shaped fruit with a distinctive smell?

Simone wipes her mouth with toilet paper and flushes. She will never eat another banana, nor will she drink champagne. Even thinking the word *champagne* makes her dry heave.

It was very bad form to get so drunk during her first weeks at work. Has she learned nothing from the past?

Simone fears she might be in over her head with this job. She's certified to teach French, but somehow the French position that was advertised evaporated (there weren't enough students interested to justify a hire; everyone wanted to learn Spanish). What Tiffin had to offer Simone instead was history—fifth-form American studies and sixth-form world cultures. Simone's mother is Quebecois and her father immigrated to Canada from Mali when he was a boy—however, this hardly makes Simone qualified to teach world cultures. She knows even less about American history.

In addition to teaching those classes, the school was looking for a dorm parent for the fifth- and sixth-form girls.

"Do you have any experience in that kind of role?" Audre asked during Simone's interview.

The answer was yes: Simone had been a floor fellow at McGill—but she had been dismissed in disgrace less than two weeks before she graduated, and so Simone had chosen to leave it off her American résumé (she'd left it off her Canadian résumé as well, but everyone in the province of Quebec knew someone at McGill, and so they'd either heard what had happened on the first floor of McConnell or seen the video, and this was why Simone had spent the past two years making latte art).

Audre must have noticed the constipated expression on Simone's face because she started throwing out prompts. "Were you a camp counselor? An au pair? Did you ever... *babysit*?"

"*Oui*," Simone said. "Yes, I babysat." She did not mention that this was a job she'd held the summer she turned twelve and was properly more mother's helper than babysitter.

But it didn't matter because Audre beamed. "Wonderful!" she said. "We'd love to offer you the position."

Upon arriving at Classic South, Simone papered the door of her room and wrote *If you don't stretch, you won't grow* at eye level in black Sharpie. Then she encouraged the girls to write their own favorite quotes. *"The people who are crazy enough to think they can change the world are the ones who do." —Steve Jobs. "There is no substitute for hard work." —Thomas Edison. "They tried to make me go to rehab, but I said no, no, no!" —Amy Winehouse.* The door has now become an attraction. The girls will stop by to see if anything new has been added, and they'll try to guess who wrote what. ("That's Tilly's, I'm pretty sure...")

There's no denying that most of the kids like Simone; her youth, to them, is a surprise and a delight. They feel that she can more easily understand their roommate disputes, menstrual cycles, and Snapchat accounts. Simone knows what "left on read" means; she might be the only faculty member at the school who does.

But there are two students who have already managed to get under Simone's skin. One is Charley Hicks. She's in Simone's F-period American history class, and—Simone will just admit it—she has a better grasp of the material than Simone does. Simone assigned a reading of Bartolomé de Las Casas on the exploitation of Indigenous people, and Charley's response to this reading left everyone in the class speechless, including Simone. After class, Simone had pulled Charley aside: *Do you have a special interest in Indigenous people?* she'd asked. And Charley had shrugged. *Not really, but*

I did the reading and I checked out some Native American creation stories.

Simone was eager to segue to the topic of Charley's behavior in the dorm. Why did she skip the ice cream social in the common room?

When Simone was leaving the dorm earlier, she noticed Davi Banerjee—whom Simone treats as an equal probably more than she should—knocking on Charley's door. Davi had one of the mesh dresses tucked under her arm, and Simone experienced a wave of relief because there was *no way* Charley would have purchased the fifth-form First Dance dress on her own.

Thank god for Davi, Simone thought.

Before Simone exits the stall, she hears a group of students enter. She peers through the crack in the door. The girls are all in tie-dye: third-formers. Freshmen.

"I heard he never comes to First Dance," one of the girls says, before pouting in the mirror to apply lip gloss.

"I heard he has a private party in his room, invitation only," another girl says.

"Should we try to crash?" a third girl asks. "I've heard he gets good drugs."

Simone nearly gasps. The girl speaking is only fourteen, what does she know about "good drugs"? Then Simone checks herself. Didn't she first try pot her freshman year? No, it was the summer between freshman and sophomore year. She was *fifteen*.

"He's not going to let us in," the first girl says. "I've heard he doesn't fuck."

"Like, at *all*? What is he, asexual?"

"He is *so* hot. The hottest guy in school."

Simone closes her eyes and shakes her head. She now knows who they're talking about: Andrew Eastman. She shoves away her absolutely inappropriate response to this chatter. *He never comes to First Dance?* A tiny, very secret part of her is crushed. Would she admit, even to herself, that she chose this dress with East in mind? He doesn't fuck? She feels an odd elation: She would have assumed he was able to seduce any girl in school, maybe even multiple girls at once.

"Honestly, I think he's kind of pathetic. He reclassed when he got here and I heard he was held back somewhere along the way, so he's nineteen. A nineteen-year-old fifth-former? He'll be twenty when he graduates. What a joke."

He's nineteen, Simone thinks. This doesn't surprise her. He seems older.

She can't linger here any longer or the girls will know she's eavesdropping, besides which, Honey and Mrs. Spooner will be wondering where she is and Spooner was already giving off some pretty judgy vibes. Simone flushes the toilet again and steps out of the stall. "Hi, girls!" she says.

"Hey, Miss Bergeron," they say. One adds, "That dress is so cute."

"Merci," Simone says. As she washes her hands, she basks in the admiring glances of the girls in the mirror. *Forget him,* she thinks. She is Miss Bergeron, history teacher, dorm parent, role model.

6. Tiffin Talks: First Dance

As usual, the first people to arrive at the dance are the third- and fourth-formers. They rush the mocktail bar, and one of the third-formers, a kid named Reed Wheeler, whose father is some hotshot real estate agent on Nantucket, spikes his piña colada with a nip of Fireball he hid in his underwear. (This kid will either end up becoming a legend in a couple of years, we think, or get Honor Boarded and expelled.) Do any of the chaperones notice the clot of boys surrounding Reed as he chugs the drink? Nah—they're completely clueless.

Two of the chaperones—Miss Bergeron and Mr. Rivera—are new this year, so they might not know what to look for. Miss Bergeron is a smokeshow in a sequin minidress. Reed, emboldened by his cocktail and not realizing Miss Bergeron is a teacher and not a sixth-former, tries to pull her out on the floor to dance to Ke$ha's "Die Young," but Miss Bergeron laughs and shakes her head. *Damn*, we think, *that would have been a conquest.*

There are actually a few fifth-formers among us already: QB1 Dub Austin sits at one of the round tables with wide receiver Hakeem Pryce and Hakeem's girlfriend, Taylor Wilson. When did *they* slip in, and why are they here so early? Some of us consider approaching the table to congratulate Dub and Hakeem on their *second win in a row*, but we can tell a visit might not be welcome. Taylor Wilson is sitting so close to Hakeem she's practically in his lap, but she's talking to Dub, reaching across the table and clenching his forearm. The mood at the table is reminiscent of those nights when our parents discussed whether they had enough money to send us to boarding school. What could these three be talking about?

"You're a cowboy, so I shouldn't have to tell you," Taylor says. "It's time to get back on the horse."

"No," Dub says.

Hakeem pinches Taylor's waist to let her know she's out of bounds. But his girl sets her own agenda; she's a hopeless romantic.

"I want you to be as happy with someone as Hakeem and I are," she says.

Dub says, "I was that happy." This is mostly true. "Nobody can replace Cinnamon. I'll never trust anyone like that again." This is completely true.

"I get it," Taylor says, though she doesn't, quite. Taylor and Cinnamon were friendly and friend-adjacent, but not really friends. They were rivals—maybe that's too strong a word?—in that they both wanted exactly the same things. They both auditioned for *Grease*. Cinnamon was cast as Sandy, Taylor as Frenchie. Cinnamon played the guitar, Taylor the piano. They both planned to run for Head Prefect or Honor Board chair; they both planned to apply to Duke Early Decision.

Taylor was just as devastated as everyone else when Cinnamon died, though her loss had a different timbre. On Miss Bergeron's door, Taylor wrote the Louisa May Alcott quote *"Rivalry adds so much to the charms of one's conquests."* Without Cinnamon around, Taylor supposes she'll get the lead in the school musical, and she'll run uncontested for Honor Board chair next year. It feels anticlimactic somehow.

"There are a lot of cute third-formers," Taylor says.

Dub scoffs. "I am *not* dating a freshman." Dub stubbornly clings to his public-school vocabulary. He still isn't sure what's meant by a "form." To him, it sounds like a mold they're all supposed to fit. He holds Taylor's gaze. "Will you please stop?"

"Just sample the buffet, bro," Hakeem says as his gaze rolls appreciatively over the dance floor. "There *are* a lot of fine third-formers this year."

Taylor elbows Hakeem in the ribs. "Keep talking like that and I'll date Dub, and you can have your little third-formers."

Hakeem laughs, though it's not entirely funny. He has long suspected that Taylor has feelings for Dub. She and Cinnamon had a frosty relationship, so the four of them could never really hang out—and Hakeem got the distinct vibe that Taylor was jealous of Cinnamon and Dub. Now she's obsessed with the man's love life. Hakeem suspects she's secretly pleased that Dub doesn't want to date again. Since the start of school, the three of them have done everything together—except football, which is just Hakeem and Dub, and C-period English, which is just Dub and Taylor. During C-period, Hakeem takes Intro to Anthropology, and when he left class on Thursday, he found Taylor and Dub strolling down the hall, heads together, laughing, until they spotted him and sobered up. Does this chafe Hakeem? Yes, a little bit. In anthropology, they've started learning about societal structures, and all Hakeem can think is that he and Taylor and Dub are practicing some kind of polyandry, which is when a woman takes more than one husband.

He notes the way Taylor and Dub are staring at each other right now.

He takes Taylor by the hand. "Let's dance."

Taylor rises with reluctance. "Are you coming, Dub?"

"Nah," he says, gazing over at the food. "I'm going to take Hakeem's suggestion and sample the buffet."

Dub is relieved when Hakeem and Taylor head off to the dance floor; being around the two of them is torture.

The DJ plays a dance remix of Lana del Rey's "Summertime Sadness."

This song reminds him of Cinnamon, but to be fair, most songs do. He's not quite sure how he's supposed to bounce back from what happened. She killed herself. It wasn't a cry for help, and it wasn't an accidental overdose. She'd left the note under the flowers he'd picked for her. *I'm sorry.*

And... there's something else eating at him.

In the hours before she died, Cinnamon sent Dub an email with an attachment. The subject of the email—which she'd notably sent to his little-used Gmail address and not his school account—was DO NOT OPEN THIS FILE UNTIL THE MORNING OF OUR GRADUATION.

The body of the email said: I mean it, Dub. Save this in the vault until May 29, 2027. You're the only one I can trust. I love you and you're going to be fine, I promise. Cin.

Dub has, of course, toyed with opening the file. What could it be? A part of him worries that it's some kind of tell-all spilling the confidences Cinnamon had been keeping, including Dub's own. But no, Cinnamon wouldn't do that. Then again, she'd already done something unthinkable.

Although his cursor has spent plenty of time blinking on top of the attachment, he hasn't clicked it open. She sent this to him—and not to Davi—for a reason. She knew he alone would keep it secret. He would do exactly as she asked him: Save the file until the morning of graduation, a year and nearly nine months from now.

Dub watches Hakeem and Taylor dance. He doesn't want to think about graduation. It will mean leaving all the people he loves.

What the hell, he thinks. When he heads out to the dance floor, everyone cheers.

Kodak Black, the Killers, Calvin Harris, Fisher: The dance is a full-on rave, and we're all out on the dance floor in one pulsing mass of sweaty teenage humanity. Mr. Rivera passes out glow-in-the-dark loops, which we fashion into necklaces, bracelets, halos. Then, finally, Davi and her entourage make their entrance—like Beyoncé at the Met Ball, Davi is always the last to arrive. The crowd parts so that Davi and all the Madisons and Olivias can take center floor. The DJ plays "Doses and Mimosas," and we pogo-jump with our fists in the air, chanting, "To all the bitch-ass hoes who hate me the most..."

The next song is Mike Posner's "Cooler Than Me," and we back out into a wide circle so that Head of School Ms. Robinson can have one dance. This year she's escorted by Señor Perez, who has moves—he twirls and dips Ms. Robinson. We hoot and cheer and take videos that we'll post later so that kids from other schools can watch them and wish they too went to Tiffin.

7. The Tunnel

Audre Robinson steps off the dance floor perspiring and exhilarated. Señor Perez is still out boogying with the kids, but Audre's tradition is one dance only. She'll be the subject of 114 private Snapchat stories, but it's all in good fun.

She grabs a box of water from a silver bowl on the buffet table (there are no single-use plastics at Tiffin) and heads to the entrance, which has now become the exit. She'll remind each student leaving the dance: *You may go only to the Grille or back to the dorms.* The school year has been without infractions so far, but Audre assumes some are coming. First Dance makes the kids horny; they're high on endorphins and sugar from the mocktails, and a few will no doubt try to sneak into God's Basement or the Schoolhouse to join the Harkness Society. Mr. James is patrolling the grounds in the Gator, but on Saturdays, she knows, he starts drinking right after lunch, so how effective will he be?

Honey Vandermeid and Cordelia Spooner are stationed by the door. Audre senses tension between them: Are they squabbling? Audre hears Honey say, "Honestly, Cord, when did you get so *needy*?"

Oh dear, Audre thinks. She knows that Honey and Cordelia are lovers; she once caught Honey emerging from Cordelia's cottage so early in the morning—and looking so ravished—that it couldn't be explained any other way. While Honey fumbled for an excuse, Audre said, "Your personal life is your own business. Just be discreet." Audre values Honey—her skills as a college counselor are unparalleled—and Audre counts Cordelia Spooner as the MVP of Tiffin's staff. Audre relies on her good judgment, her clear eye, and most importantly, her discretion. Cordelia Spooner is the only other person at the academy who has specific knowledge of the agreement with Jesse Eastman.

"Everything okay here?" Audre asks.

Cordelia whips around. "Hello, Audre."

"I'm going in to dance," Honey says.

"Please do," Audre says. "You can go too, Cordelia. I'll take over here."

"I'm sure Honey wants to dance with Miss Bergeron," Cordelia says.

"Do you hear yourself?" Honey asks.

Audre turns to inspect the dance floor and spies Simone Bergeron by the mocktail bar, talking to Rhode Rivera. He takes her hand and leads her to the dance floor.

Hmmm, Audre thinks. She knows the kids love it when the teachers dance, but she wouldn't want any rumors circulating about Miss Bergeron and Mr. Rivera.

"Looks like Simone is busy," Honey says. "Come with me to get a daiquiri, Cord."

"No, thanks," Cordelia says. "I don't *need* one."

"Suit yourself," Honey says, and she marches off.

The song changes to "Perfect" by Ed Sheeran, and Audre watches the kids pair up. She asked DJ Radio to keep slow songs to a minimum, so someone must have requested this. Audre sees Taylor and Hakeem mash together as Dub Austin slinks away. Audre wonders if Davi might come to the rescue and ask Dub to dance, but Davi and her squad are slow-dancing in a neon clot. Rhode Rivera leads Simone out to the dance floor. She looks *extremely* uncomfortable, maybe even a bit ill, as she and Rhode shuffle in a tentative circle while third-form girls film them from a nearby table.

Suddenly, Audre gets the Feeling. Something is wrong, something more than Dub's lonely heart, or a burgeoning romance between her two new faculty members, or Honey and Cordelia in a lovers' spat — but Audre can't figure out what it is. Something she's neglected or forgotten? It's a left-the-iron-on kind of feeling, though Audre distinctly remembers turning her iron off and leaving it unplugged on her granite countertop in the kitchen of the Manse.

Then it hits her. She snatches up the clipboard. On the first two pages, every name is followed by a check mark, except for one name at the bottom of the second page: Andrew Eastman. This Audre ignores. But when she flips to the next page, she sees another blank space: Charlotte Hicks.

Gah! Audre thinks. How is it that neither Simone Bergeron, Charley's dorm parent, nor Cordelia Spooner, who shares Audre's concern that Charley isn't fitting in, noticed that Charley isn't at the dance? Well, Audre supposes, the answer is they're both distracted.

Audre sighs. First Dance isn't *mandatory;* skipping it doesn't count as a missed commitment—though not attending is a red flag of sorts. The idea of Charley sitting in 111 South by herself while everyone else is here is unbearable to Audre. She would go check on her, but an unexpected visit from the Head of School at nine thirty at night will no doubt make Charley even more uncomfortable than she already is.

Audre has a better idea, one that will kill two birds. She strides onto the dance floor and taps Simone Bergeron on the shoulder. She and Mr. Rivera come to a standstill.

"Sorry to interrupt," Audre says. "Would you go to the dorms, please, and check on Charley Hicks?"

"Of course," Simone says. If Audre isn't mistaken, Simone appears relieved. "For the record, I begged her to come. Davi lent her a dress. But she said to me, and I quote, 'I would prefer not to.'"

Mr. Rivera barks out a laugh. "She's pulling a Bartleby," he says. "We read it this past week in class, and Charley had a fair amount to say about Bartleby's self-expression through passive resistance."

"That's all fine and well," Audre says. "But I would still like you to put eyes on her, Simone."

Miss Bergeron nods, and Mr. Rivera says, "Should I go too? Charley and I have a rapport."

"Just Miss Bergeron, please," Audre says. "We need you here." Taylor and Hakeem have started making out (forbidden: page 12 of *The Bridle*). There's no kissing permitted, no fondling, and certainly no grinding. Why does Audre have to be the one to police this? She sees Honey and Cordelia still bickering.

The slow song ends, and DJ Radio plays something with heavy bass next that makes the kids cheer. Taylor and Hakeem pull apart; Dub rejoins them on the dance floor. Miss Bergeron heads purposefully out the door, with the gaze of at least a dozen boys following her. Her dress is quite short and her heels quite high. Will Audre have to speak to her about appropriate wardrobe choices? Oh, she hopes not.

Simone inhales the cool night air as though she's a woman drowning. Rhode is a nice guy, he's even kind of cute for someone his age, and Simone desperately needs an ally at this place, but she gets the sense that he's into her, and that makes things *mal à l'aise.* Their conversation by the mocktail bar started out okay. Simone complained about her hangover, but this somehow led to Rhode telling Simone about his ex-girlfriend, Lace Ann, back in New York. She hit it big with her croissant business and left Rhode for one of her investors. Simone responded in the appropriate way: *Oh no, I'm sorry, I can't believe she did that,* though Simone *can* believe it, because why would Lace Ann stay with Rhode when she could bed some finance bro who had a standing reservation at Torrisi and could helicopter her out to the Hamptons?

I have this recurring fantasy where I do something extraordinary and she realizes she was a fool to leave me, Rhode says. *It's not that I even want her back. I would just like a moment of triumph.*

Did he realize he was chaperoning a high school dance? Simone wondered. And was his desire for this kind of revenge a red flag?

Simone was horrified when the DJ played a slow song. Every muscle in her body tensed, and she hoped she and Rhode could just gossip about which kids were pairing up. But as she feared, he said, "Let's go show them how it's done," and reached for her hand. It was *such* a cringey, Dad thing to say (because Rhode is *old! Four! Tee!* Nearly twice Simone's age!), but to turn him down felt unnecessarily churlish, and so Simone let him lead her to the dance floor. It was a textbook example of a woman agreeing to something that made her uncomfortable simply so she didn't hurt a man's feelings, ruffle feathers, or seem like a bitch. Simone would have counseled any of her students to say, "Thanks for the offer, but I'm not feeling it right now."

What, then, is wrong with *her*?

Simone was relieved that Rhode wasn't a flashy dancer, but it was nearly as bad that he had no moves at all. He put his hands on Simone's shoulders, and they turned in a slow circle like a couple of zombies. The kids took videos of them, and Simone wanted to vaporize.

Just as Rhode asked, "So what's your deal? Are you seeing anyone? Or were you, before you got here?"—which was a thinly veiled way of asking if she was available—Audre Robinson interrupted, and Simone was so relieved she could have kissed her.

The next time Simone is alone with Rhode, she needs to be clear that she's interested in friendship only.

The quickest way back to Classic South is across the Pasture, but Simone is wearing her stupid heels, which will sink into the grass. When she gets back to the dorm, she'll change into sneakers (all the girls were wearing sneakers with their dresses, even Davi Banerjee). Simone clips along the road, taking a moment to appreciate the beauty of the Tiffin campus: the classic brick architecture (Georgian, she's learned), the Pasture enclosed by white horse fencing, the athletic fields to her left. Simone can just make out the ghostly arms of the football goalposts in the moonlight. The bells of the chapel ring the half hour—it must be nine thirty—and the only other sound is the faint thump of bass coming from the Teddy. Tiffin exists in a bubble; it feels removed, sealed off from the rest of the world. Do traffic, pollution, poverty, pestilence, or the Olive Garden even exist? You would never know it from where Simone is standing. She is oh-so-fortunate to be here. She might be out of her depth, but she's always been a strong swimmer.

She rolls her eyes at herself.

In Classic South, most of the room lights are off—the girls are good about not wasting resources—with the exception of Simone's own room (Simone's embarrassed that she forgot to turn off her light) and one dimly lit room at the end of the hall. That would be Charley, in 111. Simone heads to her own room first in the interest of changing her shoes. Also, she needs to think about what to say.

Immediately, she notices something different about her door. There's a new quote written in red Sharpie northwest of the doorknob. *"It's better to be yourself and have no friends than to be like your friends and have no self."* The quote is unattributed; lots of the quotes on the door are; the girls find them on the internet and snatch them up like impulse buys at Target. Fine. There isn't a doubt who added this quote, especially since tonight everyone is at the dance but Charley.

Simone considers the quote as she pries off her heels—*ahhhhhh*—and slips into her Vejas. The girls love that Simone wears Vejas just like they do, though in light of Charley's quote, does she feel the pinch of conformity? Is it cool that Simone wears the same brand of sneakers that all the kids do, or is it pathetic? And why, exactly, is she checking on Charley? If Charley Hicks is happier lying in bed reading, isn't it her prerogative to do so uninterrupted? Must she be made to feel like a pariah? Audre Robinson is, no doubt, hypersensitive to the school's outliers after what happened the year before, but Charley doesn't seem sad, depressed, or even lonely. *Au contraire,* she's a strong, independent thinker.

Simone is tempted to return to the dance without laying eyes on Charley, but Audre will ask Simone for a report, and what's Simone going to do—lie? She heads down the hall, intentionally squeaking the soles of her sneakers against the linoleum so Charley will hear her coming. She pauses before Charley's door, sets an ear against it, hears nothing. There's a strip of dim light at the bottom. Charley is reading, or maybe she's fallen asleep. Simone pauses. What if she wakes Charley up?

But she has no choice, she's under direct orders from the Head. She knocks.

There's no response. Sleeping, then. Simone tiptoes away, imagining herself saying *Charley was asleep* and the expression of relief on Audre's face. Simone can't fathom what it was like to have opened that very door and found a student dead. Simone stops in her tracks and heads back to Charley's room. She knocks on the door a little louder.

"Charley?" she says. "Charley, it's Miss Bergeron."

There's no response. Simone puts her hand on the knob. This feels like an egregious invasion of privacy, though after just a week and a half of school, Simone has learned dorm culture: Girls walk in and out of one another's rooms all the time, sometimes with a cursory knock, but sometimes they just barge in like they're all siblings.

The doors in the dorm don't lock, so the knob turns easily. Simone knows that on the day she killed herself, Cinnamon Peters wedged the door shut with her desk chair. She didn't want to be saved.

"Charley?" Simone says again. "Charley, I'm coming in."

Still no answer. Simone eases open the door, pokes her head inside. The light is coming from a tiny reading lamp that Charley has suction-cupped to the wall above her bed. There's a nice seagrass rug, a framed poster of Virginia Woolf, an entire corner filled with plants. Charley has turned her milk crates into bookshelves that are stacked floor to ceiling.

The bed is neatly made with a patchwork quilt and two pillows in crisp white cases. There's a navy fleece throw blanket smoothed across the bottom of the bed; Simone sees it's embroidered with an ALE...then she figures out it's a Yale blanket. A copy of *The Talented Mr. Ripley* is open face down on the quilt, and...there's a yellow-and-pink neon tube dress crumpled on the floor.

Simone enters the room. "Charley?"

The desk chair is empty, Charley's laptop—closed—lies next to her math textbook.

Simone hurries down the hall to the bathroom, but the lights are out. She turns them on and searches the showers first, then pushes in the door of each of the toilet stalls. "Charley?" Her voice is shaking. "Charley?"

Where is she?

The common space is dark and deserted, so Simone proceeds down the hall, opening the doors to all the other rooms, but not one of them is occupied.

"Charley!" Simone is shouting now, thinking, *Is this what it feels like to be a parent?* If so, how awful. Simone won't be able to get a clear breath until she finds the child.

Simone charges up to the second floor. It's a sixth-form floor this year, many of them doubles. Fourth- and fifth-form students have singles because the workload is so intense; by sixth-form, the heavy lifting is mostly over and the girls feel nostalgic. Their boarding school days are coming to an end. What did Honey Vandermeid tell Simone? *They would all sleep in the common room together if I let them.*

The second-floor bathroom is rumored to have the best water pressure in the building; maybe Charley took this opportunity to check it out. But the second-floor bathroom is dark as well.

Simone goes back down to the first floor and checks Charley's room again. What is the room trying to tell her? It looks as though

Charley stepped out for a moment. Was she hungry? Like the rest of the kids, Charley has a mini fridge as well as hanging baskets of various snacks. Charley's tastes run toward Cool Ranch Doritos, Takis, birthday-cake-flavored Oreos. Perfectly disgusting and normal.

Simone wants to cry. Where did Charley go? Was she abducted? Maybe Tiffin isn't the protective bubble Simone thinks it is. If everyone else was at the dance, what would stop a serial killer from creeping onto campus and preying on a vulnerable girl left alone in the dorm?

But there's no sign of a struggle in Charley's room. Simone is being absurd. Maybe Charley actually went to the dance; maybe she cut across the Pasture and Simone missed her. Simone calls Rhode. When he picks up, she hears "Afraid to Feel."

"Simone?" Rhode says. "Everything okay?"

"Of course," Simone says. She doesn't want to sound any alarms just yet. "I'm just confirming that Charley Hicks ended up coming to the dance. She's there, right?"

"No," Rhode says, and Simone's hopes shatter. *Fuck,* she thinks. *Fuck!* "Why, is she not in her room?"

"She's not in her room," Simone says. "But it looks like she just stepped out for a minute. I thought maybe she was there."

"She's not, I would have noticed her," Rhode says. He pauses. "Do you want me to tell Audre?"

"Please don't," Simone says. "I'm sure she'll turn up. She probably went to the Paddock."

"The Paddock is closed," Rhode says. "I'll go upstairs and check the Grille."

"Good idea," Simone says. "Text me if she's there, please. I'll do a little walk around."

Rhode hangs up, and Simone experiences some relief, at least, in sharing the news, even if it was with someone as clueless as she is.

Charley is probably at the Grille; the food there is good, they serve smashburgers and thin, crispy fries and also a killer lemongrass chicken banh mi and sweet potato tots that Simone is in danger of becoming addicted to. Of course Charley went to the Grille. However, a second later, there's a text from Rhode: Not in Grille. Not in theater or arcade. Not in the Teddy at all.

Simone steps outside. The moon shines over the four spires of the chapel. *The chapel?* Simone thinks. Is Charley *religious*? The only thing she seems to worship is books.

Then, Simone gets it—the library! Charley probably went to the Sink. Maybe she came across something in her reading that she wanted to explore further (*but*, Simone thinks, *isn't that what the internet is for?*). Still, Simone will check the Sink. She'll probably find Charley wandering the stacks or maybe doing the unthinkable and trying out the Senior Sofa. The Senior Sofa, located on the landing that overlooks the first floor of the library, is for sixth-form students only; not even faculty can sit on it, or even stand on the Persian rug under it. The sofa is wide and deep, Tiffin green velvet with gold cord trim. As Audre Robinson explained, the Senior Sofa is a hallowed Tiffin tradition. "It's hideous and not even particularly comfortable," she said. "But because it's off-limits until the kids reach sixth-form, it's the most coveted seating in the entire school."

As Simone hurries along, far more fleet now that she's in her sneakers, she hears a mechanical whir and sees a John Deere Gator appear out of the darkness. The school custodian, Mr. James, is driving. Simone flags him down, mostly so he won't run her over. He's cruising at quite a clip.

"Hi?" she says. "I'm Simone Bergeron, the history teacher?" She has never spoken to Mr. James, and she's afraid he'll mistake her for a student.

"Yup," he says with a curt nod. "I know who you are."

He knows who she is? Should she be flattered or alarmed?

"We seem to be missing a student," she says. "A girl, tall, thin, wears glasses. Have you seen her walking around?"

"Everyone's at the dance," Mr. James says.

"Everyone except this one student," Simone says. She takes in Mr. James's appearance. He's somewhere in his early sixties, white, a bit overweight, with a military buzz cut and striking blue eyes. He has a gruffness about him, an indifference and authority that make him attractive. Simone's not sure why she's surprised. Everyone at Tiffin is good-looking; it's like some kind of requirement.

Can Simone charm him? "You're the head of security, right?"

Mr. James stares at her. "I haven't seen her, sweetheart."

Calling Simone "sweetheart" is inappropriate. Would he call a male teacher "sweetheart"?

But Simone doesn't have time to be offended. "I'm going to check the Sink."

Mr. James laughs. "The Sink is all locked up. She's not there."

Fuuuuck! Simone thinks. "Okay, then she really is lost."

Mr. James runs a shovel-sized hand over his square head. "She'll turn up," he says. He winks at Simone — again, so inappropriate — and zips off down the path.

Simone turns to watch him go. It is *literally* that dude's job to help and...he just doesn't care. Simone is appalled by his lack of concern. Or should she be heartened? *She'll turn up.*

Simone has no choice now but to return to the dance and tell Audre that Charley is missing. She'll report the interaction with Mr. James as well, though who is she kidding: Men like Mr. James are never held accountable. He's worked here 114 years and knows all the school's dirty little secrets.

As Simone pivots to head back to the Teddy, something catches her eye. There's a set of cement stairs that leads down into what must be the basement of Classic South, and Simone can see that the basement door is ajar. She stands at the top of the stairs and peers down — definitely ajar. She feels like Nancy fucking Drew, although the very last thing she wants to do right now is play girl detective and descend into the scary basement. She should go get Audre.

But instead, Simone turns on her phone's flashlight and stomps down the stairs, fueled by annoyance at Mr. James and by her desire to find Charley. (She is Charley's dorm parent. Even though she was tasked with chaperoning the dance and can't be two places at once, she somehow knows Charley's disappearance will be perceived as her fault.)

She yanks the door open and steps into the basement. It's cavernous and dark, filled with furniture, extra beds and desks. The furnace hums; she sees the hot water tanks and other inner workings of a large residential hall that she can't identify.

"Charley?" she says. She wanders to the far corner of the basement where there's a door. *A door that leads where?* she wonders. This is Edgar Allan Poe shit. She tries the knob, and although it sticks a bit, she's able to pull it open — and she's faced with another set of stairs that leads farther underground.

She hears voices. Or is she imagining things?

"Charley?" she says. "Charley, are you down there?"

Silence.

When the chapel bells chime nine, the music in the first-floor bathroom abruptly stops. *Thank god,* Charley thinks. The past hour has consisted of incessant screeching. *Take one with my phone, take one with mine.* Charley can envision the girls forming different configurations, and she laughs when she overhears Olivia H-T ask to take a pic of just her and Davi, and Davi says, "I don't think that's necessary." (Charley is reluctant to admit it because she hates going along with the group mentality, but Davi *is* kind of cool.)

The girls on her floor have now spent more time getting ready for First Dance than they'll spend at the actual dance. What a waste of time.

Charley hears the front door slam shut, and she peeks around her window shade to see the neon river flowing up toward the Teddy. *Do I wish I was with them? I do not.*

And yet...she can't stop herself from picking up the dress Davi left on her bed. It's hideous for sure, but even so, Charley tries it on. It's as snug as a wetsuit, and Charley turns in the mirror. She takes off her glasses and undoes her braids, which leaves her hair in kinky waves. She considers going into the bathroom and using Olivia H-T's makeup—Olivia is Tiffin's answer to Sephora—but Charley would need a YouTube video. She hasn't worn makeup since her ballet recital in fourth grade.

Just as she's thinking it might be amusing to shock the hell out of everyone by showing up at the dance, she hears something hit her window. It sounds like a pebble. Random? Oh, she hopes so. But then there's another strike, more forceful. Then a voice. *Hey.* Charley returns to the window and peers behind the shade.

It's East.

"Let me in," he says, pointing to the front door.

Charley imagines her mother getting a call from the school alerting her that Charley has sneaked a boy in. (Her mother would be thrilled.) Everyone is at First Dance; no one will be back in the dorm for at least another hour. But she can't let East see her like this. She shucks off the dress and pulls on her jeans and the red-and-navy rugby shirt that used to belong to her father. Replaces her glasses. Then she hurries to the foyer and peeks out in both directions before letting East inside. Without an invitation, he strides down the hall toward her room.

"Why aren't you at the dance?" he asks.

"Why aren't *you* at the dance?" Charley tries to keep her voice chill even though she's completely shook.

"I have to maintain a certain mystique," he says. "I can't be hanging around with the hoi polloi."

Hoi polloi? Charley thinks. East isn't stupid, and yet she's pretty sure he's going to fail history, which is the one class they have together. He doesn't do any of the reading. Like, none of it.

"Well, I didn't come to Tiffin to dance," Charley says. They've reached the door to Charley's room, but East strides right past it and heads around the corner toward the stairs.

"Come with me," he says. "There's something I've been wanting to check out."

"Do I need shoes?"

"You need shoes."

Charley ducks into her room and slips on her Top-Siders. She looks at the book splayed open on her bed. Has Tom Ripley been a bad influence? Is she just going to follow East into the unknown... and probably end up Honor Boarded and right back at home with her mother and Joey?

No! she thinks. But her feet don't have any sense of their own. She goes after him.

He leads her out the back of the dorm to a set of concrete steps that leads to a subterranean door. The basement, great, this is so against the rules there probably isn't even a category for it in *The Bridle*. And yet, when East yanks the door open, Charley follows. He's been here for two years, she's brand-new; if she gets caught, she'll claim ignorance. They walk through a dank, cavernous room filled with excess furniture to another door that leads even deeper into the bowels of the building.

Charley balks. "What is this?"

"Just follow me," East says. "My dad was in charge of the

renovations on campus, and when I looked at the as-built, I noticed a tunnel that connects the dorms with a secret room or something in the middle. I thought about it all summer; I just needed the right opportunity to investigate. And this, Charles, is that opportunity."

"It's Charlotte," she says.

"I know, Charles, I'm just playing. Now, let's go."

When a boy like East gives you a nickname, Charley thinks, *it's basically impossible to refuse him.* She follows him down a set of rickety wooden stairs. The door closes behind them, and Charley fears she's descending to her doom.

"So if you're not at Tiffin to dance, why are you here?" East asks.

"To get an education."

He laughs. "I'm not Ms. Robinson, you can tell me the truth."

Weirdly, she believes him. "My father died," she says. "He was having shoulder surgery and he just...never came out of the anesthesia." She swallows. "He was my favorite person in the world."

East stops on the stairs and turns to her. "I'm sorry. *That blows,* bruh. So, you came here because home had, like, too many memories?"

"I came because my mother started dating this guy who worked at her landscaping company," she says. "Then she married him. Then...some other shit happened. I applied here in May, and they miraculously had an opening."

"Yeah," East says. "Because of Cinnamon." He pauses. "You know about that, right?"

"I do," Charley says, although she didn't know about Cinnamon when she accepted the spot. She wasn't sure why she'd been admitted so late in the year, and as a junior. She supposes she believed it was because she was such an exceptional candidate that Tiffin couldn't refuse.

But this past week during Chapel, Charley opened the Book of Common Prayer and a program for a memorial service fell out.

Charley studied the front—a picture of a girl with long auburn hair and freckles, holding a guitar—and noted the name, Cinnamon Peters, and the dates, February 21, 2009–May 12, 2025. The back pages of the program had other pictures of Cinnamon—with Dub Austin at some kind of formal dance, onstage as Sandy in *Grease*, sitting next to Mr. Chuy on the piano bench during the Monday night sing-alongs, in the Grille with Davi, drinking milkshakes. Apparently, Cinnamon Peters had died while she was a student at Tiffin. Charley wondered what happened... until she saw the words written at the bottom of the back page: *If you or someone you know is in emotional distress and considering...*

Charley got a chill. Cinnamon Peters had died by suicide. A second later, it clicked: Charley had been admitted to replace Cinnamon.

"She was friends with Davi?" Charley asks.

"Best friends," East says. "But she was *nothing* like Davi. Cinnamon was chill. Really smart, musical, and she loved Tiffin. She was always giving tours for the admissions office."

Charley was tempted to ask how she did it, and where—but Charley doesn't want to be ghoulish, and also, she's afraid of the answer. She changes the subject. "Why are *you* here?"

"I got kicked out of a couple schools in the city before this."

"Don't tell me," Charley says. "You had a Chuck Bass thing going? Clubbing, drugs, older women...?"

"Is that how little you think of me?" he says, and then he grins. "It wasn't quite that bad. More like vaping, skipping school, failure to properly yield to authority. My dad sent me here to West Bumblefuck so I couldn't get in trouble."

"Where's your mom?" Charley asks.

"She lives in LA."

At the bottom of the stairs is an arched opening; East breaks a cobweb and shines his phone's flashlight into a brick, barrel-roofed tunnel. "There's a tunnel like this on the Classic North side too, but it ends at a locked door, which I'm pretty sure is some kind of secret room. Come on."

They walk down the tunnel until they come to a door. *Surely this side will be locked as well,* Charley thinks. But when East turns the knob, it opens.

And—whoa! They enter a spacious room with brick walls and a peeling linoleum floor. The room has four bunk beds against one wall, and against the opposite wall is a makeshift kitchen: a sink, open shelving, a Formica countertop with a stovetop thingy plugged in. East strides over to the sink and turns the faucet: Water runs out in a surprisingly powerful stream. When he turns the knob of the stove, a red light comes on. He shines his phone toward the ceiling: There's a single bulb with a dangling string. When he pulls it, the room is almost too bright. A door against the back wall reveals a bathroom: toilet, sink, shower stall.

"Is this, like, where they used to put kids when they were bad?" Charley asks.

East cackles. "No, Charles, it's a bomb shelter." There's a door opposite the one they entered that's bolted. "Ah, see, I tried this from the other side and couldn't get in." East unbolts the door and opens it. "Here's the north tunnel." He grins at Charley.

Charley has to admit it's cool, discovering the underpinnings of the school. "They probably built this during the Cold War."

"Must have," East says. He walks back toward her and takes one of her hands. East, she thinks, is *holding* her hand. "But we're going to turn it into something else."

Charley worries he can hear her heart beating. "What?"

"A speakeasy," East says. "We'll have a bar with real cocktails, music, couches. We'll open it after lights-out on Saturdays. Invitation only, of course."

"Of course," Charley says.

"I'm serious. I've given this a lot of thought. I want it to be upscale, civilized... Do you know about the Algonquin Round Table?"

"You mean Dorothy Parker and Robert Benchley?" Charley says. "I know about it, yes. Do *you* know about it?"

"I'm not a philistine," East says.

Charley thinks he is a philistine, but she keeps her mouth shut.

"I'm doing this," East says. "And I want you to be my partner."

"Partner?" Charley says. She tries to imagine becoming an accomplice to a wealthy New York kid who starts a speakeasy in the basement of his boarding school. It's so ludicrous, it's sort of appealing.

"If we get caught, I'll take the blame. My dad is the president of the Tiffin board. I can't get expelled."

"How are you planning on getting the alcohol?" Charley asks.

"I'll find a connection."

Charley laughs. Her night is turning out to be way more interesting than going to First Dance. "A *connection*?"

"It's going to work." He gazes around the room. "We'll make it really nice. Highbrow. Like Saint Tuesday in the city."

Charley has no idea what he's talking about. She has been to New York only once, on a school trip: Museum of Natural History, Statue of Liberty.

"Why me?" she says. "Why not Davi, or one of the Olivias?"

"Do I really have to answer that?" East says. "They're a hive mind. I need an independent thinker to partner with me on this." He pauses and squeezes her hand. "That's you. You're the only one I would ask."

At that moment, Charley hears... footsteps? Then a faraway voice calling out, *Hello? Charley?*

"Shit," East says. He ushers Charley out the north-side door. "You go this way, down the tunnel, up the stairs, out the door of Classic

North, and back around to your dorm. I'll go deal with this. I don' want anyone to see the room. Once they know it's here, it's all over. Go."

Charley goes.

Simone creeps down the stairs like the doomed heroine in a horror film. She stops halfway to text Rhode. I'm in the basement of Classic South in case I never return and people are looking for my body, LOL. She hits send, but the service is sluggish. Yeah, no shit, she's on a journey to the center of the earth.

At the bottom of the stairs is what can only be described as a tunnel, and from what Simone's weak phone light can show her, it looks pretty cool. There's a cement floor, a bricked barrel ceiling. Simone moves tentatively forward, aware that she could come face-to-face with the boogeyman at any second. She calls out for Charley; her voice bounces off the walls, back into her face. She feels ridiculous. There's no way Charley is down here.

When Simone's phone illuminates the torso of a live person, she screams.

"Miss Bergeron?" the person says. "It's me, East."

Oh god, oh god, oh god. Simone bends over in order not to faint. She can't speak, she can't breathe, and a trickle of urine runs down her leg into her sneaker. She has never, in her life, been so frightened.

"What," she says, "the *hell* are you doing down here?"

East laughs and reaches out to touch Simone's bare shoulder. "Relax," he says. "I'm sorry I scared you." He leaves his hand on her shoulder. Men are crossing all kinds of boundaries with her tonight, but now Simone doesn't move.

"Wow," he says, and he gives a low whistle. "You look *really* hot in that dress. Maybe I should have come to the dance after all."

Simone knows it's time to step away and admonish him, but when words, *You look* really *hot,* her heart revs like an engine. ⋯ute with his floppy dark hair, his dark eyes, that brooding ⋯on, that for a second, Simone feels helpless.

⋯ revisits Rhode's question. *Do you have any students who ⋯d out?*

Simone noticed East the instant he loped into her classroom. She thought he was in the wrong place: He seemed so much older than the other students, more mature, a man among boys and girls, which makes sense now that she knows he's nineteen. He didn't lift a pen or open his laptop to take a single note, but she felt the pressure of his undivided attention; every time she checked, he was staring at her. It was like some teacher-student fantasy. Simone imagined unbuttoning her blouse for him.

When he left the first day, he stopped by her desk and said, "I get the feeling this is going to be my favorite class."

Simone cleared her throat. She needed to get a grip. "Why, thank you, Andrew. I hope so."

"East," he said. "Everyone just calls me East."

After a week and a half of classes, East has yet to raise his hand in discussion, and he hasn't turned in a single response to the reading. The one time Simone called on him, asking his thoughts on Thomas Morton's reflections on the Native Americans, he'd given her a smoldering smile and said, "You know, I haven't formed an opinion one way or the other on the topic." A hoot escaped from one of the Madisons while Charley Hicks scribbled something in her notebook. Both reactions let Simone know that she should press the point—either expose East publicly for not doing the reading or ask him to stay after—but both choices felt sticky, so Simone let it slide.

"East," she says now. She means her tone to be a reprimand, but it comes out sounding like an invitation. East slides his hand up to the curve of Simone's neck. Before she knows what's happening, he bends down and kisses her.

She will push him away, she thinks. She will tell him there's no world where a kiss between teacher and student is okay. But for just a second, she lets it happen. This moment is *so* forbidden—and for that reason, irresistible. She allows his lips to linger on her lips, his tongue to seek out her tongue.

Then she hears a voice. "Simone?"

Simone pushes East away. She spins around, holding her phone up. She sees a pinpoint of light moving toward her from the direction of the stairs. It's Rhode, with his own phone, striding down the tunnel.

"Hey," she says. She's caught, she thinks. Busted. Do they subject faculty to the Honor Board? No, Simone thinks. She'll just be fired and deported, sent back to Canada to make café au lait for the rest of her life. She'll never teach again. That's the best-case scenario. Worst case is ending up like that teacher who went to jail for sleeping with her student.

"What are you doing down here?" Rhode says.

"Oh..." Simone says. She turns around, thinking she'll have to throw East under the bus to save herself. She has no choice. But East has vanished. The tunnel behind her is so impenetrably dark that Simone wonders if East was ever there or if what happened was some trick of her imagination. She takes a breath. What, if anything, did Rhode see?

"I noticed the door to the basement was propped open," she says. "So I came down here looking for Charley, but she's not here. We should go." She scoots past Rhode and heads for the stairs. "She's probably back in her room by now, and if she's not, we'll tell Audre." Simone hopes Rhode follows her instead of venturing any deeper into the tunnel. "Come on," she prompts.

Rhode stares past her into the darkness. Does he see something?

"Rhode?" Simone says.

Reluctantly, he turns to follow her.

Every once in a while, Simone thinks, the universe does you a solid.

When Simone checks Charley's room—Rhode stays out front, there are no men allowed in Classic South after eight p.m.—she finds Charley sitting on her bed, reading. She's undone her braids, and her hair runs in wavy kinks down her back. She's wearing a long white cotton nightgown with rickrack on the chest. The other girls in the dorm sleep in Roller Rabbit pajama sets. If Charley's daytime attire is from another decade, her nightgown is from another century.

"Where have you *been*?" Simone says. "I've been looking all over for you." *It's official,* Simone thinks. She sounds like someone's—everyone's—mother.

Charley regards Simone with frosty eyes. "I walked over to the Paddock for coffee, but it was closed."

"You walked there in your nightgown?" Simone says.

"Obviously not." Her voice is filled with savage disinterest. Or maybe it's pity. Simone realizes then why Charley Hicks causes her so much anxiety. She exposes Simone's impostor syndrome. Simone isn't a good teacher, she's not qualified in the subject matter, she isn't mature enough to stand up to the students, and, as the past fifteen minutes have just proven, she has grave moral failings as well. She let Andrew Eastman *kiss* her! The bald fact of this is newly appalling now that she's upstairs in the warm, well-lit dorm that houses the girls she's supposed to be in charge of. There's no way Charley could know what happened in the tunnel, but she's eyeballing Simone's party dress (Simone bought it on sale at Forever 21 for a McGill fraternity formal a few years earlier) as though she would expect that behavior and worse. Charley blinks. "I came home and changed. Did I break any rules?"

Simone tries to calculate the timing. If Charley left just before Simone arrived, walked to the Paddock, and walked back, she and Simone might have missed each other. Then when Charley would have returned, Simone would have been wandering the bowels of the building and kissing a student.

Did I break any rules?

Simone swallows. "No," she says. "I'm just glad you're safe."

Charley returns to her book without a word.

Before Simone closes the door, she says, "Did you write that quote on my door? In red?"

Charley doesn't look up. "What do you think?"

Simone thinks she should leave before she says or does anything else she regrets.

"Good night," she says.

8. Tiffin Talks: Day in the Life

After First Dance, we settle into a routine, which coincides with the shift from summer to fall. The days are still warm (hot as hell if you're on the football field wearing full pads), but we grab a hoodie when we're going to the Teddy or the Sink after dinner, and Davi Banerjee posts a thousand pictures of what she calls Tiffin's "foliage porn": the leaves of the shade maples turning colors. Our teachers finally figure out which Madison and Olivia is which, and the puny third-formers learn the shortcut from the Paddock to the art studio, where they're all required to take Visual Foundations (and they start calling it "Viszh Found" like the rest of us).

Our days at Tiffin start with breakfast, which is mandatory for third- and fourth-formers. Fifth- and sixth-formers will often roll through the Paddock for the bacon, egg, and cheese sandwiches that Chef Haz sets out. Sometimes one of us will stop to talk to Chef — he can often be found just outside the back door, smoking. Davi keeps begging Chef to appear in a TikTok — she features his food all the time — and although he has resisted so far, she thinks she's wearing him down. He finally asks if there's "any money" in being a TikTok phenom, and while the answer is yes for Davi, she has to be noncommittal with Chef. When she tells him he'd probably receive some new cookware or a case of organic peanut butter, his interest seems to fade.

On Tuesdays and Thursdays we attend Chapel, where the dress code is coat and tie or dress or skirt. Every Tuesday during Chapel we're "treated" to a senior speech. Each sixth-former is required to present a talk centered on a meaningful experience, ideally one that's led to a philosophical insight or personal growth. Favorite topics are dead grandparents, grandparents with Alzheimer's, or lessons learned at boarding school.

However, the week after First Dance, Annabelle Tuckerman captures our undivided attention with her senior speech, entitled "Three Brushes with Death." Number one is Annabelle's revelation that her mother, upon discovering that she was pregnant with Annabelle, was determined to get an abortion. She was on the partner track at a big New York law firm. "Because the world is a patriarchy," Annabelle explains, "a pregnancy would have derailed her career." We tense up: Has anyone uttered the word "abortion" in Chapel before? *Also,* we think, *what kind of mother tells her child that she was nearly terminated in utero?*

Number two: When Annabelle was eight years old, a tumor the

size of a grapefruit was removed from her abdominal cavity. Although the tumor was benign, we agree this counts as something life-threatening.

Number three: This past summer, while on Martha's Vineyard, Annabelle was the victim of a hit-and-run accident. She was biking home at midnight from her job as a food runner at the Red Cat when a car swerved onto the bike path and hit her, leaving her unconscious. When Annabelle came to, she didn't know where she was or what had happened, but she had road rash across her thigh and her bike frame was mangled. It was only later, once she limped home, that she recovered the memory of being hit by a car.

"Other than surface wounds and the temporary amnesia," Annabelle says, "I was fine." She wipes imaginary sweat from her forehead in a "Phew!" gesture. "I've been wondering what the universe is trying to tell me, and I've decided it's this: I'm built to survive whatever comes my way. It's also taught me to practice gratitude for each day I'm given. I'm lucky to be here. Thank you."

We erupt in thunderous applause while Annabelle's friends rush to give her a hug. Her bestie, Ravenna Rapsicoli, says, "Why didn't you tell me what happened on the Vineyard?" The answer is that Annabelle Tuckerman wanted to save the story for this very moment. She recognized senior speech gold when she saw it.

The only person who remains nonplussed by Annabelle's speech is Head Prefect Lisa Kim. She's scheduled to speak next Tuesday, and she'd been planning on talking about her dead grandfather. She wishes she could come up with something more dramatic, but Lisa's life has been blessed, and quite boring.

Tiffin's college counselor, Honey Vandermeid, abandons her morning swim; Jewel Pond becomes arctic in a matter of days. Honey sighs; she's too busy to swim anyway. Since Tiffin has been ranked number two, a slew of colleges have decided they'd like to visit the campus. Honey, who once had to curry favor with the Ivies, as well as places like Duke, Tulane, and "the U" (University of Miami), is now hard-pressed to find enough dates.

Honey is also busy deflecting invitations from Cordelia to spend the night in her cottage. Honey is the dorm parent for the four upper floors of Classic South (she agreed to take four instead of three because Simone Bergeron is brand-new). Surely Cordelia realizes she can't sneak out. What if someone vomits in the middle of the night and needs her help? What if there's a blow-up between roommates? What if the fire alarm goes off and Honey isn't there?

It's not like summertime, Cord. My week is full to bursting.

That's the thing about boarding school...the academic rigor, the long athletic practices, the clubs and affinity group meetings, the assignments, the tutoring and study groups, the meals and robust social calendar, are all meant to keep everyone—students and faculty alike—too busy to think about sex and romance.

On any given day, Audre Robinson can gaze out the east-facing windows of her office in the Manse and imagine the fine instruction and engaging discussions taking place in the Schoolhouse. Señor Perez is teaching Gabriel García Márquez's *Love in the Time of Cholera* to his AP Spanish class; they're fundraising to go to Barcelona over spring break, though Señor is a little disappointed that only half his class has signed up to go (and not the students who would be the most fun either; the fun kids are planning to go to Harbour Island in the Bahamas, an unofficial Tiffin tradition).

Roy Ewanick is teaching differential equations to his advanced math students—all of them sixth-formers except for Royce Stringfellow and Andrew Eastman, who is surprisingly gifted with numbers and abstract mathematical concepts, if not with turning in any of his assignments.

Simone Bergeron's students are reading Hakluyt on colonization. Simone longs to be the kind of teacher whom the students want to please, both academically and behaviorally. She feels she's succeeded on this front except in the case of Charley Hicks, whose work is impeccable (really, she could teach the class) but who glowers at Simone with barely disguised contempt.

Simone isn't sure what to do with East from an academic standpoint. With each passing day and each missing assignment, the need to speak to him alone becomes more pressing. And yet Simone puts it off because she's afraid of what will happen.

Finally, she sends him an email.

You presently have a zero in my class. If you're finding the reading challenging, I'm happy to set you up with a tutor.

He responds immediately. I'm not doing the reading LOL. Want to meet in the tunnel again tonight after lights out?

Simone gasps and deletes the email, then deletes it from the Trash folder. She can't believe he had the gall to send that on the school's server. She can't believe he had the gall to send it, period. She's particularly horrified by his use of the word "again." She can't report this email even if she wanted to, because she hasn't told a soul about finding East in the tunnel.

She has made eye contact with East once or twice per class up until now, but the next day, she avoids looking at him completely.

She sends an email to Audre that says, I have concerns about Andrew Eastman. He has yet to turn in a single assignment. What should I do?

Audre writes back, Thank you for letting me know. I'll handle.

Simone feels guilty about asking Audre to take this bit of classroom management off her plate. She wasn't looking to completely pass the buck, nor did she necessarily want to sic the Head of School on East. Oh well—what's done is done. Simone is off the hook for now.

But at the end of the third week of school, there are still no assignments from East.

Rhode Rivera is teaching the transcendentalists: Emerson and Thoreau. Their themes of self-reliance and connection to nature should resonate with Tiffin students—here at boarding school, in pastoral New England—but only a handful of kids seem to click with the material. Most find it dull and impenetrable. Madison J. raises her hand and says, "Why do we care that these old white men went out to live in the woods?"

Why, indeed? Rhode wants to be teaching Toni Morrison, Jhumpa Lahiri, Richard Wright. Following Emerson and Thoreau is Hawthorne, and then he'll tackle Arthur Miller's *The Crucible*. After his due diligence with texts that are still somehow embraced by Tiffin's board of directors, he'll move on.

He greatly envies one of the other English teachers, Ruth Wully. Ruth is married to the science teacher, Kent Wully. *They should really be named "the Woolies,"* Rhode thinks, because they both have prodigious amounts of hair and they wear what look like homespun garments. They live in an old Victorian in Haydensboro and also have a summer cottage on Sweet Pond, across the border in Vermont. Ruth teaches third- and fourth-form English as well as a senior elective called Boarding School Lit, which has a waiting list every year because who wouldn't want to spend a semester reading *The Starboard Sea* and *Prep*?

But then the magical moment Rhode has been waiting for finally arrives. Charley Hicks, Dub Austin, and Taylor Wilson get into a debate about what Emerson means by the "transparent eyeball."

"What," Rhode asks the class, "is he talking about when he writes, 'I am nothing, I see all.'"

Dub Austin—whom Rhode has perhaps misclassified as a football bro—says, "Emerson believed that when he stepped into nature alone, he achieved a greater understanding of the world. And self-awareness, maybe? I've dealt with a bunch of stuff in the past six months that...I don't know...changed the way I think about things. If you leave yourself open to learning about the world and other people, then no matter what happens to you, good or bad, you become wiser."

"Interesting answer," Rhode says. "Does anyone have other thoughts?"

Charley says, "I think what Emerson means is that, when he goes into nature alone, he loses his...ego, I guess you'd call it? And becomes one with nature and therefore closer to god?"

Taylor jumps in. "That *is* what he's saying, but it discounts the importance of individuality. Like, your personality and opinions cease to matter when you walk in the woods, and he thinks that's a good thing. To Emerson, all that matters is nature."

Ahhh, brilliant. The bell rings, class is over, the kids slap their laptops shut, pack up their books, and pull out their phones to take pictures of themselves to snap to whomever. The golden bubble they were sitting in pops, but even so, Rhode is suffused with a sense of purpose.

Maybe he should put off his lesson prep for an hour and go for a walk in the woods, he thinks. There are definitely some things he'd like to transcend—such as the unease he's been feeling since the night of First Dance and what he thinks he saw happening down in the tunnel.

After our school day ends, we transition to afternoon activities. Tiffin has a theater troupe run by Mr. Chuy—but for most of us, the afternoon means athletics.

Charley Hicks spends three weeks as a member of the Thirds field hockey team, where she reluctantly laces her cleats and charges up and down the field alongside her teammates, holding the stick backward on purpose in hopes that she might get cut. She eventually learns that Thirds field hockey is like the trap in the sink drain: It scoops up all the misfits and half-asses. Nobody gets cut.

But then one day, while they're waiting in line to do a shooting drill, Olivia H-T, a girl so annoying that Charley wills her ears to fall off every time Olivia H-T speaks, turns to her and says, "I can't believe you're not doing newspaper."

Charley knows that Tiffin has a student newspaper—it's mentioned in the brochure—but she has dismissed it because back at Loch Raven High, Charley was the editor of the literary magazine; she loved fiction, and her interest didn't extend to journalism. But with Olivia H-T's words, she realizes that "newspaper" can take the place of dreadful Thirds field hockey!

She throws her shin guards into the recycling bin and heads to the newspaper's "office" in the Teddy.

The editor of the *'Bred Bulletin* this year, Charley learns, is sixth-former Ravenna Rapsicoli, Annabelle Tuckerman's roommate and best friend. Charley also knows from listening to gossip—the other girls treat Charley like she's invisible, and she's learned an enormous amount by just keeping quiet—that Ravenna lost out as Head Prefect to Lisa Kim. Being editor of the *'Bred Bulletin* must be how Ravenna is exerting her influence. *Freedom of the press...means the freedom to criticize and oppose,* Charley thinks. George Orwell.

But upon poking her head into the *Bulletin*'s office, Charley finds that the newspaper is a complete joke. It has a staff of...three: Ravenna, and two third-form boys named Grady and Levi who have yet to go through puberty. Grady has glasses and braces, Levi a severe case of acne and a cowlick. After thirty seconds of observation from the doorway, Charley discerns the dynamic. Ravenna is the dominatrix, and Grady and Levi are her subs. They slump in their chairs around the Harkness table while Ravenna trashes their ideas for articles. Levi has just suggested doing an investigative piece about which third-form boy took a shit in the shower at Classic North; he claims to have some leads.

"That's a situation for your dorm parent," Ravenna says. "No one wants to read about your scatological issues."

Both boys stare at Ravenna with wide eyes, and Charley wants to cuddle them.

"Come up with something better," Ravenna says as she runs the thick gold cross around her neck along its chain.

Grady says, "My best friend from the city goes to Brownwell-Mather, and he said there's this app the kids at his school are posting on that's getting everyone suspend—"

"Stop right there," Ravenna says. "When you say 'the city,' what are you talking about?"

Grady swallows. "New York."

"You live in New York City?"

Grady nods.

"Where?"

"West Seventy-Eighth between Amsterdam and Broadway. I went to Ethical—"

"I live at 720 Park," Ravenna says. She seems to take new measure of Grady. "I'm confused. If you're from New York, why aren't you cooler?"

Grady shrugs.

Ravenna turns to Levi. "Where are you from?"

"Annandale," he says.

Ravenna blinks at him, then turns back to Grady. "We aren't doing an article about something that happened at Brownwell-Mather; that makes no sense. This is the Tiffin paper. Brown-Math was ranked number sixteen this year. That's way below us."

"I think it's newsworthy because—"

"An article about an app will put everyone to sleep," Ravenna says. When she turns her back on Grady, she sees Charley in the doorway.

Charley pushes up her glasses. "Hey."

It's the new girl, Ravenna thinks. *And she's wearing another inconceivably bad outfit—a red cotton turtleneck and an honest-to-god kilt, with a gold pin and everything. She's traded in her boat shoes for penny loafers with short white socks. Awful.*

And yet, Ravenna can't help but feel some relief at her presence. Ravenna was beginning to feel like a nanny. "You're the new girl, right?"

"Right," Charley says. She offers an interview hand. "Charley Hicks. I quit Thirds field hockey, and I need a new activity."

Ravenna gives Charley the up-down. "Well, I'm not putting you in charge of the fashion pages."

Charley shrugs. "We mock what we don't understand."

Ravenna laughs. Is the new girl secretly...sort of normal? Ravenna knows she's smart: Someone said she showed up to beat Royce Stringfellow for valedictorian; someone else said she has a library and a greenhouse *in her room;* and there was a crazy rumor that she was getting with East. (*Not possible,* Ravenna thinks.) "Do you have any ideas for articles? Because I was thinking about some Top Tens, What's Hot and What's Not...you know, listicles?"

Listicles? Charley thinks. Does Ravenna want to turn the *'Bred*

Bulletin into *Cosmo*? Will she include "Tips for Giving a Better Blow Job on a Harkness Table"? "Surefire Ways to Sneak into God's Basement"? Charley considers leaving, but she is the definition of desperate. "I was hoping to do book reviews, actually," Charley says. "You know, like the *New York Times*?"

"Nobody will *read* book reviews," Ravenna says. "It's too much like school. I think the reason everyone thinks our newspaper is trash—as you can see, normal people aren't exactly clamoring to join—is because the past editors wanted to make it too serious. But I'm in charge now, and I don't want the *New York Times*. I want the *New York Post*." She glares at Grady. "Please tell me you know the difference between the *Times* and the *Post*."

Grady nods. "The *Post* has *Page Six*."

"You just got your name on the masthead," Ravenna says. She eyeballs Levi. "Why should I keep you around?"

"Because I'm a computer genius?"

"Molto bene!" Ravenna says. She turns her attention back to Charley. "You live on the first floor of South, right?" She's only asking to be polite; she knows the answer is yes, this chick took Cinnamon Peters's spot in the Class of 2027. She lives in Cinnamon's room.

"I do."

"I was thinking about a deep dive into the difference between how Tiffin really is and the way Tiffin is portrayed in social media by... certain influencers."

"Certain influencers?" Charley says. "You mean Davi?"

Of course Ravenna means Davi. There have been rumblings, especially from the sixth-form girls whom Ravenna is friends with, that maybe Davi is getting a little too Insta-fabulous for her own good. Olivia H-T claims Davi took credit for Tiffin being ranked number two, which is not only shameless but absurd. The rankings aren't determined by teenage girls.

On the one hand, it's unthinkable to do a hatchet job on Davi

Banerjee—she's the queen—but on the other hand, even Marie Antoinette was beheaded.

There's no reason the 'Bred Bulletin *can't have a* Page Six, Ravenna thinks. Maybe they'll call it *Page 114* for the number of years Tiffin has been in existence. Corny? Ravenna loves the idea of publishing a gossip page. It will have to be scandalous, even salacious, for people to read it. There might be some blowback on her as editor in chief—*but,* Ravenna thinks with a sigh, *that's the life of a journalist.*

She pulls out the chair next to her and invites Charley to sit. "Welcome to the *Bulletin,*" she says.

Dinner at Tiffin starts at six, but attendance isn't mandatory. (Rumor has it other schools hold something called Seated Dinner once a week with the *faculty. Oh hell no,* we think.) In years past, we would DoorDash from either Antonio's or Moon Palace—but since Chef arrived, we not only go to meals, we get there early. There's always a line, and not just on Burger Night and Pizza Friday. A typical midweek dinner might be braised short ribs over cheddar mashed potatoes or caprese paninis made with the last of the heirloom tomatoes that Chef planted out behind the Paddock.

The Paddock is (practically) egalitarian—we can sit anywhere regardless of class, except for the sixth-form table, which is closest to the food. (Though the sixth-formers are so weird and annoying this year that no one wants to sit with them anyway.) There's one other table of distinction: the Booth. It has leather banquette seats and is tucked into one of the salvaged horse stalls from the original Tiffin farm. Tonight it's where Taylor Wilson sits with her boyfriend, Hakeem.

When Taylor leaves the Booth to toast some of Chef's homemade focaccia, which she'll spread with peanut butter and hot pepper jelly (she's trying to become a vegetarian, which is challenging because she doesn't like vegetables except for celery, and she also loves red meat), Hakeem notices that she's left her phone on the table, unlocked and unguarded. This is highly unusual: Taylor treats her phone like it contains state secrets. The other unusual circumstance is that Dub isn't with them; he stayed late after practice to talk to Coach Bosworth about the upcoming game against Northmeadow.

Hakeem peers around the walls of the Booth. All the other kids are eating, talking, laughing, and Taylor is on the other side of the room, dropping focaccia into the toaster. He edges Taylor's phone closer and peers at the screen. It's open to Snapchat, and Hakeem can't help himself. He checks her best friends list.

What the hell? he thinks. He snatches up her phone and scoots to the inside of the Booth so that he's out of her line of vision. He stares at the screen, willing it to make sense. He and Taylor snap all the time, probably 114 times a day. But...*Dub* is her number one? Hakeem obviously knows they snap, he expects them to, they're friends, but for Dub to be her *number one* means they're snapping nonstop. What makes this even more fucked up is that Taylor and Dub have three out of five classes together. They're together all damn day; why do they need to be sending each other snaps? Maybe they're bored in class, Hakeem can see that, but even so, this is *not* okay.

Taylor approaches with a plate in each hand. She sets one plate down in front of Hakeem and one in front of her place. She seems to have ditched her peanut butter toast in favor of lasagna, Caesar salad, and garlic bread.

"I got the veggie lasagna, but yours is meat, and I want to taste it."

It's sweet that she brought him dinner, and she knows he doesn't like it when his food is touching so she left respectful alleys between his lasagna, salad, and bread. The lasagna is melty and fragrant, and Hakeem loves Chef's frosted garlic bread.

But instead of digging in, Hakeem scoots out of the Booth.

"Where are you going?" Taylor asks. "There's no more bread; I got the last of it."

Hakeem shakes his head at her.

"Okay, fine, I won't have a bite of yours," Taylor says. Hakeem is always busting her for being a "fake" vegetarian. She knows he's right. She's not boycotting meat for moral reasons — well, maybe she is, a little bit — it's mostly because she wants to eat healthier. Although who is she kidding, she eats so much focaccia that after only three weeks back at school, her jeans are tight.

"I'm going to the gym," Hakeem says.

"What?" Taylor says. "Why? Did Coach text you?" She's happy that Hakeem and Dub won some games, but she isn't going to like it if they get all football-is-life on her.

Hakeem stares at her. He wants to ask about Snapchat, but who is he kidding? She isn't going to tell him the truth. Besides, he doesn't feel like making a scene here in the Paddock with the whole school watching. He'll go to the gym and bench-press his anger away. But he can't risk running into Dub because what he wants to do right now is wrench Dub's throwing arm behind his back until it snaps off.

Hakeem exhales. This kind of anger is foreign to him.

"Actually, I'm going to my room. Good night."

"Good *night*?" Taylor says. "It's a quarter after six! Are we not going to the Sink? Are we not *studying* together?" With the new school year, Taylor, Hakeem, and Dub have vowed to be more studious — fifth-form grades are the most important for college.

"Study with Dub," Hakeem says. He slings his backpack over his shoulder and leaves the Paddock.

Taylor is tempted to go after him. What is *wrong*? Then she sees her phone on the table. Did Hakeem...? She taps the dark screen and her Snapchat appears.

Shit, she thinks. She's busted. Hakeem has every right to be angry. After all, if she found out that Hakeem's number one was some little freshman hottie, she would never, *ever* forgive him.

But this is Dub. Dub is their friend, their friend who is *grieving.* Surely Hakeem can understand?

The problem, Taylor thinks, is that Hakeem most likely *does* understand.

Ugh. Taylor watches the doors of the Paddock close behind Hakeem. She sighs and takes a bite of her lasagna, then takes a bite of Hakeem's lasagna. It's so good that Taylor groans. She'll go to Hakeem's room during Intervis and work things out — but she isn't skipping dinner for him.

As usual, Davi Banerjee is surrounded by her peeps at dinner. The seat across from her is occupied by Olivia H-T. It's just weeks into the school year and Davi is already growing weary of Olivia H-T. She's just so...*obsequious* ("obedient or attentive to an excessive or servile degree"). Olivia H-T is also sort of a...*cipher* ("a person who does the bidding of others and seems to have no will of her own"). She isn't particularly bright or talented; she doesn't seem to have any interests other than Davi; she's obsessed with Davi's TikTok and Instagram; she has memorized every scrap of content, which is pathetic. Was she like this last year? Davi doesn't remember Olivia H-T last year...except for the glorious sunny afternoon of Tiffinpalooza. The lead singer of the first band to take the outdoor stage was so hot that Davi wanted to be introduced — and it turned out *he was Olivia H-T's cousin.* That was how Olivia H-T had infiltrated Davi's circle — though Davi forgot all about her over the summer. Then, when Davi returned to Tiffin, she was so...*bereft* ("sad and lonely, especially through someone's death or departure") because of

Cinnamon that she wanted as many people around her as possible—and this somehow included Olivia H-T.

The weirdest thing is that this past Sunday, Olivia H-T Ubered all the way into Springfield, saying she was bringing back a "big surprise" for Davi. Davi had hoped she'd have her cousin in tow—but instead, Olivia H-T came back with all her long, mousy brown hair chopped off. She'd gotten a bob *just like Davi's*.

Now, Olivia H-T studies Davi's plate, which is loaded up with lasagna—Davi patiently waited for Chef to unveil the third variety, a white truffled lasagna. (He'd given her the inside scoop about it earlier in the day.)

"I just don't get how you can eat all that and stay so thin," Olivia H-T says.

Across the table, Tilly Benbow snorts. According to Tilly, the most pathetic thing about Olivia H-T isn't that she copied Davi's hairstyle but how fixated she is on what Davi eats. Olivia H-T herself eats only salad, usually the baby lettuces, carrots, tomatoes, and cucumbers (which, Olivia H-T frequently mentions, burn more calories while being digested than they contain) dressed with balsamic vinegar. For breakfast, she drinks herbal tea. To the casual observer, it would appear Olivia H-T consumes almost no calories over the course of a day. And yet, Olivia H-T is...*zaftig* ("having a full, rounded figure"). Davi has heard that only a few years ago, sixth-form girls would have hazed someone like Olivia H-T, using a black Sharpie to circle the areas on her body where she needed to lose weight. Davi suspects that poor Olivia H-T has heard the stories, which led to her *ascetic* ("characterized by severe self-discipline and abstention from indulgence") diet. She probably stashes bags of chips and tubs of cake icing in her room and stuffs her face after lights-out.

This actually endears Olivia H-T to Davi. After all, everyone has secrets.

Seven o'clock brings our favorite time of day: Intervis. This is when we're allowed to visit one another's rooms, regardless of gender, for an hour. During Intervis, the door is supposed to stay "halfway open," which means "open a crack." For that reason, "Intervis" should probably just be called "intercourse," though to be honest, it's no longer cool to hook up during Intervis. Joining the Harkness Society or getting with someone in God's Basement is way more elite.

Charley Hicks is the only student on either of Simone's floors who has never exercised the privilege of Intervis—but one night, this changes. Simone is in the common room with her clipboard and a bowl of Starbursts on the table in front of her (she likes to offer the girls something sweet at the end of the day). This hour helps Simone learn the social landscape. A handful of girls—Tilly Benbow, the Madisons and Olivias—go to Davi's room, where they make Tik-Toks in front of the neon sign that says THIS IS WHERE THE MAGIC HAPPENS. Taylor Wilson goes to North to hang in Hakeem's room or Dub's room, though sometimes Hakeem and Dub come to South to hang in Taylor's room. The first time that happened, at the start of the year, Simone checked on them (two boys and one girl)—and she found Taylor and Hakeem sitting on the bed and Dub lying across the floor with his AirPods in.

Sometimes girls come to the common room to hang with Simone. This is nice (though it initially takes Simone by surprise; don't they have better things to do?). They gossip about other teachers—Mrs. Wully is a hard grader, Señor Perez is a total DILF—but it seems the real reason the girls hang out is to find out more about Simone. Specifically, does she have a boyfriend?

No, Simone hasn't been in a serious relationship since her first year at university.

Well then, they ask, *what about Mr. Rivera?*

"I think he likes you," Lisa Kim says. "He was totally into you the night of First Dance."

"He looked like he wanted to *eat* you," Annabelle Tuckerman says.

"Mr. Rivera and I are colleagues," Simone says. "Friendly acquaintances." Her tone of voice is clipped; she doesn't want to talk about Rhode. Simone suspects that the girls are right, Rhode does have a crush on her, or he *did* until he found her in the tunnel. Since then, he's been more reserved with Simone, and she's caught him looking at her strangely.

Did he see? she wonders. *Does he know?*

When Charley Hicks walks into the common room, Simone could not be more surprised. She's dressed in Levi's, a pink oxford shirt, and penny loafers. Her hair is pushed back from her face in a grosgrain headband. Behind her glasses, her expression is typically inscrutable.

"Hey, Charley!" Simone says. She can't help believing that, if she continues to try, she and Charley will form some kind of bond. "Are you... Intervissing tonight?"

"I am."

"Terrific!" Simone says. "Where are you headed?" The girls are supposed to let Simone know what room they're visiting, though if they're staying on the floor it doesn't really matter. Is Charley staying on the floor? Is she, maybe, going to Davi's room?

"North," Charley says.

Simone wants to throw a party. Charley is visiting a boy! Simone would assume this was something school-related, but for the first time ever, Charley is without a book. Does Charley have a... love interest, then? Is it maybe Royce Stringfellow? He's the top student in her class. Who else would Charley deem worthy of her time?

"Okay!" Simone says with what she's sure is a manic smile. "Be sure to check in with Mr. Rivera when you get there, and we'll see you back here at eight!"

Charley nods and leaves the room. Would it kill the girl to smile? She didn't even take a Starburst. Who passes up free candy? Simone unwraps a red one—cherry is her favorite—and once a couple minutes have passed, she texts Rhode.

Did Charley make it over there? Simone can't believe she's doing this. Charley is sixteen; North is less than fifty yards away.

Yes, Rhode texts back. She just checked in.

Who is she going to see? Simone writes. It's none of her business. Should Simone explain that this is the first time Charley has chosen to Intervis? She's mentioned to Rhode that Charley is having a hard time making friends. It's only fitting that Simone should take an interest.

Simone's phone pings. A text from Rhode: Andrew Eastman.

Simone drops her phone like it's hot.

Simone isn't the only one who's shocked that Charley is Intervissing with Andrew Eastman. Rhode can't quite believe it either.

"East?" he says to Charley.

"Yes," she says. She signs her name and writes down her destination: Room 601.

"He knows you're coming?" Rhode says.

"I'm not showing up uninvited, if that's what you're asking."

That's exactly what Rhode is asking. East is, quite literally, too cool for school. Rhode doesn't have him for English; he's apparently doing an "independent study" with Ruth Wully. Rhode asked Ruth about him the Monday after First Dance because he suddenly had a new curiosity about the kid.

Ruth said, "I've taught him the past two years, so I've learned how to handle him."

"He has remedial issues?" Rhode asks. This is the only reason Rhode can think of why East wouldn't be in the regular curriculum.

Ruth laughed. "He has issues, but he's not remedial. He's a smart kid, brilliant, even. He just doesn't want to do the work."

"Isn't he worried about getting into college?"

"He claims he's not going to college," Ruth said.

"What?" Rhode said. "Then why is he here? This is a prep school, *college* prep."

Ruth held her palms up. "You can ask someone else about East, but I'm not talking. Student-teacher privilege."

What, Rhode wonders now, *does Charley see in someone who doesn't even want to go to college? Is it the obvious? Does she think he's hot? Maybe the better question is, What does East want with Charley? Is he paying attention to her in exchange for help with his independent study? Is he using her?*

Don't go up there! Rhode thinks. *Getting involved with East is a big mistake!*

But instead, he smiles. "Have fun, see you at eight."

"Thanks, Mr. Rivera," Charley says, and she steps into the elevator.

A second later, Rhode gets a text from Simone. Who is she going to see?

Ha! Rhode thinks. Wouldn't she like to know. It gives him a perverse thrill to type the name: Andrew Eastman.

As Rhode waits for a response—what will Simone say?—there's a disruption coming from upstairs. Pounding, a girl yelling.

"Open the door, Hakeem!"

This is followed by a chorus of other voices: *Seriously? Leave the dude alone! What are you, psycho?*

Rhode trudges up the stairs, where he finds Taylor Wilson in tears.

"He won't answer the door," she says. "He won't talk to me at all, but I know he's in there." She pounds on the door again. "Hakeem, open up!"

"Try your other boyfriend!" someone calls out from the end of the hall.

Rhode says, "Guys, that's enough!" To Taylor he says, "If Hakeem isn't coming to the door, it's safe to assume he wants some space. Why don't you go back to South, and you two can chat in the morning?"

"He's mad at me for *no reason*!" Taylor says. "He was *spying* on my phone, and he misunderstood…"

"Okay, okay," Rhode says in what he thinks of as a therapist voice. He's afraid to touch Taylor, so he positions himself between her and Hakeem's door. "We'll see you tomorrow, Taylor."

"I'm going to FaceTime you in ten minutes," Taylor shouts at the door. "You'd better fucking answer!"

During Intervis, Mr. James makes his usual rounds in the Gator. First, he checks the Schoolhouse. He's too lazy to patrol the halls like he's supposed to, though he did it religiously back in the day—and caught his fair share of kids joining the Harkness Society. Most of them he barked at and let go with a warning. The only kids he turned in were the douchebags: One kid accused Mr. James of leering at his girlfriend's tits. Well, her tits were out on display, how was Mr. James supposed to avoid seeing them? Another kid called him "Mr. Jameson" to his face. (Mr. James secretly finds the nickname funny—and apt. He does break out his flask of whiskey once the sun goes down, though he prefers Bushmills.)

After the Schoolhouse, Mr. James checks God's Basement. Here, he's a bit more conscientious. He parks the Gator out front and enters the chapel. It's a soaring space that smells like furniture polish — they're fanatical about the "integrity of the woodwork" — and beeswax candles. A light is kept on above the altar at all times, which helps guide Mr. James down the aisle to the back stairs.

And...jackpot! He hears voices and footfalls on the steps. He flips on the stairwell light to see Honey Vandermeid and Cordelia Spooner. Their heads snap up in alarm. Cordelia puts a hand to her bosom and says, "Jesus, Michael, you scared the piss out of me."

Mr. James says, "You weren't who I expected to find, sorry." Cordelia seems flushed, and Honey Vandermeid — she's a fine-looking woman, Mr. James wouldn't mind having a go-round with her in God's Basement — twists her long blond hair into a bun. "Everything...okay?"

"Just fine," Honey says. "We heard a rumor about kids sneaking down tonight, so we came to check it out."

"You could have just called me," Mr. James says. "That *is* my job."

The ladies can't get up the stairs and past him fast enough, it seems, and they talk over each other: *Oh yes, we know, thanks, Michael, have a good night, good night, good night.*

"Good night?" Mr. James says. He turns to watch them skulk out of the chapel like a couple of guilty kids.

What were they doing down there? He has only one guess — but it's too wild, even for this crazy place.

At five minutes to eight, Mr. James is heading back toward the dorms and passing kids going to the Sink or the Teddy to study. *Hey, Mr. James. How's it going, Mr. James?* Mr. James lifts a hand, occasionally saying, *How's it going, Trouble?* He tries to be sparing with his greetings, since he has a reputation as a grouch to uphold. He'll return to the security office, a garage on the Back Lot, where he'll watch a couple episodes of *Yellowstone* and then do his final rounds before check-in at ten.

As he's motoring around the back of the dorm buildings, he sees two figures ascend the cement stairs that lead up from the cellar of Classic North.

What fresh hell? he thinks. *Have the kids discovered another place to sneak around?* Mr. James has spent enough time in that cellar dealing with furnace issues to know how inhospitable it is. But maybe creepy is a kink.

He slows down and confronts the two kids as they reach the path.

Surprise, surprise, he thinks. He doesn't know a lot of the students by name, but he knows this young man.

"Hey, Mr. James," the kid says.

The girl he's with, tall and thin with glasses, stares at her shoes. Mr. James has seen this girl around, always carrying books. He doesn't know her name.

"Good evening, East," Mr. James says. He nods toward the stairs. "What were you two doing down there?"

East grins. "Nothing."

Nothing? Did young Eastman really just toss him a *nothing?* God, the kid is so cocky, but something about him is likable. He's a rebel, just like Mr. James was in high school. And, of course, Mr. James knows who his father is.

"Okay, then." Mr. James won't press it; his show and his flask await. "Have a good night."

Head of School Audre Robinson cherishes her evenings. After prepping for the following day with a glass of wine and having dinner in the Residence, she takes a scented bath and reads her mystery novels (she loves Louise Penny and Selena Montgomery). She eats a couple of pieces of dark chocolate, then crawls into bed by ten thirty and prays there will be no overnight emergencies.

But a couple of times a week, Audre forsakes both bath and reading for a stroll around the campus during study hours, which are held from eight to ten p.m. She observes the kids as they do a group project for Evil and Justice or tackle an essay for Visions and Revisions. (Mrs. Wully has started out this course by having the kids compare *King Lear* with Jane Smiley's *A Thousand Acres,* sheer brilliance in Audre's opinion.) She likes to see the kids in the Grille reading *Bel Canto* while they sip dulce de leche milkshakes. She overhears Lisa Kim and Annabelle Tuckerman debating US trade policies with China. The students' young minds are discovering the poetry of Jorie Graham, the intricacies of calculus. They memorize the periodic table, the causes of World War I. As buoyed as Audre is by all the *learning* that takes place at Tiffin, she's also sadly aware that most of the facts will fall out of the backs of the students' heads in a few short years. Audre couldn't pass an Algebra II test now if her life depended on it; she's lost the basic plot of *The Old Man and the Sea*—does he die in the end? But a truly fine education teaches the students to be curious, to ask questions, to augment their understanding of the world around them and feel at ease in it.

Audre realizes not every student is immersed in academia—or is even on task. Somewhere on campus, a freshman girl is on her phone crying to her mother and begging to come home, Davi is probably giving her followers a peek at tomorrow's OOTD, and Audre doesn't even want to hazard a guess at what East is doing. But for the most part, the developing imaginations and intellects of Tiffin are engaged, the gears turning, the creative juices flowing.

When the chapel bells chime ten, both the Teddy and the Sink empty out as we hurry back to the dorms for check-in. Then we shower or snack, we complete our skin care routines, we brush our teeth and occasionally floss, then finally, finally, climb into bed.

The Academy

"*Bonne nuit, mes cheries!*" Simone Bergeron calls out as lights down the hall go out, one by one.

We've all heard about this bit of nightly theater — are the girls on the first floor living in a Madeline book? — but we're too tired to care.

Outside, the moon shines down on camp as we, the 240 students of Tiffin Academy, fall asleep.

October

9. Friday Night Lights

Audre would never say so out loud for fear of sounding both cringey and immodest, but Friday night's game against Northmeadow offers *immaculate fall football vibes.* All of Tiffin's sugar maples are aflame with color, and the brilliance of the leaves is enhanced by the sun setting over the Pasture; the evening air is just crisp enough for Audre to wear her green-and-gold Thoroughbreds sweatshirt (available from the school store for $34.95). Royce Stringfellow, in addition to being one of the top students in the fifth-form, is a gifted sports announcer; he's up in the booth with Tilly Benbow, who's in charge of the pregame pump-up songs. Three food trucks—tacos, fried chicken, and frozen custard—are set up on the far side of the home stands to feed the masses so Chef can have a well-deserved night off.

Tiffin students stomp on the metal treads of the bleachers when Tilly plays "We Will Rock You." *Is Tiffin about to make school history,* Audre wonders, *with its winningest season ever?*

She takes a sustaining breath—she can do this, she *must* do this—and strolls over to the visitors' side to greet Northmeadow's Head of School, Douglas Worth. Northmeadow students call him "Worthless"—and not without reason, Audre thinks. A caricature artist would have a field day with Doug: His abnormally large head is set on a long, slender stalk of a body. (Whenever Audre looks at Doug, she gets an involuntary vision of what his penis must look like.) Doug always wears a bow tie, even to football games. This is a sartorial affectation that Doug plagiarized from his father, George Worth, who served as Northmeadow's Head for a whopping forty-two years. There's a way in which Doug's earnest imitation of his father is both endearing and pathetic.

"Audre," Doug says, offering a long, limp hand, which Audre shakes a bit more aggressively than she needs to. "I suppose congratulations are in order."

If her years at Tiffin have taught Audre anything, it's how to offer a convincing smile. "The game hasn't even begun."

"I meant because of your number two ranking in *America Today*," Doug says. "I've been puzzling over it since the list came out, trying to figure out how Tiffin managed such a coup."

"No one was more surprised than me," Audre says. "I wish I could explain it, but as you know, the algorithm is a mystery."

"I'm not sure it's *exactly* a mystery," Doug says. "I've put a good deal of thought into why Tiffin jumped from nineteen to number two, while Northmeadow *dropped* from two to three..."

Should Audre remind Doug that Heads are supposed to be indifferent to the rankings? Though naturally they *aren't* indifferent, and especially not Doug, and especially not this year.

"...and I came up with three possible explanations."

Audre can't help but take the bait: She wants to hear these so-called explanations, but Tilly chooses that moment to blast DJ Khaled's "All I Do Is Win." Audre motions for Doug to move behind the visitors' side bleachers where it's slightly quieter.

"Oh, have you?" She looks up to see a couple members of the Northmeadow marching band peering down at them, and she realizes how unusual it must look — two Heads sneaking behind the bleachers to conduct a tête-à-tête. Audre gives the kid holding a French horn a wave, letting him know this is all on the up-and-up.

"I love that you bring the marching band. I love that you *have* a marching band. We never have enough musicians to field one."

"I suppose Tiffin students are too cool for that sort of thing," Doug says.

There's probably some truth to that statement, Audre thinks; "marching band" has a stigma that most Tiffin students would want to avoid. Audre then recalls that Doug plays the trombone; he's been known to whip it out at the Independent Schools of New England Coalition's social gatherings. "You were saying? The three 'explanations'?"

Doug squints at the players who are stretching on the field. *Oh no you don't,* Audre thinks. "You brought it up, Doug. You can't just leave me in suspense."

"Well...one explanation is that the *America Today* editors wanted to show support for diversity."

"Tiffin is no more or less diverse than other top schools..."

"I'm talking about leadership," Doug says.

Audre's cheeks burn like she's been slapped. "Me, you mean? You think our ranking rose because I'm a person of *color*?" Isn't it just like Doug to assume Audre has been rewarded solely because of her race. God, he's reprehensible.

As he sputters something along the lines of that's not, of course, what he *meant,* Audre says, "I'm in my sixth year, Doug. I hardly think that had anything to do with it." She turns away from Worthless and looks across the football field at her student body. Tiffin doesn't have a marching band, nor do they have cheerleaders, but they don't lack for school spirit: Davi and her friends are leading the crowd in some kind of chant.

Doug follows her gaze. "Then, of course, there's your TikTok phenom. She has one point three million followers. Can you imagine a sixteen-year-old girl wielding that kind of influence?"

What Audre thinks but does not say is: *You've checked Davi's following?*

"You think *America Today* ranked us above you"—Audre pauses to emphasize that she knows it's *this* fact that chafes him; if Northmeadow had been number one and Tiffin number two, Worthless would have sent Audre flowers—"because of Davi Banerjee?"

"She's very charismatic," Doug says.

Audre barks out a laugh. Has Douglas Worth watched Davi's Tik-Tok content? Her OOTDs? Her makeup tutorials? "She's one of the most dynamic students at this school," Audre says. "However, I highly doubt that's why…"

"There's only one other explanation," Doug says. "Which is that the president of your board, Jesse Eastman, bribed somebody."

Just when Audre thinks the man can't dig a deeper hole, he reaches for a bigger shovel. Audre spins on Douglas Worth and affixes him with a death stare—even though she has also wondered if this was the case. Jesse Eastman wields all kinds of power. He *could* have bribed the people who create the rankings at *America Today*. Everyone has a price, especially underpaid journalists covering the education beat. But Audre recalls how on edge Jesse was the day the rankings came out; he had sounded as shocked and incredulous as Audre herself.

"I'm going to pretend you didn't say that," Audre says.

"You can act as indignant as you want," Doug says. "But I'm far from the only Head who wonders about this."

In addition to serving as Northmeadow's Head, Douglas Worth is also the chairperson of ISNEC. He might have started a nasty text stream with the Heads of Excelsior, Brownwell-Mather, and Old Bennington positing conspiracy theories about Tiffin and maybe even Audre herself.

"Good luck in the game, Douglas," Audre says, and then she strides back to the field. She searches for Dub Austin—she wants to tell him to beat the snot out of Northmeadow—but strangely, he's not on the field.

Everyone on the Tiffin football team is out stretching, except for Dub Austin and Hakeem Pryce, who are in the locker room. Hakeem has Dub jacked up against the locker, his hand wrapped around Dub's neck.

Dub struggles for air, and yet he doesn't knee Hakeem in the groin like he probably should. Frankly, he's relieved it's come to this.

Taylor had left her phone unguarded; Hakeem looked at it and learned that Dub was Taylor's number one on Snapchat. Dub was in the library when Taylor went to Hakeem's room, so he missed the immediate drama but heard about it from Ravenna Rapsicoli. Dub and Ravenna were in the same Spanish class, but they'd never spoken. He noted her presence in the library; she was sitting close enough to him that he heard her phone buzzing and saw her checking her alerts. She looked over at him three times, then sighed and approached.

"People are saying Hakeem and Taylor broke up," she said.

Dub experienced an involuntary burst of joy, but skepticism soon followed. "Which people?"

"Only everyone in North," Ravenna said. "Hakeem saw Taylor's phone and discovered *someone else* was her number one on Snap."

Dub knew not to outright panic until Ravenna was safely back at her desk; then he collected his things and headed to Hakeem's room. Normally Dub would have walked right in, but this time he knocked. No answer. Dub cracked the door to see Hakeem lying face down on his bed. "Yo," Dub said.

"Get the fuck out of here," Hakeem said.

"Taylor is like a sister to me, man... You know I've been going through a lot."

"Get. The. *Fuck.* Out."

Dub would have confessed to Hakeem then and there—except that obviously wasn't an option. And so, Dub slunk back to his room. Because he wasn't sure what to do, he typed out a text to Taylor: What happened? Then he deleted it before sending because he didn't want to get into a whole thing with Taylor. He needed someone to talk to, but whom did he trust besides those two? Dub replayed the way Ravenna said "someone else" and realized that she knew it was him; everyone in the school knew it was him. The other day someone had referred to them as a "throuple."

Dub opened up his laptop and hovered the cursor over DO NOT OPEN THIS FILE UNTIL THE MORNING OF OUR GRADUATION. Dub caressed the words as though they were Cinnamon's cheekbone. It was a game he played with himself, of teasing and taunting. Of willpower. Could he keep the secret?

Yes, he could. He'd had plenty of practice.

He closed his laptop. He would straighten things out with Hakeem tomorrow.

He sent Hakeem a text that said, I promise to remove myself. I respect what you two have.

There was no response...which was what Dub deserved for telling a total lie.

The next morning, neither Hakeem nor Taylor was at breakfast, which was a relief. Dub had received a text from Taylor in the middle of the night that read: Hakeem is right, you are my number one, in all of the ways. Dub couldn't pretend to be surprised: Taylor touched him all the time, she leaned into him, she held his gaze, her brown eyes melting, her lips parting.

Dub left her on read. His first period was, unfortunately, English.

Instead of sitting with Taylor like he normally did, he sat all the way across the table, next to Charley Hicks. Everyone seemed surprised, even Mr. Rivera.

For the next week, Dub actively avoided Taylor—he wouldn't even look at her—and he saw Hakeem only at practice, where Hakeem iced him out. Coach Bosworth, who cared solely about beating Northmeadow, devised a new play called "Around the Apple Tree," which they ran five million times and successfully executed three. After practice, Coach called both Dub and Hakeem into his office, where he said the predictable things: *I don't care what the two of you are dealing with off the field, but you need to leave it behind for the sake of the team. Am I understood?* They both grudgingly nodded, but Hakeem wouldn't look at Dub and they did not shake hands.

That night at dinner, Hakeem and Taylor sat together in the Booth and Dub ate with his offensive line, all of them underclassmen. Taylor led Hakeem out of the dining hall by the necktie and there were cheers and whistles and Dub figured they were probably headed to God's Basement, where she would give him a blow job.

He cleared his tray. This was the way things had to be. For now and maybe forever.

Before the Northmeadow game, Dub let Teague Baldwin, the senior running back, lead the chants because he just wasn't feeling it. As the rest of the team was heading out to the field to stretch, Dub noticed Hakeem sitting on the bench with his head in his hands. He waited until everyone had left, then said, "Man, just punch me so we can get this over with."

Hakeem leaped to his feet and socked Dub in the jaw, hard. Dub, who had grown up with three brothers, instinctively hit back, and within seconds the two of them were brawling. At one point Dub got Hakeem in a headlock and thought, *What am I even doing?* So he loosened his grip, and Hakeem spun out and threw Dub up against the side of the lockers, trying to choke him.

Now, here they are: Hakeem has Dub up against the lockers. Dub closes his eyes and remembers being in this same position as an eighth grader back in Durango. A kid named Calhoun Royal, who had already gone through puberty and a growth spurt, was bullying Dub, saying he was being rewarded by the coach only because of who his older brothers were. *But your brothers aren't here to help you now, are they, little Webber?* He then called Dub a pole choker, threw him to the floor, and kicked him so hard he broke two of Dub's ribs.

Dub told the nurse in the ER that he'd taken a hit on the field, which was the same thing he'd told his mother. Karen Austin, however, was a perceptive woman: A brochure for Tiffin Academy arrived in the mail the following week. She'd already talked to Coach Bosworth, already discussed financial aid.

Massachusetts? Dub said.

You'll get a top-notch education, Karen said. *You'll get...away.*

His mother knew there was a lot Dub wanted to escape in Durango: the looming shadow of his two older brothers, Brent and Case; the encroaching shadow of his younger brother, Dallas, who was already playing better ball than Dub; Dub's father, who'd had an affair with one of the rafting guides at his outdoor expedition company, gotten her pregnant, and moved with her to Telluride; but most of all, Dub wanted to leave behind the bullies like Calhoun and his buddies who somehow sensed Dub's weakness and preyed on it.

Now, in a reedy voice Dub doesn't even recognize as his own, he says to Hakeem, "Kill me." Dying, Dub can handle. But he can't handle Hakeem hating him.

Hakeem lets Dub go and Dub coughs, bends in half, and spits on the ground. When he stands up, his vision is blurry and his jaw throbs. Hakeem has his hands on his hips and his eyes are blazing. "Man, she's *my* girlfriend, not yours."

They stare at each other for a long moment; then they hear the music out on the field and Dub knows Coach is about to come looking for them.

Dub says, "I know. I'm sorry. I'll back off. I love you, man." He isn't the kind of person who would say *Bros before hos,* but he considers doing it now, just to make things okay.

"I know you do, man, which is why I just don't fucking *get* it." Hakeem shakes his head, his hands, his shoulders. "I know Cinnamon is gone and Taylor's a nurturer and whatever the fuck, but you have to stay away from her."

"I will." Dub raises a fist. He just wants this whole thing over.

Hakeem stares at Dub a second, then grudgingly bumps knuckles. "Let's kick Northmeadow's ass."

"Bet," Dub says, and they run out onto the field.

Taylor Wilson is in the bleachers. She's wearing Hakeem's practice jersey and has his number, 62, painted on her face. But what the past week has brought into focus is that Taylor doesn't love Hakeem like she used to, and maybe not at all.

She discovered a new word on TikTok: *limerence.* It means "an intense desire for someone, marked by intrusive thoughts and a desire for a relationship and reciprocation."

This perfectly describes how Taylor feels about Dub. It's not *her* fault that Cinnamon Peters's death turned Dub into a tragic romantic hero. Underneath Dub's tough exterior, Taylor senses a swollen river of grief that draws her to him. Dub is Hakeem's *best friend,* which makes him completely off-limits. This only makes Taylor want him more.

The Tiffin team bursts onto the field to "Lose Yourself" by Eminem, and Taylor cheers along with the rest of the crowd. Hakeem seeks her out—maybe to make sure she's looking at him and not at Dub. She waves, blows him a kiss. She'll def get the lead in the musical this year, she thinks. Her acting is that good.

Chef Haz has Friday night off. He considers going to the game, though he really only enjoys sports when he has money riding on the outcome. He wonders if old Jameson wants to wager fifty bucks—Jameson will take Tiffin like the loyal dumbass he is—but before Haz can reach out to him, a text comes into his phone.

It's Andrew Eastman: Can u talk?

This is interesting, Haz thinks. *And probably not good.*

Sure, Haz says. I'm in the Back Lot having a butt.

A couple minutes later, Haz sees the glow of a single phone moving through the trees above the lot, and then East comes loping down the stairs. In the distance, Haz hears cheers: The game is underway.

"Hey," Haz says. He offers one of his Camels to East. *Corrupting a minor,* Haz thinks—except East isn't a minor, he's nineteen, and he could smoke crack and no one here would blink an eye.

East waves away the pack and sucks on his vape, also forbidden. Then he reaches into his back pocket and pulls out a thick stack of—Haz blinks—hundred-dollar bills.

"I have a proposition for you," East says.

A speakeasy. In an old bomb shelter deep beneath the dorms, connected to both Classic North and Classic South by brick tunnels. Did Haz know this place existed? No, but he's not surprised: This campus is like something out of a book, so why wouldn't there be a secret tunnel that connects the boys' dorm to the girls' with a bomb shelter in between that is fitted with both electricity and running water? East seems to think it was built during the Cold War. (Has he been paying attention in history class?) He wants it bougie, he says, with velvet and leather, brass and mahogany, soft lighting, good music, craft cocktails.

"Cocktails?" Haz says. For the last few moments, he's been able to pretend this might all be on the up-and-up, a new hangout space, a place for the kids to chill that would be an alternative to the loud, bright chaos of the Teddy. "With alcohol, you mean?"

East laughs. "Yes. Cocktails with alcohol." He flips through the bills in his hand like an old-time gangster. There's twenty-five hundred, maybe three grand there, Haz would guess.

"No," Haz says. "I am not going to help you set up a speakeasy. I am not going to buy you booze."

"You are, though," East says in that goddamned cocksure way he has. "You're going to tell me it's morally wrong; I'm going to tell you the kids drink anyway. Last year in the dorm checks, they found forty-one water bottles filled with Tito's and something like a hundred nips of Fireball. Everyone drinks, Chef, even the third-formers. This would be elevating the experience; we'd be showing the kids how proper drinking is done. I'm going to keep our clientele exclusive. This isn't a keg party. It's two hours on a Saturday night, eight or ten kids who will sneak down to enjoy a vodka martini or a Dirty Shirley, listen to music, and conversate." He hits his vape again. "Think of it as a representation of the seventeenth-century Parisian salons. Or the Algonquin Round Table. Fucking intellectual."

"Ha!" Haz says. "You're an entrepreneurial chip off the old block, that's for sure." What Haz thinks but does not say is: *I've already been banished out here to East Japip for breaking the rules once. I'm not idiotic enough to do it again.* "But I'm sorry to say, I'm not helping you with this little endeavor."

"I'll pay you twenty-five thousand dollars, cash, to provide alcohol, juices, mixers, garnishes, glassware, and specialty swizzle sticks and cocktail napkins. I'll give you twenty-five percent on top of everything you order."

Haz flicks his cigarette butt to the ground and crushes it under the heel of his clog. *Clientele,* he thinks. *Dirty Shirleys. Glassware, swizzle sticks.* Despite the chill in the air, Haz starts sweating under his chef's jacket as he fights off his worst impulses. But, as Haz has learned again and again, his worst impulses will win.

"Thirty-five grand," Haz says. "And thirty-five percent."

"Thirty grand," East says. "And thirty percent."

Haz studies the kid: He's good-looking with that dark hair, those hooded eyes, the lazy half smile. The other kids worship him, especially the girls — Haz has heard the third- and fourth-formers whispering. East's superpower is that he holds himself aloof. Haz is surprised there are eight or ten kids East would even want to hang out with.

"Why do this?" Haz asks. "Are you *trying* to get kicked out?"

"We both know that won't happen," East says. "I'm stuck here. I figured why not create something legendary, something Tiffin students will be talking about for generations to come?" East shrugs. "Plus, it'll give me a sense of purpose. I'm fucking *bored,* man."

This is as good an answer as any, Haz thinks. He nods at the money in East's hand, which in Haz's mind has taken on a radioactive glow. There, he thinks, is the start of his new life: With thirty grand, he can pay off both credit cards. With the money he makes from supplying — he'll tack on 50 percent, East will never know — he'll have a down payment for a new truck. Plus — and this is shameful as hell to admit — Haz feels the same rush that he gets when he bets on a game.

"Is that my deposit?" he asks.

"It is," East says, holding the money out.

Haz occasionally imagines opening his own place, an elevated cocktail spot. Wouldn't this, in some twisted way, scratch that itch? (If it doesn't get him fired. If it doesn't get him *arrested*.)

"I have conditions," Haz says.

East nods. "I thought you might."

"One, no phones."

"Love that rule," East says.

"Two," Haz says. "No drugs. No weed, no blow, no Molly, no gummies, and no pills. If I get any inkling about drugs, I shut it down."

"Obviously no drugs," East says. "Not after what happened."

"Exactly," Haz says. Cinnamon Peters OD'd on a combination of Valium, Xanax, and Ambien. A rumor went around the school that East sold her the drugs—because where else would she have gotten them? But Audre Robinson quickly quashed that rumor. Cinnamon had procured the drugs back in Wisconsin; the Peterses' old-school family doctor had prescribed them for Cinnamon's "mood swings," and she'd been stockpiling.

"How are you proposing people sneak out?" Haz asks.

"Do you know who the dorm parents are this year?" East asks. "Rivera in North and Bergeron in South. Both newbies."

"Right," Haz says. He'd witnessed Bergeron drunk off her pretty little ass; Rivera had basically begged Haz not to mention it to anyone. East is right: Sneaking out won't be a problem. Honey Vandermeid is a seasoned vet in South, but Haz has heard from old Jameson that Honey prowls around campus a bit herself at night. Roy Ewanick is the other dorm parent in North, but he's nearly seventy and it's unclear how effective his hearing aids are.

This could work, Haz thinks. "If you do get caught, you don't know me."

"I'll say I have a supplier in the city," East says.

Haz takes the money and shakes East's hand. "You've got a deal."

Suddenly a tremendous cheer goes up. *Tiffin must have scored,* Haz thinks. Thank god he didn't end up betting Jameson.

He's taking a much bigger gamble instead. This, he thinks, is the definition of risking it all.

The play "Around the Apple Tree" works like this:

Dub hands the ball off to Teague Baldwin and the Northmeadow defense thinks it's just another run play, but then Teague hands it off to Hakeem and Hakeem spirals a perfect pass to Dub—receiver throwing to quarterback—who is wide open in the end zone. Dub spikes the ball and the crowd goes bananas.

Hakeem leaps into Dub's arms. "We're legends, man!"

Charley Hicks loves Friday night lights. The dorm empties out and she's spared overhearing Olivia H-T trying to curry favor with Davi (Olivia's Sephora order just arrived, does Davi want to film the unboxing?) or Madison R. asking if anyone has seen her Theragun because it's gone missing from its case on top of her dresser.

Charley sets herself up at her desk with a Buffalo Chicken Caesar wrap and a Milky Way milkshake from the Grille and the copy of *Demon Copperhead* that Mr. Rivera lent her. It's a reimagining of *David Copperfield,* he said. When Charley admitted she hadn't read *David Copperfield,* Mr. Rivera said, "Well, it's just like the rest of Dickens. Bleak." Although it pained her, Charley said, "I haven't read any Dickens at all. I heard he used to get paid by the word and I like my fiction lean." Mr. Rivera threw his head back to laugh and told her she was a delight.

Her phone dings with a text but she ignores it because she's

The Academy

certain it's her mother. Fran has been blowing up Charley's phone about Family Weekend. She's insisting on coming.

Don't, Charley responded when Fran first told her. Then, to soften the blow, she said, It's not really a thing.

But of course it *is* a thing. The Head's office just released the schedule: There's a reception Friday afternoon followed by a steak dinner, and the girls' field hockey game under the lights. (This seems to be telegraphing that, at Tiffin, girls' sports are given the same attention as boys' sports, which isn't true.) Saturday goes: breakfast, Chapel, then there are some seminars (applying to college as a student athlete; an exploration of diversity at Tiffin) and rare tours of the chapel (that end with a visit to the roof), then the football game, then most kids go out to dinner with their parents to the Hobgoblin or the Wooden Duck.

I'm coming anyway, Fran said. I want to see what I'm paying for.

Of course her mother would bring up money; purse strings are the strongest tie between them.

Mom, it's actually nothing. My teachers can email you my progress reports.

I'm coming, Fran wrote. End of discussion.

Fine, Charley said. As long as you come alone.

What Charley meant was that Fran should not bring Joey.

Fran "liked" this text, and the conversation ended with a victory. Charley could maybe tolerate Fran (it might even be nice to have her mother to herself for once), but she would not — could not — abide a visit from Joey. She tries to imagine Fran and Joey on Tiffin's campus with all the other parents. Everyone would stare: Joey is fifteen years younger than Fran, he's covered in tattoos, he'll show up in cargo shorts and work boots wearing an Orioles cap over his man bun. Everything about Joey is just wrong, starting with his name. He's twenty-nine years old and goes by "Joey," like he's a character on a '90s sitcom or a singer in a boy band. He doesn't have a college degree and, as far as Charley knows, has never read a book. He has been cursed with what Charley thinks of as a "Deep Dundalk" accent. When he says, "down the ocean," it sounds like "day-yoon the aeeyou-shunn."

Once upon a time, Joey was Charley's father's project. Joey had a misdemeanor charge for dealing psychedelics; Joey's uncle was a big client of the law firm where Charley's father, Thad Hicks, worked. Thad got the charges dropped in exchange for thirty hours of community service, and then Thad invited Joey to the house for dinner, and over her famous homemade osso buco, Fran Hicks offered Joey a job at the garden center. After Joey left, Charley remembers her parents kissing and then her father saying, "Thank you for doing that. He's a nice kid, just a little misguided."

Little did her father know, three years later, Fran and Joey would be married. Joey still works for Fran: He now carries the title of project manager, on the landscaping side. His main job, Charley knows, is to drive the van around with deliveries and dig holes like a literal gopher.

Joey infiltrated all the spaces in their house where Charley's father used to be. He took over Thad Hicks's home office; it was where he played video games. Charley had caught him with his grass-stained bare feet on Thad's desk, wearing giant headphones, screaming at someone named "Ant" as he jabbed at the controller.

Charley had started researching boarding schools the day after her mother and Joey's wedding, but her mother refused to entertain the idea, even when Charley pointed out that Thad Hicks himself had gone to St. George's. *Right,* Fran said. *He was the one who said he would never want to miss a single day of your high school years. You're at the top of your class at Loch Raven. Hating Joey isn't a good enough reason for you to leave.*

The deadline for boarding school applications came and went.

Charley refused to speak to Joey; she left a room when he entered; most evenings she ate dinner at her desk while she studied.

Then came a Saturday night in mid-April: Charley and her best friend, Beatrix, had been out at a party. Beatrix had gotten wasted; she was sleeping over at Charley's because that's what she did on nights when they went out and Beatrix drank. Apparently, Beatrix went downstairs for a glass of water in the middle of the night and discovered Joey in the kitchen eating ice cream straight from the container in front of the open freezer. Beatrix said she was about to turn around and drink water from the bathroom tap, but then Joey saw Beatrix and engaged her in conversation. He fixed her not only a glass of ice water but a grilled cheese sandwich as well. As Beatrix ate, Joey asked her where she lived, how many siblings she had, when her birthday was, if she had a boyfriend. *I assume the answer is yes,* Joey said. *Since you're smoking hot.*

The next morning, Beatrix said, *I'm pretty sure Joey is obsessed with me.*

No, Charley thought. But yes, of course yes, because Joey was a lowlife!

Charley confronted her mother, who had the gall to say that Beatrix just loved drama, she was blowing things out of proportion *like she always does.* Joey had told Fran about his chat with Beatrix; he was making an effort to know Charley's friends since Charley wouldn't give him the time of day.

"Joey would never be inappropriate with one of your friends," Fran Hicks said.

Was her mother living under a rock? Just because Joey wore a T-shirt to bed that said YOU KNOW I LIKE MY GIRLS A LITTLE BIT OLDER didn't mean he wasn't a total creeper. He had been scheming Beatrix *in their own house*! Using the transitive property, it followed that Joey might also look at Charley this way. And sorry, but Charley didn't need a better reason to go away to school than that. She applied to sixteen boarding schools, from the Cate School in California to the Madeira School in Virginia.

They all said sorry, she was too late for admission in the fall.

Except for Tiffin.

At that instant, a pebble hits Charley's window, scaring the shit out of her. She checks her phone. The text is from East, not her mother.
Hey, I have good news.

The previous week, East asked Charley to Intervis and she agreed, assuming he was finally going to capitulate and ask for help with history. But instead he took her hand (again, holding hands!) and led her down the back stairs, outside to the cellar door and into the tunnel from the north side. Charley was appalled at herself for so flagrantly breaking the rules on a school night, but East assured her they wouldn't stay long, no one would miss them, he just wanted to see it again. He held her hand while they were in the tunnel and by the time they reached the bomb shelter, Charley had memorized the feel of East's warm, strong fingers intertwined with hers.

When he let her hand go to yank on the string of the overhead light, she was crushed. He started talking about building a bar— mahogany with a granite countertop, with Persian rugs and Tiffany lamps. Charley nodded along, affirming every design decision, though in her head she thought: *Granite countertops? Tiffany lamps?* Part of her was relieved his ideas were so grandiose. If he'd just been talking about a beer pong table and folding chairs, she would have been worried. That could conceivably become a reality. But a speakeasy with Persian rugs? *Never going to happen.*

Another pebble. Charley peers behind the shade and there he is, pointing at the door.

Charley wraps up her sandwich, closes her book, checks her teeth in the mirror while reminding herself that she doesn't care, she's not obsessed with him.

She goes to the front door to let him in, then stands there like a store mannequin while he walks down the hall toward her room. She's pretty sure they're breaking the rules yet again — visits during Intervis are okay as long as they're documented and the door stays cracked. East walks right into her room, helps himself to an Oreo from her hanging baskets of snacks, and flops onto her bed. "Close the door," he says.

"But..."

"Everyone's at the game."

Right, she thinks, so why do they need to close the door? But she does it anyway.

East seems different. He seems... happy. As in ready-to-explode-in-a-burst-of-piñata-candy happy. "I found a hookup for the alcohol," he says.

Charley can't believe anyone would be stupid or desperate enough to provide alcohol for a speakeasy at a boarding school. "Who is it?"

"I can't tell you," he says. "But Priorities is happening."

"Priorities?" she says. "That's the name?"

He nods. "We should have it up and running by spring."

His use of the word "we" is both delicious and deeply unsettling. He must notice the expression on her face because he says, "Don't bail on me now, Charles. You want this. Remember the literary salon? The Algonquin Round Table?"

"Is that what it's going to be like?" Charley asks. "Or is it going to be" — what comes to mind is a scene pulled straight out of *Euphoria*: Gunna thumping, the Olivias and Madisons throwing back shots of tequila and snorting bumps of cocaine off the base of their thumbs while Hakeem and Taylor fuck each other silly out in the hallway — "a place to rage?"

"I bet you" — East snaps an Oreo between his teeth, then brushes chocolate crumbs off the front of his T-shirt onto her duvet cover—"that the reason Dorothy Parker was so witty was because she'd had a martini or two."

Charley deadpans him. "A woman can't be witty when she's sober?"

"They met at a hotel bar," East says. "Because they were *drinking*."

"What if we get caught?" Charley says. She tries to imagine how *over* her life will be if she gets... *Honor Boarded*. No college for her, or not the colleges she dreams of attending. And what if she gets sent home to live with her mother and Joey?

"We're not going to get caught," East says. He bounces off the bed and, without any warning, takes her face in his hands. She holds her breath, which she fears smells like Buffalo sauce and/or Caesar dressing. "I have impunity."

Charley can't help but smile. "That's a pretty big word for someone who's failing history."

East brings her in for a hug. Charley instinctively wraps her arms around him. He rests his chin on top of her head and she closes her eyes. *This,* she thinks, *is why people write romance novels.*

"Just stick with me on this, Charles," East says. He pulls away so he can look her in the eye. "It's gonna be legendary."

After East leaves her room, Charley sits on her bed amid the chocolate crumbs and tries to steady her breathing. East is the antagonist to her protagonist: He's leading her down a wayward path. He's opening a speakeasy called Priorities in the basement of their dorm, and for some reason he wants her as his partner. Not Davi, not Tilly Benbow, not one of the Madisons or Olivias.

He's chosen her. *Just stick with me on this, Charles.*

The nickname would annoy her coming from anyone else, but now Charley can't help grinning.

Almost involuntarily, almost as if she's being manipulated by the hand of some unseen force, Charley sends East a text: I'm in.

There it is, she thinks. Her ruin, floating in a blue bubble.

There will be no more reading tonight. Charley carries the remains of her milkshake to the bathroom, where she immediately realizes she's not alone. Someone is in one of the stalls, retching.

Charley pours her milkshake down the drain and runs the water for a while, making sure there's no Milky Way residue in the sink, and then she rinses out the plastic cup. The person in the stall is probably waiting for Charley to leave, and Charley can't blame her. Doesn't everyone want privacy while they puke?

Charley shuts off the water and is about to leave when she hears more retching. She stops and thinks, *What do you care?* But tonight has taken such a bizarre turn already that Charley says, "Are you okay?"

There's no response. She should leave. But instead, she crouches down to peek under the stall. She sees a pair of lavender Adidas Gazelles. It's Davi.

Whoa, Charley thinks. Not who she expected. She has, of course, heard about girls at boarding school who develop eating disorders, but she assumed Davi Banerjee would be above all that. Isn't Davi celebrated in the Paddock for her appetite? Isn't she Chef's favorite?

"Davi?" Charley says.

There's a rustling, then the toilet flushes, then the stall door opens and Davi stands before her, eyes shining, strands of hair caught in her mouth.

"The barbacoa from the food truck was bad, I think," she says. "I felt sick right away." As she washes her hands, Charley holds her gaze in the mirror.

"What?" Davi says. "I'm fine."

"Okay."

"You don't have to pretend to be *worried*," Davi says. She scoops water into her mouth, rinses, spits. "I know what you think of me."

Charley blinks. "What do I think of you?"

"You think I'm shallow. You think I whore myself out for clicks and follows."

"Maybe that's what you think about yourself."

Davi turns to her. "She was my best friend, you know. My best *fucking* friend—and I didn't know there was anything wrong. She was engaged in life, she played the guitar and sang, she was with Dub. Did she have moments? Yeah, but we all have moments."

Charley nods. "I'm sorry. I wish I'd known her." Everything Charley has heard about Cinnamon Peters makes Charley believe she would have liked Cinnamon better than anyone else in the school.

"Paradox," Davi says. "There's no way you would have known her. If she were alive, you wouldn't be here."

"You're right."

Davi pulls a pack of mints out of her pocket and crunches one between her teeth. "I just really want to know why you think you're superior to the rest of us."

Charley tilts her head. "You have over a million followers on TikTok, Davi. Your parents own a fashion label. You live in London and have an accent that I'm sure everyone in this dorm tries to imitate when they're alone. People at this school *worship* you." Charley pitches her rinsed plastic cup into the recycling bin a little harder than she means to. "I do *not* think I'm superior."

"You don't *have* to be weird, is the thing," Davi says. "I can help you with your clothes, your hair, your makeup. I can turn you into a total smokeshow."

Charley nearly laughs. Becoming a "total smokeshow," which she understands to mean looking like a clone of Davi and her minions, is the last thing she wants. Does this make her superior?

"I'm good, thanks," Charley says. "I just wanted to make sure you were all right."

Davi turns back to the mirror and wipes under each eye. "Never better." She sighs. "If you could just not..."

"Don't worry, I won't tell anyone," Charley says, though she considers texting Beatrix at home. I caught Davi Banerjee puking in the bathroom. But Charley would feel disloyal sharing this even with Beatrix—and the barbacoa *might* be the reason.

Charley heads back to her room and closes the door. When she checks her phone, she sees a text from East. You're the fucking best, Charles.

In that moment, she feels strangely bonded to Davi. They both have secrets.

There's no better sport, Simone Bergeron decides, than American football. When time runs out on the clock—Tiffin 14, Northmeadow 10—Tiffin students rush the field. Simone watches Taylor Wilson jump into Hakeem's arms. This is exactly what Simone dreamed boarding school would be like: teenagers in love celebrating a big win on a crisp autumn night.

"Good luck to us getting everyone in for dorm checks," Rhode says.

Simone doesn't care about dorm checks. Some of her girls asked if they could swing by the Grille for a milkshake on the way home and Simone said *oui,* as long as they returned *tout de suite.*

At halftime, Rhode plunked himself down next to Simone in the bleachers, and the cluster of third- and fourth-formers who were sitting with Simone scattered. They all fully believed that Mr. Rivera was scheming Simone. Simone wanted to call the girls back—*Please stay!*—but that would have made things awkward, and they wouldn't have listened anyway.

Rhode nodded at the cup of hot cider Simone was holding.

"I have something for that," he said.

Simone wasn't sure what he meant; she was too busy thinking about how to make a graceful exit—she could go sit with Mrs. Spooner and Honey Vandermeid a few rows below—when Rhode pulled a silver flask from the pocket of his quilted jacket and poured something into Simone's cider.

"What are you *doing*?" she hissed. She looked around, but they were sitting pretty high up and everyone's attention was on the field. "What is that?"

"Bourbon," Rhode said. "The good stuff, Buffalo Trace." He took a swig from the flask himself before tucking it back into his jacket. "It'll take the edge off."

Simone wanted to say that she wasn't feeling any edge, the night was perfect, she'd been looking forward to drinking her cider once it cooled. She wanted to say that they were teachers, and new teachers at that; they couldn't just drink on the job. She still felt chagrined about their night out at the Alibi back when school first started.

But instead, Simone took a sip of the cider, which made her throat and chest blaze like an orchard fire. She nearly shared this image with Rhode—he might appreciate it as a writer—but in the end she just held out her cup for more.

When the game ends, she's not drunk-drunk, just slightly out-of-body. She joins the throng of kids heading toward the Teddy and the dorms. As she tosses her cider cup in the trash, she considers ending her night with a glass of *vin rouge*—she keeps a bottle stashed inside one of her Hunter boots in her closet—though she's certain that if she indulges, there will be some kind of emergency in the middle of the night for which sobriety is required. She can't be sporting blue teeth and a headache. Her college days are, for better or worse, behind her.

She shepherds the girls into Classic South. It's up to the floor prefect, Madison J., to make sure everyone checks in; Simone will be contacted only in case of emergency. Her night is therefore over, though she should review for class the next day; they've finished up with Native Americans and moved on to the original thirteen colonies, and Simone is on shaky ground.

Simone chastises herself for leaving her room light on—she thought for sure she'd turned it off; she's leading by piss-poor example in energy conservation—when she opens the door and screams: Andrew Eastman is lying on her bed, vape pen in hand, blowing smoke at the ceiling.

Simone knows the proper course of action: Demand that he leave and report him to his dorm parent, Roy Ewanick. However, when East says, "Close the door, please," she complies, though not before checking that both her window shades are down.

"What," she hisses, "are you doing here?"

She puts a hand out to stop him as he approaches her, but he takes her hand and presses her palm to his mouth. She fights off a very strong, very forbidden wave of desire. She pulls back her hand as though she's been bitten by a snake and he laughs. "Relax."

He's calm, she thinks, because he can't get into any trouble. But she, of course, can. She ignores how handsome he is, how he's broad and strong without being bulky, how he fills out his jeans perfectly, how he managed to pair a ratty Vampire Weekend T-shirt with a vintage Rolex on a weathered leather band.

She can't relax. How is she going to get him out of here? The dorm is crawling with girls sharing bags of Takis, getting ready to watch the last episode of *Love Island* in the common room, or vying for one of the sinks to start their fifteen-step skin care routines.

"You have to go—" Before Simone can say another word, East's lips are on hers, and if it's possible, it's even hotter than when he kissed her down in the tunnel. It's lips and tongue and a playful bite and a hip lock; she can feel him through his jeans. Is she in a puddle on the floor? No, apparently she's still upright, still making out with East, a student, her student, as the predictable excuses roll through her head: The age difference between them is only five years; she's French Canadian, she views things like this differently. Brigitte Auzière was once Emmanuel Macron's high school teacher, and now she's Brigitte Macron, the well-regarded First Lady of France.

Simone also thinks: *This isn't happening.* Or it won't be happening in a second; she's going to push him away.

She hears Olivia H-T's voice, perilously close to her door. "Has anyone seen Davi? She never came back to the game."

Madison J. says, "She wasn't feeling well. She went to bed."

Simone snaps back to reality and pushes East away with both hands. "Stop," she whispers. "You have to get out of here right now."

"Okay, okay," East says. "Chill."

Chill? she thinks. She wants to smack him. How dare he sneak into her room—how did he even get into the dorm when everyone else was at the game?—and compromise her job, her good name, her entire future? He's too young to consider the consequences of his actions. He's immature, rash, destructive, entitled—and so, so hot.

East snaps off the light: Oh no, he's not luring her to bed. That's absolutely not happening...is it?

No—East lifts the shade, peers outside, then opens the window and climbs out. She hears a soft thud when he hits the ground.

She closes the window and locks it. Then, without turning the light back on, she fumbles through her closet, reaches a hand into her boot, and pulls out the hidden bottle of cabernet franc, which is, thankfully, a screw-top. She swigs directly from the bottle. Her phone dings with a text, which strikes a dissonant chord in her chest—there's no way it's a text she wants to read—and she takes another swig.

The text is from Rhode. Great, she thinks. He was outside, he saw their shadows or he watched East drop from Simone's window, her life is over. She could claim her reckless behavior was Rhode's fault: Who knew what was in the flask? It could have been something stronger and stranger than bourbon.

The text reads: Is East in your dorm? Roy Ewanick can't find him.

Simone blinks. Not here! she types. Although this is presently the truth, she hesitates before sending it. There's still time to come clean — tell Rhode that she came home to find Andrew Eastman in her room and when she asked him to leave, which she obviously did right away, he leaped out her window like a little boy with Spider-Man fantasies. But there would be follow-up: Audre might go through the motions of disciplining East (would she?). He might counter by describing exactly what happened with Simone in her room. It would then turn into a he said/she said, and the whole school would be ablaze with it like... an orchard on fire.

In the end, no reply is necessary because Rhode texts again: Never mind, he just turned up. Have a good night!

Simone brings the wine bottle to her mouth with one hand and with the other hand types: You too!

10. Family Weekend

Greetings, Tiffin families!
We look forward to welcoming you to our esteemed academy this weekend. The foliage on campus is at its peak, and we

have a full slate of fun and enriching activities planned for you to experience with your students. To view the weekend schedule, click here.

Audre pauses. Her backside is heating up like there's a gas burner under her chair. In theory, this should be the most successful (and lucrative) Family Weekend ever; after all, they've been ranked number two in the country! Cordelia Spooner informed Audre that campus tours and interviews are up by 208 percent...and Audre has replaced two dinosaurs on the faculty with dynamic young teachers. (Privately, Audre worries that Simone Bergeron is *too* young. Audre will recommend that she dress conservatively this weekend and hope Simone doesn't push back.)

The only thing tempering Audre's anticipation of the weekend ahead is an email she received late the night before from Douglas Worth, acting in his capacity as chairperson of ISNEC, "courteously" informing Audre that the coalition is making an official inquiry into Tiffin's ranking in *America Today*.

Audre had gasped out loud. Was Douglas Worth so bitter and jealous that Northmeadow had been supplanted from the number two spot that he was starting a *witch hunt*? Apparently so. This was a *blatant* exploitation of power. ISNEC was a *coalition;* the purpose was to *support* one another. Audre wonders if Douglas's inquiry will gain any traction. Audre counts the other Heads of ISNEC as friends or friendly acquaintances, and she's always assumed the feeling was mutual. But maybe the other Heads liked Audre only because they felt their schools were superior to Tiffin.

Even though it was late (Douglas no doubt sent the email at night in order to ruin Audre's sleep), Audre forwarded the email to Jesse Eastman with the subject line: Do we need to be concerned about this?

A response came right away: Hell no. Sour grapes.

This was the answer Audre was hoping for. If Big East is unconcerned—if he didn't have anything to do with manipulating the rankings—then Audre won't worry.

Except, of course, that she will. Boarding schools have been historically rife with scandal; Audre has heard some chilling stories over the years. For example, a student at one of the oldest, most prestigious schools took a spring break trip to Venezuela and returned with three hundred thousand dollars' worth of cocaine that he'd (rather ingeniously) stuffed inside tennis balls, which he then sewed back up and transported in their cans. He was caught with the drugs at Logan Airport, and further investigation revealed a spreadsheet on the student's laptop with the names of a dozen other students who had paid him for the cocaine in advance.

There was an incident at a different school where a student made chloroform in the chemistry lab, soaked a rag in it, and placed said rag under another student's pillow in what was termed an "attempted murder."

Audre experienced a certain amount of schadenfreude (a word that may have been invented for Heads of Schools) when she heard these stories: Thank god them and not us. Tiffin became the recipient of ISNEC's thoughts and prayers last May when Cinnamon took her own life, though Audre knew what the other Heads were thinking: *Thank god them and not us.*

This year, in addition to certain cosmetic improvements (Audre had the cushions of the Senior Sofa restuffed and reupholstered in the same green velvet with gold cord piping) and the promising athletic contests (the field hockey and football teams are playing Colbert, the same school they played every year during Family Weekend because it's the only one they can reliably beat), there will be a seminar focusing on mental health, led by the chaplain, Laura Rae. Audre felt this was appropriate, though she's already received an email from Dub Austin's mother, Karen, asking why Audre hasn't hired a proper school psychologist to lead the seminar. Audre wrote back that they do have a school psychologist on call, but unfortunately, Dr. Pringle's son is getting married this weekend in La Jolla, hence, Laura Rae will be stepping in.

Karen Austin wrote back that she'd expected more from Tiffin, more from Audre *personally,* since the mental health of the students was at risk. And what could Audre do but respond: You're absolutely right, Karen. I'm doing the best I can under the circumstances. Please know that the students' mental health is of paramount concern to everyone here at Tiffin. I'm confident Laura Rae will conduct a meaningful discussion.

Karen sent back the thumbs-up emoji, which might as well have been a middle finger.

Audre could use some help on the front lines, and so she texts Big East: What time will you be arriving on Friday?

Not coming, Big East responds. I'll be in Tokyo.

Audre blinks. Not *coming*? Big East *loves* Family Weekend. The past two years, he lorded over every event, showing off all the places where his money had made a difference. (Audre will admit, it's a lot of places.) It must be killing Big East to miss it and yet, when Audre does a gut check, she finds she's more glad than sad. Big East won't be around doing his usual crowing. (It bugged her that Audre was the person with boots on the ground but Big East claimed all the glory.)

Audre will ask Cordelia to serve as her lieutenant. Honey Vandermeid will be swarmed by fifth-form parents asking her opinion of the ACT versus the SAT. ("Which test is easier?")

The Academy

Audre looks out the window of her private library across Jewel Pond, which reflects the scarlet and gold leaves of the surrounding woodlands. She recalls her predecessor, Chester Dell, telling her that the key to a successful year was keeping the school running smoothly until Family Weekend. After that, Chester said, the wheels can fall off the bus. *The parents won't be back until they come to pick up their little darlings for the summer. As long as they're dazzled by the foliage, can celebrate wins for the teams, and are plied with plenty of top-shelf liquor, and as long as the faculty mention how much they've enjoyed getting to know young Melissa and David in class, these parents will leave contented and will write a nice check to the Annual Fund before they go.*

Although Audre found this advice shabby at first—it was her intent to not only uphold Tiffin standards but improve on them every single day—she now understands he was, for the most part, correct. She just has to keep things sunny and upbeat through the weekend.

She clicks out of her letter and rereads the ISNEC email. Douglas Worth is using the power granted to him as chairperson to invalidate the great strides Audre has made with the school since she took over as Head. How *dare* he! There's a reason the students call him "Worthless": They can smell his underlying insecurity. *America Today*'s rankings must give his life more meaning than Audre even realized. A part of her is tempted to stroke his ego. Should she reach out to Doug privately and remind him that the Tiffin students gave rousing applause for Northmeadow's marching band, even though their rendition of "All of the Lights" was a bit anemic?

No, she won't. She's above that. *Let them inquire all they want,* Audre thinks. *Tiffin was ranked number two fair and square.*

At least, she hopes so.

The day before Family Weekend begins, the atmosphere in the *'Bred Bulletin* office is tense.

"We're fucked," Ravenna Rapsicoli says. Ravenna is wearing one of her mob-wife outfits: black leather pants and a red satin bustier that shoves her breasts forward in a way that's impossible to ignore. She lords these breasts over Levi, who is sitting at the student paper's massive computer terminal arranging the layout. (Levi is the only one who understands how to operate the software.) "We're supposed to publish the first edition of the *Bulletin* in time for Family Weekend and we have almost no content."

They do have content, Charley thinks. There's the lead article about Tiffin being ranked the number two boarding school in the country by *America Today* with quotes from students and faculty, all of whom expressed the predictable joy as well as some bemusement. "It doesn't make any sense," fifth-former Tilly Benbow said. "I'm not sure we're better than Hill School or Middlesex—but whatever, I didn't make the list."

There's also an article about the football team winning the most games since the school's inception. Grady wrote this article, but it doesn't include quotes from Coach Bosworth or any of the players because Grady—who's five-foot-two, weighing in at 107 pounds—was too intimidated to go into the locker room after practice.

Ravenna was incredulous. "Athletes love journalists."

Grady shook his head. "Athletes strip journalists naked, tie them up with jump ropes, and throw them in the showers. That's what happened to my friend at Brownwell-Mather; he was too afraid to tell anyone, but it came out on that app I was telling you about—"

"Oh my god, enough already about the app," Ravenna said. She decided to just run the football story without any quotes.

What Ravenna means when she says the paper has no "content" is that it has no gossip for her baby, *Page 114*. Ravenna wrote a juicy bit about the breakup of "Tiffin's cutest couple," and somehow Taylor

Wilson got wind of it and confronted Ravenna, saying that if she printed it, there would be consequences. (Taylor's mother, Kathy Wilson, is a litigation attorney in Philadelphia and sits on Tiffin's board, so this felt like more than an empty threat.)

"There has to be other stuff going on," Ravenna says. She eyeballs Charley. "You live on the first floor of South; that's where all the drama is. Davi and her minions. Any secrets there?"

Charley does her best to convey nonchalance. "Secrets with Davi? You're kidding, right? If her period comes a day early or the guavaberry hair mask she ordered arrives, one point three million people know about it instantly."

"One point four," Levi says. "She's up to one point four on TikTok."

"But still only one point three on Instagram," Grady says.

"It's pathetic that you two know that," Ravenna says. "And yet you're both completely useless in the gossip department."

Grady gives Ravenna a pair of puppy dog eyes. Levi sighs and turns back to the computer.

"How's your list coming?" Ravenna asks Charley.

Charley is supposed to be writing the "In" and "Out" columns for the fall of 2025. Charley has, ironically, put "in and out lists" in the "Out" column. Below that, she has written, "Family Weekend."

Ravenna reads over Charley's shoulder and barks out a laugh. "Funny!" she says—and for a second, Charley feels seen. "But you can't put Family Weekend in the 'Out' column. Parents are boomers, and boomers are sensitive."

"Millennials are sensitive," Charley says. "They're the ones who got all the trophies. My mother is Gen X. She doesn't have feelings."

"My mother is Gen X too," Levi says. "She was a latchkey kid who ate Stouffer's French bread pizza and watched reruns of *The Brady Bunch* after school."

"That sounds tragically suburban," Ravenna says. She turns back to Charley. "Put some things in the 'In' column."

"Like what?" Charley says. "Stanley cups? Ten-year-olds shopping at Sephora?"

"Why did I put you in charge of this list?" Ravenna says. "You don't have the first fucking idea what's in. I'll have to do it."

Charley doesn't take offense; Ravenna is right. Though Charley takes a certain satisfaction in knowing what will be in next semester if East is to be believed—Saturday nights at Priorities.

The night before Family Weekend, Cordelia Spooner and Honey Vandermeid are eating dinner at Moon Palace, a kitschy Chinese restaurant they frequent in Capulet Falls, which is one town over from Haydensboro. Honey feels Haydensboro is too close to campus, someone might see them, and for Honey, privacy is very important. *Too* important, in Cordelia's opinion. Who cares if someone sees them? But Cordelia likes Moon Palace; the hostess, Pammy, always gives them the same red leather booth and without asking knows to bring them a chardonnay (Cordelia) and a Manhattan (Honey) and a dish of the crunchy wonton snacks, which Cordelia will devour and Honey won't touch.

This dinner is meant to be a chance to connect before they're pulled in two different directions this weekend. Cordelia will serve as Audre's *consigliere,* and Honey...well, poor Honey will be divebombed by every sixth-form parent in attendance. Honey's especially dreading her interactions with Annabelle Tuckerman's parents—both Princeton alums—who will grill Honey on Annabelle's "chances." Honey will think but not say, *It depends how much you've been donating the past eighteen years.* There's nothing worse for Honey than a student who has her heart set on one school. Annabelle has no interest in attending her targets or likelies; she wants only Princeton. And Princeton is a reach.

Cordelia and Honey raise their glasses. "To surviving," Cordelia says. "It's only two days."

"Easy for you to say." Honey takes a sip of her cocktail, then pretends to study the menu, though they always order the same things: the egg rolls to share, the Singapore chow mei fun for Cordelia, and the shrimp with lobster sauce for Honey.

Cordelia reaches across the table for Honey's hand, but Honey pulls away as Pammy approaches to take their order. Cordelia tries not to take offense, though she feels the chasm between herself and Honey growing greater and chillier with each passing day. Honey hasn't come to Cordelia's cottage even once—she's too busy with sixth-form application deadlines, hunting down teacher recs, analyzing their test scores, editing their essays, prioritizing their extracurriculars, and managing their expectations, not to mention all the responsibilities that come with being a dorm parent for two-thirds of Classic South. Cordelia and Honey haven't been together in weeks, since they sneaked down to God's Basement under the guise of checking for students who were "making a public space private," and where they then proceeded to do that themselves, furtively getting each other off on an old recliner that groaned under their weight.

When their egg rolls are delivered, Cordelia dips one into the apricot-hued duck sauce and then takes a bite, even though it's so hot she burns her tongue. She tends to eat too quickly when she's nervous, and she's very nervous now. She wants this dinner to go smoothly; she wants to get their glow back.

"How is Simone adjusting?" Cordelia asks. She tries to keep her tone light, though Simone's mere existence is a pebble in Cordelia's Skechers. Sultry, nubile Simone, whose sexual orientation has yet to be determined, sleeps in a room directly below Honey's three floors down. There are limitless chances for a rendezvous, something Cordelia obsesses about as she shivers alone in her bed halfway across campus.

"The girls love her," Honey says. "Because why wouldn't they? She's fun, she's beautiful..."

"She's their age," Cordelia supplies.

"They look up to her the way we used to look up to our babysitters," Honey says. "They're positively obsessed with her love life. They're all convinced Rhode Rivera wants to fuck her."

Before Cordelia can stop herself—she had a glass of chardonnay (two) before she came out tonight, so she's feeling both uninhibited and combative—she says, "Do *you* want to fuck her?" Her cheeks immediately burn with embarrassment. Revealing her jealousy only gives Simone—and Honey—power.

Honey laughs. "Everyone wants to fuck Simone," she says.

When their meals arrive, steaming and fragrant, there's a flurry of activity—unsheathing chopsticks, passing the sticky bottle of soy sauce between them—and although Cordelia wants to stop talking about work, she can't help but say, "Jesse Eastman isn't coming to Family Weekend."

Honey blows on a shrimp. "You've got to be kidding."

"Not kidding. He has business in Tokyo. Audre is relieved and so am I."

Honey frowns. "Sometimes I don't understand you, Cord."

"What? The guy is a megalomaniac."

"He's a *father*," Honey says. "How do you think East feels about him not showing up?"

Cordelia admits she hasn't considered East. She didn't think she needed to consider East—he's the most independent, self-sufficient student at Tiffin. He's nineteen, an adult.

"There are other parents who won't come," Cordelia says, though she knows that historically over 90 percent of students have at least one family member in attendance. Davi Banerjee's parents fly in all the way from London.

"The parents have already shipped their kids off for someone else to raise," Honey says. "The least they can do is clear their schedules one weekend a year. Taylor Swift had 'business' in Tokyo, she was on tour, and she made it to Vegas to watch her boyfriend play in the Super Bowl."

"Jesse Eastman is no Taylor Swift," Cordelia says. She makes a clumsy attempt to snatch up noodles with her chopsticks, then gives up in frustration—she only uses them to impress Honey—and spears a sliver of pork with her fork. They have arrived at the launchpad of their favorite argument: Why do parents send their children to Tiffin? Cordelia believes that the parents see it as a sacrifice made in service of their child's education. Kids who attend boarding school not only face greater academic rigor than their public school counterparts, the course offerings are wider and deeper. Cordelia hears from former students all the time and, to a person, they tell her that Tiffin was more challenging than college. Another advantage is that the students learn how to converse with adults. The relationships between students and teachers are more intimate than at public schools, thanks to the small class size (an 11:1 ratio, as Cordelia tells parents in the information sessions, with some classes as small as eight students). *No one falls into the cracks at Tiffin,* Cordelia had been fond of saying—though she hasn't used that line this year because of what happened with Cinnamon Peters. Boarding school also teaches kids how to live away from home; it fosters independence and self-reliance. Cordelia wholeheartedly believes that sending a child to boarding school is an act of selfless love; the parents have only their child in mind.

But oh, does Honey disagree! She views the parents as lazy and selfish. Since they have the money, why *shouldn't* they remove the unpleasantness of teenagers in the house—the smells, the attitude, the girlfriend hiding under the bed, the vomiting in the kitchen sink after a night of drinking pilfered Bacardi 151 in a field, the gym socks stiff with dried cum among the bedsheets, the tears when their honor roll daughter is deferred from UMiami, where she applied ED because she wants to be just like Alix Earle—and pawn them off on a bunch of underpaid, overstressed strangers to raise?

Cordelia will then point out that many Tiffin parents went to Tiffin themselves. They enjoyed it and they want the same experience for their children. Besides, you can't expect someone who grew up at 720 Park Avenue (like Ravenna Rapsicoli) to attend the New York City public schools.

Definitely not! Honey will exclaim in mock horror. By all means, keep the successful parents away from the public school system, where they might actually be able to effect some positive change!

Cordelia will then mention students like Dub Austin, who are on scholarship: Tiffin is a tremendous opportunity for them.

Honey will scoff and say Dub's mother sent him to Tiffin so he would succeed at football and not have to live in the shadow of his brothers, all of whom are better at the sport than he is.

Is that such a bad thing? Cordelia will counter. Cordelia reads these kids' applications, and she always begins with the personal statement. The prompt is: *Describe your reasons for wanting to become a Tiffin student, focusing on the ways you will contribute to the community.* Cordelia has seen plenty of kids phone it in because of course there *are* kids whose parents nudge them toward boarding school against their will. But Cordelia weeds them out just as she sifts out those kids who have cut and pasted essays they used for admission to St. Paul's and Taft, simply changing the name of the school (or, in the case of one student also apparently applying to Deerfield, not even bothering to change the name). Cordelia makes certain that every student she accepts specifically wants to be at Tiffin. A new thought comes to her: Maybe *that's* why they were ranked number two. Maybe it's because Mrs. Cordelia Spooner, head of admissions, has done her job so adroitly. Tiffin Academy is a place where student and school have a remarkable synchronicity. (Cordelia would never suggest this possibility to Honey; she's not sure "synchronicity" is the right word, anyway.)

If Cordelia reminds Honey that she reads the children's essays, Honey will say, *If I know anything, it's that kids stretch the truth in their essays. They embellish, exaggerate, and fabricate. And by* fabricate, *I mean that they, yes, flat-out lie.*

Cordelia polishes off her chardonnay. She will end the imaginary argument before it begins. "You're right. Tiffin parents are selfish assholes who ship us their kids either for some pumped-up notion of prestige or because they're just too afraid or exhausted to do the job themselves. If the kids turn out poorly, they can blame someone else. They can blame us."

Honey stands up and Cordelia thinks, *Now I've done it. Honey detected the sarcasm and she's leaving in the middle of dinner. She'll return to campus and poke her head into Simone Bergeron's room, maybe stay for a moment with the door closed so she can fill in Simone on what to expect over Family Weekend from the callous parents.*

But instead of leaving, Honey slides into the booth next to Cordelia and plants a juicy kiss on her cheek. "I love it when you're feisty," she says, and Cordelia decides to bask in the golden warmth of Honey's favor while she has it.

As Charley leaves the Schoolhouse after English class—the academic day is over and afternoon activities are canceled today to make time for the family reception, followed by a steak dinner in the Paddock, followed by the under-the-lights field hockey game against Colbert—she sees a crowd of students gathered around a table, snatching up copies of the *'Bred Bulletin*. There was talk of sending the paper to each student's inbox electronically, but Ravenna, who (lest anyone forget it) is a New Yorker, still believes in the power of newsprint.

Ravenna was apparently right, but all Charley can think is, *Prepare to be underwhelmed.*

Charley manages to procure the last copy of the paper, which she stuffs in her backpack. She'll show it to her mother as proof that she's participating, even if it is the most pathetic student newspaper of all time, and will probably be used to start the bonfire later.

Charley can't believe it, but she feels a burst of excitement about seeing her mother. Before she left English, Mr. Rivera said, "I look forward to meeting your mom, Charley. I can't wait to rave about you."

Fran Hicks will be expecting such raves; she has always been in awe of Charley's intellect. *Book smart, like your dad.* Fran's intelligence runs more toward brass tacks, common sense. She understands the physical and natural world, she knows the names of a thousand plants and where to place them so they thrive, also the correct way to lay irrigation hose, and she can instantly determine the provenance of stone or wrought-iron garden fixtures: antique, or simply fashioned to appear antique?

As Charley walks toward the dorms, she gets glimpses of other people's parents: The dads are in navy blazers and expensive loafers without socks; they place proprietary hands on the backs of the mothers, who are older versions of the Madisons and Olivias with their cute white jeans and Golden Goose sneakers, their long hair flowing over the collars of their puffy SAM vests. Fran Hicks will stick out like a scruffy mutt among sleek golden retrievers, but Charley doesn't care. She can't wait to feel her mother's strong arms around her, and inhale the cedar scent of her hair.

Charley enters Classic South as Davi exits, followed by a trio of the most stylish people Charley has ever seen. Unlike the majority of other parents, who favor khaki and navy blue, Davi's people are in black and white. Her father is a slender Indian man with close-cut salt-and-pepper hair. He's in a black suit with a black shirt open at the collar, and he wears black velvet loafers. Davi's mother is in black jeans, over-the-knee black boots, and a black cashmere poncho. There's another woman with them — she's white with hair dyed the color of a marshmallow. She's in a white tank, a white tutu, white footless tights, and a black motorcycle jacket.

Charley takes heart: No matter what Fran Hicks wears, she'll fit in better than these people. They're so unlikely, they might have just stepped off a spaceship. But wow, they're gorgeous and fabulous and Charley is dumbstruck as they execute a do-si-do, the Banerjee party coming out, Charley going in.

Davi's mother smiles warmly at Charley and offers a hand. "How do you do, I'm Ruby Banerjee."

Charley looks quickly to Davi, who is scowling. Davi's mother has mistaken Charley for someone who matters.

"This is Charley, Mama," Davi says. "The one who wrote the In and Out list in the paper."

"Ohhhhh," Ruby Banerjee says. "I see."

Before Charley can explain that she didn't actually write the In and Out list — the editor, Ravenna Rapsicoli, did — Davi says, "We have to go. Ms. Robbie is waiting." Then she raises a microbladed eyebrow at Charley. "You're just full of surprises."

Once in her room, Charley decides that her outfit of corduroys, a turtleneck, and a Fair Isle sweater will probably be fine for the reception — but is the steak dinner more formal? She has no idea of the dress code for any of this, nor does she particularly care; her disinterest in fashion has been proven. Why did Davi say that

Charley had written the In and Out list? And what did she mean by "full of surprises"? Charley pulls the *'Bred Bulletin* from her backpack. There, on the front page, is the anodyne stuff about the rankings and the football team. She has to go to page 3 to find the In and Out list—and there it is:

Fall 2025 In and Out List
By Charlotte Hicks

In	**Out**
Saying no	Makeup
Staying in	Exes
Vodka Red Bulls	Crying
Reading	Drama
Hating people	Buying drinks
iMessage	Chasing
Sunscreen	Broke men
Pulling people for chats	Outfit slideshows
Orgasms	School spirit
Fifth-form repeats	Gratuitous posting

Charley reads the list three times, her hands trembling more visibly each time. She wants to open her window and yell, *I didn't write this! Ravenna wrote this!* Charley doesn't have Ravenna's cell number; otherwise she would be calling her right now. The worst thing about this list is that enough of it tracks (In: staying in, reading, hating people; Out: makeup, crying, drama, outfit slideshows, school spirit) that most people will believe Charley wrote it. The item that addles Charley the most, of course, is *orgasms.* What does Charley know about orgasms? Nothing. Also, vodka Red Bulls? Fifth-form repeats? (*Like East,* she thinks. *Oh god, oh god, will people think that's a coded allusion to East?*)

A text comes into her phone from her mother: In the reception tent, where are u?

In my room, packing, Charley wants to respond. *We have to go home.*

Can you come to the dorms, please? Charley texts. She's going to have to spend all of Family Weekend with her mother in 111 South.

You said to meet you at the tent, her mother writes back. I'm at the tent. I have wine. Just come here, please.

Charley pulls on her peacoat. Her life, she thinks, is over.

Charley trudges across campus toward the tent on the front lawn of the Manse, worried that her mother is standing in a corner by herself, waiting for Charley so that the two of them can stand in a corner together, gazing out at the other kids and parents socializing in bunches because they all know each other already—not only from previous years' Family Weekends but because they all have houses in the Hamptons and on Nantucket and they spend Christmas in Palm Beach or Lyford Cay. There's a sticky web of wealth and privilege for the East Coast boarding school elite, and all these people are caught in it. Then there's Davi, who exists on an even higher plane. In summer, she goes to Tuscany and hangs out with actual aristocracy; at Christmas, she skis in Courchevel.

Charley feels clammy with anxiety as the tent comes into view; she hears chatter and laughter and a tinkling piano (Mr. Chuy must be playing). The only reason she's going into the tent, if she's honest, is so she can pull Ravenna aside for a chat and demand that she print a correction on the author of the In and Out list. That can't wait until the next issue; it will have to be sent via email so that Charley's name is cleared. *She did not come up with* orgasms *or* fifth-form repeats*!*

Olivia H-T emerges from the tent with two bullfroggish adults who must be her parents—it's funny how they both look like her in different ways—and she beams at Charley.

"Charley!" she says. "Hey!"

"Hey?" Charley says. Olivia H-T isn't usually friendly to Charley, but maybe now that the parents are here, the rules have changed? Or maybe Olivia H-T read the list and she too feels like orgasms are In? Does Olivia H-T know anything about orgasms?

Charley enters the tent and is immediately offered a glass of wine off a tray by one of the catering staff. The dude mistakes her for a parent, maybe because she looks like she wants to kill someone (Ravenna). "No, thank you," Charley says curtly.

She sees Madison J. and Tilly Benbow with their parents, and both Madison and Tilly wave to her. To *her*? Charley turns around to see if there is someone else—someone normal—standing behind her. Nope, they're waving at her. What the hell is going on? She feels a hand at her elbow and turns to see Taylor Wilson with a woman—her mother, obviously—in a skirted business suit, pearls, and heels. Taylor is in three of Charley's classes and has always been perfectly nice, though, again, they don't speak except about school-related things.

"Charley, this is my mother, Kathy Wilson."

Kathy's handshake is warm. "Hello, Charley. I sit on Tiffin's board of directors. Taylor tells me you're one of the brightest students at the school. I've been eager to meet you."

"Oh...?" Charley feels a flush of pleasure, and she dearly hopes neither Kathy nor Taylor has seen the *'Bred Bulletin*.

"I know it must be hard entering Tiffin as a fifth-former," Kathy Wilson says. "I went here myself, Class of 1987, and there was one girl in my year who entered as a fifth-former. I was so sick of everyone else by that point that she ended up becoming my best friend." Kathy pats Charley's shoulder. "So that's one advantage. You're a fresh face."

Charley isn't sure how she's supposed to respond to this, but Taylor saves her. "Your mom is here. She was looking for you."

"Well," Charley says, "I guess I'll go find her." She wanders away, scanning the crowd for Fran. There's a huge floral arrangement in the middle of the tent surrounded by tiers of boards and platters: cheeses, crackers, sliced meats, spring rolls, deviled eggs, tea sandwiches, and crab cakes. There's a line of parents at the bar. Charley sees Levi from the *Bulletin* with his parents, and she considers going over to ask if he was in on the plot to mortify her, though she realizes Levi is powerless when it comes to Ravenna. She notices Davi's parents talking to Ms. Robinson. She overhears one of the mothers say, "If you haven't booked spring break in Harbour yet, you might be too late. Everything sells out."

Suddenly, Charley hears someone calling her name and she cranes her neck to see her mother standing in a circle of people, waving. Charley threads her way over, but when she's a few yards away, she stops. Her mother looks stunning—she's had her hair blown out and she's wearing a forest-green wrap dress (so Tiffin) and big gold hoops and lipstick. She's surrounded by the girls on Charley's floor—Willow Levy, Madison R., Olivia P., and even two sixth-formers, Annabelle Tuckerman and Tiffin's Head Prefect, Lisa Kim.

Then Charley blinks. *No,* she thinks. She feels like her hair is ablaze. A *WHAT THE FUCK* forms in her brain, but she can't even whisper it to herself because she has too much to process. There's a man standing next to Charley's mother, and that man is...Joey, though he's almost unrecognizable. First of all, he's cut his hair. Gone is the man-bun; his hair is now short in the back with floppy bangs in the front. *Like East's hair,* Charley thinks. Except East's hair is dark and Joey's hair is a coppery brown that has been sun-bleached to almost gold. He still has a tan on his face and his neck, which pops against the navy of his button-down shirt. He's wearing a pair of brick-colored canvas pants—Nantucket Reds, Charley realizes—with tasseled loafers that look casually worn in. The cuffs of his shirt are turned back at the wrists and all his hideous tattoos are covered up.

A voice in Charley's ear says, "Oh my god, he *is* hot." Charley turns: It's some third-form girl Charley doesn't even know. The girl looks at Charley and says, "Everyone in this tent is scheming your stepdad."

Charley studies the girls surrounding her mother and Joey. *Oh my god,* she thinks. *They think Joey is a DILF.* She recalls the glint in Beatrix's eyes when she said, *I'm pretty sure Joey is obsessed with me.*

Charley spins around and goes back the way she came. She sees an abandoned glass of wine on a clearing tray and snaps it up, taking one giant swallow, then another. She sets the glass back down before anyone can see. The wine spreads through Charley's chest like warm syrup, which is nice, though it does little to blunt the fact that she's living in a nightmare. As if the In and Out list wasn't traumatic enough, her mother brought Joey to Family Weekend.

"Charley?"

Mr. Rivera has appeared out of nowhere. "Hey," she says.

"Is your mother here?" he asks.

"She is," Charley says. She waves a hand in Fran's general direction. "She's over talking to..." Charley wonders if Mr. Rivera has read the *Bulletin.* Oh god. *Orgasms.* Her face burns. "I have to go."

"Go?"

"To the ladies' room," Charley says. She beelines out of the tent as her phone starts humming. That will be her mother, but there's no way she's picking up.

Where can she go? Not the dorms, there will be too many stragglers; the girls on Charley's floor take forever to get ready. (Because of their *makeup,* Charley thinks. Because of their *gratuitous posting.* Everyone definitely believes she wrote that list.) She can't go to the

Teddy; the third- and fourth-formers will be showing the Grille and the arcade to their parents. Charley passes the Paddock, where they're setting up for the steak dinner; she can smell meat grilling and her stomach grumbles. But there's no way in hell she's sitting down with her mother and Joey—and now, a bunch of Joey stans.

Her last option is the Sink, which should be deserted. *Nobody* will be at the library right now, and there's a bathroom on the third floor. Charley takes the stairs two by two and weaves through the stacks and around the corner to the ladies' room, which is cool and quiet. Charley closes herself in a stall, sits on the toilet, and starts blasting her mother.

You lied to me, tricked me, you know I can't stand him and DO NOT want him here. He's the reason I left home in the first place. What is wrong with you?

There's no response. Of course not. Fran is probably getting off on all the attention. Does she not realize she looks like a hardcore cougar?

Charley's phone buzzes. I'm sorry. He really wanted to come. He made an effort to clean up for this.

I don't care! Charley texts back. That makes it worse!

The next text says: I know you miss your dad. I miss him too, but he would want us both to move forward.

Charley wipes at the tears dripping down her face. She hates that she's crying on Family Weekend (Out: crying)—she feels like a cliché. But Fran is right: Charley does miss her father. She wants to edit not only this weekend but also the past several months so that her father doesn't have shoulder surgery, or he has the surgery but wakes up like he's supposed to. Fran doesn't start dating Joey, doesn't marry Joey, and for fuck's sake doesn't bring Joey to Tiffin Family Weekend.

Charley texts back: I will not spend one second with you while he's here. But that won't be a problem because it seems like you've found plenty of other Tiffin students to hang out with.

Charley's phone rings. Charley declines the call. I'm not talking to you. If you want to see me, he has to leave.

You're being unreasonable.

Is Charley being unreasonable? Joey told Beatrix she was hot—and sorry, but that's gross. Even if Beatrix was exaggerating or flat-out lying (which isn't impossible), Joey still has no redeeming qualities. Except that, for some reason, he makes her mother happy. (But that seems to indicate that Fran's judgment is impaired.)

Charley wipes at her face and is about to head back to the dorms—she'll barricade herself in her room (forbidden: page 5 of *The Bridle*, "doors must not be obstructed or padlocked")—when she hears someone enter the bathroom.

Not possible, she thinks. Nobody uses this bathroom. Hardly anyone knows it exists.

A second later, Charley hears retching in the next stall, then, unmistakably, a splash of vomit hits the toilet bowl. Charley remains silent and raises her feet off the ground so they won't be seen. The vomiting stops as abruptly as it started. There's a flush, then water runs at the sink. Charley peers through the gap by the door hinges and sees...Davi.

Well, Charley thinks, if she wasn't sure about Davi before, she is now.

After Davi leaves the bathroom, Charley's phone buzzes with a text. It's her mother. Joey is going back to the hotel for the night. Please come to the dinner with me.

Charley is so shook about what she just witnessed that she types: Ok, be there in 5.

There's no one else in the library, or so Charley believes until she passes the Senior Sofa on the second-floor landing and sees a girl lying across it, eyes closed, arms crossed over her chest like a corpse in a coffin.

Am I in a Wes Anderson film? Charley wonders. The corpse is Ravenna Rapsicoli.

"Hey?" Charley says, though she means to say, *HEY!*

Ravenna opens her eyes. She looks as miserable as Charley feels, but Charley won't let that distract her. "You put my byline on the In and Out list," she says. "You have to send a retraction, like, right now. Email everyone. People think I'm claiming orgasms are In! People are going to think I'm scheming"—Charley swallows East's name; she will not say it—"a fifth-form repeat."

Ravenna blinks. "I was trying to help you. You have this whole librarian-core thing going and I'm sorry, but people think you're a freak. The In and Out list is cool, it's funny. It'll make everyone reconsider their opinion of you. They won't believe you wrote it..."

"Because I *didn't* write it!" Charley hisses.

"But you *are* cool and funny," Ravenna says. "Better than funny—witty."

Charley refuses to be won over. "Bullshit," she says. "You wanted to print something people would talk about, and since we didn't have any items for *Page 114,* you turned me into clickbait. Vodka Red Bulls? I don't drink Red Bull, much less vodka. Print a retraction, Ravenna."

Suddenly, Ravenna starts to cry, and Charley would like to snidely remind Ravenna that crying is Out—but then she wonders why Ravenna is alone on the Senior Sofa when she should be at the reception.

"What are you doing here?" Charley asks. "Where are your parents?"

"They didn't come," Ravenna says, wiping at her tears. "I have a brother who's a fourth-former at Pomfret and it's his Family Weekend as well."

"But you're a senior."

Ravenna grimaces, and what can Charley think but that the elder Rapsicolis are like characters from *The Godfather*—her father is obsessed with the son and the bloodline; her mother has been silenced with gifts of furs and diamonds.

"They chose Dante," Ravenna says.

Charley wishes there were something she could say, but of course there isn't. If there was more room on the sofa, and if the sofa wasn't strictly for seniors only, Charley would lie down next to Ravenna.

Charley's phone buzzes. Her mother: I'm at the Paddock.

Charley looks at Ravenna and almost mentions the retraction one more time, but Ravenna has closed her eyes and Charley decides to let it be. They both have bigger things to worry about.

At the welcome reception, Davi leaves her parents and Saylem (introduced as "our creative director") talking to Ms. Robbie and fixes herself a plate. She smears golden crostini with creamy brie, then takes a scoop of hot artichoke dip, a handful of pita chips, a few coins of Italian salami, and a couple of crab cakes, which she dollops with mustard sauce before devouring the finger sandwiches: two cucumber, two egg salad, three pimento cheese. She plucks a coconut shrimp off a tray, drags it through sweet and sour sauce, and pops it in her mouth. Delicious.

Mrs. Spooner appears at Davi's elbow. "I'm envious," she says, eyeing Davi's plate. "You can eat whatever you want and still stay so thin."

Davi struggles to keep her expression neutral. People have been saying this, or similar, the entire time she's been at Tiffin. She has been celebrated, not for having a healthy appetite, but for having a healthy appetite and staying thin. If she were plump (like Mrs. Spooner or like Olivia H-T), people would look at her plate and frown. Davi wants to ask Mrs. Spooner if she would make that same comment to Dub Austin. Of course she wouldn't. Boys can eat whatever they want and look however they want.

But this reception is neither the time nor the place to engage in a debate about food, gender, and body image. Davi just wants to stuff her face. She gives Mrs. Spooner a conspiratorial smile and wink as if to say, *Yes, I know. I'm SO lucky.* She hoovers everything on her plate, then checks on her parents. Her mother is gone (probably at the bar) so Ms. Robbie talks only to Davi's father and Saylem. Is Ms. Robbie wondering why the hell her parents brought their "creative director" to Family Weekend?

Davi sets her plate down and leaves the tent. A third-former enters with her parents in tow. She gives Davi a timid smile and nudges her mother. As soon as Davi passes by, she hears the girl whisper, "That's Davi Banerjee, the influencer. She's a queen."

Not a queen, Davi thinks as she hurries down the path before cutting into the Sink. She was a queen, maybe, this time last year. Davi's TikTok had gone viral; she was pursued by everyone from Kylie Jenner to Anthropologie. She remembers how hyped she and Cinnamon were when Anthropologie delivered a full-length Luisa mirror to Davi's dorm room for free.

The internet realizes that influencers aren't always what they seem. However, Davi is hiding some awfully big things. For starters, her *egregious* ("notable for a negative reason") verbal score on the PSAT. (Posting her score might have brought awareness to people who don't "test well," but Davi doesn't want anyone questioning her intelligence.)

Then Cinnamon died and Davi went dark, claiming the need for a "social media cleanse." (Posting about Cinnamon might have been an opportunity to highlight mental health issues, but Davi needed to respect the privacy of Cinnamon's family.)

Davi spent a quiet summer at her parents' villa in Tuscany, where she sat by the pool; practiced her Italian by flirting with Paolo, the eighteen-year-old who tended their olive trees; walked to the Piazza Grande with her father for an afternoon espresso; and took pasta-making classes with her mother. All of it was hashtag wholesome — and Davi enjoyed keeping it private.

She resurfaced on Instagram and TikTok at the end of the summer when she documented a weekend trip to Ibiza with her European friends. It was a whirlwind of champagne, clubs, dancing, and three outfits a day, but what Davi's followers didn't hear about was her *ennui* ("boredom"). At sixteen, she was already world-weary.

And there was *no way* Davi would ever reveal what she discovered when she returned to London to pack for school and finish her summer reading.

Namely, both her parents in bed with Saylem.

Davi bursts into the third-floor bathroom of the Sink and sticks her finger down her throat. As her food comes back up, she replays her parents' explanation: They're polyamorous. Saylem — some random *American,* from *Cincinnati,* who got a summer job *interning at the British Museum* — is now their girlfriend and should be treated with respect.

She's our third, Ruby Banerjee said. *Maybe not forever, but for now.*

It was evident from her parents' tone that they expected Davi to handle this announcement with *equanimity* ("mental calmness and composure"). After all, the Banerjees were fashion people, constantly on the lookout for new creative inspiration. That's all this was, really, Davi's father assured her. An outlet for their artistic personalities. Out of Office's brand tagline was "where cutting edge meets comfort," and though a third person added to their romantic and sexual relationship might seem odd at first, Davi would grow used to it.

Davi was repulsed by what she witnessed in the house the days before she returned to Tiffin. She had hoped Saylem (the name alone made Davi shudder) would slip in and out of the house discreetly, but she was everywhere all the time—in the kitchen at six a.m. completely nude, preparing a pot of tea that she then carried on a tray to Davi's parents' bedroom; kissing Ruby's neck while Ruby checked her email, which would then turn into a full-blown make-out session. The house suddenly had a musky, nearly fishy odor, and Davi would hear her father moaning behind the closed door of his office. Davi fought back images of lips and tongues and engorged genitals, her parents intertwined with this alabaster foreigner like slippery eels. Saylem was like a siren who was luring Davi's formerly cool and aloof parents to the underworld. (Davi had chosen *The Odyssey* for her summer reading.)

It might have been more palatable if Saylem had been interesting, but she was nothing more than a very pale, extremely affected mynah bird who repeated Davi's parents' thoughts and views back to them in a way they must have found seductive.

The day before Davi flew back to school, she cut off all her hair. Her parents barely noticed.

Davi started puking the first week of school, though not all the time, not after every meal—just when she felt the urge to be empty. To be cleaned out. To be in fucking control.

Now she's familiar with every out-of-the-way bathroom on campus, though her preference is this one, on the third floor of the Sink. No one is ever here.

Davi rinses out her mouth, washes her hands, regards herself in the mirror. She has scoured both Meditation TikTok and Mindfulness TikTok, but neither helped.

As she leaves the Sink, she receives a text from Willow Levy: Charley Hicks's stepfather is a total daddy. Come see.

It figures, Davi thinks. It figures that Charley Hicks, who is too arrogant to care what anyone here thinks, would have a hot stepdad while Davi has her parents' human sex toy to contend with.

She can't wait for this weekend to be over.

By the time Simone Bergeron reaches the top of the fifth flight of winding, wrought-iron stairs that lead to the roof of the chapel, she's sucking wind—but not so for Mr. Stringfellow, Royce's father, who informs Simone that he rises every morning at five to ride his Peloton, then goes for a three-mile run along the Charles, no matter the weather. He checks his Fitbit as Simone catches her breath.

Mr. James, who leads a tour to the chapel roof only during Family Weekend, pushes open a heavy metal door and Simone and the parents step out into mellow sunshine.

There are oohs and aahs as the parents move toward the crenellated walls and gaze out at the campus, spread below them like a patchwork quilt. They have a bird's-eye view of the playing fields, the Pasture, the long drive lined with white horse fencing, the Schoolhouse, the Manse, the Paddock, the Sink, and the Teddy. They can see the white tent where everyone else is gathered for the reception. (Simone should be there, but Cordelia Spooner assured her that the tour was a better use of her time. *Just don't stand too close to the edge!* Cordelia said, in a voice that made it sound like that was exactly what she wanted Simone to do.)

For some reason, Simone thinks, Cordelia Spooner has it out for her.

The Academy

The parents whip out their phones and Simone does as well, but there's a bottleneck at the best vantage point, so she ventures to the adjacent wall, which overlooks the dorms.

She sees someone—a student? A faculty member?—heading down the outdoor stairs in the rear of Classic South, the stairs that lead to the cellar. Simone zooms the lens of her phone in. It's East.

Simone waves to Mr. James. "Thank you so much for this, but duty calls." She tries to pull open the metal door, but it won't budge, so she's forced to accept help from Mr. Stringfellow.

Mr. James calls out, "Be careful going down, missy. Watch your step."

As Simone hurries down the staircase, she considers bringing a complaint against Mr. James for the inappropriate way he addresses her (first "sweetheart" and now "missy"?), though Simone knows she won't do this because she is far from innocent herself.

She race-walks over to the dorms, praying that nobody from the chapel tour sees her the way she saw East. And also, what is she doing? The sun is starting to set, and she's expected at the Paddock for the steak dinner; she'll go straight there as soon as she figures out what East is up to.

She descends the outdoor stairs and yanks open the cellar door. She turns on the light of her phone, though this time she knows where she's going—to the door in the far back corner. She opens it and descends the stairs until she's in the brick tunnel.

"Hello?" she calls out. "East?"

She hears nothing so she moves forward and *bam*! Out of nowhere, there he is in front of her. She nearly drops her phone.

"*Merde!*" she says. "What are you doing down here again?"

He gives her a lazy grin. "What are *you* doing down here again?"

Does she need to remind him that she's the teacher and he's the student? He has one hand behind his back; he's hiding something—an unlit joint, a flask of Jim Beam? Simone grabs his arm. "*Qu'est-ce que c'est?*" she asks.

"Keska say," he mimics, switching whatever he's holding into the opposite hand, laughing.

"What is it, East? Hand it over, now." But Simone's voice is more playful than it should be, and East keeps switching hands until Simone backs him up against the brick wall. She gazes up at him. "I'm serious. Give it."

He holds out something shiny and made of metal. It's a...tape measure?

"What's this for?" she asks.

He pulls the end out and pretends to measure the distance between Simone's shoulders. Then he shoves the tape measure into his back pocket, takes Simone's face in his hands, and kisses her.

This, she thinks, is why she came down here. Not to catch Andrew Eastman doing something but to kiss him in this brick tunnel. She presses up against him and wonders if there's a way to measure desire. Does it have a scale? Because right now she wants Andrew Eastman more than she's ever wanted anyone in her life.

She runs a hand over the fly of his jeans and he says, "Hey now, Ms. Bergeron."

"It's okay," she whispers, though of course it's *not* okay, it's the opposite of okay, a fact East seems to be more cognizant of than she is because he backs off, tucks in his T-shirt, and runs a hand through his bangs, suddenly cool. He knows Simone wants him.

"You shouldn't be down here," she says, angry now and embarrassed by his rejection. "You should be at the Paddock at dinner."

"I'm good," East says. "My dad didn't come this weekend."

"He didn't?" Simone says. She thought all the Tiffin parents came. And isn't East's father the...

"He's in Japan for work." East shrugs, and Simone tries to discern if this is bravado or if he doesn't actually care.

"Your mother...?"

"Ha," he says flatly. "No."

"Okay, well, you still shouldn't..." She peers down the hallway into the dark. "What are you doing down here, East?"

"Just dreaming," he says.

Simone's phone buzzes with a text. She doesn't have to check it to know that it's Rhode. He wants to sit together at dinner, present a "unified front" as dorm parents, as fifth- and sixth-form teachers, English and humanities, with their complementary curricula.

"I have to go," Simone says. She turns to head back the way she came, but instead of following her, East stays where he is. When Simone reaches the bottom of the stairs, she looks back. He's gone.

10A. The Parents

Karen Austin, Mother of Dub

In years past, Karen and Dub went to dinner the Saturday night of Family Weekend with Hakeem Pryce and his parents, Ray and Alysha, at a place called the Wooden Duck Tavern. The Wooden Duck has a rustic Yankee aesthetic—Windsor chairs, heavy brocade drapes, ivory tapers in glass hurricanes on the tables—and it serves things like pot roast and broiled scallops. It isn't overly fancy or intimidating, but Karen suffered through dinner the two previous years because Ray Pryce was a wine guy who dug deep into the Wooden Duck's cellar, and all Karen could think was that she would be paying for half of a bottle of Château Latour Bordeaux that she had three sips of and didn't appreciate. Her anxiety evaporated at the end of the evening when Ray Pryce insisted on taking the check. But last year, after having been his guest twice, Karen said, "Next year is on me."

Next year is now this year and financially, Karen is worse off than she was last year because her ex-husband's rafting company went belly-up, he got his skanky girlfriend pregnant (they're having a girl, bless their hearts), and his child support payments have dried up. Dub is at Tiffin on a full scholarship; he's ostensibly given a stipend, but that stipend is only two hundred dollars a year. Karen sends him care packages of ramen noodles and protein bars, but she's had to warn him against buying milkshakes at the Grille every day after practice.

For this reason, she should be relieved when Dub tells her that they won't be having dinner with the Pryces this year because the Pryces are eating with Hakeem's girlfriend, Taylor, and her mother instead.

"At the Wooden Duck?" Karen asks.

"Yep."

Karen thinks but does not say, *And we weren't included?*

"Is everything okay between you and Hakeem?" Karen asks. The football game was low stress; the other school could barely field a team, so it was a chance for Dub and Hakeem and the senior running back (sorry, but Karen will never use the phrase "sixth-form"; she finds it obnoxious) to put on a fireworks display. The boys' dynamic on the field seemed okay, but when Hakeem came out of the locker room, Karen opened her arms for a hug and — maybe she was imagining things — he seemed a bit cool. He chatted with her distractedly for a moment before announcing that he had to "find Taylor."

"Everything's fine," Dub says.

"Fine" is the only word Karen's other three sons seem to know, but Dub is more articulate than his brothers. He knows "fine" isn't a satisfactory answer.

Finally, he looks at her. "Some stuff was going on," he says. "But we resolved it. And no, I'm not offering any more details."

Fair enough, Karen thinks.

She and Dub end up going to dinner at the Alibi in Haydensboro, which is a dive bar with a better-than-it-needs-to-be roast beef sandwich on the menu. They sit at a sticky table. Karen orders a beer and Dub a Coke, and only then does she see his shoulders relax.

"It's nice," he says. "Being off campus."

During dinner, Karen asks questions: *Tell me about math. What's the new English teacher like? Which class is your favorite?* She's warming up to the big one, which she finally broaches once they have demolished their sandwiches (Dub eats three) and are splitting a brownie sundae. "How's it been?" Karen pauses. "Without her?"

Dub digs his spoon into the sundae so that he gets a good ratio of brownie to ice cream to hot fudge to whipped cream. But before he eats, he flicks his eyes at her, exhales, and says, "If I tell you something, do you promise to keep it secret?"

"Of course."

Dub tells her about a computer file that Cinnamon sent him before she died. DO NOT OPEN THIS FILE UNTIL THE MORNING OF OUR GRADUATION.

Karen feels like she's been plopped right into the middle of a teen drama on TV. "You haven't opened it?"

"I have not."

"What do you think it is?"

"I don't know, Mom." When he looks at her, she takes in his handsome face, cheekbones and eyelashes any girl would kill for, the square jaw replicated in her two older sons, the pimples that remind her he's still a kid—but what kid has the willpower to obey such a request? Karen isn't sure she'd be able to do it herself.

"There's something else," Dub says, and he sets down his spoon, sundae suddenly irrelevant. *Here it comes,* she thinks. He's finally going to tell her.

She waits. And waits. She wills herself not to force it out of him but she can't help saying, "I'm a safe place, Dub. My love is unconditional."

These feel like the right words, but it's as if she's poked a turtle with a stick. He retracts back into his shell.

"Whatever." He resumes his careful excavation of the sundae. "I'm going to honor her wishes."

In the end, Karen thinks, it wasn't a *bad* weekend. The Thoroughbreds won the game (it amused her how little the other Tiffin parents knew about football) and she left without a six-hundred-dollar charge from the Wooden Duck on her Visa. But she had hoped for better. She had hoped Dub would finally tell her the truth.

Vikram Banerjee, Father of Davi

Vikram Banerjee is many things, but an idiot isn't one of them.

His wife, Ruby, tried to persuade him, back when Saylem first entered their lives, that Davi "wouldn't bat an eye" at the new arrangement.

"I'm sure she's experimented herself," Ruby said. "She goes to boarding school, darling."

Was that what they were paying for at Tiffin? Vikram asked his wife. Davi's sexual experimentation?

"It's part of growing up," Ruby said. What Ruby meant was that it had been part of *her* growing up while she was a student at King's School, Canterbury. When Vik and Ruby first met, stories about Ruby's exploration with the girls in her house were fuel for the already considerable desire Vik felt for Ruby. Not once in twenty years has Vik felt jealous of those long-ago school friends, nor of any other woman in his wife's orbit.

Saylem, however, is different.

Ruby brought Saylem home from the Portobello Road Market one Saturday in late summer as though she were a silk scarf or vintage mirror. Davi was off in Ibiza and Vikram was on the phone with China, trying to find a reasonably priced cotton vendor for Out of Office's new line of cropped tees, and he didn't have the bandwidth to wonder who the young woman in their kitchen was. When he finally hung up to make himself a cup of tea, Ruby introduced him to "our new friend, Saylem." *Our new friend?* Vik thought. Curious choice of words. Before he could even put on the kettle, Ruby and Saylem started kissing, Saylem's hands traveled up inside Ruby's blouse, and a moment later, they pulled Vik in.

He couldn't pretend to be *completely* surprised; he and Ruby had recently discussed the idea of a third in order to spice up their sex life. Vik had been thinking of a late-night tryst at a good hotel, preferably in a foreign city—Rome, Marrakesh, New York—after several bottles of champagne were consumed. Not a middle-of-the-day sober situation in their family home.

Ruby and the stranger from Portobello Road lured Vik to the master suite, where he came so quickly and so explosively in Saylem's mouth that he spent the remainder of the interlude watching Saylem and Ruby fondle and tongue each other, which was captivating certainly, though his mind eventually wandered back to his Chinese vendors.

He expected Saylem would leave before dinner, never to be seen or heard from again. He and Ruby would open a bottle of cold

Sancerre and toast to checking that particular adventure off their list.

But Ruby wanted Saylem to stay—not just overnight, but indefinitely. Saylem moved her things—which all seemed to fit in one roller bag—into their guest room, though she spent every night in bed with them. Vik went along with it because Davi was due home from Ibiza, at which point, he was certain, the fantasy would end.

"You'll have to leave tomorrow," Vik told Saylem over an improbably domestic scene of toast soldiers and fried eggs. "Our daughter is coming home."

Saylem sucked on her vape and looked to Ruby. Vikram pulled a twenty-pound note from his pocket and said, "Would you run to the shops, please, and get us a dozen oranges? I'll make juice."

Saylem blinked as if to say she wasn't there to run errands, though who knew? She'd spoken very little since arriving.

"Thank you," Vik said, to put a point on it.

Once Saylem left, Vik asked Ruby what the hell she was thinking, Saylem wasn't a new puppy to show Davi, she was a human being. How were they going to explain a third person to their sixteen-year-old daughter?

We'll tell her the truth, Ruby said. She then went on about TikTok and *Euphoria* and some article in *New York* magazine and Davi not batting an eye.

No, Vik thought. It was wrong, Davi was still a child. She was sophisticated, yes, but their family life had a sanctity, one they would irreparably damage if they introduced Saylem to Davi.

"We can't do it," he said. "I'll die on this hill. It was fun while it lasted, but Saylem has to go."

Ruby laughed, which was another way of saying *Die if you must, Vikram.* He had no veto power—not in their marriage, not in their business partnership. Ruby's family had fronted the money to start

Out of Office, and their homes in Belgravia and outside Montepulciano had been gifts from Ruby's parents, now deceased (so Vik couldn't even appeal to the traditional values of his in-laws). Vikram had often joked that his last name might as well be Singh. Ruby was both queen and king of their castle.

Saylem would stay.

Did Vikram feel vindicated when Davi reacted to Saylem's presence exactly the way he had feared—with visceral disgust, confusion, and finally anger, expressed by slamming doors and chopping off her beautiful long hair? He did not; he felt only guilty and complicit. He longed to pull Davi aside and explain that this was all her mother's doing, but he and Ruby vowed long ago to present a united front where Davi was concerned. And so, he told her a lie about Saylem bringing a much-needed boost to their creativity.

He offered to fly to America to accompany Davi back to school but she said no thank you, she'd prefer to go alone. Vik booked her a first-class ticket to Boston and arranged for car service to transport her to Tiffin. He even instructed her driver to make a stop at Chick-fil-A because this, Vik knew, was her American favorite.

By the time Family Weekend rolled around, Ruby and Saylem were inseparable—but even so, there was no universe in which Saylem would accompany them to Massachusetts.

Except yes, apparently, she would.

"Are you *mad*?" Vikram asked Ruby. "What are we going to tell people?"

"We'll tell them she's our creative director," Ruby said.

Vik supposed he should be relieved that Ruby agreed to a cover story. He'd feared she would simply say to the other Tiffin parents, "This is Saylem, our lover. We're polyamorous."

He insisted that Ruby be the one to tell Davi that Saylem was coming, which she did from the insulated comfort of their Mercedes. Vikram opened the garage door to see Ruby in the car with her head pressed back against the rest, eyes closed as she talked, as though willing herself to remain calm. When Ruby opened her eyes and saw Vik watching her, she waved him away.

"How did it go?" Vik asked later.

"Poorly," Ruby admitted. "But please don't forget, Vik. We're the parents and she's the child."

As much as Vik dreads the weekend, it ends up being fine. Davi greets Saylem with a formal handshake and a *Good to see you again,* and then they proceed to lie to everyone they meet about Saylem being OOO's new creative director. In years past, Ruby had been secretly disdainful about how bucolic and "quaint" western Massachusetts is. ("Not a bottle of Dom Pérignon within two hundred miles of here," she'd said, probably accurately.) But this year, with Saylem in tow, Ruby delights in the foliage, the equestrian-themed needlepoint kneelers in the chapel, the boisterous cheering at the American football game (a sport Ruby doesn't understand, but when Saylem tells them that she's a "Cincinnati Bengals fan," Ruby pretends to know what that means).

Vik doesn't care about Ruby and Saylem. (He booked two rooms at a local inn and sleeps in the second room alone.) He cares only about Davi. Her grades are, by all accounts, good, she's surrounded by friends at all times—the other girls stick to her like lint to a sweater—and she even takes a selfie with Vik in front of the student union and posts it to her Instagram stories. (There are no pictures, nor is there any mention, of Ruby or Saylem.)

But did Davi seem…happy? She'd lost her closest friend the spring before. Back then, both Vikram and Ruby were keenly attuned to Davi's moods. They asked if she wanted to see a therapist but she declined; she preferred to sort it out on her own.

Now, however, Vik notices that the light in Davi's eyes has dimmed—or perhaps just changed. It isn't genuine, he can tell.

He informs Ruby that he's going to attend the seminar called Your Child's Mental Health, a conversation facilitated by the school chaplain.

"What on earth *for*?" Ruby says.

How can Vik explain? He knows there's something wrong with Davi and he suspects it's their fault.

"Doesn't she look... *thin* to you?" he says. "And off-color?"

"She'll kill you if you go to that seminar," Ruby says. "Everyone will think she's unwell. That's the last thing she wants."

Vik has to admit this is probably true.

"I think she looks *amazing*," Saylem says, and it takes enormous willpower for Vik not to snap, *You don't get a say when it comes to our daughter, sorry.* "And she's been eating. She has an impressive appetite."

Vik wonders if he's worrying about nothing. Davi *has* been eating. She does have an impressive appetite.

Family Weekend Steakhouse Menu

Friday, October 17

Popovers, Parker House rolls, freshly churned butter

STARTERS
Colossal shrimp cocktail with three sauces

SALAD
Spinach salad with cherry tomatoes, warm bacon dressing or buttermilk ranch

ENTRÉES
Grilled rib eyes or cauliflower steaks, béarnaise or green peppercorn sauce

SIDES
Jacket potatoes, thick-cut onion rings, roasted asparagus, sautéed brussels sprouts

DESSERTS
Coconut cream pie, seven-layer chocolate cake

Fran Hicks, Mother of Charley

When Fran tells Joey that Charley is drawing a line in the sand—she won't see Fran unless Joey leaves—Joey handles it with unexpected maturity. He says he'll go back to the hotel (a Hampton Inn fifteen minutes south) and hit a Mickey D's on the way, and then when Fran is ready, he'll come back and pick her up.

Fran kisses him, grabbing the back of his newly shorn head. This haircut makes him look ten times as handsome, and apparently the female population of Tiffin agrees with her. Within seconds of entering the tent, Fran and Joey were surrounded by pretty young faces attached to nubile bodies clad in cropped sweaters and tight skirts. Were these friends of Charley's? It didn't seem so; one girl said she knew Charley from "around the dorm," and another said "she reads a lot." The girls, Fran realized, were hanging in their orbit because of Joey; one willowy blond girl asked if Joey was Fran's son. Instead of slapping her, Fran offered a tight smile and said, "Husband, actually."

"Thank you," Fran says to Joey now, "for understanding." She doesn't remind him that this is why she begged him to stay in Baltimore.

"It's chill." His good mood is due, she's certain, to his newfound popularity.

At the steak dinner, Fran and Charley sit alone at the end of one of the long tables. The family next to them has a third-form son whom Charley doesn't know and also two daughters aged eight and ten, who are seated next to Fran and Charley. It's a bit awkward—they're isolated but not alone, so Fran doesn't have a chance to find out how Charley is really doing. She asks about Charley's participation in the school newspaper and Charley says, "I don't participate. The editor is a direct descendant of Mussolini."

Fran laughs. "Will I be able to read—"

"Absolutely not," Charley says, and before Fran can react to having her head bitten off, a gentleman approaches the table, hand outstretched.

"You must be Charley's mother," he says. "I'm Rhode Rivera, Charley's English teacher." Mr. Rivera then goes on and on about how, when he accepted this job—he was a Tiffin alum himself, Class of 2003—he dreamed of having students like Charley, kids who are eager to engage with the material, kids with natural curiosity, kids who are motivated enough to do the extra reading. Charley is a superstar, he says.

Fran's happy to hear this. She wasn't sure Charley would continue to stand out once she got to Tiffin. Fran's main argument for Charley staying home was big fish–small pond (appropriate for Fran, who knew a thing or two about ponds, haha). Charley is now a big fish in a more elite pond.

Mr. Rivera turns his attention to Charley, who is intent on scraping the inside of her baked potato skin clean. "Have you seen East?" he asks.

Charley's head snaps up. "East? No."

Mr. Rivera gazes over the rows of tables where, Fran notices, people are much more convivial; by comparison, she and Charley look like they're awaiting dental surgery. "What about Miss Bergeron? Neither of them were at the reception."

"I didn't notice," Charley says.

"Oh, *there's* Simone," Mr. Rivera says. He turns to Fran. "If you'll excuse me."

"Excused," Fran says. "It was a pleasure..." But Mr. Rivera is on the move.

An instant later, he's replaced by the same blond girl who asked the obnoxious question about Joey.

"Where's your stepdaddy?" she asks Charley. "Did he leave?"

"He did," Charley says. "You're free to go back to scheming Royce."

"Awesome," the girl says. "And you can scheme your fifth-form repeat. Hmmm, wonder who that could be?"

"For the record, Tilly," Charley says, "I didn't write that list. Ravenna did."

"For the record," Tilly says, "you should just pretend you wrote it. It'll make you seem normal. More normal, anyway."

As Tilly walks off, Fran regrets not slapping her earlier like she wanted to. "Who *is* that?"

"No one you need to worry about," Charley says, frowning. "Do you mind if we skip dessert? I'd like to call it a night."

"Oh," Fran says. "Okay?" She peeks down the table at the decadent wedges of chocolate cake and decides she'll take a piece to go, for Joey. "Will I see you tomorrow?"

"I have zero interest in the football game," Charley says. "But we can go out to dinner tomorrow night."

"Wonderful!" Fran says.

"As long as you're alone," Charley says.

The next day Fran and Joey go for a drive to admire the foliage, then they find a bar with college football on TV. During a commercial break, when Joey orders nachos, Fran tells him she and Charley are going to dinner alone.

"No prob," Joey says. "I have plans." Turns out one of the other fathers — some guy Joey bonded with during the reception — invited Joey to dinner with his wife and daughter. *You'll keep me from being outnumbered,* the guy apparently said.

"What's this guy's name?" Fran asks. "Which one was he?"

"Jimbo, I think he said? He looked like everyone else — thinning hair, navy blazer?"

Fran finds it very strange that Joey is going out to dinner with one of Charley's classmates' family but what can she say? Charley doesn't want him around.

Fran and Charley score a last-minute reservation at a place called Hobgoblin, which is an Asian fusion restaurant randomly plunked inside a haunted-looking Victorian two towns away. As they're being seated, they pass boisterous tables of ten or twelve, clearly other Tiffin families who are eating together, but Charley doesn't wave or even acknowledge any of the other students and Fran is relieved when they're seated at a two-top in a remote alcove, though she suspects they'll be overlooked by their server.

Fran doesn't have to wonder how to start the conversation because Charley plunges right in.

"I don't understand why you married him," she says. "He's half a generation younger than you; he'd be in jail if it weren't for Dad, he's... beneath you, Mom. You deserve better."

Right, Fran thinks. After Thad died, she should have dated men north of fifty-five who had established careers and grown children. But she had been so, so lost. Thad had gone into one of the country's top hospitals for routine shoulder surgery. Fran had stayed at the hospital only until Thad was admitted, then she'd driven to a client meeting out in Glen Burnie, a meeting that was interrupted by a phone call from the doctor, informing her that there were unforeseen complications with the anesthesia. Thad hadn't survived.

Fran didn't grant herself the luxury of falling apart; she had Charley to think of. She made funeral arrangements, she dealt with the paperwork of death, and, eventually, she went back to work. Work proved to be a refuge; the acts of planting, watering, weeding, and installing soothed her. At the time of Thad's death, Joey had been working for Fran for about a year and they'd developed something of an unlikely friendship. Fran knew Joey loved the Dropkick Murphys and disliked girls his own age who, he said, were all in love—first and foremost—with their phones.

At the annual end-of-season party for her staff held at Bertha's Mussels in Fells Point, Fran got drunk, and long after everyone else went home, Joey remained. Fran and Joey stumbled down the street to the Horse to listen to some live music, and the next thing Fran knew, they were making out in an alleyway. Fran registered the absurdity of it: She was kissing wayward Joey, whom she'd hired only as a favor to Thad. But now Thad was dead, so what did it matter? What did *anything* matter?

Fran woke up the next morning with a skull that felt like cracked concrete and a burning sense of shame. She had kissed Joey, her employee.

She prayed Joey would laugh it off (and not, for example, sue her for sexual harassment). What she never could have predicted was the way Joey love-bombed her, claiming he'd had a crush on her since the night Thad brought him to the house for dinner. He dreamed about Fran, he said. Fantasized about her. The reason Joey had been the last to leave the staff party was because he wanted to be in Fran's presence any moment he could.

Fran was embarrassed to tell Charley now how vulnerable she was. That she was attractive to someone so much younger was too seductive to ignore. Fran and Joey started sleeping together and it quickly became an addiction. She knew she was too old for him, too "good" for him, yes she got it, she was a successful business owner, a professional, and the mother of a talented, intelligent daughter who needed her to set a good example. But Fran's body wanted Joey. Her heart... well, even to this day, her heart belongs only to her late husband. She likes Joey, enjoys his company, and tells him she "loves" him, though what she means is that she loves how much he loves her. He's crazy about Fran, besotted with her. He's her puppy.

Still, Charley has a point: Fran didn't have to marry Joey. Joey proposed with an earnest attempt at a ring—bigger than he could afford; Fran knew that much and figured Joey had worked out a payment plan—and Fran was touched and overwhelmed and visited again by the idea that *nothing mattered* since Thad had died, so what did it matter if she married Joey? There was also an element of self-preservation in her decision. Joey would stay with Fran after Charley left for college; he would take care of Fran when she was old and sick. She wouldn't have to die alone.

Fran gives Charley a level look. Charley is wearing a monogrammed cable-knit sweater that used to belong to her grandmother Catherine Eaton Hicks (they have the same initials) over a turtleneck. Her hair is in two braids; the low lighting makes it impossible to see her eyes behind the lenses of her glasses. Fran noted all the other girls at school with their long flowing hair, their impeccably applied makeup, their flirtatious outfits, and she is glad (she thinks) that Charley isn't like them. Her daughter was born a middle-aged woman; Fran and Thad used to laugh about it, but her exacting judgment puts Fran on the defensive. She can't get any shoddy behavior past Charley; she can't lie or be disingenuous. Charley will call her out.

"He makes me happy," Fran says. "Doesn't my happiness matter to you?"

"I hate him," Charley says. "He hit on my best friend…"

"He did *not*," Fran says. "I appreciate your loyalty to Beatrix but even you have to admit, the girl has always been an unreliable narrator."

"Joey is the reason I'm at boarding school." Charley leans across the table. "Doesn't *my* happiness mean anything to *you*?"

Fran sighs. Some parenting experts might side with Charley and say that Fran should put the happiness of her child first. They might believe that since Charley hates Joey, there must be something wrong with him. (Fran would argue Charley hates that Joey isn't Thad.) There's another school of thought that Fran should make herself happy so that she can be a better parent. What do they tell you on an airplane? Secure your own oxygen mask first, then tend to your child. Charley hates Joey now, but down the road, she'll be relieved that she isn't saddled with a lonely, unhappy mother she feels responsible for.

"Your happiness matters a great deal," Fran says. She reaches across the table for Charley's hand but Charley pulls back. "That's why I agreed to Tiffin. I wanted you to have the best education."

Charley cackles. "You agreed because now you get to be at home alone with Joey, which is disgusting, but at least I don't have to bear witness to it. That you would bring him *here* when you know how I feel about him only proves that you're the worst mother in the world."

The worst mother in the world. Fran realizes it's almost a rite of passage to be called this by your teenage daughter, but it guts her nonetheless.

She casts around for their server. As she predicted, they've been summarily ignored. They don't even have menus. "Let's just enjoy our dinner," she says.

Fran makes it back to the hotel room long before Joey. She wakes up briefly when he staggers in reeking of alcohol and falls like a tree onto the other side of the bed. He had a far more festive night than she did, good for him.

A buzzing punctuates Fran's dreams and when she gets up to use the bathroom, she sees the buzzing is coming from Joey's phone. Who is texting him in the middle of the night?

She almost checks, but she isn't that kind of wife. As she sits on the toilet, she remembers that Dispatch is playing at the Power Plant back in Baltimore tonight. His buddies are probably texting to let him know what a great time he is missing. He could have stayed home like Fran suggested—but instead he's here in the wilds of northwest Massachusetts in a Hampton Inn, sleeping next to the worst mother in the world.

Jesse Eastman, Father of Andrew

When Jesse's plane lands in New York from Tokyo, he wakes up and reads Audre's email to the parents—standard stuff—then her personal email to just him. They raised 246,000 dollars in donations over the weekend and a lovely time was had by all.

Nothing but good vibes, Audre wrote.

Jesse responds: Happy to hear it. Thank you, Audre.

Now, 246 grand is nothing to sneeze at, though Audre is no doubt aware this isn't enough to run a school on. Tiffin would probably shut down were it not for Jesse's deep, deep pockets.

Jesse texts his son: How was Family Weekend?

There's no response. Jesse noticed a large withdrawal from East's trust—thirty grand—but East was given full control over his accounts when he turned eighteen, so Jesse can't interfere, and he's not going to ask because, honestly, he doesn't want to know.

Nothing but good vibes, Jesse thinks. Which must mean that East is behaving himself.

Dear Tiffin Families:
Thank you for participating in the most successful Family Weekend in our academy's long history

Audre stares at the blinking cursor. What makes a Family Weekend successful? They did hit an all-time fundraising high, but it feels mercenary to equate success with the money flowing into Tiffin's coffers. Was it a success because both the field hockey and football teams won? (Losing to the Colbert School was essentially impossible.) Was it a success because the mental health symposium led by Chaplain Laura Rae had only three parents in attendance (meaning, Audre assumed, that the other parents felt confident about their child's overall happiness)? Was it a success because everyone raved about the steak dinner? (*Really,* Audre thought, *Chef deserves a bonus.*) Was it a success because Rhode Rivera and Simone Bergeron hosted an open classroom on Saturday morning, explaining how they were (finally) updating the curriculum? Was it a success because, thanks to Jesse Eastman's absence, Audre was allowed to shine and take credit for all the positive things happening on campus?

Talk about egotistical! Audre laughs at her own hubris just as Cordelia Spooner walks by her open office door.

"Cordelia!" Audre calls out. Cordelia pokes her head in. She was an enormous help this weekend, essentially serving as Assistant

Head. Cordelia also deserves a bonus and Audre considers buying her a gift certificate to the spa in Haydensboro. "Do you think it's hyperbole to say it was the best Family Weekend in the school's history?"

Cordelia had a fabulous weekend as second-in-command; she tried to keep the power from going to her head, then thought, *Why bother?* She had been at the school a long time, she knew where the bodies were buried, it was time she got her flowers. Honey, on the other hand, had barely survived; the Tuckermans were like gum on her shoe.

"It went very smoothly," Cordelia says.

"Should we send out a survey?" Audre says. "Ask the parents what they enjoyed, what could be skipped or enhanced?"

Cordelia raises an eyebrow. "Do we really want to know what the parents think?"

Audre sighs. "We do not," she says.

November

11. Zip Zap

The Zip Zap app Tiffin Academy edition is now available for free download.

Audre receives another email from Douglas Worth in his role as chairperson of ISNEC.

WTF? she thinks. She can't deal with the inquiry into *America Today*. Are the other Heads really wasting their time with this nonsense? Wouldn't it make more sense for them to put their energies into their respective schools so that their own rankings might rise?

But then Audre notes the subject line: A new pandemic. *What's this?* Audre thinks. Did she miss something in the news this morning? She groans inwardly, recalling the year of lockdown across campus. The masks, the social distancing, the incessant testing and quarantining, the parents who came out as staunchly anti-vax. Those were the days before Chef Haz arrived. They all ate boxed meals of cheese sandwiches and Campbell's tomato soup for the better part of a year. Roy Ewanick, one of the math teachers, got sick and Audre feared they were going to lose him.

She clicks on the email, steeling herself, but quickly realizes she misunderstood. The "pandemic" in question seems to be something called the Zip Zap app, which popped up at the Excelsior School over the weekend "and has likely spread to other boarding schools in the coalition."

The Zip Zap app is designed for closed communities such as high schools and colleges, with a "geo-fence" of five miles. That would mean only Tiffin, Audre thinks. The nearest town, Haydensboro, is six miles away. The danger with the app is that posts are anonymous and, in past incarnations of similar apps, there have been strings of abuse, cyberbullying, racial and sexual harassment, and bomb threats. Users can vote "up" or "down" on the posts and comment anonymously.

Lots of room for damage and distraction, the email says. I encourage all Heads to be vigilant in quashing student use of Zip Zap. I would suggest a no-tolerance policy. Here at Northmeadow, students who are discovered to have downloaded the app will be disciplined immediately.

Audre scoffs. Isn't it just like Douglas Worth to tell them all how to do their jobs? He's a Nervous Nellie, and an alarmist. He led Audre to believe there was something to actually worry about—and instead she's being fed this nonsense about something called Zip Zap.

As Audre clicks out of the email—she's certainly not going to respond, nor will she read the reply-alls that will inevitably clog her inbox, thanking Doug for the "heads-up" and his hypervigilance—there's a knock on her door.

"Yes?" Audre says.

Cordelia Spooner enters holding her cell phone, her eyes as round as plates. "Audre?" she says. "You need to look at this."

Tiffin somehow has its own Zip Zap app and there's already one anonymous post.

It reads: "Mrs." Cordelia Spooner (who, for the record, has never been married) admits students to Tiffin based on their appearance.

Audre laughs out loud, though she can see Cordelia isn't amused.

"Surely you're not concerned? Really, Cordelia, do you think anyone is going to believe you admit students based on appearance?"

Cordelia's hand wavers a bit as she holds up the screen. "It's gaining traction," she says. It has thirty-seven "ups" and one comment: I can think of a few Tiffin students who prove this theory wrong. Has anyone checked out the third-form boys?

"Aw," Audre says. "I think the third-form boys are cute."

Cordelia frowns. "I can't believe you aren't taking this seriously."

"That's been a rumor for years," Audre says. "Everyone always jokes about how attractive our student body is."

Right, Cordelia thinks. She feels an itchy warmth prickling the skin of her chest and neck; she's certain she's splotching pink. It has been mentioned before, but nobody has ever connected her name with the phenomenon.

"What about the dig at my name?" Cordelia says.

"Name?" Audre says. "Oh, you mean the 'Mrs.'? I'd hardly let that bother you."

Cordelia checks her phone. "It's at sixty-eight 'ups.' How did the kids find out about this?"

"I received an email from Douglas Worth." Audre grimaces; the man's name leaves an acidic taste in her mouth. "The app is apparently popping up at all the schools. It spreads like a virus...and you and I both know you can't treat a virus, you have to let it run its course. The kids will grow bored with this soon enough. But let's keep an eye on it to make sure no one gets hurt."

Cordelia bursts into the college counseling office but has to wait because, through the glass wall, Cordelia can see Honey is in with... yes, Annabelle Tuckerman. As she waits for them to finish, she checks her phone: 112 "ups." Another comment: **Those third-form**

girls, tho. This is followed by the fire emoji. Then, to Cordelia's horror, a third comment: Maybe "Mrs." Spooner prefers girls...

Cordelia is about to suffer from full-on hives.

When Annabelle Tuckerman leaves Honey's office and sees Cordelia, she beams. "Hey, Mrs. Spooner! If you need any help rating applicants, just let me know." She nudges Cordelia's arm. "That was a Zip Zap joke."

"Good morning, Annabelle," Cordelia says crisply. She enters Honey's office, closing the door behind her.

"You know I don't like it when you bother me at work, Cord," Honey says. "But today, I owe you a thank-you. That child is relentless. I'm tempted to offer the Princeton rep a blow job to just let her in already."

Cordelia pushes her phone across the desk. "Have you seen this? The Zip Zap app?"

Honey reads the screen and laughs. "On their *appearance*?" She passes the phone back and studies Cordelia. "Why do you look like you need a cortisone shot? You're not *upset* about this, are you? You're the one who always says the kids treat you like a piece of furniture..."

Cordelia blinks. She has said this in the past, yes—since present Tiffin students have already been admitted, Cordelia is no longer of any use to them. They look right through her. (Except for her corps of tour guides, though this group isn't the same without Cinnamon Peters's big Tiffin energy.)

"...so you should be flattered they noticed you."

"They claim I've never been married!" Cordelia says.

Honey lowers her voice. "Well, that's the truth, isn't it?"

Yes, Cordelia thinks, *but the students aren't supposed to know that.* Cordelia has been working at Tiffin for twenty-two years, longer than anyone except Roy Ewanick and Mr. James. When Cordelia interviewed for the job, Chester Dell was Head and he was a man with traditional values. Cordelia used the title "Mrs." and invented a story about a husband who died only months after their wedding of... testicular cancer. This did the trick: Chester Dell waved a hand as if clearing the mention of testes from the air, and Cordelia knew her marital status would never be broached again. She goes by "Mrs. Spooner," and this has effectively served to keep questions about her sexuality at bay. How did the students uncover this long-ago lie? It's troubling, but apparently only to Cordelia.

"Well, what about the other part?" Cordelia says. "The part accusing me of admitting students based on appearance."

"Preposterous," Honey says. "Why are you worried about *that*?"

"They're insinuating that I'm... *corrupt*."

"This has nothing to do with you, Cord," Honey says. "Teenagers are narcissists. They're feeling themselves. You admit students based on appearance and they're here, which means they're good-looking."

"So you don't think they *know* anything?"

"What could they possibly know?" Honey waits a beat. "Cord?"

"Nothing. Obviously nothing," Cordelia says. "I'm sorry I bothered you at work."

Cordelia hurries back to her office and logs on to her computer. She has a group of thirty people attending the information session at ten; she needs to move fast.

She googles "how to clear your search history" and follows the instructions. Only once it's done (Right? She was successful? It's been cleared?) does she sink back in her desk chair.

No one can *prove* anything, yet it is deeply disturbing because... well, because Cordelia does occasionally check out an applicant's photo before deciding whether or not to admit. She does this when an applicant is on the cusp—maybe her SSAT score is underwhelming but her grades are promising or vice versa; maybe there's a problematic disciplinary infraction in an otherwise sterling application; maybe the essay, while technically sound, lacks inspiration. Cordelia will, on such occasions—assuming the child hasn't interviewed at the school in person (which is true for over half the applicants because Tiffin is so far out in the boonies)—find the student on Instagram or TikTok and poke around. Many times the student's account is private and so Cordelia will hunt down the parents on Facebook and look at pictures of the prospective student that way. Is it a pretty face she's searching for? Not exclusively, though physical beauty certainly doesn't hurt. She's moved by overall appearance: Does the student look like she'll fit in at Tiffin? Cordelia eschews students who are too pale, too pimply; she's not fond of overbites, or worse, underbites. She once turned down a repeat fourth-former with an unironic mullet. Really, she thinks, she's doing these children a favor, sparing them high school trauma.

But let Cordelia again state: She looks up only the students who might need something to push them over the line. Tilly Benbow, for example. Mediocre academically, but an astonishing beauty. Tilly has managed her academics just fine, she's in charge of the music at the football games, she's part of the tight-knit group of girls on the first floor of Classic South. Admitting Tilly had been a good decision.

Is admitting a student based on looks any worse than admitting a student because her mother is the US ambassador to Ireland or her father runs the third-largest hedge fund in New York? Cordelia somehow senses the answer is yes. What she's been doing is shameful, so shameful that she would deny it even if polygraphed.

The perplexing question is: How did someone discover this well-guarded secret? Cordelia has never confessed this shameful habit to anyone—not Audre, not even Honey. She reassures herself that nobody "found out." Honey is right, the kids are simply giving themselves props and Cordelia became collateral damage.

She checks her phone again. The post now has 202 "ups" and so many comments that, if Cordelia read them all, she would miss the information session.

She thinks, *202 is a concerning number.* Nearly the entire school is now on Zip Zap.

The second post on Zip Zap arrives bright and early the next morning.

Annabelle Tuckerman's senior speech about her "three brushes with death" was fabricated. Annabelle has had...zero brushes with death. The entire speech was a lie.

Audre reads the post with her first cup of coffee. *Who has a beef with Annabelle?* she wonders. *Who would post something so damaging?* Audre can come up with only one answer: Lisa Kim, the Head Prefect. Lisa and Annabelle are "friends," but they're also neck and neck for valedictorian. But would Lisa, as the chosen student leader, blaspheme a classmate and risk being Honor Boarded and removed from her position? She would not. It wasn't Lisa Kim. But who else would have it out for Annabelle? Audre had been so impressed with Annabelle's senior speech that she mentioned it to Annabelle's mother over Family Weekend. Carolyn Tuckerman asked if Audre would send the video, which Audre remembered to do the week following with the subject line: Proud mom moment ahead!

Annabelle Tuckerman reads the Zip Zap post only moments after opening her eyes. She hears a gasp from the bunk above her and realizes that her roommate, Ravenna, must have seen the post as well.

Ravenna hangs her head down into Annabelle's air space. She's wearing a silk bonnet to protect her long dark hair from overnight breakage; it makes her look like Red Riding Hood's grandmother. "Uh... did you...?"

Annabelle has to decide quickly: Should her reaction be righteous indignation or should she brush it off as no big deal? She's too addled to figure out what an innocent person would say.

Her eyes fill with genuine tears, and all she can hope is that Ravenna doesn't construe these as tears of admission.

Because... Annabelle *did* fabricate some/most of her senior speech. First off, her mother never considered having an abortion. By all accounts, when Carolyn Tuckerman found out she was pregnant, she jumped at the chance to pursue a non-partner track at Echols & Diamond and she has enjoyed a happy, stress-free, and fulfilling career at the firm in contracts. Annabelle might make the argument that her mother at least privately considered terminating the pregnancy—but Carolyn has been vocal about work-life balance and how getting pregnant with Annabelle was the best thing that ever happened to her.

Annabelle, at the age of eight, did not have a tumor removed from her abdominal cavity, though she did have tubes put in her ears, which was scary at the time but not life-threatening.

And finally, this past summer, Annabelle did fall off her bike on her way home from working at the Red Cat in Oak Bluffs, but she wasn't the victim of a hit-and-run. She scraped her knees and took all the skin off her palms.

Annabelle made up her senior speech and fully intended to get away with it, because who would ever know? What Annabelle didn't anticipate was Ms. Robinson talking with Annabelle's mother over Family Weekend and then sending Carolyn Tuckerman the video of Annabelle's speech. Last week, Annabelle received an email from her mother with the video attached, subject line: You made up your senior speech?!??! The body of the email read: Don't call me for a few days. I need to process that my daughter is a liar.

But Annabelle called her mother as soon as she could, in the afternoon while Ravenna was at the *'Bred Bulletin* office. She cried and begged forgiveness and tried to explain that she had no choice, senior speeches had to be about something dramatic, nothing had ever happened to Annabelle, she had never known hardship. *Which is such a disadvantage! You don't realize how challenging it is to be a normal suburban kid, how am I supposed to stand out? You and Dad put so much pressure on me. Princeton is never going to take me, they wouldn't take either of you today, it isn't 1987 anymore!*

Her mother repeated three times that she was "very disappointed" and then she said that thing about having to face yourself in the mirror every morning, but she admitted that she and Annabelle's father were, perhaps, guilty of pushing Princeton, they just wanted Annabelle to have the same stellar collegiate experience that they'd enjoyed.

Carolyn Tuckerman said, "I'm not going to tell Ms. Robinson about this," and Annabelle breathed out a substantial sigh of relief. She knew her mother *should* tell Ms. Robinson; the correct course of action from an *integrity* standpoint was to come clean. "But, Anna, you can't use any iteration of this speech in your college essay. Am I clear?"

"Yes," Annabelle said. Except she had already turned the speech into her college essay. Ms. Vandermeid said it was "very strong," that it was "by far" the most compelling part of Annabelle's application.

Annabelle could still use the essay—parents aren't privy to them—but Annabelle believed in karma. If she included the mendacious essay in her Princeton application, she would get rejected. And so, for the past few days, amid studying for her government test and carrying the group project for Spanish on her back, Annabelle has been writing a new essay about her summer service trip to Ecuador. Annabelle thought writing a new essay from scratch would be the only repercussion.

But now she's been exposed by Zip Zap.

The only people who know that Annabelle lied are Annabelle's parents—and they certainly didn't post.

"Somebody has it out for you," Ravenna says.

"Who?" Annabelle says.

"Oh, come on," Ravenna says. "Isn't it obvious?"

By the end of first period, everyone has read the Zip Zap post and drawn the conclusion that the anonymous poster was Lisa Kim. Lisa coolly addresses the allegations at lunch. "It wasn't me," she says as she blows on a spoonful of soup. "Although I wouldn't be surprised if Annabelle did lie about all of it. That speech sounded like performance art."

That afternoon in the *'Bred Bulletin* office, Ravenna is *a fuoco*.

"Everyone's taking sides," she says. "Annabelle or Lisa. I would suggest we run a poll in the paper, but I'm afraid Annabelle would lose and she's my roommate, so..."

Annabelle would definitely lose, Charley thinks. Charley isn't privy to *all* the gossip, though she does use the first-floor bathroom in South, so she's heard plenty. People believe that Annabelle made the speech up and that Lisa is getting blamed.

"We should do an article about Zip Zap," Ravenna says. Gone is the corpse Charley found flung across the Senior Sofa over Family Weekend. Today, Ravenna wears a Gucci belt and new Gucci logo boots, which were gifts from her parents to make up for their absence. "I'll investigate it myself. How great would it be if the *'Bred Bulletin* uncovered the identities of the anonymous posters!" Ravenna's cheeks have color, her hair has luster, Charley can practically see the adrenaline pumping through her veins. Grady and Levi turn their homely young faces to bask in her glow. "This is the most exciting thing that's happened all year, and something tells me there's a lot more to come."

That, Charley thinks, is what she's afraid of.

12. Tiffin Talks: Ghost in the Machine

None of us have any idea who's behind Zip Zap.

As part of her investigative reporting, Ravenna Rapsicoli tries to post on the app herself but she gets shut out. So... the new posts are coming from... where? The ether? From Ralph Waldo Emerson's transparent eyeball out in the woods, watching us?

A third post announces that Tilly Benbow has been sexting with someone outside the school, and this somehow leads to a first-floor Classic South scandal. Madison R.'s long-ago-missing Theragun is found by Olivia P. in Tilly's room, and everyone suspects that Tilly has been using the Theragun to masturbate while sexting.

Tilly confesses to the sexting but not to the Theragun theft or masturbation. Instead of treating her like a pariah, the fifth-form girls celebrate Tilly for her sexually adventurous relationship. Olivia H-T and Olivia P. both ask her who the guy is and Tilly turns pink beneath her Flawless Filter and says, "None of your business," which is highly unusual because Tilly loves to overshare.

Zip Zap seems intent on unearthing all our secrets. It reminds some of us of the hypnotist who came to campus last winter. He chose people to go up onstage and put them under his spell. Some of them cried, one of them clucked like a chicken, and last year's Honor Board chair, Vanessa Kendrick, told the whole auditorium that she still wet the bed. Vanessa ended up leaving school right after that, and we overheard Ms. Robinson telling Mrs. Spooner that the hypnotist would never be asked back.

Charley hopes she falls beneath the consideration of the Zip Zap app because she too has a secret: On Tuesday and Thursday nights, she signs out of the dorm saying she's going to the Sink to study, but instead she sneaks down to the tunnel, where she's helping East renovate the bomb shelter. Tonight they move the mattresses off the bunk beds and transport them up to the cellar, where they get tossed among the extra furniture. Then, using a power drill, East dismantles the bunk beds themselves until they're just a pile of metal frames. Charley is freaked out by the sound of the drill—someone is going to hear it—but East assures her the shelter is soundproof.

It's gratifying, watching the space morph into something else—Charley has never seen a single minute of HGTV, though she now understands the appeal—but the real reason she's there is to be with East. She won't deny that she's attracted to him, but she's also not delusional. She knows that when he looks at her, he sees only a brain, and once she learns to relax around him, he'll see a sense of humor. East is extremely intelligent, though you would never know it from his lackluster performance in history class. He confides that because Tiffin is his third high school, he's covered all the material before and sees no point in doing it again. He doesn't do the reading or turn in written work or participate in class, but he'll ace the midterms and squeak by with a passing grade.

"Don't you want to go to college?" Charley asks.

"God, no," East says. "I know you're going to tell me this is a college preparatory school and I'm going to tell you that the deal I have with my father is I have to graduate, then I can go to him with a business plan and he'll back me."

Charley could never, ever fall in love with someone who doesn't want to go to college. And yet, she finds herself relishing the moments of physical proximity with East—for example, when he hoists her up to the counter so she can lift the open shelves off their brackets and hand them down to him. Once, he rubbed his thumb over the corner of her mouth and showed her a crumb—focaccia—saying, "You saving this for later?" Another time, when Charley's hands were full, he pushed up her glasses, which gave such sweet rom-com vibes that Charley giggled, possibly for the first time in her life. She was more embarrassed about the giggle than she was about food on her face.

Occasionally she'll catch him looking at her—she pretends not to notice, though she turns the color of a raspberry—and one night he says, "Remember when I first brought you here and you wore your hair down? I liked it that way."

Charley tries not to go up in flames. East noticed her hair when it was out of its braids the night of First Dance?

"I keep it back so it doesn't get in my face," she says.

"Would you wear it down for me?" he asks. "Maybe on Thursday?"

They're standing side by side in the doorway as they give the area one final look for the night. The room has been stripped bare. It's uglier than it was before, but that's the process: It has to get worse to get better.

"I'll wear my hair down Thursday if you raise your hand in history tomorrow," she says.

"Oh yeah?" he says. "That would be a turn-on? To hear me bloviate about the Articles of Confederation?"

Charley nearly comments on his use of the word "bloviate," but she tries to imagine how one of the girls on her floor would respond.

"The *biggest* turn-on." She holds his gaze. The moment is so loaded, Charley can nearly hear the air between them crackle. *Kiss me!* she thinks. He takes a breath and — is she imagining it? — leans in. Charley panics and bolts for the middle of the room, where she pulls the string that leaves them in darkness.

"Ready to go?" she asks. "I think it's late."

He gives a brief laugh. "Okay, Charles."

East turns on his flashlight and leads Charley through the tunnel, up the stairs to the cellar. This is chivalrous because he exits out the other side to his own dorm. She can't believe the way she just sabotaged her own dreams. What is *wrong* with her?

He says, as he always does, "Have a good night, Charles."

Charley, desperate to pretend like none of this matters to her ("chasing" is Out), says, "Night."

When Charley looks at her phone, she sees it's ten past ten. She has two texts, one from the floor prefect, Madison J., and one from Miss Bergeron, asking where she is.

Nobody could find you at the Sink, Miss Bergeron says.

Shit! Charley thinks. She runs around Classic South and tries her key card on the pad but the light flashes red and the speaker burps at her. Charley tries to flag down Davi, who's in the hallway — *ugh* — but Davi ignores her.

Madison J. finally comes to let Charley in. Madison is a cool person, serious but kind: perfectly suited to her role as first-floor prefect. Charley knows that Madison J.'s mother was the first Black female graduate of Tiffin back in the 1980s; there are pictures of her in the class composites lining the hallways of the Schoolhouse, one of the few Black faces in a sea of white.

"You have to report to Miss Clavel," Madison says. (This is how the girls on the first floor have started referring to Simone Bergeron—it's a *Madeline* reference.) "Also, where *were* you? You weren't at the Sink like you said. I was there all night."

What the actual fuck? Charley thinks. She basically moves through her day like the Invisible Woman, which is why she felt comfortable slipping down to the tunnel. Who would ever notice she was missing? The answer was nobody... if she'd gotten back on time.

"Oh," Charley says. "I was out, you know, drinking vodka Red Bulls, having orgasms."

She watches a smile tug on the corners of Madison's lips. "I'd let this slide," she says. "But it's not up to me. You have to go check in with Bergeron."

Miss Bergeron is alone in the common room, picking Starburst wrappers and kernels of popcorn up off the floor. "Charley!" she says. "Where *were* you? I was worried."

"The Sink," Charley says.

"Nobody saw you at the Sink."

"I have a spot that's tucked away," Charley says. "Because even though it's supposed to be a *library*, it gets pretty social."

Miss Bergeron studies her. *Please,* Charley thinks, *don't press.* At the beginning of the year, Miss Bergeron was so fervent about Charley having a social life that Charley almost feels as though she could tell Miss Bergeron the truth—*I was down in a tunnel below the dorms with Andrew Eastman*—and Miss Bergeron would be happy for her.

"It's quarter past ten," Miss Bergeron says. "The Sink kicks everyone out at nine fifty-five. Where have you been the last twenty minutes? You know check-in is at ten sharp. Frankly, I can't believe we're having this conversation."

Frankly, Charley can't believe it either. "I took a walk." This is a standard Tiffin excuse when people aren't where they're supposed to be because they're in the Schoolhouse joining the Harkness Society or hooking up in God's Basement. She considers saying *It's my dad's birthday*—but she can't bring herself to invoke her dead father as a cover and so she says, "I had some things on my mind."

Miss Bergeron sighs. "I have to give you an infraction. You'll be restricted to the dorm tomorrow night. I'm sorry."

"I'm the one who's sorry," Charley says. She will happily study in her room tomorrow night, as long as she can check out Thursday.

Thursday afternoon at the *'Bred Bulletin* office, Ravenna says that she's asked multiple people to try posting on Zip Zap and none of them have been successful. "This means someone has hijacked the app. Or there's a ghost in the machine."

Grady says, "You mean the ghost of Cinnamon Peters?"

Ravenna snaps her fingers in his face. "Hey," she says sharply. "Respect."

"It could be Mr. James," Levi says. "He knows a lot of secrets."

"Hahaha!" Ravenna says. "That dude does know a lot of secrets, but I doubt he knows how to post on the Zip Zap app." She pats Levi on the head.

Levi looks like he's gonna pop a boner—Ravenna is touching him!—and Charley takes that as her cue to leave early. "I have to go," she says. "I have to study."

"Keep your ears open on the first floor," Ravenna says. "My money is on a fifth-form girl. Your class is a bunch of troublemakers."

Charley takes a shower, washes her hair, and does the extra step of combing through her conditioner. Back in her room, she rummages through the bottom of her closet for the blow-dryer and round brush her mother gave her as a going-away-to-school present, "just in case you ever want to do something different with your hair." Charley knew Fran had been stalking other Tiffin students on Instagram and noticed they all wore their hair down.

Charley clicks on YouTube, searches for "How to Achieve the Perfect Blowout," and gets to work.

Half an hour later, she gazes in the mirror. Her hair, which might generously be called "dishwater blond," now has hints of honey as it flows over her shoulders. Is this her? She takes off her glasses. Her mother also sent her with five pairs of disposable contact lenses, but Charley hates them; they feel like suction cups on her eyeballs.

The hair, she decides, is enough.

She skips dinner; she doesn't want to be seen, and so she nibbles at crackers as she waits for East to text. He normally reaches out between seven thirty and eight with the downward arrow emoji. When, at eight twenty, she hasn't heard from him, Charley texts him the down arrow emoji followed by a question mark.

He responds: My bad. I'm getting extra help from Bergeron tonight.

Charley flinches like she's been smacked and emotion rolls over her like Attila the Hun invading Gaul. She went to all this trouble and he's *canceling*? The end of the semester looms, but why didn't he get extra help *last* night? Of course, as soon as she admits to herself that these meet-ups are important to her, he backs off. He was going to kiss her Tuesday night, she's sure of it, but she torched the moment.

Maybe he's pissed, maybe he figures she's not into him. She snatches up her backpack and storms into the common room to check out to the Sink—but instead of finding Bergeron, it's Ms. Vandermeid.

Right, Charley thinks. *Because Miss Bergeron is with East.*

"I'm going to the Sink," she says. "Charley Hicks."

"You're new this year," Ms. Vandermeid says. "How are you liking Tiffin?"

"I'm not," Charley snaps.

Ms. Vandermeid studies Charley long enough for Charley to feel like a petulant child. She probably should have played along, Ms. Vandermeid is the college counselor and will be in charge of Charley's future next year.

Ms. Vandermeid nods. "I feel that way too sometimes. You're free to go. Have a productive night."

Fuck Priorities, Charley thinks as she bolts for the Sink. It's never going to happen anyway; how is he going to get materials downstairs—flooring, paint, a slab of granite, furniture—without anyone finding out? At the very least, Mr. James will notice. East claims he's been on DIY sites learning how to install light fixtures and put up wallpaper, but there's just no way. Priorities is going to end up being a nothingburger. Charley should be glad she isn't wasting her time.

Except she's not glad. When she walks into the Sink and sees Taylor and Hakeem studying side by side—they're doing problem sets for pre-calc, which Charley needs to finish as well, she's behind—she feels like someone is choking her. East doesn't like her, he was teasing about her hair, he would never like her, she has prided herself on not being delusional and here she is, fucking delusional.

She races up to the third-floor bathroom; it's as good a place as any to cry, but when she pushes in, she hears someone retching.

"Davi?" she says.

The toilet flushes and Davi emerges, eyes watering. She moves past Charley to the sink, where she rinses her mouth and washes her hands.

"Barbacoa again?" Charley says.

Davi holds Charley's gaze in the mirror. "It's my business, okay?"

Charley knows the right thing is to offer help: *I'm here for you if you want to talk,* or *Do you want me to help you find counseling?* But she knows nothing about eating disorders and she can't exactly judge Davi when she's such a mess herself.

"Okay," Charley says. "I just came up here so I could cry in peace."

"I thought I was the only one who knew this bathroom existed," Davi says.

"Well, you're not."

"Cinnamon and I had some of our best talks here," Davi says. "Out of the dorm, you know. Away from everyone else." Her eyes narrow. "You hair looks...amazing. Did you blow it *out*?"

Charley shrugs.

"Well, if you ever want to do makeup..."

"I'm good, thanks," Charley says.

"The only reason I don't like you," Davi says, "is because you don't want me to like you."

Fair enough, Charley thinks.

"However, I do respect you," Davi says.

Charley considers this. "Thank you," she says. "That means a lot. Especially tonight."

"Did something happen?" Davi asks.

Charley imagines confiding in Davi Banerjee about East. Hahaha! Never in a million years. "Nothing happened," Charley says. She pushes out the door, but not before catching a glimpse of herself in the mirror. She will tackle pre-calc, she thinks. She and her amazing hair will have a productive night.

There are only four weeks left in the semester and if Simone doesn't intervene, East will fail her class. When F-period ends, she says, "East, will you please stay?"

She waits until everyone has emptied out (is it her imagination or is Charley Hicks lingering?) and then Simone closes the door.

"You have a zero in this class," she says. "If you don't start producing, you'll fail."

"I won't fail."

His cockiness enrages her. "I'm not on your father's payroll, Andrew," she says. "I *will* fail you."

He seems amused by this, which is the opposite of what she wants. She wants fear, deference, respect.

"Maybe I do need extra help," he says. "What about tonight during Study Hall? I can meet you here at eight."

"Here?" Simone says. "No. I'll meet you at the Sink."

"I can't let anyone see me actually studying," East says. "It'll ruin my reputation."

"What about the Grille?"

"Nah, I'll meet you here."

Why is Simone letting him set the terms? She should say, *We need to meet in a public place so nothing happens.*

But she doesn't.

Simone can't be surprised when East shows up without books, without a laptop, without anything. Before she even opens her mouth to speak, he turns off the light in the classroom and locks the door.

Simone stands up from her desk. Is she going to stop this? There's no one else in the Schoolhouse—she was careful to check—though she knows Mr. James swings by once or twice a night. But does he check every single room? Does he even bother to come inside?

Simone isn't thinking clearly; she's mortified to admit it, but she finished the bottle of wine hidden in her closet before she came. The wine has impaired her good judgment—isn't that what she was hoping it would do?—and so when she feels East's hands on her waist and his mouth warm and firm on hers, she lets it happen. As they kiss, East runs a light finger over her nipple. She wore only a camisole beneath her blouse instead of a bra; every choice tonight was in subconscious anticipation of what's happening right now. Simone can't believe how skilled East is: Other boys his age would grab or tug, but East's touch is a barely there graze, a tease that makes her groan into his mouth.

He leads her over to the Harkness table where she moderates discussions during class. He hoists her up so that she's sitting in her usual spot and he slides off her jeans before kneeling before her.

Oh my god, Simone thinks. His tongue is slow at first but then he goes faster in just the right spot; she hates that he's good at this. When she comes, she claps a hand over her mouth to muffle her screams.

He pulls away. By this time, Simone's eyes have adjusted to the dark; she can see the outline of him heading for the door.

"Thanks for the extra help," he says. "I understand the material much better now."

Simone waits fifteen minutes, twenty, she's shaking with fear and shame. What has she done? Did she learn nothing from the debacle at McGill? She was lucky to get this job, lucky that Audre Robinson didn't dig any deeper into her background. Simone's intention was to shine at Tiffin—and hasn't she been doing just that? The girls in the dorm *love* her. Most of them, anyway. She has diligently studied all the material she's presenting in class and the kids—most of them, anyway—respond to her teaching style. They have thought-provoking conversations. "History" isn't just facts and dates. It's up for interpretation. Whose perspective is represented, whose is ignored?

None of this matters, however, because Simone Bergeron is a criminal.

When she feels enough time has passed to put a cushion between East's departure and her own, she leaves the Schoolhouse. The second she steps out into the raw evening—November has arrived like the grim reaper; all the trees are bare, the wind howls at night, the skies have been brooding and gray—she hears her name and nearly jumps out of her skin.

She turns: It's Rhode, coming from the Teddy.

"Hey," he says. "What are you doing here? I thought you had dorm duty."

"I thought *you* had dorm duty," she says.

"Roy covered for me. I met with a student who wanted me to read her college essay." He pauses. "But it turned into a therapy session. It was Annabelle Tuckerman, poor kid. Zip Zap ripped her apart. She confided that the post was true. She did make up her whole senior speech."

"Wow." Simone doesn't like how close Rhode is walking to her. She worries she's giving off a scent of wine, sex, and immorality.

"So what are you doing out?" he asks again.

She can't tell him the truth. As far as she's concerned, she hasn't seen Andrew Eastman tonight. "I forgot some materials in my classroom."

Rhode says nothing and Simone wonders if he knows she's lying.

"Listen." His tone changes and she stiffens. He knows. Rhode saw East go into the Schoolhouse while on his way to meet Annabelle at the Teddy. Why hadn't Simone considered this possibility? "I'd really love to take you out this weekend. We could go somewhere nicer than the Alibi. The kids said the Hobgoblin was good. Or the Wooden Duck? Would you like to do that on Saturday night?"

Oh my god, Simone thinks. Rhode is asking her on a date.

"I'm not sure it's allowed?" Simone says. "Two teachers on a date?"

"It's *not* not allowed," Rhode says. "I looked into it. The Wullys met when they were both single teachers here and now they're married."

Simone nearly laughs. Does Rhode imagine the two of them will have a love story like the Wullys? Although they're colleagues, Simone is way closer in age to East.

Simone has learned that, when it comes to Rhode, she has to be firm. She can't leave any room for interpretation. "No, I don't think so, Rhode, I'm sorry."

An excruciating silence follows, but Simone won't fill it. She won't try to make Rhode feel better; that's not her job. She has done everything wrong tonight, but this she'll do right.

Finally, he clears his throat. "If you change your mind, let me know."

Simone isn't going to change her mind. "I sure will," she says.

In the morning, there's a new post on Zip Zap. **Last night, the hot new history teacher gave "extra help" to the notorious bad boy fifth-form repeat in a dark classroom in the Schoolhouse. Or was it the student who gave the teacher extra help?**

Simone wakes up with a start, her mouth chalky, her head throbbing, but oh god, the rush of relief she feels when she realizes it was just a dream. Right? Simone picks up her phone and clicks on the Zip Zap app. There are no new posts. She scrolls up and down to make absolutely certain. This app is a ticking time bomb for her. She's new, she's young, and the kids, at least, think she's hot. She's an easy target.

The best defense is an offense, Simone thinks. Should she give the kids something to talk about? Something that isn't *not* allowed?

She texts Rhode. I thought about it overnight and decided that dinner on Saturday night sounds fun. If you're still up for it?

Rhode answers immediately. Still up! Way up!

This response makes Simone think of an erection. *Ew, ew, ew!* What has she done?

I think we should cover our bases, Simone says. Will you please check with Audre to make sure it's okay? I won't feel right otherwise.

Happy to! Rhode answers and he includes the big smile emoji, which makes her cringe.

Ew.

Cordelia Spooner is at her computer reading the application of a Charlie Norton from Milton, Massachusetts: He's obsessed with aviation, tracks every flight in and out of Logan, has a flight simulator on his Xbox, and is asking for flying lessons for his fifteenth birthday. His essay is about facing an "excruciating" decision: Should he become a commercial pilot or an air traffic controller?

Cordelia loves nothing more than a student with a passion. She admits Charlie Norton from Milton. She considers checking Instagram for a picture of Charlie—she just wants to see if he's as darling as he sounds, it has no bearing on his admission, he's already in...but she stops herself. She might take a peek at his mother's Facebook, however. Is it not perfectly natural to want to see a picture of the student she's admitting? She goes to the search bar and types Kath—

"Cordelia?"

Cordelia jumps. Audre has poked her head into Cordelia's office without knocking—almost as if she's trying to *catch* Cordelia doing something.

Nothing to see here! Cordelia thinks, minimizing the page.

"Hey, boss," she says, swinging around in her office chair. "What's up?"

Audre comes in and closes the door. "Delicate question."

Cordelia wills herself not to get splotchy. She waits.

"I just got a text from Mr. Rivera," Audre says. "He wants to take Simone Bergeron on a date Saturday night, somewhere off camp."

Cordelia exhales. Nothing to do with her and nothing to do with that abhorrent Zip Zap app. Cordelia takes a moment to process: Rhode wants to take Simone on a date? This is fabulous news! It will dash any interest Honey might have in Simone. "What's the question?"

"It felt like he was asking my permission," Audre says. "There are no rules against the staff or faculty dating. Rhode mentioned this was how the Wullys met, though that was before my time."

"Yes," Cordelia says. "I remember the Wullys at the Move-In Day cookout way back when. Ruth had been here a year or two, Kent was brand-new. They got together right away and nobody was surprised."

"Chester didn't mind?"

"He thought of himself as a matchmaker," Cordelia says. "He presided over their wedding at Jewel Pond the day after school let out."

"Hmmm," Audre says. "I almost wish Rhode hadn't asked. I prefer a Don't Ask, Don't Tell approach. What you do in private is your own business, you know?"

Yes, Cordelia *does* know.

"Well, I think it's marvelous," Cordelia says—though only in this self-serving instance. In principle, Cordelia thinks faculty dating other faculty is a recipe for disaster. She should have steered clear of a love interest at her place of employment because it's distracting — and, in Cordelia's present situation, not in a good way. Knowing that Honey is only a few hundred yards away is torture. "I hope you told Rhode it was okay. Did you?"

"Not yet," Audre says and she winks at Cordelia. "I needed to check in with my voice of reason. Thank you, Cordelia."

As soon as Audre closes the door, Cordelia texts Honey. I guess Rhode Rivera and Simone Bergeron are dating.

That's on Zip Zap? Honey responds.

Real life, Cordelia says. Confirmed by Audre.

Three dots rise, then disappear. Cordelia wonders if Honey is bothered by this — and if so, *how* bothered.

New on Zip Zap: Everyone be extra nice to Chef Haz today. Although he's a (Draft) king, he lost his most recent (Fan) duel. He par-laid an egg.

What the hell? Haz thinks. It's no secret that Haz is a betting man. He asks the kids who they like in Sunday's game and would they take the points. Haz has formed a connection with the kids that way; he knows it's not exactly wholesome, but he has never shared a single detail about his own personal betting habits, wins, losses, or otherwise.

How then would anyone at the school know that Haz took a chunk of the money he got from young Eastman and, despite his vow to quit gambling, bet it on the Philadelphia Eagles beating Houston on Thursday night? And then, when the Eagles were up by ten at the half, parlaying that bet on the over/under. At the start of the third quarter, Jalen Hurts got sacked and fumbled, Houston recovered, the momentum of the game changed, and Houston ended up winning by ten, leaving Haz out twenty-five hundred bucks.

The wound of the loss was bad enough, but now he's the hot topic on Zip Zap? Seriously?

We *are* extra nice to Chef on Friday morning: Davi Banerjee gives him a hug after breakfast service, and someone overhears Olivia H-T wondering if we should start a GoFundMe for Chef. (*What? Girl, no.*)

In between classes, third-former Reed Wheeler passes through the Paddock just so he can tell Chef what a beast he is. Reed expects to find Chef preparing the dough for Friday pizza lunch, but instead he spies him in some kind of meeting with Mr. Rivera. Reed overhears Mr. Rivera say, "I have a business proposition for you." Then Mr. Rivera lowers his voice, which gets Reed's attention—but he can't make out what Mr. Rivera is saying. He does hear Chef respond with "Hell yes! Let me pull together some numbers and I'll get back to you."

Reed slinks out of the Paddock undetected, grabbing a breakfast sandwich (meant for upperclassmen) on his way out.

Is this "business proposition" anything we'd care about? *Probably not,* we think, but if so, we'll hear about it on Zip Zap.

13. Limerence, Part I

Rhode's former girlfriend Lace Ann marries her bakery investor, Miller. It's a lavish affair downtown—rehearsal dinner for forty in a private back room at the Lowell, ceremony at St. Patrick's, reception at MoMA. Rhode scrolls through the pictures on Instagram and thinks how, if he and Lace Ann had gotten married, it would have been City Hall followed by Korean BBQ. He's able to think this dispassionately. He can see that Lace Ann looks beautiful but he feels nothing.

His romantic interests now lie elsewhere.

Taylor Wilson, who is one of his top students, showed him a poem that she'd written in her class journal entitled "Limerence." Rhode was unfamiliar with the word, but when he looked it up ("a desire to form a relationship with the object of love and also to have one's feelings reciprocated"), he thought of Simone. He sees her all the time, every day, and when he's away from her, he's thinking of her.

She turned down his offer of a date—the rejection felt like she walloped him with a two-by-four—but then in the morning, she texted to accept his offer. *What changed her mind?* he wonders.

Doesn't matter. They have a date for Saturday and Rhode is going all out.

Simone asks Rhode the dress code for Saturday night and he says, *I'm wearing a jacket and tie.* Simone dies inside and considers wearing jeans, but she reminds herself this date has a purpose. She tells the girls on her floor that she's going out to dinner with Mr. Rivera and could they help her choose what to wear?

OMG. The girls shriek and raid their closets. Simone ends up borrowing an Out of Office original from Davi—a jade-green bias-cut slip dress, which Simone pairs with her nude stiletto sandals and a faux fur wrap that she borrows from Tilly. Madison J. does her makeup and Olivia H-T lends her a beaded clutch.

Simone offers to drive but Rhode says he has it covered (a relief, since Simone won't make it through the date without drinking). She figures he'll call an Uber—but instead she finds he's rented a luxury SUV with heated leather seats and a new-car smell. *Extravagant,* Simone thinks, *but nice and toasty.* Rhode opens the passenger door for her (the car is already running, seat heated) and waits for her to arrange her dress, her feet, her purse on her lap.

"Have I mentioned?" Rhode says. "You look beautiful."

She smiles. Rhode's hair is spiky with product. She bows her head until he closes the door.

They head off into the dark country night, two teachers on a date. Simone longs to be back in the dorm, eating popcorn in the common room, watching *Love Island.* "Where are we going?" she asks. He'd mentioned the Hobgoblin and the Wooden Duck; she hopes for the Wooden Duck because it's closer. She's been on this date for five minutes and can't wait for it to be over.

Rhode has his phone synced with the car radio; he's playing Billy Joel. *Okay, Grandpa,* Simone thinks.

"It's a surprise," Rhode says. "I wanted to do something special."

Simone turns off her heated seat and unzips the faux fur; she's suddenly roasting. The road in front of them is illuminated only by their headlights. Out here there are no homes, no streetlights, no gas stations or convenience stores. It's woods, farmland, ponds, and creeks; they go over a little bridge and Simone thinks how easy it would be for Rhode to murder her. She pulls her cell phone from her clutch; she has no service.

"Everything okay?" Rhode says. "I'm sorry I'm not much of a conversationalist but I need to watch the road. The last thing I want to do is hit a deer." The rental cost Rhode so much money that he decided to decline the collision insurance.

"No, I get it. It's fine, I'm fine," Simone says. They ride along in silence except for Billy Joel's piano: He is the entertainer... waving Brenda and Eddie goodbye... while the lights go out on Broadway. Where the hell are they going? A sign in the distance reads VERMONT WELCOMES YOU!

We've crossed state lines? Simone thinks.

Rhode slows down, takes a right onto a gravel road. "Almost there."

Up ahead, Simone sees a pair of headlights coming toward them, the first vehicle they've encountered since pulling out of the Tiffin gates. Rhode slows down as they pass; he waves to the driver of a crappy gold pickup. Simone watches the driver respond in kind. This will be the witness authorities call upon when Simone's body is found.

They trundle down the road through dense woods until the landscape opens up and Simone sees a body of water before them—a big pond or small lake, it's hard to tell—and a row of cottages. Rhode parks in front of the only cottage with lights on. "Made it," he says. He feels like his tie is strangling him; he's desperate to remove it.

"What is this?" she asks. The cottage has gingerbread trim, like something out of a fairy tale. There's smoke coming out of the chimney.

Rhode opens Simone's door. "You'll see."

Ten minutes later, Simone is sitting at a table for two by a roaring fire, Sinatra is playing on a bona fide turntable, and Rhode is wrangling the cage off a magnum of very cold Veuve Clicquot. The cottage—it's the Wullys' vacation home—is charming and cozy with big plate-glass windows that overlook Sweet Pond. The champagne improves Simone's mood; the bottle is the size of a small child.

Rhode says, "I remembered that you like champagne. You know, from that night at the Alibi."

"Oh god," Simone says, and for the first time all night, she smiles. "The Pour Deux."

Rhode raises his flute. "Here's to us," he says.

Simone drinks.

Rhode hasn't stopped at champagne. There's a tin of caviar on the table that they eat with crème fraîche and homemade potato chips.

"It's royal osetra," Rhode says, then worries it sounds like he's flexing. The caviar was Chef's idea; he shamed Rhode into adding it to the menu. Chef also upsold him with the champagne. Rhode had suggested prosecco (*good* prosecco) and Chef had laughed.

"This is over the top!" Simone says. "You shouldn't have gone to so much trouble."

"I wanted to," he says. "You're worth it."

The champagne goes straight to Simone's head. She *is* worth it! She digs into the caviar. Rhode escapes to the kitchen, where he whips off his tie and pulls the appetizers from the toaster oven, burning his finger on the sheet pan.

Rhode presents Simone with asparagus wrapped in puff pastry and oozing nutty Gruyère.

"*Incroyable!*" she says. "Did you *make* these?"

"I considered booking at the Hobgoblin or the Wooden Shoe—"

"Duck," Simone says. Suddenly, she's giggling. "The Wooden *Duck*. I think the Wooden Shoe is a restaurant in... Amsterdam? Sorry, dad joke."

She's loosening up, Rhode thinks. He feels better too, without the tie. He settles into his chair by the fire and replenishes their champagne. "But then I thought, why go to a restaurant when the best chef in the western half of the state is at Tiffin? So I hired Chef Haz to make dinner. That was Chef who passed us in the truck."

"Oh!" Simone is relieved that Chef Haz knows she's here, and the Wullys too, of course. She and Rhode will be an item on Zip Zap tomorrow for sure, and then the whole school will know Simone and Rhode went on a date, including East. East will leave her alone, Simone thinks as she drains her second glass of champagne. Simone will have saved herself before something *really* bad happened.

Rhode should have taken Haz up on his offer to stick around and serve them (for an additional hundred dollars per hour). It wasn't so much the cost that deterred Rhode but, rather, the idea of having a third person in the cottage—and someone from school to boot. But right now, Rhode could use an extra set of hands. He clears the asparagus appetizer but leaves the caviar, refills their glasses, and fetches more ice for the wine bucket because the champagne isn't as cold as it was. The Sinatra record ends and the silence feels awkward, so Rhode chooses another album. He'll stick with Sinatra but only too late realizes he's chosen a Christmas album. Oh well, it's nearly Thanksgiving and Simone doesn't seem to notice. She's drinking her bubbly, gazing into the fire, which could use another log. Rhode grabs one in a hurry and gets a splinter in the same finger that he burned, but he can't tend to it now because he has to plate and serve the roasted beet salad with goat cheese, toasted pistachios, and a blood orange vinaigrette. He checks on the beef Wellington warming in the big oven as well as the spinach soufflé—has it fallen? No, it's perfect.

He brings the salads out to the table and takes a breath. Does Simone need more champagne? She'd love some, she says. When Rhode lifts the bottle, he notices it's significantly lighter than he expected. Have they really drunk a magnum already?

He picks up his fork and considers the plate before him, but he's too nervous to eat. "Bon appétit," he says.

"I thought when you drove me out to the woods that you were going to kill me," Simone says. Beet juice drips from her mouth like blood. Rhode looks away. She's getting drunk, but what did he expect, he's left her alone with nothing else to do.

"Murder is not on the menu tonight," he says. "I was hoping to get to know you better. How did you end up teaching at Tiffin?"

Simone would love to shock him with the truth: After what happened her final semester at McGill, she couldn't get a teaching job at any school in Canada so she applied for positions in the States, where most people didn't even know what McGill *was*. Simone had left all mention of being a floor fellow off her résumé and Audre was none the wiser.

She says, "I can't believe you went to so much trouble with this dinner. Did you make grand romantic gestures like this with Lace Ann?"

Rhode doesn't want to talk about Lace Ann. "Wait until you see the entrée." He clears their salad plates — hers ravaged, his untouched — and heads into the kitchen. *Simone is just a human being,* he thinks. He has built her up into some kind of mythical creature because of her beauty. He hasn't gotten laid in nearly a year, he lives in the middle of nowhere, he and Simone have a lot in common — first-year teachers, dorm parents.

Rhode slices into the beef Wellington. It's rosy, with layers of foie gras pâté and mushroom duxelles wrapped in golden, flaky pastry. Worth all the money he paid for it, though there's enough here for ten people. He scoops two servings of the spinach soufflé, which is fragrant with onion, garlic, and nutmeg.

He ventures out to the living room to find Simone turning the magnum upside down in the ice bucket.

"Dead soldier," she says. She's swaying dangerously close to the fire while Sinatra sings, "Oh, by gosh, by golly, it's time for mistletoe and holly..." and Rhode wonders how it's possible that Simone finished an entire magnum of champagne — minus two glasses — in under an hour.

"Dinner!" Rhode says. He waits for Simone to sit before he sits himself. This whole attempt at a romantic evening is beginning to feel like a very expensive mistake.

Simone says, "Is there anything else to drink?"

"Maybe we should eat something first," he says.

"This would be nice with a red wine."

"I have a bottle of Châteauneuf-du-Pape, actually," Rhode says. "But it should probably breathe. You dig in." He returns to the kitchen where the wine waits next to a "decanter," which is actually one of the plastic water pitchers from the Paddock. Chef Haz offered to provide a crystal decanter "for an additional fee," but Rhode told him that was unnecessary.

He opens the wine and glugs it into the pitcher, which is cloudy from seventeen thousand trips through an industrial dishwasher. Maybe he should have sprung for the decanter? He hears Simone humming along to "The Christmas Waltz" and hopes she's eating.

When he brings out the wine, he finds she's only taken a single bite of food. She picks up the pitcher and pours herself a healthy glass of wine.

"That needs to breathe, Simone."

She hoots. "You sound like a teacher."

He studies her. She is so lovely, even in her increasing disarray. He looks at his plate and is suddenly ravenous, though he senses now is the moment to make his move.

"Would you like to dance?" he asks.

Simone springs from her chair, wineglass in hand. She's so drunk that everything seems fabulous and amusing. As soon as Rhode takes her in his arms, however, she remembers how awkward he is—she learned that at First Dance—and she twirls herself out, nearly knocking over her chair, saying, "Loosen up, Rhode!"

Rhode would very much like to loosen up but he just can't. He looks longingly at dinner growing cold on the table. Maybe he should have a nice big glass of wine himself—but there's the matter of the luxury rental car in the driveway and the long, dark drive home. He watches Simone doing a spinny, trippy dance all by herself.

He pretends to cast a fishing line and reel her back in, and this, improbably, works: A second later, she's back in his arms.

He has a question for her, one he was going to ask only if he saw the right opening. Her joyfully drunken state, he decides, is that opening.

"Do you remember when I came to find you in the basement of the dorms?" he says. "Down in that brick tunnel?"

"Mmmmhmm." Her mouth is pressed against the front of his shirt and the vibration of her lips travels directly down to his cock. He is instantly hard. *Don't say another word,* he thinks. *Just enjoy this.* But what he thought he saw going on in the tunnel has been plaguing him. He has to ask.

"Were you down there with East?"

She snaps her head back. "East?"

"Andrew Eastman? I'm pretty sure I saw you in the tunnel with Andrew Eastman." He swallows. "East."

Simone grabs Rhode's face and kisses him. Rhode opens his mouth too wide, he uses too much tongue, and their teeth click; his erection presses into her leg. Awful, all of it—however, Simone is pretty sure all thoughts of her with Andrew Eastman in the brick tunnel have flown from his mind.

Rhode slips one of the delicate straps of Simone's dress off her shoulder to expose her breast. He takes her nipple in his mouth and bites—why, *why* do men feel the need to do this? It hurts and Simone carefully pulls away.

"I think we should sit down," she says.

Yes, yes, Rhode thinks. He leads her over to the sofa, a threadbare creature that has seen its share of pond-wet bathing suits over the years. It smells like algae, but hopefully Simone won't notice.

Simone *does* notice: The smell is a medley of mold, mildew, fungi, decay, water murky with insect carapaces and fish eggs. She ate fish eggs tonight, a lot of them, black and glistening. This suddenly turns Simone's stomach, it's roiling, roiling, she can't think about the—

"I need the—" But before she can ask for the powder room, she pukes in Rhode's lap.

Rhode ends their romantic evening by rubbing Simone's back as she vomits a magnum of champagne and four ounces of royal osetra caviar into the Wullys' toilet. She's crying and begging his forgiveness, then she's accusing him of intentionally getting her drunk so he could seduce her. He doesn't respond; his mind is, frankly, elsewhere. It's on the three hundred dollars he owes for the rental car (more for cleaning if Simone barfs in it on the way home) and on the whopping seventeen hundred dollars he owes Haz. He has enough beef Wellington left over to feed the first floor of Classic North, though the boys won't appreciate it. There are two gorgeous chocolate caramel tarts waiting in the fridge; those he'll take home to feed his feelings of utter failure.

Simone sleeps until noon on Sunday and awakens feeling like dog shit—not only physically but emotionally. So many things went wrong: She got wickedly, mortifyingly wasted, she puked, she kissed Rhode and let him fondle her in a desperate attempt to eradicate Rhode's notion that he saw Simone and East together.

Rhode *knows*—not everything, but something.

When Simone finally emerges from her room, the girls on the first floor are all over her like ants on a picnic. *How was it? Was it fun? Where'd you go, what'd you do? DID YOU GET WITH HIM?*

Simone has, at least, come up with a spin. "I had a lovely time, Mr. Rivera is quite the romantic. The details are private." When she sees Davi, she says, "I'll return your dress after I've had it cleaned." (It's splattered with vomit and Simone worries it won't come out.)

"Keep it," Davi says. "It'll always remind you of your first date with Mr. Rivera."

That's what Simone is afraid of. "Thank you," she says. She will throw the dress away.

The next day, Simone checks Zip Zap—and the next, and the next, but nothing appears about Simone and Rhode. After all she went through, Zip Zap doesn't give a flying fuck.

14. Limerence, Part II

Hakeem is leaving on a recruiting trip—first to Princeton, then Columbia, Harvard, and Dartmouth.

The night before he leaves, things get very hot between him and Taylor during Intervis and they go almost all the way.

"Come on, baby," Hakeem says. "You can't make me leave for these recruiting trips as a virgin."

"I'm not ready," Taylor says. "And I don't want it to be like this, with the door cracked and Mr. Rivera down the hall."

"We could go to God's Basement," Hakeem says.

"Hakeem," Taylor says. "No."

Later, Hakeem stops by Dub's room. Dub thinks maybe Hakeem feels bad because while he has four Ivies interested in him, Dub hasn't been contacted by any college scouts. Or, possibly, Hakeem wants to review the playbook because he's missing practice all week and their final game—against longtime rival Old Bennington—is on Saturday.

But it turns out, Hakeem is there to talk about Taylor.

"She won't give it up to me, man," he says. "I just turned seventeen. It's embarrassing that I'm still a virgin."

Dub can't believe Hakeem is confiding in him like this; he thought those days were over forever.

"How did you convince Cinnamon?" Hakeem asks.

"I didn't. We never..."

"You never slept with her?"

"No," Dub says. He understands why Hakeem finds this shocking: Dub and Cinnamon Intervissed every night and there were plenty of weekends when Dub sneaked into Classic South and spent the entire night with Cinnamon. But there had been no sex on those nights. Cinnamon was just really sad and wanted Dub to hold her.

Hakeem says, "There's a chick I've been texting with at Dartmouth. She's a freshman, a student athletic trainer for the team."

"You're not thinking about... I mean, dude, you wouldn't cheat on Taylor, would you?"

Hakeem says nothing, which means yes.

Wow, Dub thinks.

The Academy

The second Hakeem's car service pulls out of the Tiffin gates the next morning, Dub gets a text from Taylor: Piano Bar tonight?

Dub isn't sure how to respond. He and Taylor haven't spoken much since the episode in the locker room. That was the price of restoring peace with Hakeem: Dub and Taylor couldn't be close. But with Hakeem gone, the restriction feels silly and pointless. Dub hasn't been to Piano Bar all year, though as a fourth-former, he and Cinnamon never missed it. Cinnamon was Mr. Chuy's favorite.

Ok, Dub responds.

Since they're going to Piano Bar in the Grille, they end up eating dinner together beforehand in the Paddock. They don't take the Booth, that would be too high profile; instead they find seats among the randos of the fifth-form (some of whom Dub has never exchanged a word with). It's Burger Night, so he and Taylor get their usual: Angus burgers medium rare with cheddar, bacon, pickles, and an extra side of special sauce. Hakeem always ate his burger in a lettuce wrap without cheese or sauce because, he said, his body was a temple.

They don't talk about Hakeem, however. They don't need to, they've never needed to.

Taylor tells Dub about the spring musical. Mr. Chuy has chosen *Mean Girls,* and Taylor can't decide whether to go out for the part of Cady or the part of Regina George.

"Cady," Dub says. "More complex."

"I love that you know the roles in *Mean Girls,*" Taylor says. She dips one of her french fries in his ketchup. "I've missed you."

When they get to the Grille, Dub buys Taylor a peppermint stick milkshake even though he's down to the last ten dollars on his stipend and the school won't deposit more money until next semester. When Dub doesn't order a milkshake of his own, Taylor buys him an Oreo one on her account.

At the piano, Taylor takes a seat on the bench next to Mr. Chuy and Dub stands at her side. A few minutes later, the third- and fourth-formers arrive, along with the theater kids and Annabelle Tuckerman, Lisa Kim, and Ravenna Rapsicoli. The sixth-formers are starting to get nostalgic; they have only six months left at Tiffin and they want to enjoy every second. There's a third-form kid who plays on Dub's offensive line named Benj; he looks surprised as hell to find Dub Austin at Piano Bar, and he gives a tentative wave as if to say, *Are you really doing this?*

Dub nods. There's no reason to be embarrassed.

Mr. Chuy launches into "Wagon Wheel," and they're off! Dub knows he has a good voice. They sing "Don't Stop Believin'," then "Can't Stop the Feeling." Then Mr. Chuy asks Taylor and Dub if they want to duet on "Shallow," and honestly, they sound so freaking fantastic together—Taylor knows how to harmonize—that when the song is over, everyone cheers. Dub takes Taylor's hand and helps her to her feet so she can bow.

The hour passes too quickly. Mr. Chuy plays "Friends in Low Places," because he knows Dub likes country music, then he segues into Taylor Swift's "Love Story," always the final song of the night.

Dub and Taylor walk back to the dorms together, both of them on an adrenaline high. It's an even better buzz than the one he gets when he runs off the field after a game. He should have been singing every Monday all year. What was he afraid of?

Taylor links her arm through his. "That was fun."

"Thank you for dragging me."

Taylor is quiet but Dub thinks nothing of it. What he likes best about Taylor are their companionable silences.

Suddenly she says, "Hakeem wanted to have sex last night. He pressured me but I held out."

Dub inhales the cold night air through his nose.

"I don't want to lose my virginity to Hakeem," she says.

"Taylor," Dub says. "Tonight was amazing, and probably just what I needed. But I'd rather not talk about Hakeem. Okay?"

"Okay," she whispers.

Later that night, as Dub is climbing into bed, he gets a text from Taylor. I want to lose my virginity to you. Dub stares at the text for a long while, but he doesn't respond, and although he knows he should, he doesn't delete it.

The days pass quickly. Dub and Taylor return to their usual routine: They sit together in English, history, and Spanish, they eat lunch together, once even claiming the Booth. Dub practices hard after school — if there was ever a year they can beat Old Bennington, this is it — and then he meets Taylor in the Paddock for dinner. A couple of nights they go straight to the Sink to study. But they don't Intervis and Dub is careful not to touch Taylor, even casually. He pretends she never sent the text and she doesn't bring it up.

Hakeem is due back to school on Saturday at nine; kickoff against Old Bennington is at noon. The rest of the school has been gearing up all week, making posters that say PULVERIZE THE POETS! (Old Bennington is where Robert Frost is buried. Their mascot is, yes, a white-haired dude in a suit.) Dub used to dread Rivalry Weekend not only because he was embarrassed to be consistently whupped by a team called the Poets but also because he didn't want the season to be over. (In the winter, Hakeem plays hoops and, on advice from Coach Bosworth, Dub does strength and conditioning.) But this year, Dub is pumped! They could win. They *will* win!

When Dub wakes up on Saturday morning, he sees the alert: **New** post on Zip Zap. He thinks Zip Zap is as annoying as hell, but he clicks into it anyway.

Fifth-former Taylor Wilson wants QB1 to pop her cherry.

Before they dress for the game, Coach Bosworth calls both Dub and Hakeem into his office. "We're not going to have a problem on the field today, are we?"

"No, sir," Dub and Hakeem say in unison.

On the way back to the locker room, Dub says, "Bro, you know that app is bullshit."

"The funny thing is?" Hakeem says. "It has yet to be wrong."

"I haven't touched her, bro."

"But you hung out all week."

Hakeem had spies, Dub thinks. *People texting him, sending videos.* "Nothing happened. We studied, we ate, we went to Piano Bar."

"You sang a duet, I heard." From Benj, the offensive lineman, Dub thinks, who was only masquerading as an ally.

"Hakeem."

"She's saving herself for *you*," Hakeem says. "You, not me." He runs a hand over his head; somehow, Dub is only now noticing that Hakeem got a fresh cut while he was away, his number, 62, shaved into the side fade. Dub also notices the puffiness around Hakeem's eyes and that he reeks of alcohol. "But it's no big deal. I fucked that Dartmouth chick."

Dub flinches. "You did?"

"I did," Hakeem says. He holds out a fist. "So we're good, bro."

But they're not good. Hakeem misses two catches in the end zone and blames both on Dub's throws. (Dub's throws were perfect.) Then, in the second half, Hakeem catches the ball but fumbles it running; it's recovered by Old Bennington and returned for a touchdown.

Tiffin loses 7–0.

Win some, lose some, Audre thinks as she strides across the field to shake hands with the Old Bennington Head, Mikayla Ekubo. Mikayla is the newest and youngest Head in ISNEC — like Audre, she took over from a long line of staunchly conservative white men. In Mikayla's case, taking the helm was more daunting... because Old Bennington has long been ranked the number one boarding school in the country.

Audre has done her best to serve as a mentor to Mikayla; she counts her as a friend.

"Good game!" Audre says, opening her arms. "Are you ready for Thanksgiving? I know I am."

Instead of embracing Audre, Mikayla offers a stiff hand. *Hmmm,* Audre thinks as she shakes it. She gets the Feeling.

"You should know, Audre, that I signed the inquiry letter," Mikayla says.

Audre drops Mikayla's hand. Why would Mikayla sign the letter? Old Bennington was ranked number one, so why would anyone else's placement on the list matter? Is Mikayla worried that Tiffin will claim the top spot next year? Does she prefer to be the sole female Head in the top five? (So much for women polishing one another's crowns.)

"It's a witch hunt," Audre says.

"You have to admit, Audre, a seventeen-spot jump is puzzling when there have been no discernible changes here in the past year," Mikayla says. "Everyone knows the head of your board is problematic."

"Why?" Audre says. "Because he's rich?"

"He's a robber baron," Mikayla says. "He got his start buying up low-income housing and transforming it into luxury apartments, displacing thousands of innocent tenants."

Did Mikayla do a deep dive into Jesse Eastman's business? Or is this something Douglas Worth dug up and shared with everyone on the council?

"None of that has a single thing to do with our ranking, Mikayla," Audre says.

"I just think it warrants looking into," Mikayla says. "For due diligence's sake." She points a finger at Audre. "Also? Rumor has it, Tiffin has a Zip Zap problem."

There's a bonfire down on the beach by Jewel Pond—this is a tradition on Old Bennington weekend, win or lose—but Dub doesn't go.

Taylor sent him a barrage of messages: Did you show my text to anyone? I'm confused. Why would you do that? Did you tell anyone? Hakeem blocked me. He'll never speak to me again. Dub? Hello? WTF?

It wasn't me, he finally responds. I told no one, showed no one. He wants to say that he's just as freaked out by this as she is. Whoever is running Zip Zap is like a sniper, strategically assassinating characters all over the school. I'm sorry about Hakeem. He'll get over it.

But a little while later, Hakeem posts a picture on his Snapchat story of him with his arm around a third-form girl named Cassie Lee at the bonfire.

Alone in his room, alone in the entire dorm, Dub opens his laptop. The file from Cinnamon is where it always is, in the upper right-hand corner of his screen. DO NOT OPEN THIS FILE UNTIL THE MORNING OF OUR GRADUATION.

This file is his last link to Cinnamon, and Dub needs her tonight more than ever. He rolls his cursor over the file. One click and he would be in touch with her again.

He sighs, then opens his email instead. He writes to Ms. Robinson.

> Can you please shut down the Tiffin Zip Zap app? It's bad for the school.
>
> Sincerely, Dub Austin.

15. Thanksgiving

After Olivia H-T asks 114 times if Davi will come home with her for Thanksgiving, Davi relents. Four and a half days isn't enough time to make a trip back to London worthwhile, and her family doesn't celebrate Thanksgiving anyway.

The year before, Davi went to Wisconsin with Cinnamon. That Wednesday night they went to a fish fry at a place called the Moose Club, which ended with Cinnamon's father and his cronies, some of whom wore trucker hats, hoisting their draft beers in plastic cups while singing along to "Pink Houses." Davi took a video and posted it to TikTok.

Thursday at Cinnamon's parents' farmhouse was a three-ring circus: grandparents and little cousins and a twenty-eight-pound turkey with two kinds of stuffing, mashed potatoes, candied yams, green bean casserole, cranberry sauce with indentations from the can, four kinds of pie, and American football games on all day in the den where the uncles drank Leinenkugel's and ate cheese curds. One of the uncles asked Davi where she was "from," and when she said London and he said, "No, really *from,* before that," Cinnamon stepped in and said, "Your fly is down, Scottie," then she pulled Davi outside where they walked down a dark country road and smoked a joint that Cinnamon had stolen from Scottie's jacket pocket, which was good enough revenge for Davi.

Now, Olivia H-T's parents hire a black car to transport the girls from Tiffin to Beacon Hill in Boston. The H-Ts' brownstone on Mount Vernon Street is five floors of refined understatement. (Davi finds this puzzling since nothing about Olivia is understated.) Its most impressive feature is a curving white marble staircase with an ebony banister that ascends all the way to the top floor (though there's also an elevator). Davi admires the fine rugs and antiques; Mrs. H-T has a *plethora* ("excessive quantity") of clocks—grandfather, grandmother, banjo, mantel, nautical, carriage—that give the house a soundtrack of ticking and chiming. Davi is tempted to whip out her phone and take pictures of the hand-painted mural in the foyer (Boston Harbor, 1830s) and the stained glass windows in the library, but she can sense Olivia *wanting* her to do this. With unconcealed pride, Olivia shows off a bronze bust of Charles Bulfinch, the architect who designed the Massachusetts State House. When she twists Charles's head, a secret door opens to reveal Mr. H-T's elegant man cave. There's a wet bar and a glass-fronted cigar humidor.

"Isn't this *fierce*?" Olivia H-T says. "I'm not even allowed in here."

Davi imagines posting from Mr. H-T's secret inner sanctum—he's a top executive with Fidelity—but she fears she'll be asked to leave before the turkey is carved. She can't help feeling that Olivia H-T has brought her to Boston because Olivia wants to be Davi's content.

Davi's mind revisits the In and Out list that Charley Hicks published in the *'Bred Bulletin*. "Chasing" is Out—and yet this is exactly what Olivia is doing.

Olivia leads Davi to the kitchen, which is in the basement. It has brick walls, wooden beams, and a fireplace with an iron pot hanging from a hook. This is where they find Mrs. H-T, whose body type can most accurately be described as a bowling ball on toothpicks. Mrs. H-T has had a lot of work done on her face; her upper lip juts out like a shelf.

"I made you girls dinner," she says. "You should eat something before you go out." She presents a platter—clearly prepared elsewhere—of veggies with a doll-size dish of hummus.

"Thank you," Davi says. She's starving. On the drive, she asked Olivia if they could stop for lunch and Olivia said, *I'm not hungry, are you?* in a way that sounded *truculent* ("aggressive or hostile").

Davi snatches up a celery stick and drags it through the hummus while Mrs. H-T brings them two glasses of ice water with nearly translucent slices of lemon.

"Enjoy!" Mrs. H-T says before she disappears, and Davi gets the feeling that this is it—the vegetables and the dollop of hummus are dinner. She gazes around the kitchen—the pot in the fireplace is a design element, a prop, a nod to the days when the only people in this kitchen were servants—and finds no evidence of any other actual food. A bowl on the counter holds wooden apples. The bread box is empty.

"We're going out?" Davi says. She hopes for one of the sports bars near Fenway; she would kill for some loaded potato skins.

"Yes, Klatsch in the South End is all over TikTok." Olivia eats a plain sliver of red pepper. "We should finish up here and get ready."

Finish *up*? Davi attacks the veggie platter—cauliflower, broccoli, carrots. She uses a coin of cucumber to swipe up the last of the hummus. "Does your mom cook on Thanksgiving?" she asks Olivia.

"God, no," Olivia says, and Davi, who is British and therefore shouldn't care about Thanksgiving, feels duped. "Come on, let's go."

At Klatsch, the line snakes down the block. Davi wants to suggest they go elsewhere but Olivia is locked in. "Do you have your fake? My fake is really good."

Davi has her fake, though she doesn't like to use it. She has 1.3 million Instagram followers, she's basically a public figure; there's always the chance the bouncer will recognize her and know she's sixteen.

Davi therefore finds it hard to match Olivia H-T's enthusiasm about seeing the inside of Klatsch. She's freezing: She went with a Guizio mini, boots, a cropped sweater, and a leather jacket, which are no match for the icy hatchet of wind blowing down Tremont Street. A quick check of her phone reveals a cluster of restaurants nearby: dumplings, oysters, a French bistro.

"I'll pay for all the drinks," Olivia says. "And we should come up with a code word if we want to get with a guy."

Davi presses her tongue against her teeth to keep from being mean: *No one is going to want to get with you, Olivia.* Although, who knows? Olivia's mother managed to snag Mr. H-T, who has done very well for himself. The other people in line at Klatsch are in their twenties and thirties; the guy in front of them is giving MIT super nerd—maybe he'd be into an awkward, insecure teenager.

"Code word 'Amsterdam,'" Davi says. This is the word she uses with her friends in London and Ibiza when she's peeling off for the night.

Olivia beams. "Amsterdam!" Her breath forms a silvery cloud in the cold.

In London and Ibiza, Davi doesn't wait in line; she's whisked in because someone always has a connect. What, Davi wonders, is she *doing* here? She'd far preferred the Moose Club, and Uncle Scottie with his basic racism.

Finally, it's their turn. Olivia H-T turns her ID over to the bouncer, who Davi is surprised to find is a woman. She's over six feet tall with sharp Slavic cheekbones and eyes the color of stainless steel.

A woman, Davi thinks, is bad news.

She looks Olivia up and down and, without even glancing at her ID, says, "No."

"But . . . ?" Olivia says.

The bouncer eyes Davi. "You." She nods toward the door.

"Oh," Davi says, "I can't leave my friend."

"Just go," Olivia says. "I'll meet you at home. You have the address, right? Go have fun, I'm sure you'll know people." Her eyes are glassy with tears; she has lipstick on her teeth.

Davi hears a remix of "Rich Baby Daddy" coming from inside; she feels a blast of seductive warm air, sees a sexy red glow, smells expensive perfume. She *could* go in; the idea of an MIT genius is sort of appealing. Surely Olivia considered this might happen?

"Please," Olivia says. She must want to serve a good time even if she can't be part of it. She wants Davi to tell everyone back at Tiffin how much fun she had in Boston.

Across the street, Davi sees a restaurant called Picco; a couple step out holding a large, flat box. She grabs Olivia's hand. "Forget the club," she says. "We're getting pizza."

Although the H-T home is pleasant the next morning — there's classical music playing and sunlight streaming through the big bay windows — there are no trappings of what Davi has come to expect at Thanksgiving: no preparations to run a Turkey Trot, no Macy's parade on TV, no shift at the local soup kitchen to serve those less fortunate, no football, no relatives. (Davi had secretly hoped for a meet-up with Olivia's cousin who played at Tiffinpalooza the year before.) There are also no cooking smells. Breakfast is black coffee and a banana—half a banana for Olivia. Davi is worried they won't have a meal at all until Mrs. H-T pokes her head into the library where Davi and Olivia are lounging on their phones in front of the fire and says, "We're leaving for dinner in an hour, girls."

When Davi enters the Bristol Lounge at the Four Seasons, she perks up. She's back in her element: servers in crisp uniforms pulling out her chair, asking the table if they'd prefer still or sparkling water. Beyond the other tables of well-heeled patrons, Davi sees bronze light over a carving station. She exhales: There's a buffet.

Davi met Mr. H-T five minutes before they left the house. He shook her hand and asked her name; he seemed unaware Davi was staying with them. During the drive, Mrs. H-T told her husband that Davi was Olivia's "best friend" from school, that she lived in London, that her parents owned the fashion label Out of Office ("Do you remember the pink knit jacket I wore to the Friends of the Public Garden benefit?"). She then turned around to Davi in the back seat and said apologetically, "Thomas isn't on social media."

The H-Ts order a bottle of red wine and the server tells them to help themselves to the buffet when they're ready. Davi wants to race to the front of the line but instead she waits for the bit of theater surrounding the opening and tasting of the cabernet. Then a toast: "Happy Thanksgiving." At Cinnamon's house, Mr. Peters gave the blessing, then they went around the table and said one thing they were grateful for.

Finally Mrs. H-T scoots back her chair. "I guess we should..."

Davi loads her plate like a person who might not eat the rest of the weekend. She starts at the bread station, selecting a warm sourdough roll and a slice of moist pumpkin bread along with five pats of butter. Then it's on to a bowl of butternut squash bisque. She delivers these back to the table and returns to the line for turkey, stuffing, mashed potatoes with gravy, brussels sprouts, and a cranberry compote. There's a cheese station—Davi is tempted but decides to save the cheese to have with her dessert.

By comparison, Olivia is *abstemious* ("not self-indulgent"). She has taken two slices of turkey with no gravy, some brussels sprouts, and green salad with no dressing. Mrs. H-T's plate looks much the same, though she added cranberry sauce.

Mr. H-T, thankfully, eats like a normal human being, and when he sees Davi's plate, he smiles. "It's nice to see a young lady with an appetite!"

Davi butters the pumpkin bread and tries not to shove it in her mouth as she wonders how long it will take for...

...Mrs. H-T to say, "I don't know how you do it, Davi. Eating so robustly and staying so thin."

"Metabolism," Olivia says morosely.

When they get back to the house, Davi is pleasantly full but not stuffed. She slowed down once she realized she could bring home a to-go container. For the first time in a long time, it feels good to have food in her stomach. She hasn't purged once since she's been here; there's been so little sustenance, there's been no reason.

Olivia wants to watch *The Holiday*—the H-Ts have a home theater on the fourth floor—and Davi remembers how, the instant Thanksgiving is over, Americans jump with both feet into Christmas. All across the country, people are driving to Best Buy.

"Do you want to call your parents before we start the movie?" Olivia asks. "You haven't talked to them yet today."

Davi hates how Olivia monitors her every move—she's such a stalker—though she understands it must seem odd that Davi hasn't phoned her parents on the holiest of family holidays. She nearly explains that, to Davi's parents, it's just another Thursday. However, this is a chance for some much-needed alone time, so Davi says, "Let me call them and dress down and I'll meet you in the theater."

Olivia pats her midsection and groans. "I have such a food baby."

As Davi changes into sweatpants and a Tiffin T-shirt, clocks throughout the house chime. It's only six o'clock, still so early. Davi sits on her bed and scrolls through other people's Thanksgiving TikToks, which evoke an unexpected longing for her own parents. *Should* she call? She has communicated with them only by text since Family Weekend; she hasn't yet acknowledged her father's email about her travel plans home at Christmas.

Davi checks her Snap Maps to see where her parents even are; they like Paris in November. Vikram's avatar (brown skin, graying hair, all-black outfit) turns up in the 8th arrondissement at the Plaza Athénée. But Davi's mother isn't with him. Ruby isn't in Paris; she isn't in London. Davi zooms out, checking her mother's other haunts—she's not in Tuscany, not in Morocco. When she clicks on Ruby's avatar, the map reorients.

Ruby is in the US. She's in... Kentucky?

Davi burps. Her mother is in some town called Covington, Kentucky. But this can't be right.

Davi dials her mother, gets her voicemail, calls back. After four rings, Ruby picks up; it sounds like she's eating. "Darling?" Ruby says. Davi hears her swallow. "Is everything all right?"

"Where are you?" Davi says.

"I'm at Saylem's family's house, darling," Ruby says. "In Covington. I had no idea Kentucky was so close to Cincinnati, did you?

We're just in the middle of a gorgeous dinner. I tried sweet potato with marshmallow topping. I thought it sounded dreadful but it's actually..."

Ruby is with Saylem's family for Thanksgiving.

Davi feels her stomach lurch. She claps a hand over her mouth and dashes for the bathroom.

December

16. The Holly and the Ivy

Charley takes an Uber from the Springfield bus station back to school the Sunday after Thanksgiving. When Horace's Toyota RAV4 pulls up to the entrance, Charley gasps. The gates are decked with evergreen garlands, white lights, and a pair of wreaths with green-and-gold tartan bows. In the middle of the Pasture stands an enormous Christmas tree strung with golden lights. There are candles and tiny wreaths in every single window across campus—in the Teddy, the Sink, the Schoolhouse, the Paddock, and Classic North and South.

Horace whistles. "This is a *high school?*" he says.

"Yes." In that moment, Charley understands how privileged she is.

A wreath and single candle have been placed in Charley's room. They give such a festive vibe that Charley forgives whoever entered her space while she was away.

As she's unpacking, Miss Bergeron pokes her head in. "A bunch of us are going to watch *Love Actually* in the common room," she says. "We have popcorn and I'm making hot chocolate." She smiles tentatively. " 'Tis the season."

"I want to read," Charley says, though as soon as Miss Bergeron retreats, Charley wonders if she should join everyone else. It sounds cozy and Charley has reached the point where Tiffin feels more like home than her actual home.

Over Thanksgiving weekend, Charley hung out with Beatrix, who filled her in on every nonevent at Loch Raven High School, then ever so casually mentioned that Joey had "visited" her at Towson Hot Bagels. She gave him a free coffee and he winked at her.

"He winks at everyone," Charley said. This wasn't true, but she needed to shut Beatrix down. Why did Beatrix give him free coffee? She should have refused to wait on him.

Then Beatrix asked about Davi again. Had Charley been invited to her room to film a TikTok? Had she seen the neon sign that read THIS IS WHERE THE MAGIC HAPPENS?

"Nope," Charley said.

Beatrix sighed. "Maybe I can visit you next semester?" They had talked about this over the summer, before Charley left. But in this moment, when Charley imagined Beatrix sitting in on Mr. Rivera's English class or coming to the *'Bred Bulletin* office to meet Ravenna, Grady, and Levi, or tasting Chef Haz's peanut butter pie or... introducing Beatrix to East and watching as Beatrix's eyeballs popped out of her head because she had "literally" never set eyes on a more gorgeous human, she thought, *No way.*

"Having friends visit isn't really a thing," Charley said. "Nobody does it. I'm not sure it's even allowed."

Beatrix pulled a face and started scrolling through her phone.

"But I can check *The Bridle* and maybe ask Miss Bergeron," Charley said.

"See, I don't know what *The Bridle* and who Miss Bergeron even are," Beatrix said. "It's like I'm losing you."

Just as Charley decides she *will* join everyone in the common room (she knows the girls on her floor expect her to be a grinch and she wants to surprise them by wearing the new candy cane–printed pajamas she bought at the Owings Mills Mall over the weekend), her phone pings with a text. Charley assumes it's her mother making sure she got back okay on the bus, but when she checks, she sees East's name and the downward arrow.

Her heart soars like Santa's sleigh.

But...it's almost nine, which is kind of late to check out for the Sink. Charley pokes her head into the hallway and realizes everyone is packed into the common room, where the lights are off and the TV is glowing with scenes of horny people bustling through the snow-flurried streets of London with their parcels. Charley smells the popcorn and imagines her floormates burning their tongues on watery Swiss Miss. Nothing can tear their attention away from *Love Actually.*

Jolly good, Charley thinks. She pulls on her peacoat and absconds out the back door.

East meets Charley outside the bomb shelter. His hair is a mess and he has scruff on his face, which Charley is dismayed to find only makes him hotter.

When he sees her, he breaks out into a huge smile. "Hello, Charles, how was your turkey?"

"Dry as dust," Charley says, which is a lie. Her mother and Joey did the trendy thing and deep-fried their turkey—they sell the fryers at the garden center—and it was the best turkey Charley had ever tasted, which only intensified her resentment. "How about yours?"

"I smashed some KFC," East says. "There's one in Haydensboro."

"Wait," Charley says. "You didn't go to New York?" She'd imagined East celebrating the holiday in some glass-walled penthouse overlooking Central Park with servants lifting silver domes off trays and dinner guests like Selena Gomez and Benny Blanco.

"I stayed here," East says. "And worked on this place. Wait until you see it. Are you ready? Close your eyes."

Charley obeys. East takes her hand and guides her forward.

"Okay," he says.

Charley opens her eyes. The room, *their* room, now has new wood floors. They look antique, though they're polished and give off a strong smell of varnish. But the more astonishing thing is the *chandelier* that has replaced the single bulb in the middle of the room. It resembles an upside-down wedding cake with descending tiers of crystals. It's classic Art Deco style and Charley immediately thinks of the F. Scott Fitzgerald story "The Ice Palace."

"Oh my god," Charley says. "Who did this?"

"I had some help from a couple of townies who were looking for work," East says. "I was supposed to drive home to New York, but when I realized everyone was going to be gone until Saturday—Ms. Robinson, Spooner, even Mr. James—I turned around. These floors came out of an old mill in Dalton, Massachusetts, which is where they used to make paper for the US Mint, the paper money is printed on."

"Provenance doesn't get any better than that," Charley says.

East tugs on one of her braids. "Charles appreciates provenance?"

Charley's cheeks heat up. "Where'd you get the light fixture?"

"I ordered it from a decorator-only site," he says. "I...kind of have someone helping me. This person has a really good eye and she has professional accounts so I can access stuff nobody else can get."

"Who is it?" Charley asks. Her voice is spiked with jealousy. "I thought we were the only two people who knew about this."

"We are," East says. "Except for the two guys who helped the other day, but they think this is a sanctioned school project."

"Plus the decorating consultant," Charley says. "You realize the more people you tell, the greater chance we have of getting busted."

"The decorating consultant won't tell anyone," East says. "Trust me."

"Is it Davi?" Charley asks. Davi certainly has a good eye, and she might have access to design accounts through her parents.

East takes Charley by the shoulders and looks her in the eye. "It is not Davi. It would never be Davi."

Great, Charley thinks. *It's probably some glamorous chick East knows from the city.* She eyes the chandelier. There can be no arguing: It's fabulous.

"Well, she has exquisite taste," Charley says. "She'll be a real asset to you down here."

East bursts out laughing. "You are so *territorial,*" he says.

"I'm not—"

"It's my mother," East says. "Lori Litavec, formerly Lori Eastman. She's an interior decorator in LA."

"Your *mother*?" Charley says.

"She also thinks it's a school-sanctioned project," East says. "Which just goes to show how little she knows about Tiffin. But she's very happy to help us with design elements."

"Oh my god," Charley says. Not Davi, not some Gen Z Kelly Wearstler. East's *mother* is helping them decorate an illegal speakeasy in the bomb shelter beneath their boarding school dorms.

"All I could think about over the weekend was how much I wanted you to see this," East says. "But we should probably go back up."

"I'm sorry if I sounded territorial," Charley says. "This is your project..."

"*Our* project," East says. "Next I have to work on the bathroom, build a bar, create a template for the granite, and get some furniture down here."

Even though Charley is impressed by the floors and the chandelier, she holds no expectations of these next steps happening.

"There was something else I wanted to ask you," East says.

She cocks an eyebrow. Part of her is always waiting for East to ask her to write one of his papers or dig him out of his hole in history class.

"Do you know about the Kringle?"

Charley blinks. The only Kringle she knows about is the breakfast pastry filled with almond marzipan that they sell at Trader Joe's over the holidays. Her father used to eat the entire thing by himself.

"It's the night before we leave for break," East says. "Evensong in the chapel followed by a party in the Egg. People dress up; it's upperclassmen only. And I was wondering if you wanted to go with me."

Charley stares at East, trying to determine whether or not this is a joke. She has never heard of the Kringle, though who would tell her? She has no friends. Is East asking her to attend a school function with him? This is a prank or a gotcha, or something crueler. This is Stephen King's Carrie being crowned prom queen before they dump a bucket of pig's blood over her head.

East takes a step closer and lays a hand on her cheek. "Just say yes."

His expression is earnest. Either that or she's the world's biggest idiot. If that's the case, so be it. All the girls on her floor are watching *Love Actually*—but Charley is living it. This is love, actually.

"Yes," she says.

Zip Zap alert: **Royce Stringfellow turned in a Hawthorne paper that he wrote using ChatGPT.**

When Rhode Rivera reads the post, he thinks, *Shit.*

He's making himself a cup of instant coffee in his room because he's trying to avoid bumping into Chef Haz at the Paddock; Rhode still owes him a balance of eight hundred dollars for the disastrous dinner date with Simone. Rhode goes to his laptop and brings up Royce's essay, which compares Hester Prynne to Anna Karenina. Rhode had been so impressed by the choice of topic, never mind the essay, that he'd awarded Royce an automatic A. Rhode rereads the essay: Does it sound like AI wrote it? The vocabulary is impressive, the structure impeccable, the comparisons between the heroines elite — but these are hallmarks of Royce's usual work. Does it sound like Royce's voice? Rhode would have to go back and read Royce's other essays, and who has time for that? Not Rhode. He has to wrap up Hawthorne this week and get through *The Crucible* before Christmas break. (He has dedicated an entire semester to old white men at the board's insistence, but next semester will be different!)

Rhode isn't going to discipline Royce Stringfellow due to some baseless claim on Zip Zap.

Before Rhode's C-period class begins, Royce comes skulking into Rhode's classroom.

"Mr. Rivera," he says, "I came to beg forgiveness. I did use ChatGPT to write my essay."

Rhode stands up. Royce Stringfellow is aptly named — he's tall and rangy with pale hair and pasty skin. Today, he has brown circles under his eyes and a mess of cowlicks. "You're an exceptional student, Royce. Why would you do that?"

Royce sits on the Harkness table, letting his long legs dangle. "Woman trouble," he says. "I've been hanging out with Tilly Benbow since the start of school and, as you probably saw on Zip Zap, she's been sexting with someone off camp."

Yes, Rhode saw the post, but he doesn't want to know any of the particulars. "I can empathize with woman trouble," he says. Rhode hasn't had a meaningful conversation with Simone since their date; if he thought that being a good sport about her poor showing would win him points, he was wrong.

"I'll rewrite the essay on a different topic," Royce says. "Maybe compare Hester Prynne with Emma Bovary? I'll write it in front of you." Royce gives Rhode a beseeching look. "Just please don't give me a zero. My GPA is basically my only friend right now."

Rhode considers this request. The kid blatantly cheats, gets caught by the mysterious, omniscient eyes of Zip Zap, but instead of denying it (which is what Rhode himself might have done), Royce admits the truth and offers to correct his ways. Rhode thinks of Tilly Benbow sending nudes out into the scary world beyond Tiffin.

"That's fine, Royce," Rhode says. "See me after school and you can write a new essay in here."

Royce blinks away tears. "Thanks, Mr. Rivera," he says. "You're a king."

Zip Zap alert: Our beloved academy's name has been dragged through the national mud. Click here for link.

Audre exhales. What is *this* all about? She opens the link and is taken to an Instagram post of The Cut, *New York* magazine's online style/culture/power brand. The headline reads: "Is Tiffin Academy's #2 Ranking in *America Today* a Sham?" The caption goes on to describe ISNEC's inquiry. "The coalition believes the number two spot may have been bought rather than earned, and they're seeking answers from journalists at *America Today*. How did the school jump seventeen spots in only one year?"

Audre clenches a fist. As if the inquiry itself isn't bad enough, now the whole world knows about it. It doesn't matter what the inquiry reveals, the mere suggestion of pay-for-play will be all anyone remembers. *Well,* Audre thinks, *Worthless has exacted his revenge: Tiffin's reputation has been effectively sullied.*

Before Audre can call out for Cordelia, she appears in the doorway of Audre's office. "There's a reporter from the *New York Times* on the phone," she says, "asking if you have a comment on The Cut's post."

"No comment," Audre says, which takes all her restraint. What she'd like to say to the paper of record is that Douglas Worth is jealous. And for good reason: Tiffin bumped him out of the number two spot. Jesse Eastman is automatic clickbait because of his conspicuous wealth; Audre dearly hopes *New York* mag doesn't do any more digging and discover the unorthodox arrangement they have in regard to East. Audre studies Cordelia, who hides a lockbox of secrets behind her somewhat dowdy exterior. "Tell Laura Rae I'd like to speak at Chapel this morning after the service."

"Very good," Cordelia says. Audre hears her say, "No comment, thank you, goodbye," as Audre rifles through her drawer for a copy of *The Bridle*. Surely something in here will save her.

The chapel is glorious at Christmastime. The pews are hung with garlands; the altar is blanketed with red poinsettias. A wreath hangs from the pulpit. Because it's a gray, drizzly day, they light all the candles, which cast the sanctuary in a golden glow.

All this coziness feels at odds with what Audre is about to do. She should be announcing that Piano Bar on Monday will include carols; she should be reminding fifth- and sixth-formers about the Kringle and lauding the squash team for their excellent showing at the Winter Invitational.

Instead, Audre says, "Some of you may have seen the latest post on Zip Zap about an official inquiry into our number two ranking. The inquiry is real, though baseless." At least Audre hopes so. In the moments before Chapel, she sent the link to the Cut post to Jesse Eastman with a text that said, Please reassure me again that you had nothing to do with our ranking, Jesse. "We earned our ranking, fair and square."

In the front row, Annabelle Tuckerman breathes a sigh of relief. She's hoping that a GPA of 3.95 from the number two boarding school in the country might have more weight with the Princeton admission counselors than a 4.0 from a lesser school.

"The more insidious problem," Audre says, "is that of Zip Zap itself. As per page one of *The Bridle,* there is to be no hateful rhetoric used at Tiffin—racial, sexual, ethnic, religious, or otherwise. In accordance with this most important of rules, I demand that all students delete the Zip Zap app from their phones."

A ripple of chatter rolls through the chapel.

Audre raises her voice. "If it's discovered that you still have the Zip Zap app on your phone—and every faculty member is authorized to conduct random checks—you will face an immediate Honor Board hearing."

The chatter quickly becomes mayhem.

"Whoever is responsible for administering the Zip Zap app will be expelled from school."

Sixth-former Teague Baldwin raises a hand. "What if the person behind Zip Zap is an adult?"

Audre blinks. She hasn't considered this, but just because *she* would be unable to navigate an app like this doesn't mean someone else on her payroll couldn't. "That person will be dismissed." Before the uproar can get any louder, Audre says, "You are excused. Off to A-period. Thank you."

Mr. Chuy plays "Abide with Me" on the organ while Audre silently congratulates herself. She knows that Excelsior and Brownwell-Mather managed to vanquish Zip Zap, and although Audre wasn't able to ask how they did it, she has found her own way.

That afternoon at the *'Bred Bulletin* office, Ravenna is incandescent with rage—and, Charley thinks, glee.

"She can't do this," Ravenna says. "Do you know why, Grady?"

Grady beams. "Censorship?"

"Finally, we have a story!" Ravenna says. "I don't like sending out email blasts, but I have no choice. Ms. Robinson can't *force* us to delete Zip Zap. Our phones are our personal property. We have rights!"

"Yeah, rights!" Levi says. He's at his post in front of the computer. "What do you want me to say?"

"'Tiffin students resist censorship,'" Cordelia Spooner reads aloud when the email appears in her inbox. The entire student body is up in arms; the Honor Board is threatening to resign.

"'None of us intend to delete the app,' Head Prefect Lisa Kim announced. 'The administration can't dictate what we consume on our personal time.'"

Cordelia finds Audre in her office with her head in her hands.

"I assume you saw the email?" Cordelia says.

Audre looks up. "We have to find out who has control of the app." She pauses. "It might entail getting our hands dirty."

Bring it on, Cordelia thinks. She'll do whatever it takes to catch the little fucker.

Fifth-form English students are assigned Arthur Miller's *The Crucible.* A "crucible," Mr. Rivera tells them, is "a test designed to bring about change or reveal an individual's true character."

Their essay prompt, due the day before Christmas break, reads, "*The Crucible* details the effects of the witch trials in Salem. How do these trials affect the community? Government and authority? The Church? Individuals?"

Taylor Wilson is studying in the Sink with Dub and Charley Hicks. She hasn't spoken to Hakeem since before Thanksgiving. He is fully with third-former Cassie Lee; they Intervis every night. Taylor is surprised by how jealous this makes her. Chasing Dub is an exercise in frustration. They're together all the time, but he has yet to make a move. He probably doesn't want to piss off Hakeem. The three of them are victims of Zip Zap—just like Annabelle

Tuckerman, just like Royce Stringfellow, just like Chef Haz, and just like poor Mrs. Spooner.

Taylor reads the essay prompt once, then a second time. She leans in.

"You guys?" she says. "Is it just me or is Zip Zap kind of like the Salem witch trials? We don't know who will get accused next, or why."

Charley had been thinking the exact same thing: The similarities between the themes in *The Crucible* and what's happening now at Tiffin are uncanny.

"Mr. Rivera has access to our journals," Dub says. "Do you think he's..."

"Conducting a social experiment?" Taylor says.

"I love Mr. Rivera," Charley says. "He is *not* behind Zip Zap."

Love is blind, Dub thinks. The second he gets back to his room, he emails Ms. Robinson with their theory.

17. The Kringle

In the second week of December, packages from Revolve, Retrofete, and Reformation pile up on the mail table outside the common room of Classic South, overtaking the gingerbread house display. The parcels contain prospective dresses for the Kringle—and the first-floor hallway soon rivals a runway at New York Fashion Week.

The Academy

Davi has been dreaming about the Kringle since she got to Tiffin: a special evensong service for fifth- and sixth-formers followed by an elegant holiday party. Students dress up; some go with dates.

Davi and Cinnamon had shopped for Kringle dresses as early as the previous Christmas. Davi bought a half dozen, which now hang in her closet. She hears other girls out in the hallway modeling for one another. She knows they're waiting for her to poke her head out and offer a blunt assessment in the style of Nicky Campbell. But Davi is uninspired. She feels a fresh wave of grief about Cinnamon and she can't bear to think about the holiday break—three weeks stuck with her parents and Saylem.

On the other side of the door, she hears *ebullient* ("extremely lively, enthusiastic") squealing. Sixth-former Teague Baldwin has asked Madison J. to go to the Kringle with him. Davi rolls her eyes; everyone is reacting as though Madison J. just got engaged.

Maybe Davi should get a date for the Kringle. Maybe if she has her own relationship to focus on, she'll be better able to stomach her parents' threesome. The question is who? The boys at this school are children. She'd happily ask her father to fly Paolo in from Italy for the event (the other girls would *die*) or ask Olivia H-T to set Davi up with her cute cousin (Olivia owes her after that weird Thanksgiving)—but the Kringle is for Tiffin students only.

Hakeem Pryce is a possibility. He's with that third-former, Cassie Lee, a future queen bee, but third-formers aren't allowed to attend the Kringle even as guests. So, Hakeem and Davi could go as friends. Taylor can't get bent about it; she'll go with Dub. But does Davi really want to insert herself into that messy situation? She does not.

There's only one other person at Tiffin who's worthy of Davi Banerjee...and that's East. Davi sort of resents the guy. He's been granted all kinds of special privileges—he keeps his truck in the Back Lot and he takes English as an independent study, which is basically a joke—because his father is president of the board and the biggest donor Tiffin has seen in the past 114 years.

Davi will overlook these annoyances: East is older, he's hot, they'll look good in the pics, her followers will eat him up.

She sends him an iMessage because he's not on Instagram or Snapchat. Do you want to go to the Kringle together? She hesitates before she sends this; she has never before texted East. They'd exchanged numbers during the Move-In Day cookout when they were third-formers and Davi assumed they'd be friends. They are not friends. Davi became internet famous, East became an *enigma* ("a person or thing that is mysterious, hard to understand").

She edits the text to read, Hey East, it's Davi. Do you want to go to the Kringle together? She presses send. She doesn't feel weird about being the one to ask; she knows she's intimidating and not even East would be brave enough to ask her.

He texts back right away: Hey Davi, thanks, good idea. But I already have a date.

Shit, Davi thinks. She wasn't expecting this because East never mingles with Tiffin commoners. Were the rules bent for him again? Is he importing someone from New York? Coco Arquette? Lexi Underwood?

Davi texts back. I love that for you!!! Who are you taking?

Three dots appear, then disappear. He doesn't want to tell her. Or maybe there isn't anyone. Maybe he just said that because he doesn't want to go with Davi.

There it goes, she thinks. The last of her self-esteem.

Then her phone buzzes with a text: I'm taking Charley Hicks.

Davi marches down the hall, passing Olivia H-T, who is modeling a holly-green knit dress with faux fur at the cuffs and hem. The fur is a fun touch, but someone with Olivia H-T's body type should *not* be wearing a knit.

"You can do better," Davi says.

"Wait, Davi!" Olivia H-T says. "Can you—"

But Davi is on a mission. She opens the door to 111 and finds Charley lying on her bed reading *The Crucible.* Shocker.

Charley's eyes flick over the pages to Davi. "What?"

"I can't believe you aren't using the SparkNotes," Davi says. "But of course that's what makes you you. You read the original."

"I feel seen, thank you," Charley deadpans.

Davi steps in and closes the door behind her.

"By all means, make yourself at home."

Davi smiles. Any other girl at Tiffin would kill to have Davi Banerjee in her room—but not Charley. She's *impervious* ("immune") to Davi's charms. "Are you going to the Kringle with East?"

This gets Charley's attention. She sits up, sets the book down. "Where did you hear that? It's not on Zip Zap, is it?"

"No," Davi says. "East told me himself. I asked if he wanted to go together and he said he was taking you."

Charley sinks back into her pillows. "Yeah."

"Can I just ask? What's up with you? You've been asked to the Kringle by the hottest guy at Tiffin and you don't even look excited. You look *bored.* Do you think you're too good for East? Too good for any of us?"

Charley studies Davi for a second. "I do not think that, no. I'm just socially awkward."

"I figured that much out day one," Davi says. "But you don't even try."

"Chasing is Out," Charley says. "I figure if I present my authentic self, my people will find me."

"Is that what happened with East? He found you?"

Charley's eyebrows rise and her lips turn up just a tick. "I have no idea. He's hard to read."

"Amen to that," Davi says. "So what are you going to wear?"

"Wear?"

"To the Kringle?"

Charley glances toward her closet, which was what Davi was afraid of. "No. You can't wear a khaki skirt and monogrammed sweater to this." She pauses. "Come to my room."

"I will," Charley says, "under one condition."

Under one condition? Davi thinks. *Are they on the CW?* "Which is?"

"You have to get help with your...issue."

Whoa! Davi nearly storms out of the room. Davi's "issue" is none of Charley's business. "Forget it," Davi says. "You do realize I came in here to help you, right?"

"I want to help you too," Charley says. "I don't even really like you, Davi. But I can acknowledge that you have some great qualities—you're strong, charismatic, a natural leader. I'm sure you feel pressure to be perfect on the outside—"

Davi holds up a hand. "Don't psychoanalyze me, please. You don't know anything about my life. Nobody does. I'll handle my own issues if and when I fucking feel like it."

Charley studies Davi for one unsettling moment. "That's a more honest answer than I expected, I guess," Charley says, swinging her feet to the floor. She sighs. "Fine. I'll let you dress me up like a doll."

Preparation for the Kringle is a lot like the scene before First Dance: *Les filles* crowd into the bathroom, vying for sink space, while the JBL speaker blares "I Can Do It with a Broken Heart" followed by "Oklahoma Smokeshow." Simone thought the girls might listen to holiday music, but she was naïve.

Simone is wearing a long black dress with long sleeves and the slightest boatneck. She received a terse email from Cordelia Spooner a few days earlier, reminding her that although she's young, she should dress "modestly and appropriately" for the Kringle. *The dress you wore to First Dance was several inches too short,* Cordelia said. *We like all faculty to lead by example, especially someone as influential as you.*

When the girls see Simone, they shriek. "That dress is *so Crucible*-core."

Yes, Simone thinks. She feels like she's back in the seventeenth century being disciplined by the town elders.

What's different about the Kringle is that Charley Hicks is participating (rather than holing up in her room with Dickens's *A Christmas Carol,* as Simone expected). She took one of the first showers, then slipped into Davi's room.

The other girls appear in the hallway, hair half up or in curlers, in bras and panties; Tilly Benbow wears her "transitional garment" — an old dress shirt of her father's, which hangs to her knees and has Flawless Filter smudged all over the collar. She likes it because it buttons, so she won't mess up her hair taking it off. The girls are trying to appear like they're not loitering around Davi's closed door.

Simone overhears Olivia H-T say, "I don't get it. The girl is *such* a freak."

"Olivia," Simone says sharply.

A little while later, nearly everyone is ready. Madison J. puts on a parka over her little black dress and waits for Teague Baldwin by the front door. Madison R. is in her white robe because she sings in the choir; Olivia P. wears a red robe because she is in the handbell choir.

"Do you have a date, Miss Bergeron?" Willow Levy asks.

"I do not," Simone says, though of *course* Rhode suggested that they "go together." Simone told him she didn't feel that was appropriate. The majority of girls on her floor were going solo and Simone didn't want them to feel awkward about it. "I'll just see you there," she said.

At ten minutes to seven, it's time to head over to the chapel.

"Allez!" Simone calls out. Everyone puts on coats, slips into heels or boots. The air in the hallway is thick with Flowerbomb perfume.

Finally, the door to Davi's room opens and Davi steps out wearing a tiny red crushed-velvet dress and a pair of sky-high black Louboutin sandals with studded straps. She's stunning and sophisticated, but this, Simone expected. Davi closes the door behind her.

"Is Charley not coming?" Simone asks.

"Oh, she is," Davi says.

A second later, the door opens again—and Simone gets goose bumps. Charley emerges in a skintight white silk dress with a black lace deep V. Her hair flows down over her shoulders. She has ditched her glasses. Her makeup—smoky eye, glossy lip—is worthy of a supermodel. She's breathtaking.

All the girls in the hall turn around. There's one second of pin-drop silence—and then they cheer. Simone feels herself choking up. Charley Hicks is a total smokeshow, and although Simone believes that the only beauty that matters comes from within, she couldn't be happier.

Simone pulls Davi aside. "You worked some kind of magic," she says. "Charley should be going to this thing with Prince Charming."

"Hotter than Prince Charming," Davi says. "She's going with East."

Simone jerks her head back. "What?"

"Charley," Davi says. "She's going to the Kringle with East."

"Wasn't that service magnificent?"

Simone is darting from the chapel over to the Teddy for the soiree in the Egg when she turns to find Honey Vandermeid at her elbow. Honey is wearing opera-length pearls and a camel hair coat; her hair is in a chignon. She emits a timeless elegance that Simone will never achieve. Honey must have left the service at the first possible opportunity and moved at quite a clip to catch up with Simone.

"*Magnifique,*" Simone says dully. Her eyes are blurred with tears, which could easily be blamed on the bitter cold.

Simone barely paid attention to the service. She only remembers the choir singing "Angels We Have Heard on High," and the handbell choir, predictably, chiming out "Carol of the Bells." *Ding-dong, ding...dong.* Chaplain Laura Rae recited the entire Christmas story according to the Gospel of Matthew while Simone stared across the aisle at Charley Hicks and Andrew Eastman sitting side by side. East occasionally leaned in and whispered in Charley's ear and Charley smiled each time. Once, she swatted East's leg.

Simone was consumed with a sick green jealousy. She would never have put East and Charley together, but now she realizes that out of any girl in the school, it's Charley she's most envious of. If East had chosen someone beautiful but silly like Tilly Benbow or someone too-cool-for-school like Davi, Simone wouldn't mind quite so much. The problem with Charley Hicks is that she's quality. She's brilliant and hardworking and self-possessed. Girls like Olivia H-T call her a "freak" because she doesn't care about the things other teenage girls care about. She's mature, more mature than Simone herself.

Simone should be *glad* that East likes Charley. This is how it's *supposed* to be—students dating students. But Simone replays the scene in her classroom: Simone on the Harkness table, East's head between her legs.

As the choir sang "Silent Night" and the congregation passed a flame from one handheld candle to another until the sanctuary was aglow, Simone thought, *East is mine. He's mine.*

Simone attempts to escape from the chapel in order to be alone with her agony, but Honey seems intent on chitchat. Where is Simone spending her *Noel*?

"At home in Montreal with my parents."

Will she ski? Honey loves Mont-Tremblant. Does Simone's mother make any traditional dishes at the holidays?

"My father cooks a goose for Christmas lunch," Simone says. "On Boxing Day, we have the neighbors over." For a moment, Simone is comforted by thoughts of home. Her parents were scandalized by what happened at the end of Simone's senior year at McGill, and they barely tolerated her presence at home the years after she graduated when she worked as a barista. But now she'll be able to regale her parents with all her Tiffin successes: She taught a full semester of *l'histoire des États-Unis;* she has become a beloved dorm parent.

Simone should be glad nothing else happened between her and East, and relieved that they didn't get caught. *East and Charley together is a blessing,* she thinks. *A Christmas miracle.*

Simone enters the Egg, which exudes tasteful Christmas: green-and-gold tartan tablecloths and hundreds of electric pillar candles. The mocktail bar serves cranberry-ginger shrubs, honey vanilla cider, and "Grinch punch," which is bright red with a green sugar rim. Servers pass trays of mini lamb chops with mint aioli and filet mignon sliders. In the middle of the high-top tables is an elaborate cheese fondue set up with chunks of baguette, veggies, and sausages for dipping.

DJ Radio is back. After the kids get mocktails and dunk pieces of bread into the bubbling fondue, they hit the dance floor. Simone keeps her eyes pinned to East and Charley. She tries to catch East's eye; she wants him to know she's watching him, but he seems to be studiously avoiding her. Or maybe she's flattering herself. Maybe he isn't thinking of her at all. He seems locked in on Charley.

Honey appears at Simone's side, offering a gingerbread latte, which Simone has no choice but to accept. "I've been trying to catch the kids sneaking alcohol," Honey says. "But I haven't seen any suspicious behavior. They're probably afraid of Zip Zap."

Yes, Simone thinks. It's a little disconcerting now that Zip Zap seems to be watching them.

Simone feels a tap on her shoulder. It's Rhode. "You owe me a dance," he says.

Simone blinks. She probably owes him *something* for the fiasco at the Wullys' cottage, but his smug expression and his bow tie printed with snowmen hit exactly the wrong way.

She lowers her voice. "I don't owe you a thing." She nearly adds that he's a terrible dancer, his shameless pursuit of her is off-putting, and if he wants to get laid, he should go on the apps because he's fifteen years too old for Simone, but even if he was younger, she wouldn't date him because he's smarmy and reeks of desperation.

Rhode opens his mouth to speak, but at that moment, Audre appears out of nowhere and takes his arm. "Mr. Rivera, may I pull you for a quick chat?"

Relieved, Simone turns back to Honey, but she's involved in some kind of quarrel with Cordelia Spooner.

"Could you be more obvious?" Cordelia hisses.

"Oh, Cord, stop it," Honey says.

By the time Simone checks the dance floor, East and Charley are gone. Simone spins around. They aren't at the fondue table, they aren't sitting at a high-top. Where did they go?

Simone slips out the door without her coat; if anyone asks where she's going, she'll say she needs air. Because her dress is long, she wore sneakers, so she runs across campus, hugging herself against the cold. She passes the Sink, the Schoolhouse, and the Paddock remembering how she traveled this same path in pursuit of Charley

Hicks the night of First Dance. She was new then, clueless and naïve, but not anymore.

When she reaches the dorms, she descends the outdoor steps, pulls open the door, and shines her light into the cellar. Then it's down the scary steps to the tunnel. Does she hear anything? No. Did East take Charley somewhere else, maybe to God's Basement? Simone heads through the tunnel until she's pretty sure she's gone too far, but then she sees a faint stripe of light underneath... a door? Simone turns the knob and eases the door open just a crack, enough so that she can see a room with a wood floor and a crystal chandelier.

Beneath the chandelier, East and Charley are kissing.

Simone opens her mouth to speak. This is *against the rules;* they could both be written up for leaving a school event without permission and for being in a place they don't belong. But Simone is struck by how beautiful the two of them look. The kissing is sexy; every second that Simone doesn't announce herself, she becomes more of a voyeur. When East kissed Simone, it was never romantic like this. It was, she realizes now, *strategic.*

The strategy worked: If Simone busts East and Charley, she'll end up in trouble herself.

Gently, nearly tenderly, she closes the door.

Audre doesn't want to deal with a school matter during the Kringle. What she wants is to devour the white chocolate macadamia petit fours that Chef has handcrafted. But campus will clear out in the morning, so Audre has no choice but to confront Mr. Rivera in the hallway just outside the Egg.

Audre says, "One of the students brought to my attention that you're teaching *The Crucible.*"

Rhode bobs his head. "I meant to get to it around Halloween, but things took longer than I anticipated."

"I'm not concerned about the timing," Audre says. "Though I am curious about the context. The play deals with paranoia and scapegoating." She pauses. "Which could also describe our campus in the past few weeks."

He tilts his head. "I'm not sure I follow?"

"This student suggested you might be conducting a high-concept thought experiment. Trying to make a profound statement. I'm aware, Mr. Rivera, that you're a novelist and therefore quite creative..."

"High-concept thought experiment? Profound statement? What are you talking about, Ms. Robinson?"

"Zip Zap," Audre says. "Some of the students seem to think you're behind it."

"Me?" Rhode says. He looks baffled and almost flattered—then he chuckles, which annoys Audre. Initially, she thought Dub's theory was preposterous, but the more she considered it, the more she hoped Rhode was the culprit. She would have to fire him, yes, but then the matter would be resolved.

"This student said you require them to keep journals," Audre says. "Which would make you privy to their innermost thoughts..."

"I encourage them to keep journals for their own edification," Rhode says. "But I only read what the students want to share. I'm not privy to their secrets, nor would I want to be."

"So you're not behind Zip Zap?" Audre says.

"I am not."

Audre isn't sure she believes him, but there's nothing more to be done on the topic tonight.

"Very well," she says. "I hope you have a safe and joyous holiday."

"And you," Rhode says.

Audre returns to the Egg just in time for the biggest moment of the night, the biggest moment of any holiday party across America:

The DJ plays Mariah Carey. Students rush the dance floor, hands in the air, singing along. *All I want for Christmas...is you!*

At that moment, Audre's phone buzzes. She holds it at arm's length so she can see the screen; she's come to the Kringle without her glasses.

It's an alert from Zip Zap. **Update on the Ranking Scandal: It seems Head of School Ms. Robinson believes Tiffin's board president Jesse Eastman had something to do with our #2 spot.**

What? Audre thinks. Then she remembers the text she sent to Big East: Please reassure me again that you had nothing to do with our ranking, Jesse. Does Zip Zap have access to her *phone?* It's always in her possession; she charges it at night next to her bed. Audre searches the Egg for Mr. Rivera and finds him attacking the last of the fondue. There's no way he could have posted so quickly. Most of the fifth- and sixth-formers are out on the dance floor, so she has to rule them—her likeliest suspects—out as well.

When the song ends, so does the Kringle. The lights come up, the kids scatter in search of their coats and the few remaining petit fours. It's Audre's tradition to return to the Residence, pour herself a glass of wine, and blast the "Hallelujah" chorus to mark the end of the first semester.

But now, Audre feels defeated. All she wants for Christmas, she thinks, is for things to be like they were last Christmas: Before Cinnamon Peters killed herself, before Cordelia Spooner and Honey started quarreling, before Audre hired either Mr. Rivera or Miss Bergeron, before Tiffin was ranked number two and became the subject of an official inquiry. Before Zip Zap. *Is that too much to ask?* she wonders. She fears the answer is yes.

January

18. Resolutions

The Tiffin Academy brochure shows the campus in high autumn when the foliage is at its peak—campfire orange, buttery yellow, deep crimson—and in late spring when the wildflowers in the Pasture bloom like pastel fireworks. There are, however, no photographs of Tiffin in January when the students return for second semester: colorless skies, barren trees, dead grass, Jewel Pond brown and muddy with a patchy skin of ice. The Thoroughbreds are facing three months of frigid wind and a new semester of academic rigor without much to distract them. For sports, it's either squash or basketball, and both basketball teams are historically dreadful. Not even Hakeem Pryce's natural athleticism or Annabelle Tuckerman's occasional luck behind the three-point line can save them.

Despite this, the Thoroughbreds are happy to be back! Charley races up the steps of Classic South, nearly slipping on the ice. She lugs her duffel—filled with new, slightly more stylish clothes—to her room and seconds later, Davi appears. "Let's go to the Grille."

Charley is supposed to meet East in the tunnel as soon as it gets dark; he wants to show her the work he did over break. It's quarter to four; Charley has an hour until the sun sets.

"Okay," she says.

At the Grille, Charley gets a birthday cake milkshake even though it's twenty-two degrees outside, and Davi orders a grilled cheese with bacon on Texas toast and a side of onion rings.

The morning of Christmas Eve, Davi texted Charley out of the blue, asking if they could FaceTime. Davi was barefaced and Charley had her hair down and her contacts in, so for a moment it was as though they'd switched roles.

"I'm just going to tell you what's going on with my family," Davi said—and she explained about Saylem, her parents' third, who was now sleeping in the primary suite with her mother while her father slept in the guesthouse out back. "It feels like my father and I are living with a couple of newlyweds. My mother and Saylem are all over each other all the time. So now everyone at Out of Office knows, and it's all over Annabelle's."

"Annabelle's?" Charley said.

"Their club," Davi said. "Have you never heard of it?" On the FaceTime, Charley watched Davi shove a lamington into her mouth. "What are things like at your house?"

Charley told Davi about her father's death, then about her mother and Joey and Joey's possible fascination with her best friend, Beatrix. "I hate him," Charley said. "I stay in my room and read."

"Notice the look of surprise on my face," Davi said.

But whereas things stayed miserable for Davi—Saylem accompanied Davi and her parents on their annual ski trip to Courchevel—the situation at Charley's house improved on December 27 when Joey announced he was driving up to Connecticut to spend the new year with friends and wouldn't be back until after Charley left. This came as a surprise not only to Charley but to Fran Hicks as well, who said, "You're doing *what*?"

With Joey gone, Charley could breathe again, though she spent just as much time in her room because she wanted to avoid her mother's sighs and barbed comments. "I hope you're happy. You drove him away. He knows you hate him."

Charley *was* happy! She *did* hate him!

On New Year's Eve, Charley and her mother celebrated the way they used to celebrate when Charley's father was alive: with pizza and sparkling cider while watching the ball drop in Times Square on TV. At midnight, Charley received a text from East that said, I wish I was kissing you right now. Happy New Year, Charles.

Her mother called Joey and got his voicemail. She left a message that started out angry then devolved to weepy and pathetic. Fran Hicks had by then switched from sparkling cider to prosecco, and she refused help when Charley tried to get her up to bed.

It was Charley's first lesson in Be Careful What You Wish For.

Now, in the Grille, Davi says, "I made a resolution. I'm going to do less posting and more studying."

Charley says, "My resolution is to lighten up."

When the two of them leave the Teddy, they lean into each other like real friends. Charley can't get over how the start of this semester differs from last semester. Everything has clicked into place.

But then Davi peels off when they reach the Sink, saying she'll see Charley back at the dorm. Although Charley is relieved — she's going down to the tunnel to see East — she's also concerned because she knows Davi is going to the third-floor bathroom to puke up her grilled cheese and onion rings.

Suddenly the new year seems slightly less promising.

Simone Bergeron's New Year's resolution is not to obsess about East, or about East and Charley together — but by the end of the first week back, she has broken this resolution 114 times. Every F-period, East and Charley enter class together, they sit next to each other, they walk out together, leaving Simone to steep in her envy. East turns in written responses to the reading for the first time all year. Simone assumes Charley is doing his work for him — until she calls on East in class and he gives an answer so eloquent and informed about the causes of the War of 1812 that Simone feels defeated. All it took for East to turn things around academically was the good influence of Charley Hicks.

Simone now *hates* Charley, though she tries to tamp down her pettiness and treat Charley like the other girls. But one day, as she's hunting through her desk, she comes across a copy of the *'Bred Bulletin* from Family Weekend and she remembers something.

The In and Out list that Charley wrote.

Simone notes the items of the In column that track for Charley: *staying in, reading, hating people.* Simone's eyes then drift down to the last two items: *orgasms* and *fifth-form repeats.* Charley's scheme was coded right there in the newspaper back in October.

During Family Weekend, East kissed Simone in the brick tunnel. To think of it now is like a straight pin through her heart.

Also on Charley's list is *vodka Red Bulls.*

Which gives Simone an idea.

As if East and Charley getting cuffed isn't enough, a troubling email lands in Simone's inbox. It's from Jasper Stiefel, a person so problematic from Simone's past that she's tempted to delete the email without reading it. The subject line says: I'm sorry. Out of pure curiosity, Simone clicks on it.

> Hey Simone.
> I tried sending a letter to your parents' house in Saint-Henri but I heard nothing back, so I tracked down your mother at her medical practice and she gave me your new email. I hope you read this apology, even though it's long overdue.
>
> I want to say how sorry I am for being a part of that horrible night in your final semester at McGill. I heard you were

disciplined harshly and lost your position as floor fellow. Lars told me they let you graduate, but not walk with the rest of the class. I assume since you're now working at an American boarding school, everything turned out okay?

I have no excuse other than that I was young—too young to resist the temptation of hanging out with you. Even as it was happening, I knew what we were doing was wrong and I'm sorry you alone had to pay the price.

I hope you can bring yourself to forgive me, and that you've dusted yourself off from the debacle of that night in McConnell and moved on.

All best, Jasper

Simone reads the email twice, the first time incredulous, the second time merely enraged. Jasper must be going through a twelve-step program and this must be part of his amends. He *should* be sorry! If he and Lars hadn't appeared at her room with their mischievous grins and their bulging backpacks, Simone would have graduated with honors, a shining paragon of hard work and leadership.

Instead, she left *entaché*.

Simone can't blame anyone but herself; she was the floor fellow. She should have turned Lars and Jasper away but didn't.

She reads the email a third time and feels a deep mortification.

She would like to say she dusted herself off from the debacle of McConnell and moved on. But she hasn't changed, not really.

Simone won't respond right away; she's learned that much. She'll think on it for a couple days.

All week, Charley signs out to the Sink, but instead of going on the scheduled trip to the cineplex in Capulet Falls Saturday night— Simone has learned they save trips to the movie theater for the dead of winter—Charley opts to remain in the dorms. She says she wants to read.

Simone isn't naïve; she knows what this means. Davi and all the other girls are going to the movies, which means that Charley is planning to link up with East—and Simone will be damned if she's going to let that happen.

Simone steps out into the hallway as the girls scurry among one another's rooms getting ready; rumor has it boys from the nearby public schools frequent the cineplex and the Five Guys next door. "Room check!" she shouts.

Everyone freezes. Simone has never done a room check; she has been too intent on winning the girls over, making sure they're happy, becoming their bestie. But what did Simone learn that terrible night in McConnell? She *isn't* their friend. She's a figure of authority. Someone to be respected, even feared.

Simone notices a squeamish expression on Tilly Benbow's face. Ditto, Willow Levy. Their mini fridges are probably packed with cans of passion fruit Truly. Madison J. gives Simone a quizzical look. As prefect on the floor, she's supposed to be informed when a room check is about to take place (so she can give the girls a heads-up, which is why nobody at Tiffin ever gets in trouble).

Simone ignores Tilly, Willow, and Madison J. and marches down the hall to Room 111. She flings open the door without knocking to find Charley—not reading like she claimed, but rather, on her phone. Simone already feels justified: Charley was lying (though *Real Americans* by Rachel Khong is splayed open next to her on the bed).

"Charley," Simone says. "I'm conducting a room check."

Charley rises to stand in the doorway, as is protocol, phone still in hand. Simone wants to grab it. *Is she texting East? Making a plan to meet later in that room down below?*

Simone opens Charley's mini fridge to find six cans of A&W Root

Beer, a package of Boursin cheese, and...an opaque white bottle. Drugs? Simone snatches it up. This is beyond her wildest dreams. What if Charley Hicks is not only Honor Boarded but expelled as well? The bottle has a typed label, listing the scientific name of the contents.

"Qu'est-ce que c'est?" Simone asks. She shakes the bottle. It's a powder, not pills.

Charley smirks, and Simone wants to slap her. How dare she make light of keeping a bottle of whatever this is in her fridge after what happened to Cinnamon Peters in this very room?

"What is it?" Simone demands. She hears whispers coming from the hallway; the girls are watching all this unfold like it's tonight's movie.

"Plant food," Charley says.

Simone deflates. Plant food—for the parlor palm, the fiddlehead fern, and all the other greenery that, for the first semester anyway, counted as Charley's only friends.

Simone replaces the plant food and slams the fridge door closed. She ransacks Charley's dresser drawers. There is vodka here somewhere, she knows it. She tears through the closet, rummaging in the duffels on the floor. She hears Olivia P. in the hall say, "Buh-bye, Miss Clavel; hello, Dolores Umbridge." In Charley's mirror, Simone sees the other girls huddled around Charley, watching as Simone rifles through Charley's boat shoes and L.L.Bean moccasins.

The Dolores Umbridge crack stings, but Simone will not be deterred. She abandons the closet and targets Charley's desk. She pulls open the top desk drawer and...stops short.

She pulls out a shiny metal tape measure, just like the one East had down in the tunnel.

Slowly, she holds it out to Charley. "What is this?"

Charley blinks. "A tape measure."

"Where did you get it?"

"I brought it from home."

A lie, Simone thinks. *She got it from East.* Simone is convinced it's the same one East used to measure the distance between her shoulders.

"What are you doing with it?"

Charley points to the wall next to her bed. "I hung up a poster I got for Christmas. I wanted to make sure it was centered."

Simone follows Charley's finger. Next to Charley's poster of Virginia Woolf is a new poster of the Brontë sisters—Charlotte, Emily, and Anne—which is annoyingly on-brand. Simone recalls hearing that Charley was named after Charlotte and Emily Brontë.

Simone squints. "Did you use *tacks?*"

"Putty," Charley says. "As specified in *The Bridle.* The kind that won't stain the paint."

Simone huffs, then resumes checking the desk drawers—extra notebooks, printer cartridges. She inspects Charley's hanging baskets, peers under the bed. Where is the vodka?

"Fine," she says, standing up. The girls in the doorway disperse. She's given them plenty of time to dispose of any contraband in their own rooms—but she doesn't care what anyone else is hiding.

Out in the hall, Madison J. touches Simone's arm. "Miss Bergeron?" she whispers. "Are you okay?"

Zip Zap alert: Turns out, Miss Bergeron wasn't always such a sterling role model. She lost her floor fellow position in her final semester of college and was disciplined by the university.

Early on Sunday morning, Simone is awakened by her phone ringing. She can't lift her head off the pillow and her mouth is chalky.

After the room check, Charley decided to go to the movies after all; the other girls treated Charley gingerly, as though she'd been the victim of some gross abuse. Olivia H-T said she felt a migraine coming on, which was just the excuse Simone needed to hang back as well, and in the darkness of her room, she drank the new bottle of wine that she'd stashed in her Hunter boots.

It was shameful, but at least she'd resisted the temptation to text East.

She grapples for the phone. It's Rhode.

Ugh, she thinks. *At eight o'clock on a Sunday morning?*

"You've been Zip Zapped," he says.

Cordelia Spooner has made a resolution: She will fix things between herself and Honey.

She invites Honey over to her cottage for Sunday supper. *I'm making my pimento cheese dip and the ham and poppy seed sliders you like. We can watch the Wild Card games in front of the fire.*

Honey says: *Sounds heavenly. I'll be over at five. Go Bills!* followed by blue and red hearts.

But five o'clock becomes five thirty, the Bills game is at halftime, the sliders are warming in the oven, and Cordelia has to put the dip back in the fridge because it's growing too soft. When is it reasonable to text and ask Honey when she's coming?

Cordelia waits until six fifteen; the Bills are up by three but the Texans are driving. She sends Honey a text: All good? She knows only too well how many last-minute distractions can pop up when you're a dorm parent for so many girls.

It takes twelve minutes for Honey to respond. I'm not going to make it, Cord. I have Simone here in my room and she's in bad shape. You saw Zip Zap?

Oh yes, Cordelia saw Zip Zap. She was secretly overjoyed to find Simone Bergeron was the victim. Something happened during her final year in college; she lost her position as floor fellow (which Cordelia assumes is similar to a prefect) and was disciplined. Is Honey getting the story?

Why don't you and Simone both come over? Cordelia writes. We can talk her through it.

Good idea! Honey says, and Cordelia pulls the dip from the fridge again. She and Honey will serve as sounding boards for poor, maligned Simone. She's so young. A person's prefrontal cortex isn't fully developed until the age of twenty-five. Simone still has an entire year to go before she reaches the age of reason.

A little while later, Honey texts again: She doesn't want to come. Sorry, Cord. Rain check.

60 Minutes is starting. Cordelia sits down in front of the TV and eats all the pimento dip herself.

On Sunday, the girls on the first and second floors give Simone side-eye—and when she suggests a group order from Moon Palace that they can eat in the common room while they binge *Below Deck,* everyone declines.

Fine, Simone thinks. She has work to do anyway.

There's a knock on her door and Simone opens it to find Ravenna Rapsicoli, pen and pad in hand.

"I'm here in my role as editor of the *'Bred Bulletin,*" she says. "Would you like to comment on either the Zip Zap post from this morning concerning the incident at the end of your collegiate career, or on your behavior during the room check last night, which certain anonymous sources called 'hostile' and 'unhinged'?"

"No," Simone says. As she closes the door in Ravenna's face, a text comes in. She hopes it's East but fears it's Rhode.

It's neither. The text is from Honey Vandermeid: If you need a friend, I'm here.

Simone has never been to Honey's room and is surprised to discover it's a suite—a bedroom and a sitting room with a kitchenette.

"Tea?" Honey says.

"Please." Simone settles on the buff suede love seat, moving a needlepoint pillow that says, *I literally can't right now.* She accepts a mug of jasmine tea from Honey.

The tea reminds Simone of her *maman,* though she's very glad her parents aren't here to witness any of this.

"I heard about the room check," Honey says. "Charley Hicks? What prompted that decision?"

"Her list in the *'Bred Bulletin,*" Simone says. "It included vodka Red Bulls."

Honey blows across the surface of her tea. Even on a Sunday in the middle of winter, Honey is impeccably put together. She's wearing an ivory cashmere turtleneck with an assortment of gold bangles on one wrist and an Apple Watch with a tortoiseshell strap on the other. Cute jeans, ballet flats. Simone is in sweatpants and her Expos T-shirt; it's what she slept in.

"Charley didn't write that list," Honey says. "Ravenna Rapsicoli did, in an attempt to make Charley seem a little more relatable to her peers."

"Ravenna wrote the whole thing?"

"The whole thing."

Ravenna was the one who wrote *orgasms* and *fifth-form repeats?* *Hmmpf.*

"Charley has been acting differently this semester," Simone says.

"She's figured it out. She's become friendly with Davi now and she's hanging with East." Honey winks. "I'd say she's too good for him but I'm kind of obsessed with him myself. Give me naughty over nice any day. More interesting."

For some reason, this makes Simone feel better. Honey is north of forty-five and she's "kind of obsessed" with East, which makes Simone being full-on obsessed with East seem almost reasonable.

"Do you want to talk about Zip Zap?" Honey asks.

Simone regards the needlepoint pillow. *I literally can't right now,* she thinks—but Honey is waiting for an answer. "It's just so... *violating,*" she says. "I'm pretty sure someone read through my email. Is that *possible*?"

"So it's true?" Honey says. "You got into some kind of trouble your final year at college?"

Oh yes, big trouble. Simone was a floor fellow at McGill, in a dorm called McConnell. A floor fellow was less than a dorm parent, but it was still a position of responsibility. Simone went through hours of training and, in return, received free room and board and a small stipend. She dealt with roommate squabbles, homesick kids, breakups, failing grades. She passed out condoms, organized ride shares for kids to get home at the holidays, sponsored taco and sushi nights, created a community. Her door had been papered and graffitied with quotes then too.

McConnell was composed of mostly U1 students, all of whom seemed impossibly naïve; Simone felt like she suddenly had twenty-four younger siblings.

The drinking age in Canada is eighteen but drinking was forbidden in the dorms, a rule that was broken every single night. Simone turned a blind eye as long as no one threw a banger.

Simone's year unfolded beautifully until reading week in May, which preceded finals and, for Simone, graduation. Simone was in her room studying for her Byzantine art final—she was scrutinizing picture after picture of the Hagia Sophia—when there was a *knock knock knock* at her door.

It was Lars Kelley, a freshman on her floor, and his friend Jasper

Stiefel, who was a junior on the hockey team. Simone knew Lars had a crush on her and she, in turn, had a crush on Jasper.

"Can I help you gentlemen?" she asked.

"We came to see if you wanted to hang," Jasper said. He opened his backpack to reveal the makings for chocolate martinis, which at that time were Simone's favorite drink if someone else was paying.

The answer should have been no. She could meet up with Lars and Jasper later at Gerts. But Simone was weary of Constantinople and Justinian I, it was spring semester, she had less than two weeks of university life left before she had to face the real world, so... what the hell, she let them in.

Jasper mixed the drinks on Simone's desk, pouring the martinis into red Solo cups. Lars declared his too sweet and produced a bottle of cheap tequila from his own backpack. Simone put on a dance mix and shed her hoodie; after a couple of martinis, she and Jasper were bouncing on her bed, Simone in just a cami and cutoffs. Lars was on the floor with the bottle of tequila. Simone remembered checking on him a couple of times to make sure he wasn't filming her. She didn't want to show up in his Snapchat stories.

The song playing was "Hello" by Martin Solveig and Dragonette. Simone and Jasper were grinding together, completely shit-faced. Simone checked on Lars but saw only his legs; his head and torso were blocked by Simone's overflowing laundry basket. She and Jasper started making out, but as soon as Jasper slid his hand up her camisole, she nudged him away and said, "Let's get Lars out of here."

They couldn't wake Lars up. At first, Simone thought he was playing around or intentionally cockblocking Jasper—but then Simone started to panic. *Call 911!* she told Jasper. Lars was completely unresponsive.

The paramedics came; the entire dorm clotted the halls. A girl named Celine, who had a robust Instagram following, took a sweeping video of the empty bottles, the Solo cups, Simone's duvet on the floor, and the McConnell floor fellow Simone Bergeron in her cami and cutoffs, crying into her hands.

Lars's blood alcohol was 0.42. He'd imbibed over half the bottle of tequila while in Simone's room.

Simone immediately lost her fellow position and had to move out with less than two weeks of school left. After Celine's video circulated, none of Simone's friends wanted to shelter her, so she ended up confessing what had happened to her parents and moving back home to Saint-Henri. She bombed her finals, her GPA suffered, and she met with the provost, who said she would receive her diploma but would not be allowed to walk at graduation. Lars's parents filed a civil suit against Simone, and Simone had to hire a lawyer. The suit went nowhere because Lars was eighteen and had bought the tequila himself. There were moments when Simone felt indignant: *I did nothing wrong! They interrupted me! It was all their idea!* Simone didn't force or even encourage Lars to drink the tequila.

But she was the floor fellow. It had all happened in her room while she was present. Her job was to make sure the students on her floor *didn't* go to the hospital with alcohol poisoning. She had failed.

"There was an incident in the dorm where I was a floor fellow," Simone tells Honey now. "A kid drank too much on my watch. He was fine, but the university needed someone to blame." She hates making it sound like she was scapegoated—but she can't very well tell Honey Vandermeid the truth. It would make Honey think that Simone had issues with alcohol and younger men.

Honey leans in and gives Simone a hug. "You poor thing," she says.

Bright and early Monday morning, Cordelia Spooner calls the provost at McGill, identifying herself as the "Assistant Head" at Tiffin

Academy. "We recently realized we missed an important piece of due diligence," she says. "Could you fill in some blanks for me about a 2023 McGill graduate named Simone Bergeron? We've learned she lost her position as floor fellow, and I'm hoping you can share what happened. I ask because Miss Bergeron is now teaching at our academy and also serving as dorm parent to forty teenage girls."

Audre is at her laptop googling *Tiffin Academy*. Nothing worrisome turns up—and the post in The Cut about the inquiry has magically disappeared.

Audre releases a breath. Jesse Eastman must have called a fixer and scrubbed the internet of any bad press regarding *America Today*.

If Jesse is capable of this, Audre thinks, *what else is he capable of?* She's becoming more and more concerned that he had something to do with Tiffin's ranking.

"Audre?"

Audre spins in her chair to find Cordelia Spooner in the doorway. "Tell me some good news, Cordelia."

"The Bills beat the Texans," Cordelia says, though she knows Audre is a fan of the New Orleans Saints, a team for which there is presently no hope. "Other than that, I'm afraid the news is not so great. I assume you saw yesterday's Zip Zap about Simone Bergeron?"

Audre closes her eyes and nods. She's been trying not to think about this because, back in August, she was in such a hurry to fill the history position that she didn't confirm *any* details on Simone's résumé; Simone could be Anna Delvey for all Audre knows.

"I just spoke to the provost at McGill," Cordelia says. "Simone served as a floor fellow in the dorms, and at the end of the year she entertained two male students in her room, one of them a freshman on her floor. The student drank himself unconscious, and Simone and the other student were, apparently, too intoxicated themselves to notice. Simone was dismissed from her position, although she was allowed to graduate."

Audre exhales. Thank god for that much. "The student survived? He was okay, no brain damage?"

"He was fine, as far as I know," Cordelia says. "The parents filed a lawsuit, which was dismissed."

Also good news, Audre thinks.

"I found a video online of the scene in Simone's room that night," Cordelia says. "It's pretty incriminating. Would you like to see it?"

"Absolutely not."

"Audre, this is a person we've put in charge of our students…"

Audre says, "Simone Bergeron has done a good job since she's been here. She deserves a little grace for past lapses in judgment." Audre pauses. "We all do."

"Very well," Cordelia says. "I just thought you'd want to be aware."

"Thank you, Cordelia," Audre says. When Cordelia leaves, Audre thinks how remarkable it is that Cordelia Spooner could dig up all that information before the day has even begun. With those kind of sleuthing skills, why can't she figure out who's behind Zip Zap?

February

19. That's So Fetch

No one ever asks Olivia H-T for her opinion. It's just assumed by the girls on the first floor of South (which basically constitutes Olivia's entire universe) that Olivia thinks whatever Davi thinks.

But with the announcement of the school musical, this changes.

Mr. Chuy has chosen *Mean Girls.* Everyone predicts that Taylor Wilson will play Cady and Davi will play Regina George. Olivia H-T will probably end up getting the part of Regina's lackey Gretchen, which would be the definition of typecasting.

The night before tryouts, Davi shocks everyone by saying that she isn't going out for the musical this year because she wants to focus on her studies.

Olivia H-T is hurt enough that she closes the door to her room so no one sees her tears. Davi isn't just choosing her studies over the musical; she's choosing Charley over Olivia. Davi and Charley had a random bonding moment right before the Kringle, one Olivia H-T hoped would vanish once Davi realized how truly weird Charley was. (She's a plant lady! A bookworm!) But in the new year, Charley has emerged victorious—not only because she has somehow won Davi's devotion but also because she's hanging with East, which Olivia H-T can't believe is a real thing.

Olivia knows everyone expects her to say she's not going out for the play either—but for once, Olivia H-T is going to do something on her own.

And guess what? She slays her audition, and despite the fact that Olivia H-T does not fit the role in either traditional beauty or social status, she is cast as Regina George.

Olivia pretends it's no big deal as everyone on the floor—including Davi, including Charley, including Miss Bergeron—congratulates her. But as soon as she's alone in her room, she jumps up and down, silently screaming, *That's so fetch!*

Zip Zap post: The Harkness Society would like to welcome new members... Hakeem Pryce and Cassie Lee.

The newest Zip Zap post comes out on a Saturday evening in February. Valentine's Day has come and gone (Head Prefect Lisa Kim mentioned something about Candygrams one morning in Chapel, but then she got deferred Early Decision 2 at Tulane and was so despondent about it, she forgot to order the candy), and it's weeks until spring break. In other words: Welcome to Tiffin's bleakest time of year.

Taylor Wilson receives the Zip Zap alert just like everyone else. Hakeem and Cassie have joined the Harkness Society. Taylor isn't sure why she's so jealous. Hakeem and Cassie are always breaking the No PDA rule (forbidden: page 3 of *The Bridle*) and making out in the halls of the Schoolhouse, so joining the Harkness Society is the obvious next step. Taylor supposes she's jealous because Hakeem has now lost his virginity and Taylor hasn't. She hasn't even come close.

The alert addles Taylor so much that she considers going home for the weekend, but home is Philadelphia, which isn't realistic. So instead, Taylor plucks a well-hidden "water" bottle from the back of her mini fridge. It contains Casamigos tequila that she pilfered from her parents' bar cart over the holidays. She grabs a bag of tortilla chips and a jar of salsa from her hanging baskets and texts Dub. I'm coming over.

K, Dub responds.

When Taylor gets to Dub's room, he's lying in the near-dark playing "exile" by Taylor Swift and Bon Iver. He has the room lit only by the electric candles they used at the Kringle; he'd swiped a bunch at the end, telling Taylor they would be such a vibe in his room this winter. He was right: They add a romantic glow to an otherwise dreary evening. Are the music and the candlelight for her? Oh, how she wishes this were true, but somehow she knows they're not.

"Hey." She closes the door because Mr. Rivera wasn't at his post and didn't see her come in. She plops in the middle of the floor and opens her backpack. "Trifecta," she says. "Tequila, Late July salt and lime chips, and Mikey V's seven-pot salsa."

"No way." Dub joins her on the floor. She hands him the bottle and he takes a slug. "Woof. Limes would have been nice."

Taylor swallows some tequila herself. It's sooooo gross. Tequila tastes like dirt and Taylor can't understand why the world doesn't agree with her, but it's her parents' preferred poison, and beggars can't be choosers.

"You saw Zip Zap?" She pulls open the bag of chips.

"Yup."

"I can't believe he lost his virginity to a random third-former," Taylor says. She dips a chip into the salsa, which sets her mouth ablaze; the discomfort is welcome.

"It wasn't his virginity," Dub says. "Probably hers, though."

Taylor pulls from the tequila again. "It *was* his virginity."

"No," Dub says. "He told me he lost it to some chick at Dartmouth. The student athletic trainer. During his recruiting trip last semester."

Involuntarily, Taylor moans.

"I'm sorry I didn't tell you," Dub says. "I wasn't sure you'd want to know."

"I don't care," Taylor says. To prove her point, she dips another chip and chases it with more tequila. She's starting to feel it now. "I'm the reason he and I aren't together anymore." She looks at Dub, who is staring at his knees. Since football season, his hair has grown back all curly and wild and she longs to run her hands through it. "I don't want Hakeem, Dub. I want…"

"Today is Cinnamon's birthday," Dub says. "February twenty-first. She would have been seventeen."

"Oh god," Taylor says. "I didn't know." But then she recalls the year before, Cinnamon's sweet sixteen. Davi made a pink balloon arch outside 111 South. Cinnamon and Taylor had both been in rehearsals for *Grease,* and Dub had shown up in the auditorium with an ice cream cake from the Carvel in Haydensboro.

"It's okay," Dub says, though obviously it's not okay. This explains the darkened room, the candles, the maudlin playlist. The song now playing is "Jar of Hearts."

Taylor offers Dub the bottle again. He drinks, then attacks the chips and salsa. Taylor watches him eat the snacks she brought him; she feels like such a trad wife.

She hits the tequila for what is probably the fourth or fifth shot; she's to the point where she doesn't even notice how disgusting it is.

Taylor is smart like Cinnamon, she now has the lead in the musical like Cinnamon, she even considered dyeing her hair auburn over the holidays, but then decided that was psycho.

Taylor's and Dub's hands brush when they both reach into the chip bag; Dub pulls away, saying, "Go ahead."

Taylor lifts his chin so he's looking at her. "Why do you never touch me?"

Dub chugs what's left in the water bottle, then shakes his head and gasps. "I have something to tell you," he says. "But you can't tell another fucking soul."

"Okay?" Taylor says.

"Taylor."

"Okay!" she says. "I won't, I promise."

He studies her, shakes his head.

"Do you not trust me? We're best friends, Dub."

She's nearly drunk enough to say *I love you,* but not quite.

"Fuck it," Dub says. "I have to tell someone because this thing is eating me alive."

"What is?"

He opens the laptop on his desk. He brings up his Gmail account and scrolls through a thousand marketing messages from every athletic brand in America: Nike, Under Armour, Rawlings. He dives all the way back into the previous spring. Taylor makes two fists. May 20, May 17, then finally, she sees it. May 12 from Cinnamon Peters. Subject line: DO NOT OPEN THIS FILE UNTIL THE MORNING OF OUR GRADUATION.

He clicks on the message and Taylor reads:

> I mean it, Dub. Save this in the vault until May 29, 2027. You're the only one I can trust. I love you and you're going to be fine, I promise.
>
> Cin.

Below is an attachment.

"What is it?" Taylor says.

"I haven't opened it, obviously."

"What do you *think* it is?" Taylor asks. "A letter, maybe, to our class?"

"I don't know, Tay," he says. "She asked me not to open it until next May and I'm not going to." He runs a hand down his face. "But just having access to it is driving me fucking crazy."

Right, Taylor thinks. *It's the ultimate clickbait: a message from beyond the grave. It has to be a suicide note, right? An explanation? No wonder it's driving Dub crazy.* Taylor would have opened the attachment the minute she saw it. Cinnamon forfeited her right to tell anyone what to do when she took the pills. But Dub, of course, doesn't see it that way. Dub is a person of honor and integrity who will obey Cinnamon Peters's final wish.

"Thank you for sharing it with me," Taylor says. "I'm a safe place."

Dub nods solemnly and clicks out of his email. "I feel better now that you know," he says. "I told my mom too, but that's not the same."

"You didn't tell Hakeem? Or Davi?"

"Hell no."

Taylor grabs Dub around the midsection and presses her head against his chest. His arms close around her just as she hoped, but she can feel the tension in his muscles — it's restraint, maybe even resistance. The reason he never touches Taylor has nothing to do with some bro code or his devotion to Hakeem. Dub never touches her because this other thing has him all knit up.

He's obsessed with a ghost.

When Charley walks into the *'Bred Bulletin* office, she sees Grady and Levi huddled together in front of the computer. As soon as they notice her, they click out of whatever they were ogling and try to act casual.

"Where's Ravenna?" Charley asks.

"She has rehearsal every afternoon from now until the musical," Levi says.

That's right, Charley thinks. Ravenna was cast in *Mean Girls* as the weirdo outsider Janis, a role she's been coveting since attending theater camp on Broadway when she was ten.

"So it's just us," Grady says.

"What were you two doing just now?" Charley asks. "Playing video games?" Both Grady and Levi are regulars at the arcade in the Teddy.

"No," Grady says.

"Were you...watching porn?"

"Orgasms are In," Levi says, which makes Grady hoot.

Charley can't believe she's been left to babysit these two.

"Do either of you have ideas for articles?" she asks. "We should try to get an issue out before spring break."

"Ravenna wants a review of the musical," Grady says. "But she told me she's going to write it herself."

"Unbiased journalism is a hallmark of the *'Bred Bulletin*," Charley deadpans. The boys just bob their heads. "Anything else?"

"Why do *we* always have to come up with ideas?" Levi asks. Clearly, Ravenna's absence has emboldened him. "We're third-formers. You're a fifth-former."

"Your life is more interesting," Grady says. "Especially now."

Charley doesn't have to ask what he means. He means now that Charley has become Davi's confidante, now that she and East are hanging out.

Charley can't very well write an article about herself, although she'll be the first to admit, her transition from friendless weirdo to a person who is in the company of the two most popular kids at school is newsworthy. And yet, Charley is wary. She knows that at any moment the spell could break — Davi could drop her, or East could. For this reason, she's tried to remain indifferent to both Davi's and East's attention. Charley and Davi study together at the Sink. Sometimes East joins them, sometimes he doesn't. Some nights East texts Charley the green downward arrow and on those nights she lies to Davi, saying she's staying in her room to read when really she's sneaking down to the bomb shelter. Davi never questions this and

Charley knows it's because she's too busy guarding her own secret. There are now calluses on Davi's knuckles, which is a bulimia tell. When Charley ran a gentle fingertip over the calluses, Davi snatched her hand back and said, "They're rough from the cold. They always get like this in winter."

"Davi," Charley said.

Charley can sort of understand why Davi likes her. Davi is sick of everyone else on the floor, she's tired of people like Tilly Benbow and Olivia H-T tracking her every move.

East is harder to figure out. Every night before Charley falls asleep, she wonders, *Why me?* She knows he likes spending time with her and they definitely have chemistry, but doesn't East have chemistry with *everyone*? There's no *way* Charley is the only girl in his life; she figures he must have girlfriends everywhere — back in New York City for sure, maybe at other high schools and colleges. Charley is just the person he's passing the time with while he's stuck at Tiffin.

The only place East ever kisses her is in the bomb shelter. "Are you embarrassed to kiss me aboveground?" she asked him one night. Her tone is light but she wants to know: Why can't they just Intervis like other couples?

He'd kissed her eyelids, the tip of her nose, and then, very lightly, her lips. "Everyone hooks up during Intervis. Only you and I come down here. It's our place. It's special. Do you really want me to take you to God's Basement and have Mr. James catch me with my hand down your pants?"

Charley had blushed; they haven't gone that far yet. Tiffin doesn't have an ice hockey team but East jokes that Charley is the best goalie in the school. She allows above-the-waist touching only, although she's always wet straight through the crotch of her pants; she can feel East's erection against her leg and sometimes her belly. She wants him — but she fears that as soon as she gives it up, he'll drop her. With each passing day, the idea of life without East becomes more unthinkable. For the first time, Charley understands her mother and Joey. This kind of desire changes your brain chemistry. It makes you do stupid things.

To Grady and Levi, Charley says, "My life isn't that interesting." She sighs. "Ravenna likes listicles. Why don't you guys rank every flavor of milkshake at the Grille?"

They look at her, then at the computer in front of them.

"Fine, stay here and watch more porn, what do I care? *I'll* go get a milkshake." Before she leaves the office, she tries to imagine what Ravenna would do. "No whacking off!" she calls out over her shoulder.

They're so engrossed by the screen, they don't even hear her.

March

20. Mean Girls

The school musical runs the first weekend of March. On Friday night, all Tiffin students are required to attend.

At the entrance to the auditorium, Madison J. hands out programs. Students normally come to the auditorium for second-run movies and assemblies—guest speakers, the ill-fated hypnotist, a visiting local author who read for an entire hour (fifty-nine minutes too long)—but tonight, the usual laughing, roughhousing, and jockeying for seats are replaced by respectful whispers and an underlying thrum of anticipation: Everyone wants the cast to succeed.

Davi buys a pack of Twizzlers from the concession stand but Charley grimaces and says, "I hate licorice."

"I wasn't planning on sharing," Davi says.

They find seats close to the stage but far enough back that they won't have to crane their necks. The other girls from their floor—those who aren't in the cast—have claimed the front row of the balcony, but Davi has no interest in joining them.

Davi stands back and lets Charley sit. "I'm an aisle hog, sorry."

When the house lights dim, the audience goes wild. Mr. Chuy comes out onstage and runs through etiquette reminders: No catcalling, no cell phone usage of any kind, but especially no flash and no name-shouting. "I know it's rousing to see your classmates onstage when you're used to seeing them in the Paddock and the dorms," he says, "but it's distracting and may cause our actors to involuntarily break character, which no one wants to see happen." He brings his hands to prayer. "Thank you in advance for your courtesy and attention. And now, it is our pleasure to bring you... *Mean Girls*!"

During the ensuing cheers, Davi tears open the package of licorice and shoves a piece in her mouth while Charley tries to mask her revulsion; it smells like plastic.

When the curtain lifts, all thoughts of licorice and Mr. Chuy's unfortunate choice of the word *rousing* evaporate and Charley becomes engrossed by what's unfolding onstage. She has seen the movie *Mean Girls,* though it's not a religion for her the way it apparently is for Davi. ("I can recite every line verbatim," Davi said earlier. "Please don't," Charley replied.)

Taylor Wilson is a natural as Cady Heron, the new student who shows up straight from Africa. (This has always seemed like such a random thread of the plot to Charley. Whose parents are *zoologists*?) Ravenna Rapsicoli is serviceable as Janis, though Charley fidgets in her seat, wanting to shout out director's notes: *Clearer! Snarkier!* She feels like she's watching her own child onstage.

The most curious casting, of course, is Olivia H-T as Regina George. However, the second Olivia steps onstage, she commands attention. Her carriage is haughty, her tone catty but somehow not abrasive. She's trailed by her lackeys Gretchen (Willow Levy) and Karen (Annabelle Tuckerman, who plays a bubblehead with sharp comic timing).

With each passing scene, Charley grows more and more uncomfortable. She can't help feeling that, in her portrayal of Regina George, Olivia H-T is channeling Davi. Davi is, after all, Tiffin's queen bee. Davi makes the rules, not anything as overt as "On Wednesdays, we wear pink," but she sets the agenda and influences the school's taste in all things. Charley sneaks a look at Davi, who is stuffing licorice in her mouth while watching the stage. She seems unbothered, but can she be blind to the parallels? Is anyone else in the audience connecting the dots between Regina George and Davi? Then Charley is struck with an even worse thought: If Davi is Regina George, then Charley is Cady Heron, the new girl who shows up from a faraway land (such as Towson, Maryland) and gets sucked into Regina's orbit.

Is Charley being ridiculous? She can't tell. She wishes East were here. The "entire" school is required to attend the musical—skipping it would result in a missed commitment—but East is, as ever, exempt from this rule. Charley knows he's down in the bomb shelter installing trim around the doorframes and replacing the industrial stainless steel sink with a hammered copper basin.

During intermission, Davi stands up and stretches. "I'm getting Milk Duds," she says. "Want anything?"

"No, thanks," Charley says.

Backstage, Olivia H-T is so high on adrenaline she feels like she's levitating. The audience loves the show. They love *her*. Olivia H-T only cares what Davi thinks. Olivia H-T projects all her lines toward Davi; she sings every song for Davi. And for Charley as well. Olivia wants Charley to realize that Olivia is a force.

In the second act, during Olivia's big number, "World Burn," Davi gets up and walks out of the auditorium. Olivia H-T tries not to let her attention wander; she needs to stay locked in, maybe it wasn't Davi, maybe it was someone else who left, the lights are in Olivia's eyes, and she has to focus on hitting her notes. But when the song ends and the audience cheers, Olivia H-T sees that Davi's seat is empty and Charley's neck is craned toward the exit. Then Charley too gets up and leaves.

What the fuck? Olivia H-T thinks.

Charley checks the girls' room outside the auditorium but finds only third-former Cassie Lee crying to one of her little friends. "Hakeem can't stop saying how good Taylor's acting is!" Cassie says. "I'm so over it!"

Charley checks the bathroom upstairs next to the Grille. Empty.

She rushes outside and runs down the path to the Sink. She takes the stairs two at a time and pushes into the third-floor bathroom in time to hear the strangled sound of Davi purging.

Charley waits in silence until Davi emerges.

"Fuck," Davi says.

"I'm not standing by one more day." Charley's eyes burn with tears. "You need help." Davi's skin is gray and all she wears now are oversize sweatshirts so nobody will see how thin she's getting. "If you don't seek help tonight, I'll tell someone. I'll tell Miss Bergeron and Ms. Robinson. I'll tell the whole school."

Davi stares at Charley in the mirror. She wants to tell her to go to hell. Charley doesn't need to save Davi. It's the other way around — Davi's saving Charley from being the single weirdest person ever to attend Tiffin.

But the thing is, Davi *wants* to stop purging. The licorice came back up in lurid red clumps, nearly choking her. Her teeth feel perpetually furry and she's pretty sure she's destroying the lining of her esophagus. Maybe the resentment she's feeling toward Charley right now is just her denial of the obvious: She has to stop.

"Okay," she says. "I will."

"You can't just tell me that and..."

"Charley," she says. "I promise."

When Davi and Charley walk into Classic South, everyone is giving Taylor and Olivia H-T their flowers, literally and figuratively. Olivia H-T is still in her stage makeup and her costume.

Charley squeezes Davi's hand, then retires to her room. Davi navigates the mayhem, grateful that in all the celebration, no one noticed she and Charley were missing.

Miss Bergeron enters with a box of cheeseburgers and fried chicken sandwiches, courtesy of Chef Haz. "Feast in the common room!" she says.

Davi slips into her room and closes the door. She gazes at her pink neon wall sign that reads THIS IS WHERE THE MAGIC HAPPENS and thinks, *I'm such a phony.*

She opens her laptop and composes an email to Dr. Pringle, the school psychologist. He and Davi had a series of conversations after Cinnamon died. The last time they spoke, Dr. Pringle patted Davi on the shoulder and said, "You're a well-wrapped young lady, Davi Banerjee."

This is one of the best compliments Davi has ever received. *Well-wrapped:* It spoke to her curated appearance but also acknowledged that her insides were in order, her priorities straight, her vision unclouded.

In the subject line, Davi types: Unwrapped.

> Dear Dr. Pringle—
> I'd like to schedule an appointment to chat on Monday if possible.

Davi stares at the blinking cursor. Dr. Pringle obviously knows about Cinnamon and also about Davi's dreadful PSAT score, but he knows nothing about the situation with her parents. Davi shudders as she imagines telling him.

What Davi wants is a referral to someone else, a stranger.

> Since the start of the school year, I've had trouble keeping food down. I wouldn't say I have a full-blown eating disorder,

but I should probably talk to someone before it gets any worse. I'm hoping you can refer me to a specialist? My free period is D or I can make myself available after school.

Thank you.

Davi Banerjee

Just as Davi hits send, the door to her room flies open and Olivia H-T steps in. Davi blinks: Normally, girls on the floor knock before they come into Davi's room in case she's filming a TikTok. Being the star of the musical has given Olivia H-T some *moxie* ("force of character, nerve"). Her eyes are flashing, her cheeks blaze bright pink — or maybe that's just her makeup.

"Hey," Davi says. She quickly checks the screen: message sent. Then she pauses. Did Charley tell Olivia H-T?

"You left the show," Olivia H-T says. "Right in the middle of my song."

So much for leaving undetected, Davi thinks. "I know, sorry. I had to go to the bathroom, then it was so close to the end, I didn't think it was worth disrupting to come back in."

Olivia H-T glares at her. "You'll come back tomorrow night?"

Again? Davi thinks. Saturday night the musical opens to the public; all the olds from Haydensboro and Capulet Falls come.

"My cousin Roddick will be there," Olivia H-T says.

Roddick: the cute singer from last year's Tiffinpalooza. It's tempting, sort of.

"Thanks," Davi says. "But I have to study."

"Don't you want to see the end of the show?" Olivia asks.

Davi gives Olivia the most patient of smiles. "I know how it ends. Thanks, Olivia."

Zip Zap alert: Finally, an answer to the question everyone has been asking all year. How does Davi Banerjee eat so much and stay so thin? She sticks her finger down her throat.

Saturday morning, Charley holds her breath as she opens the Zip Zap alert. East seems pretty confident he's immune to Zip Zap, but Charley thinks his attitude is naïve. Zip Zap doesn't care who he is. Nobody at Tiffin is off-limits.

Charley reads the post and—although she considers herself above dramatic gestures—screams into her hands. She races down the hallway; it's so early, nobody else is awake. She taps lightly on Davi's door before easing it open.

Davi is sitting on her bed in her pale pink Roller Rabbit pajama set, which reveals just how thin she's gotten. Charley has noticed that lately, in the bathroom, Davi always wears her bathrobe.

She's bent in half, staring at her phone.

"Davi," Charley whispers. "Oh my god."

Davi raises her face; her eyes look like obsidian marbles. "Get out."

"What?" Charley says. "Davi, it wasn't me. I didn't say a word to anyone, I swear."

"Get the fuck out," Davi says. "Nobody *knew* except you. You threatened me! Maybe you thought I didn't take you seriously but I came home and emailed Dr. Pringle..."

"Maybe Dr. Pringle told someone," Charley says.

"Dr. Pringle didn't tell anyone," Davi says. "Have you never heard of HIPAA?"

"It wasn't me," Charley says. "I swear on my life."

"You told East."

"I didn't!"

"You're the only person who knows," Davi says. "Or you were, until now." Her eyes fill with tears. "It's a private issue and now all of Tiffin is going to be gossiping about it, pretending to *pity* me but deep down, thinking I'm pathetic."

Charley can't deny this is probably true. Maybe the girls on the floor weren't asleep; maybe they were just afraid to come out of their rooms.

"I care about you too much to have betrayed your confidence like this," Charley says. "We're friends, Davi."

"We *were* friends," Davi says. "But you can go back to your plants and your books. I'm done."

"I can't believe you think this was me," Charley says. But, looking at it objectively, who else could it be? The timing is so incriminating. Charley cringes as she replays her words: *I'll tell the whole school.* "I'm not Zip Zap and I don't know who is. It's like Big Brother is out there, watching us. They probably read your email to Dr. Pringle."

"Charley," Davi says, and her voice sounds sort of normal, which gives Charley hope. "Would you please get the fuck out?"

That night, it's Charley who sends the green arrow to East. She's been holed up in her room most of the day; the one time she ventured to the bathroom, she bumped into Tilly Benbow, who wrinkled her nose and said, "You're disgusting."

Charley, who has always found Tilly irrelevant and vacuous, was surprised at how much those words hurt. "It wasn't me, Tilly," she said, but Tilly sniffed and stormed out.

The first-floor girls' take on that morning's Zip Zap is that Davi deserves to deal with her eating disorder discreetly and Charley made it public in the most grotesque way. She won't be able to dissuade them from this position, at least not until the person behind Zip Zap is outed.

Charley is friendless now, just as she was for most of the first semester—but it's worse now that Charley knows what having a friend feels like.

She hears the girls leave for the auditorium. Everyone is being extra solicitous of Davi, who, apparently, will be sitting with Olivia H-T's super-hot cousin at the second night of *Mean Girls*. *Good for her,* Charley thinks. As soon as everyone has left the dorm, Charley pulls a red Sharpie from her desk drawer and marches down to Miss Bergeron's room. Miss Bergeron repapered her door at the start of the new term and it's still mostly blank; writing down quotes has lost its novelty.

Charley picks a spot at eye level and writes: *"I think most of humankind would agree, the hard part of high school is the people."* —Demon Copperhead, *Barbara Kingsolver*

By the time she gets back to her room, East has liked her text. Charley exhales and heads downstairs.

She planned on using their time as a distraction—going down to the tunnel is like leaving Tiffin altogether—but as soon as Charley walks into the bomb shelter and sees East hand-sanding the pieces of door trim, she bursts into tears.

"Oh, Charles," he says, opening his arms. "Come here."

He runs his hands up and down her back and breathes into her hair. She bawls in a way she hasn't since her father died, and this thought alone makes the tears subside. What does any of this matter, compared to losing her father? It's a tiny blip. Davi is upset, she's going through something hard, and now the whole school knows it. Of course she's angry, of course she's blaming Charley.

East goes to the bathroom for toilet paper so Charley can blow her nose.

"Do you want to talk about it?" he asks.

Charley can't imagine boring him with the whole story. East goes to school with them but he seems above the fray; it's what she loves most about him.

She can't believe she just thought the word "love."

"No," she says nasally.

"Okay, then," he says, kissing her eyes, her nose, her lips. "Come help me sand."

21. Head's Holiday

The Zip Zap post about Davi Banerjee sends Audre into a tailspin. Is *nothing* off-limits? She reaches out to Big East, describing the problem and asking for solutions. Does he know anyone who can figure out how to shut Zip Zap down?

I tried to ban the app schoolwide, she writes, and got called out for censorship.

Jesse Eastman responds: It took six seasons to figure out who Gossip Girl was.

Audre shows the email exchange to Cordelia Spooner. "This response is so absurd that I wonder if *Big East* is Zip Zap."

"He can't be," Cordelia says. "Remember the geofencing." She lowers her voice. "It's someone in our midst."

As if Zip Zap isn't bad enough, Audre receives a letter from ISNEC secretary Mikayla Ekubo saying that *America Today* has agreed to comply with their inquiry and be fully transparent about how the rankings were decided upon this year. Audre considers responding with bravado: *Wonderful, I look forward to seeing our legitimacy verified!* But she can't quite bring herself to do it.

On Tuesday morning, not long before spring break, Audre awakens to a startling sight out her bedroom window. After months of freezing rain, sleet, bitter winds, gunmetal skies, and flurries, Tiffin has been blessed with a proper snow. The entire campus is blanketed in white.

Audre hurries to her computer and sends a schoolwide email.

> Today will be a Head's Holiday: All classes and commitments are canceled. Enjoy the snow, Thoroughbreds!

By midmorning, the Pasture has been turned into a toboggan run. Sixth-former Teague Baldwin finds a couple of Radio Flyers and a half-dozen plastic saucers in the field house storage room, and the third- and fourth-formers go rocketing down the hill, then run back up. Rhode Rivera watches the kids from his window; he fondly recalls snow days when he was a student at Tiffin—which gives him an idea. He texts Simone: Want to go cross-country skiing? I know some trails behind the school.

He expects her to decline with some feeble excuse—she's organizing a knitting circle for the girls on her floor—but the response he receives is Oui! I have skis, where should I meet you?

There's something magical about a snow day, Cordelia thinks. She takes a long, hot bath accompanied by an Irish coffee, then bundles up in cozy layers: cotton turtleneck, ancient L.L.Bean fisherman sweater, down parka, long johns, snow pants, duck boots. She sets out feeling unfettered for the first time in months; she has no agenda other than to wander the campus and appreciate the beauty of the day. The sky is a lovely pewter color and snowflakes drift gently down, distinct against the stark black woods. The first two people Cordelia encounters are Mr. Rivera and Miss Bergeron on their cross-country skis. They're chugging along, red-cheeked and smiling, Simone in a cute hat with a pom-pom.

Hello! Bonjour! Exhilarating... such good exercise... just out for a walk myself, wish I had snowshoes... have fun! Cordelia is delighted to see Rhode and Simone together. Maybe a romance is brewing after all...?

She passes Taylor Wilson and Dub Austin overseeing a bunch of the underclassmen football players in the making of a giant snowman outside the Teddy. She waves and carries on. Mr. James is out on his riding snowblower, clearing the paths.

Cordelia pretends like she doesn't have a destination, but of course she does: Jewel Pond. This is where Cordelia finds Honey figure skating. Annabelle Tuckerman and Ravenna Rapsicoli are out on the ice as well, and while they're both competent skaters, they aren't nearly as skilled or as elegant as Honey. She skates backward and executes an axel jump, then goes into a sitting spin. Cordelia claps and cheers. She's consumed by love.

East texts Charley the downward arrow. Charley had planned to dive into *Doctor Zhivago,* but instead she gets dressed and heads to the cellar. Even though it's the middle of the day. Even though anyone could follow her footprints. Head's Holiday feels like a free-for-all; nobody is checking where they are, it's an opportunity they would be stupid to waste.

When Charley gets to the bomb shelter, she finds that East has unrolled a Persian rug and on top of the rug, a fleece blanket from his room.

Lana Del Rey plays from a wireless speaker, and the chandelier is set low on its dimmer.

East kisses her and they lie down side by side on the fleece blanket. *This is it,* Charley thinks. *The seduction scene.*

The instant Charley strips off her sweater and turtleneck, East's mouth is all over her. He takes off his own flannel and T-shirt. Their bare chests touch for the first time and it's both so tender and so erotic, Charley wants to cry out. East fiddles with the button of her jeans, and she grabs his wrist.

"Is it okay?" he asks.

"If we do this, you can't break up with me," she says. "You can't ghost me. You can't *hurt* me, East."

"I won't, Charles," he says. "Trust."

Is there a more romantic way to lose her virginity than in the bomb shelter with East on a Head's Holiday while the rest of the school is having a snowball fight?

She pushes off her jeans, then her underwear. She keeps her eyes open because this moment happens only once in a person's life and she wants to remember everything.

Dinner Service, Snow Day!

Tuesday, March 10

Cheesy breadsticks and frosted garlic bread

SALAD BAR

Tonight's additions: grapefruit and blood orange segments, fresh sliced avocado, chili-crunch cucumbers

SOUP OF THE DAY
Vegetarian chili

ENTRÉES
Chicken pot pie with herbed pastry, beef stew

DESSERTS
Snow cones (grape, cherry), Baked Alaska

When Rhode and Simone enter the Paddock for dinner, Simone scans the room for East. She finds him cozied up in the Booth with Charley. Simone immediately senses something different about the two of them. A new intimacy. East buries his face in Charley's hair; the two of them are sharing a bowl of stew, a plate of salad. The Booth is high-profile seating. They're Tiffin-official.

"The chicken pot pie sounds amazing," Rhode says. "Where should we sit?"

"I'm going to sit with my girls," Simone says.

"But..." Rhode says. "We had such a nice day together."

"We did," Simone says. "Thank you for inviting me skiing, it was just what I needed." The snow day made Simone feel like her younger self. In college, Simone used to cross-country ski up Mont-Royal, then go for a beer and *frites* on rue Bishop. She enjoyed Rhode's company while they were skiing—why can't that be enough? Why does he always have to act like she owes him something more?

She watches East feed Charley a section of orange with his fingers.

"Actually I think I'm going to take dinner back to my room," Simone says. "I'm beat."

Rhode's expression is one of barely concealed annoyance. "Have a good night," he says.

Oh, she will, she thinks. The wine in her boot awaits.

Zip Zap post: When Andrew Eastman asks Charley Hicks to "go down," she likes it.

When Charley gets up to pee in the middle of the night, she bumps into Tilly Benbow in the bathroom. Normally they would ignore each other, but this time, Tilly says, "Hey." Charley turns to look at her in the mirror. Tilly makes a lewd hand gesture while poking her tongue into her cheek.

This is a new low even for Tilly, who is famous for being vulgar, but it's two in the morning, so maybe Tilly is sleepwalking, or Charley is dreaming.

But after Charley wakes up and reads the new Zip Zap post, it makes sense. **When Andrew Eastman asks Charley Hicks to "go down," she likes it.**

Zip Zap has seen the downward arrows East texted her, and her response of thumbs-upping them, and Zip Zap thinks it's a reference to blow jobs. Charley knows she should be embarrassed, but all she feels is relief that their real secret is safe.

Then the comments start rolling in.

I knew that girl was a freak in the sheets!

I'd love her to polish MY knob.

East can do better (and probably does).

Charley pretends to be elevated but she's as common as a back-alley whore.

Charley suspects this last comment is Davi, though she has no way to prove it. She needs to remain stoic; however, it feels supremely unfair that the Tiffin community, who haven't commented on a Zip Zap post since Annabelle Tuckerman, are now piling on her.

There's a knock at the door. Charley holds out hope that it's Taylor or Madison J. or someone else offering support and solidarity (this is textbook slut-shaming!)—but when Charley opens the door, she finds Miss Bergeron.

"Yes?" Charley's tone is icy; she hasn't forgiven Miss Bergeron for the arbitrary room search.

"You do realize I could write you an infraction for making a public space private," Miss Bergeron says.

Charley takes her time gathering her hair in a ponytail. "I'm sorry, what?"

"The Zip Zap post," Miss Bergeron says. "You and East?"

"Wait, I'm confused," Charley says. "You're threatening to give me an infraction because of something that was posted on Zip Zap?"

"Everything on Zip Zap has turned out to be true," Miss Bergeron says. "So I assume that's the case here. You've been breaking school rules."

Charley shrugs. "Zip Zap got it wrong this time."

Miss Bergeron glares at her with what seems like contempt. But why? Because Charley doesn't like to rot her teeth with Starbursts or her mind with *Love Island*? Because Charley alone *doesn't* think Miss Bergeron is fierce? She's a mediocre teacher and she tries too hard to be liked by the girls on the floor. The Zip Zap post about Miss Bergeron herself must have been true—she got disciplined in college and lost her floor fellow position. Did anyone write up an infraction for *that*?

"I'm watching you," Miss Bergeron says, and Charley tries not to laugh. Are they in a movie?

The sound of rushing water and the roar of the hair dryer from the bathroom break the tension. Charley says, "If you'll excuse me, I have to get ready for class."

The only reaction to the Zip Zap post that matters to Charley is East's: He might not love that his sex life is trending. But as Charley is walking to the Schoolhouse for English, he calls for her to wait up.

He grabs her hand and kisses her neck, just under her ear. "We dodged a bullet," he whispers.

"I know," Charley says. "I just have to endure the entire school thinking I'm a back-alley whore."

He squeezes her hand. "Nobody actually thinks that."

"Bergeron came to my room threatening to give me an infraction for making a public space private. She has it out for me for some reason."

East pulls Charley close, wrapping his arm around her. The paths of the school are now slushy and Charley's toes freeze in her boots. "Zip Zap has to go," he says. "I'll handle it."

"How are you going to handle it?" Charley asks.

East pulls out his phone and starts texting.

As soon as Audre gets off the phone, she hurries to the admissions office to find Cordelia.

"I just hung up with Big East," she says. "He's sending a computer forensics expert to the school over spring break. A woman named Laurie Hummel. She lives in New York, and she's an IT security consultant to all the Wall Street banks. She's going to put an end to Zip Zap."

"We don't have to be here to welcome Ms. Hummel, I hope?" Cordelia says. She knows that Audre is heading down to New Orleans for break. Honey, meanwhile, has invited Cordelia to go to Naples, Florida, to visit her mother, who has Alzheimer's. Cordelia is so happy to spend time with Honey that she doesn't even mind that much of her vacation will be spent in a memory care facility. But if someone needs to stay behind, Cordelia knows it will have to be her.

"No," Audre says. "Jesse told me it's like having the exterminator come. It's better if nobody is here."

"Wonderful!" Cordelia says. "Let's hope she gets the little rat."

22. Spring Break

Charley, who has never before cared about social media, spends the majority of her spring break scrolling through Instagram and Snapchat.

She starts with posts of the sixth-form trip to Harbour Island in the Bahamas, a long-standing Tiffin tradition. The only sixth-formers Charley knows well are Ravenna Rapsicoli, Annabelle Tuckerman, and Lisa Kim, who have rented a villa called At Ease. (*With those three in residence, the villa should be named Not At Ease,* Charley thinks. *Are they talking about anything other than college admissions?*)

Charley gorges on photo after photo of pastel bungalows with wide front porches, conch shells on windowsills, clear turquoise water, girls riding horseback on a stretch of pale pink sand. In Harbour, everyone drives golf carts; Ravenna posts a video of Teague Baldwin and six of his friends packed into a cart meant for two, cruising the wrong way down a narrow one-way lane. In one of Annabelle's posts, Charley sees the back of a familiar-looking head.

Wait, what?

A little creeping reveals that both Davi and Tilly Benbow are in Harbour crashing the sixth-form trip. *Of course they are,* Charley thinks. It looks like they're staying at some fancy hotel called the Dunmore. Davi posts pictures of her and Tilly eating mango and croissants on the waterfront veranda and of the two of them playing pickleball in matching white skirts and navy visors.

The Academy

Everyone from Tiffin gathers for happy hour at a place called Valentines, where there's a DJ; Teague Baldwin is shown shucking off his polo shirt and whipping it in circles over his head. After happy hour, there are cocktail parties hosted by the sixth-form parents. Every single night ends at a club called Daddy D's. These late-night photos are dark and blurry, but Charley gets the gist: Everyone grabs a rando at the end of the night and makes out on the dance floor before heading to the after parties, which mostly seem to take place at the Doll House, the villa where Teague and his football teammates are staying.

Charley keeps herself from feeling jealous and morose by imagining how jealous and morose Olivia H-T must feel. Olivia H-T's Instagram shows pictures of her shopping at the Chanel boutique on Newbury Street with her mother. Willow Levy comments: So wholesome! ♥. Charley wonders if buying a 6,000-dollar bag and a 150-dollar lipstick can be considered wholesome.

When Charley runs out of student content, she stalks the teachers. Ms. Robinson is in New Orleans. There's a picture of her on a balcony with gingerbread trim and window boxes dripping with ivy, another of the line outside Acme Oyster House, and a video of a brass band marching down Chartres Street in the French Quarter.

Mr. Rivera is in New York City. He posts a selfie at an event with the writer Dani Shapiro at the 92nd Street Y, then another selfie taken outside the Frick Collection, then a video of the St. Patrick's Day Parade with the caption Green and drunken hell.

Charley goes hunting through Instagram for Miss Bergeron, but comes up empty. Is there a universe where Miss Bergeron doesn't have an Instagram account? Or maybe she does, and she's blocked Charley? That would be weird.

Finally, Charley stumbles across a little-used account belonging to Mrs. Spooner. Ha! Charley would have guessed that Mrs. Spooner stayed at Tiffin throughout spring break (somehow Charley can't imagine her anywhere except campus). But from the look of things—a stretch of beach crowded with olds, an alligator in the middle of the road—she's somewhere in Florida. The most intriguing photo is of two drinks side by side—a glass of white wine and something rust-colored with maraschino cherries—on a balcony with a setting sun in the background. The caption is one red heart.

Even Mrs. Spooner is having a romantic break, which Charley finds annoying.

All this snooping is meant to serve as a distraction from Charley's longing for East. He flew to LA to see his mother and then his plan was to return to school early to work on the bomb shelter. He was building the main bar; the granite would be delivered during the one week Mr. James left campus to visit his daughter in St. Charles, Missouri.

Charley's former high school, Loch Raven, isn't on spring break, so Charley sees Beatrix only once, when Beatrix asks, "So what's up with Davi?"

Charley rears back. "What do you mean?"

"Her posting," Beatrix says. "It's changed. It's all sponsored stuff. No new organic content."

"I wouldn't know," Charley says. "I don't follow her." Her words are sharp; she doesn't want to talk about Davi.

Charley gets so bored at home—not even reading holds her interest—that she considers going back to Tiffin early. Her mother obviously knows how long Charley's break lasts (she made a snide comment about how the more expensive a school is, the less a student actually has to attend), but Charley thinks she might be able to claim an independent study that needs her attention. When she imagines two or three days alone on campus with East, she slips her hand down into her underwear.

March is Fran Hicks's busiest month of the year. She and Joey leave the house long before Charley gets up and they get home after Charley has made herself dinner and closed her bedroom door. However, one night, Fran makes a reservation for two at Sabatino's in Baltimore's Little Italy, the restaurant she and Charley go to for special occasions.

It feels good to get dressed up and head downtown in Charley's father's Audi instead of one of the garden center vans. It feels good for it to be just the two of them. A part of Charley wants to tell her mother about East, but the other part of her fears that as soon as she claims she's in a relationship, the relationship will end.

At Sabatino's, Fran orders a glass of Chianti and a Coke for Charley. The table next to theirs is just receiving their entrées—bowls of clams with linguine, a chicken parm so big it hangs off the plate. Charley is suddenly ravenous, so she orders the special shrimp to start, then the Florentine steak with a side of gnocchi. Bread is delivered along with a dish of olive oil sprinkled with Parmesan cheese.

Right after Charley and her mother touch their glasses for a toast, Fran says, "I think Joey is having an affair."

"What?" Charley says, leaning in. She thought six months at Tiffin had desensitized her to drama, but she is *shook*. "What makes you say that?"

"He's become very weird about his phone," Fran says. "He's always texting and he changed his passcode." Fran takes a deep drink of wine. "I showed up unannounced at a project he's overseeing and he was off by himself, basically *hiding,* on the phone. He hung up as soon as he saw me, and when I asked him who it was, he said Ant, which I knew was a lie." Fran shrugs. "I assume he's found someone younger."

Well, Charley thinks, *it's unlikely he's found someone older.*

Charley's immediate next thought is that Joey is having an affair with Beatrix. Beatrix didn't bring up Joey during their chat, which was a relief—but now Charley wonders if that was intentional. Oh god.

"You're too good for him, Mom," Charley says. "You're a fully formed adult with a successful business and a home and an awesome daughter." Charley reaches across the table for her mother's hand. "You've given Joey this whole life that he never would have had. I can't believe he'd be stupid enough to cheat on you." Charley can totally believe it. Trash takes itself out.

"I knew it was a risk, obviously, when I married him." Fran sighs. "Part of me wishes I'd just left it as a fling, something to bring me back to life after your father died. I can't believe I *married* him."

Charley is about to say *That makes two of us,* but suddenly her mother is using her white napkin to wipe away tears. "He's probably not cheating. He's pretty obsessed with you."

"He *was,*" Fran says. "Like a puppy dog, always at my heels, always asking me for one more kiss, always trying to get me to stay in bed…"

"Ew," Charley says, waving a hand. Her shrimp arrives but Charley is too grossed out at the moment to eat.

Fran reaches over and helps herself to a shrimp, which drips white wine sauce on the tablecloth. "Your father was a rare breed. Most men can't be trusted. It's not entirely their fault. It's their biology."

Charley would accuse her mother of making sweeping generalizations, but she wonders if this is what Fran needs to believe right now to keep herself sane. Joey is so much younger, maybe he did wake up one morning and realize he was married to a middle-aged woman. Maybe he would like kids of his own. Part of Charley wants to rejoice—if Fran is right, she and Joey will divorce and Charley will be rid of him forever!—but she can't stand to see her mother so upset.

That night, when Charley gets home, she texts Beatrix. Have you seen Joey recently?

No, Beatrix responds. Why, did he ask about me????

Charley exhales. It's not Beatrix.

Simone has no money for a proper vacation and so she goes home to Montreal to stay with her parents, which is fine right up until the day Simone wakes up and finds that both her parents have stayed home from work because they want to talk to her.

"We think you're drinking too much," Simone's father says.

Simone goes to the kitchen for coffee, which in her parents' house means dealing with a candy apple–red De'Longhi espresso machine that they bought the same week Simone left for Tiffin. (*Meet our replacement child!* Simone's mother joked at Christmas.) Simone snaps right back into barista mode, brewing up a double shot with steamed milk; the ritual gives Simone time to process her father's words. They think she's drinking too much? Both of them drink one and sometimes two bottles of wine with dinner — Sancerre, Château Margaux — because they're French Canadian, it's the culture. Naturally, Simone has joined them. Then, some nights she's hit the bars on Crescent, she met some old McGill friends at Gerts, and she had one epic night clubbing at La Voûte, but that was MDMA and a little coke, not alcohol, or not much. (She ended up going home with some corporate attorney named Sharif who lived in Old Montreal.)

She returns to the living room with her cappuccino. "I guess I'm not sure why you say that? I drink the same amount as both of you."

Her mother frowns. "I found four empty *bouteilles de vin* in your room, Simone. As well as all of these…" She empties a reusable grocery bag full of nip bottles onto the table. There are easily three dozen — Jägermeister, Bacardi, Grand Marnier — as well as an empty fifth of Cîroc vodka.

"I'm twenty-four years old," Simone says. "I can do what I want."

"*Oui, mais pas chez nous,*" her mother says.

"We're concerned about you, Simone," her father says.

There are still two days until Simone needs to be back at school, but she flees that afternoon, packing up her RAV4 and stealing a case of wine from her parents' collection. If they want to see a drinking problem, she'll show them a drinking problem.

She pulls onto campus as the sun is descending. All traces of the snowfall are gone, though it might be optimistic to call the weather springlike. Simone relishes the peace and quiet; she'll have the whole campus to herself.

She regards the roller bag, duffel, and case of wine in the back of her car. She'll have to make two trips, which is a drag, but she has nothing but time. She takes her luggage and leaves the wine, checking the Back Lot for Mr. James—but the garage that serves as the "security office" is all closed up.

She enters Classic South using her ID, hoping there isn't some rule against returning early. (How would she explain? *I had to leave home before my parents sent me to rehab?*) The first floor feels cold and foreign without the energy, laughter, and constant babble of *les filles*. But Simone decides to embrace the silence.

A few minutes later, as she's lifting the case of wine out of the back of her car, a black pickup pulls into the lot. *Abort!* Simone thinks. But it's too late; the truck swings into the spot right next to hers. The back of the truck holds a bundle of two-by-fours, a sawhorse, a circular saw. This is someone doing maintenance work, maybe, a random contractor who could give two shits that a teacher at school is carrying a case of wine up to her room. But does Simone need to worry for her personal safety?

The driver gets out, taking a good long time to come around. Should Simone hurry away? Yes—but she can't seem to move. Then she sees that the driver *isn't* some random carpenter. It's East.

"Hey," he says.

"Hi?" Simone says.

East's gaze lands on the wine bottles in the box. "You throwing a party?"

She hates that she's already on the defensive. She hates that East has gotten a tan wherever he's been—*Did he go to Harbour Island with the sixth-form?*—and that he looks even hotter than normal. She hates that she finds him hot normally.

"What are you doing back early?" she asks.

"What are *you* doing back early?"

Her eyes flick toward the stairs that lead to campus. "Is anyone else back? Ms. Robinson? Mr. James?"

"Nope."

"In that case," she says, "want to come to my room for a glass of wine?"

East raises his eyebrows. "I don't think so."

"Oh, that's right," Simone says. "You're with Charley now."

He stands up a little straighter. "That I am."

Simone is crushed by this answer. She expected him to hedge, to say he and Charley were "just talking," to say it wasn't a big deal, possibly even to tell Simone things had cooled off over the break. She wonders if there still might be a little wiggle room. With nineteen-year-old boys, there usually is.

Simone checks out the building materials in the back of his truck. "What's all this?"

East shrugs. "I'm helping Mr. James with a project."

"I thought you said Mr. James wasn't here."

East licks his lips; for one second, he looks nervous. "He's not. That's why I'm helping him."

"Doing what?"

"You sure ask a lot of questions," East says. He presses his key fob to lock his truck, and the electronic chirp reverberates in the empty lot. He says, "I'll see you, Miss Bergeron."

As he's walking away, Simone says, "You know what I think you're doing? I think you're building a little love nest below the dorms."

East turns around and, after the briefest pause, starts back toward her. The expression on his face is psychopath-calm, and for a second Simone wonders if he's going to hurt her. But instead, he takes the case of wine from her and says, "Why don't we have a drink up in *my* room?"

Rhode posts pictures of himself all over New York City in hopes that Lace Ann might see them and decide to reach out. He tells himself that Lace Ann must be growing weary of Miller the finance bro, who is probably hip-deep in his March Madness bracket right now or planning a guys' trip to Augusta for the Masters.

When Rhode's posts don't garner any attention from Lace Ann (or anyone else, really), he considers casually bumping into her near her new storefront on Ludlow, but he fears she'll think he's stalking her — and he's not desperate.

He is, however, broke — so broke he has to cut his trip short. He can't help but bitterly dwell on the two grand he spent on the date with Simone. With that money in hand, he could have stayed at the Warwick, or at least the Belvedere, instead of surfing the couches of old friends who barely concealed their bemusement about where Rhode's life had taken him.

He has just enough money left for a bus ticket to Springfield, an Uber to campus, and a couple days' worth of DoorDash from Moon Palace.

Rhode arrives on campus after dark and, he's not going to lie, walking through the gates and across the deserted campus is spooky. While Rhode was in the city, he met up with his former editor, Oscar, who suggested that Rhode try his hand at writing a boarding school novel, an idea that caused Rhode to rear back in revulsion.

"You mean write YA?" he said.

"No, man, I mean *A Separate Peace,* but bring it into the 2020s. There must be hella drama in your day-to-day that you could mine."

Rhode wasn't sure anything "literary" could be drawn out of reading fifteen ChatGPT papers about *The Crucible* or overhearing the noises Royce Stringfellow made as he jerked off in the bathroom stall. There *was* the whole situation with Zip Zap. Maybe Rhode could exploit that? Would readers care about a high school terrorized by an app? They might... but Rhode would be fired for sure.

It's only now, as Rhode wanders past the darkened Schoolhouse and locked-up Teddy that he realizes there *is* some intrigue here—not only with the students but with the faculty as well. Rhode could write the hell out of a scene about a well-meaning English teacher who tries to impress a hot young colleague with the world's most expensive dinner date only to have said colleague puke her guts up all night.

Ha.

Rhode enters Classic North, but the hall light isn't working. Maybe he should write a horror novel set at Tiffin, because entering the empty dorm in the dark is terrifying.

It's not quite as terrifying as his finances, however—but at least Rhode opted to amortize his salary over twelve months instead of taking it all in nine. It's less money per month, but he won't be completely destitute over the summer. The best thing that happened to Rhode in the city was that he lucked into an unbelievable sublet situation: Some chick named Josephine manages a boutique on Bleecker and will be managing the East Hampton branch of the same boutique all summer. She advertised a one-bedroom on West Fourth for fourteen hundred a month. (The rent is actually twice this, but Josephine needed someone right away to appease her parents. "They really don't want to pay for an empty apartment, so half is fine!") Even so, Rhode will have to take on some tutoring clients, but that will still leave him with plenty of time for writ—

"Whaaa!" Rhode screams. A shadowy figure appears in the hall, then moves into one of the doorways. Part of Rhode wants to run out of the building rather than become the doomed main character in his own unwritten novel. He scrambles for the light on his phone. "Hello?"

There's no response. Is Rhode imagining things? He creeps down the hall, holding his lit phone out like a cross to ward off a vampire. "Hello? It's me, Mr. Rivera."

The figure runs to the other end of the hall. Rhode, in a moment of uncharacteristic courage, drops his bags and takes chase. He sprints after the figure and catches him leaving out the back door. In the moonlight, he sees it's not a him after all, it's a her.

"Simone?" he calls out.

She stumbles in the grass, which gives him time to catch up.

"Oh, hey," Simone says, righting herself. She puts a hand to her chest. She's wearing a soft purple sweater, her braids are collected in a bun, she's wearing eye makeup. She's panting and Rhode sort of wants to laugh, but what the actual hell?

"What are you doing?" he asks.

"Doing?"

"You came back early?" he says.

"Oh yeah, I did. I was home with my parents and it was just...a lot. So, yeah, I came back early."

Her voice is thick and slurred. Is she drunk? Rhode wonders. "What were you doing in North?" he asks.

"Oh, well, I...I was bored and I went for a walk and that's where I ended up. When I heard you, I got scared and I hid. I thought maybe you were Mr. James. I did *not* want to get caught in a dark hallway with that dude." She smiles. "Sorry I ran."

"How did you get into the dorm?" Rhode asks. "Wasn't it locked?"

"It was locked, but my key card worked."

"It *did*?"

"I mean, yeah, how else would I have gotten in?"

Rhode doesn't have an answer to this, but there's no way Simone's key card worked at North. The key cards are *stringently* building-specific, otherwise the kids would be sneaking into the other dorm nonstop. This was also true of the faculty's key cards—to ward off parents' concerns about male faculty members randomly entering their daughters' dorms. The only people with full access to Classic North and South were Audre Robinson, Cordelia Spooner, and Mr. James.

"Let me walk you back to South," he says.

"You don't have to."

"I want to," Rhode says. "I'll help you fend off Mr. James."

As they amble over to Classic South, Rhode wonders if this is his chance. They're all alone on campus.

"Do you want to hang out tomorrow?" he asks. "We can get lunch, or go to the movies?"

"Thanks," Simone says, "but I have a lot of prep work."

When she goes to swipe her key card, Rhode grabs her by the wrist. "Let me try mine," he says. He waves his key card in front of the pad. A red light flashes and emits an angry burping noise. Access denied. "Hmmm, that's interesting. You're *sure* your card worked in North?"

"It did, yes, Rhode," Simone says snippily. She flashes her own key card and gets past the other side of the door, pulling it closed behind her as though Rhode is some kind of predator. She doesn't wave or anything.

It did, yes, Rhode, Rhode mimics as he walks back to Classic North.

When he gets to his room, everything is in order, but he can't help feeling something is amiss. Simone was just out for a *walk,* and ended up in the hall of the boys' *dorm?* Was she checking the rooms for cash, valuables, *contraband?* Did she find someone's hidden flask? Because she was definitely intoxicated.

Rhode decides to do his own walkabout, floor by floor. The dorm has been cleaned over break; each hallway smells like artificial pine.

It's only when Rhode reaches the sixth floor that he sees a light and hears faint strains of a Tame Impala song. He's not sure why he's surprised; deep down, Rhode knew Simone's presence in the building had something to do with Andrew Eastman.

Rhode knocks, thinking, *You are so busted, buddy.*

But when East opens the door, he's as chill as ever; he has a copy of *Demon Copperhead* in one hand. Over East's shoulder, Rhode sees a neatly made bed; the pillow holds the soft indentation of someone who was lying down reading.

The desk and dresser are clear, the trash is empty.

"Hey, Mr. Rivera," East says. "You just get back?"

"I did." Rhode clears his throat. "What are you doing here? Students aren't supposed to return yet."

"Yeah, I know," East says. "I was out in LA with my mom, but it's a long break, so we mutually decided I should come back early."

"Ah, okay...?"

"My mom told the school, I think?" East says. "Or she told my dad and my dad told Ms. Robinson, I'm not sure which. But yeah, I've just been chilling. I have a truck here so I've been hitting KFC pretty hard."

Why does Rhode always feel so off-balance around this kid? Maybe because East reminds Rhode of the guys at Tiffin twenty-some years earlier who intimidated him: Todd Littman, who defined BMOC, and Curt Barker, who mercilessly teased Rhode about being a virgin.

"Have you seen Miss Bergeron?" Rhode asks. "Since you've been back? Was she... *here* tonight?"

A bland, baffled expression crosses East's face. "Miss Bergeron? Nope, haven't seen her."

Rhode holds East's gaze. Is the kid lying? There's no way to tell.

But then, Rhode sees something on the floor over by the foot of East's bed: a wine cork.

"Excuse me," Rhode says, and he nudges past East to pick the cork up. "What is *this*?"

East gives Rhode his seductive half smile. "It's a cork."

"What is a wine cork doing on the floor of your bedroom?" Rhode asks, though he knows. Obviously! Simone was up here drinking wine with East — and maybe more than that. It's no *wonder* Simone lost her floor fellow position at McGill.

"It must have fallen out of my duffel," East says, reclaiming the cork from Rhode. "My mom and I went to Pasjoli in Santa Monica. Have you ever eaten there?"

"No," Rhode says. He's never been to LA, though there was, for a hot minute, talk of adapting *The Prince of Little Twelfth* into a feature film. But that had died on the vine.

"Well, you should," East says. He palms the cork. "Thanks for checking in, Mr. Rivera. If you need me to run you to the market tomorrow for provisions, just let me know."

Rhode thinks, *I will not be distracted by your charming use of the words "market" and "provisions"! I know you're lying to me. I just can't prove it.*

"Thanks," Rhode says. He has no option but to leave.

The instant he gets back to his room, he texts Simone: Guess who else is back early? Andrew Eastman! Hard to believe you didn't bump into him when you were prowling around North. Rhode adds the head-scratching emoji.

Three dots rise, then disappear, which is all the confirmation Rhode needs. Simone's key card didn't work at Classic North. East let her in and they drank wine!

Rhode may not be justified in calling Simone a bitch — if she doesn't like him, she doesn't like him — but he feels just fine calling her a liar.

23. Ivy Day

Honey Vandermeid wakes up with a fuzzy head. She took two Ambien the night before, a completely irresponsible move when she was in charge of eighty girls' welfare (thank god there wasn't a fire drill or some other middle-of-the-night emergency). But history had proven that, above all else, Honey needed a good night's sleep in order to face whatever news was delivered on March 28.

Ivy Day.

Honey allows a moment of nostalgia for the good old days of college admissions, back when schools—the private institutions, at least—notified applicants of decisions by letter on April 15. It was well-known that if you received a thick letter, it was an acceptance; a thin letter meant rejection. When Honey was a student at the Winsor School in Boston, she had gotten into Harvard (where her father was an endowed chair) and Davidson; she had been wait-listed at Brown (her mother's alma mater) and rejected from Cornell, which was Honey's first choice. Due to her burning desire to get away from Boston (and her parents), Honey attended Davidson, where she ended up being very, very happy. She regularly shares her own experience to make a point: The Ivy League isn't always the best answer. Most kids agree with her; the typical Tiffin student prefers to apply to "fun" schools like Tulane, Miami, SMU.

But for Annabelle Tuckerman, it's Princeton or the apocalypse.

Decisions usually arrive at five o'clock, but because the

twenty-eighth falls on a Saturday this year, the release time is eight a.m. EST.

It's now five minutes to seven.

Honey wonders how Annabelle Tuckerman is faring. Did she sleep last night? Honey should have checked in, but that would have been showing blatant favoritism.

The biggest surprise of Honey's year is that Annabelle Tuckerman *has* sort of become Honey's favorite—all thanks to Zip Zap. Annabelle had flat-out fabricated her senior speech, "Three Brushes with Death," then planned to use it as the topic of her college essay. When Zip Zap called this out, Annabelle confessed to Honey: She'd lied. That meant it was back to the drawing board on the essay. Annabelle had so many false starts on her new essay (first, she wrote about her decision to go to boarding school, then about her attachment to her teddy bear, then about her summer service trip to Ecuador) that she missed Princeton's Early Decision deadline. Not applying ED would set Annabelle back even further, Honey knew, though she respected Annabelle's decision to get her essay right.

Only a week before Princeton's regular decision deadline, Annabelle emailed Honey her new essay with the subject line I'm using this one.

The title was "Zip Zapped." The essay told the whole sordid story about how Annabelle had lied in her senior speech and her original college essay—because she wanted to stand out and seem extraordinary—and how she'd gotten busted by Zip Zap, then faced scrutiny and scorn from the entire Tiffin community.

I didn't want anyone at Princeton to find out about this, Annabelle wrote. But then I realized that college admissions officers understand they're admitting human beings who are not only learning, winning, and succeeding, but also failing, losing, and making mistakes. I'm sure most students don't amplify their failures, but I'm doing so because getting caught in this lie is the most significant thing that has ever happened to me. It changed how I viewed who I am, and more importantly how I visualize the person I want to become.

Wow, Honey thought when she finished. It was a gamble for sure; the Ecuador essay, although run-of-the-mill, might be a safer bet. But Annabelle was resolute.

I'm using this one.

Now Honey texts Simone Bergeron: How's Annabelle doing?

Simone answers: Okay, I guess. Why?

Does Simone not realize it's Ivy Day? Honey thinks. She's Canadian, so maybe not.

Simone texts again: I'm actually not doing so great. Do you have time to talk today, or tonight?

Tonight, Honey and Cordelia are supposed to go to the Wooden Duck. It's their standing Ivy Day tradition, though Honey has lost all enthusiasm where Cordelia is concerned. During their time in Florida over spring break, Cordelia was saintly with Honey's mother—but Honey knew that Cord expected emotional reciprocation. *I'll do the heavy lifting with Sarabeth as long as you love me like you used to.* Cordelia wanted hand-holding and cuddling and early morning sex and walks on the beach and cocktails at sunset. Honey went through the motions, trying to ignore her growing ick.

She no longer felt the way she used to about Cordelia. There was no explanation, nothing had happened. Cordelia's ardor had grown and Honey's had diminished. It happened in relationships all the time, every day. Honey felt guilty about it, which turned her off even further.

She texts Simone: I'll find time. Let me see how this morning goes with Annabelle.

Simone texts back: Kk.

Dear god, Honey thinks. She really has no idea what today is. She's either living under a rock... or *very* preoccupied with something else.

Honey is so suffused with anticipation and anxiety (Annabelle's safety school is West Virginia, chosen solely because if Annabelle can't have Princeton, she wants to party her face off) that she swings by the chapel to light a candle. She then stops at the Teddy for a banana-pineapple smoothie. These are delay tactics: Honey doesn't want to be sitting at her desk when the decisions come out.

The year before, Ivy Day was a cause for massive celebration: Honey had eleven kids apply to the Ivies and eight got in. Willow Levy's older brother, Adam, got into Harvard, Yale, Princeton, *and* the Naval Academy (which was where he ended up). Honey needs only a fraction of that success today. Just one kid, one school. Is it too much to ask?

As she waits for her smoothie, the chapel bells chime. *Do not ask for whom the bell tolls,* Honey thinks. *It tolls for thee.* Her heart is beating so fast it probably counts as a medical condition. Her phone buzzes: This is it, then. The answer.

She checks her texts. It's Cordelia, with a row of question marks.

Honey huffs. Doesn't Cord realize she'll text as soon as she hears? While Honey has her phone out, she logs on to TikTok. It's only 8:03, but the first posts are already up. A boy named Michael Josephson from Methacton High School in Fairview Village, Pennsylvania, films himself opening an email from Columbia. Rejected! Honey scrolls: A girl named Lucy Love in Grand Rapids, Michigan, opens an email from Yale. Rejected! Then Lucy opens an email from Dartmouth: Rejected!

What has Honey been telling the sixth-form parents? College admissions get tougher every year.

Honey's smoothie is finally ready. There can be no more stalling; it's off to work she goes.

Honey can see Annabelle through the glass of her office window, hunched over, sobbing.

Shit, Honey thinks. *Shit, shit, shit.* She feels bad for Annabelle, but also for herself. She has never, in all her years at Tiffin, had a student want a school this fervently; she should have done more. She should have called Princeton one more time on Annabelle's behalf, although sometimes, she knows, pestering them too much can lead to a rejection.

When Honey opens the door, Annabelle rushes into Honey's arms. Honey absorbs her sobs and runs a hand down the girl's spine the way she senses a mother would.

"It's okay," Honey says. "Everything is going to be okay." She considers singing "Almost heaven…West Virginia…" but this definitely counts as "too soon."

Annabelle finally lets Honey go and breaks into a smile as tears stream down her face. "I got in," she says. "I don't know how I can ever thank you."

Whaaaa? Honey thinks. *She got* in*?* In the next instant, both Annabelle and Honey are jumping up and down, screaming at the top of their lungs. Honey makes Annabelle show her the email… because frankly, Honey doesn't quite believe it. But there it is: Congratulations, Annabelle Tuckerman! We'd like to offer you a spot in the Princeton University Class of 2030.

It's real, Honey thinks.

When Annabelle leaves Honey's office — she's late for Diff EQs — Honey collapses in her office chair.

She should text Cordelia first. Cord has been at Honey's side through this journey since last spring; nobody will understand what this means to Honey more than her.

But instead, Honey texts Simone: Annabelle got into Princeton! What do you say we go out tonight to celebrate? The Alibi, maybe? Leave around six, back by nine?

Simone texts back a thumbs-up, and Honey beams. Now she just has to figure out how to break her date with Cordelia.

Honey insists that they Uber to the Alibi so they can both have a cocktail or two. "I'm in the mood for ice-cold Veuve Clicquot," Honey says. "Too bad the Alibi doesn't serve champagne."

Simone wants to gag, remembering the two bottles of Pour Deux she demolished by herself when she and Rhode went to the Alibi at the beginning of the school year.

The same grizzled gentleman, Jefferson, is behind the bar when they arrive. He doesn't seem to recognize Simone, but his eyebrows lift when he sees Honey. "Hey, Hon," he says. "What'll it be?"

"Maker's Mark old-fashioned for me, Jeff," she says. "And for my friend...?"

Simone knows she should stick to wine, but what are the chances they have even a decent bottle of chardonnay? "The same."

Jefferson mixes up the cocktails, which come in smudged highball glasses, though Honey doesn't seem to mind. They toast at the same moment the colored Christmas lights over the bar come on.

"Here's to Annabelle," Honey says. "Lordy, what a day. I try not to judge my performance in terms of acceptances and rejections, but today was a definite win."

"Here's to you!" Simone says. She takes a sip of her drink and gasps. It's *strong*.

"*And* to Annabelle's parents, who had a four-hundred-dollar orchid delivered to my office by noon," Honey says. She looks at Simone. "Were the girls celebrating when you left?"

"Annabelle and Ravenna were," Simone says. "I didn't see Lisa."

Right, Honey thinks. *Lisa is probably sulking. She didn't get into Harvard (she applied just for kicks) and she also didn't get into her first choice, Tulane. She did, however, get into the University of Virginia, George Washington, and Emory, which are all prestigious schools—though they might not feel that way on Ivy Day.*

The admissions chat, while endlessly fascinating to Honey, is probably putting Simone to sleep. "So what's up with you? You wanted to talk?"

Simone considers her drink; she wants to slam the rest of it back. "It's about Rhode."

"Rhode?"

"He's obsessed with me," Simone says. "At the beginning of the year, I thought we could be friends." She gazes down the bar. "The two of us came here, actually. We bumped into Chef Haz, thank god, because I got tipsy and if Haz hadn't seen us, I think Rhode might have taken advantage of me."

Honey notes Simone's trembling lip and the discomfort in her eyes. "But I thought... I mean, I *heard* the two of you were dating? Or had gone on a date?"

"One date," Simone says. "I figured I'd humor him, get him off my back." She pours the rest of her drink down her throat; Honey spins her finger in the air and mouths *Another round* to Jefferson.

"So tell me what's going on, exactly," Honey says. She's been the college counselor for eight years, though she was trained as a good old-fashioned guidance counselor, which is the kind of work she wishes she did more of.

Simone has to be so careful. It's risky talking to Honey about Rhode without mentioning East. "He's always been inappropriate," Simone says. "During First Dance he asked if I had a boyfriend. I said no, though now I wish I'd invented one. He then told me in excruciating detail about his breakup from some chick back in New York."

Honey rolls her eyes; she can just picture it.

"Then, at one of the football games, he plunked himself down next to me and spiked my hot cider with whiskey. I didn't notice until I'd taken a sip."

"At a *Tiffin* football game?" Honey says. "On school grounds?" She knows she sounds aghast, though she isn't. Cord occasionally brings a S'well bottle filled with wine to the games. But spiking Simone's drink without her permission is one step away from drugging her!

"He's always texting me, watching my every move, asking where I've been. During Family Weekend, I was a few minutes late to the steak dinner because I took the chapel tour with Mr. James, and Rhode acted like he wanted to give me a missed commitment."

"Come on," Honey says.

"Back in November, I agreed to a date. I vowed to be open-minded. Rhode rented a fancy car, which was thoughtful, but instead of going to the Wooden Duck like we'd agreed..."

At the mention of the Wooden Duck, Honey drinks. Breaking her date with Cordelia had *not* gone well. Honey's excuse was that she needed to spend the evening in the dorms. Cord has no idea that Honey is out tonight and hanging with Simone, though Honey doesn't care if she finds out. They aren't married, they aren't even openly dating. Honey prefers to think of them in the "friends-with-benefits" space. They've never had a conversation about being exclusive... but that's primarily because there was no one else in the Tiffin bubble to consider.

"...he drove me to Vermont!" Simone says. "He borrowed the Wullys' vacation cottage and had Chef Haz drop off a gourmet dinner. Caviar and champagne! Beef Wellington."

"Wow," Honey says.

"I was *so* uncomfortable," Simone says. "We were all by ourselves, across state lines, in the middle of the woods."

"Did he *try* anything?" Honey asks. She finds herself growing angry—and a little jealous—at the thought.

"He kissed me," Simone says. "It made me sick. Literally: I vomited everything up. And that ended the date."

Their drinks are gone. Honey orders one more round, which will have to be their last. They can't return to Classic South completely wrecked.

"So he got the hint?" Honey asks.

"I thought so," Simone says. "During the snow day, we went cross-country skiing together, which was fun. He kept things light. But then he wanted to sit together at dinner and when I told him I was tired and taking food back to my room, he got pissy with me."

"That's crazy!" Honey says. "It's as though he thinks you *owed* him something."

"But the reason I wanted to talk to you," Simone says, "is because of what happened last weekend." She takes a swallow of her new drink, which is—*eeeee!*—even more potent than the first two. "I came back to Tiffin early from break. I was out for a walk, fully believing I was the only person on campus. It was getting dark and all of a sudden I heard footsteps and heavy breathing and I saw someone chasing after me. It was Rhode."

"No!" Honey says. "What was he doing there?"

"Stalking me!" Simone says. "He asked where I'd been, what I was doing, if I wanted to go out with him. He followed me all the way back to Classic South under the guise of 'walking me back.'" Simone's eyes brim with tears. "I wasn't sure what he was capable of. I did not feel safe with him. He's such a...predator."

"That's exactly the word I was about to use," Honey says.

"Later that night, he texted me all of these ugly, accusatory things."

"I hope you saved the texts," Honey says.

"I didn't," Simone says. "I deleted them immediately. I couldn't have his voice lurking on my phone."

In reality, Simone deleted them because of how they implicated her. She was lucky she'd left East's room when she did. They had split a bottle of wine—Simone had four glasses to East's two, or possibly five to his one—but when it became apparent East wasn't going to even kiss her, Simone stormed out, hoping he might change his mind. But he hadn't—and as soon as Simone got down to the first floor, she bumped into Rhode. It was, absolutely, the worst-case scenario: Nothing had happened between her and East, but she had brought alcohol into his room and drank it with him.

"Do you want to talk to someone about this?" Honey asks.

"I'm talking to you," Simone says.

Honey covers Simone's hand with her own. "It's safe with me."

She motions to Jefferson for the check...but instead he shows up with two shots of tequila. "From the gentleman at the end of the bar," he says. "He's picked up your tab as well."

Honey peers down to the end of the bar, afraid she'll see Rhode Rivera himself, or Mr. James, or Jesse Eastman. But the "gentleman" in question is a stocky, bearded guy wearing a flannel over a stained gray T-shirt. Some Alibi regular who wants a couple of new friends. Honey holds her shot glass up to him and says, "Thank you! My kid got into Princeton today!" Then she and Simone throw back the shots and Honey says, "Let's get out of here before he comes over to ask what she got on the SAT."

Maybe it's the safety of the dark back seat of the Uber or maybe it's the mix of bourbon and tequila, but Honey starts blabbing on the way home. She compares the guy at the end of the bar to Rhode: Men can't just do something nice, it's always transactional. They expect a return and that return is access to women's bodies.

"I say 'men,' but it's not just men, it's people." Then, in a roundabout way, she tells Simone about Cordelia. *This person I was in a relationship with feels differently for me than I do for them, which has put me in an awkward spot. I'm not sure how to tell this person to back off without hurting their feelings.*

Simone grabs Honey's forearm. "So you do understand. You

understand exactly." Simone holds Honey's gaze and Honey senses Simone's face moving closer. Of course this is where the night was headed from the very beginning, it's Honey's dream, if she's being honest. Honey closes her eyes as she brings her lips to meet Simone's.

There's a gasp, then a firm hand planted on Honey's chest as Simone pushes her away.

"No," Simone says. Then, a bit softer, "I'm sorry, was I giving that kind of energy? Because I'm not...I don't..."

Oh god, Honey thinks. *What have I done?*

Honey pulls her lipstick out of her clutch. "No need to be sorry," she says. "Simple misunderstanding, is all."

Simone rests her forehead against the cool glass of the car window. When she closes her eyes, her head spins.

April

24. Zip Zapped

"Laurie Hummel is on the phone for you," Cordelia Spooner says, and Audre thinks, *Finally.* Over a week has passed since they returned from spring break, and although there have been no additional Zip Zap posts, Audre hasn't heard from the so-called computer forensics expert that Jesse Eastman hired. Did she even come? Audre asked Jesse in a text. Yes, Jesse responded. Laurie Hummel had been to campus, she was able to download the Tiffin Zip Zap app on her phone, and she got down to business.

Now, Audre hopes they have some answers.

"Good morning, Ms. Hummel," Audre says. "This is Audre Robinson, Head of School."

"Ms. Robinson, hello," Laurie Hummel says. "First, my apologies for taking so long. I spent a few hours at Tiffin, but then I had an emergency call from the Joint Chiefs of Staff and I had to hightail it back to DC. I realized last night that I'd neglected to connect the dots between the app administrator's IP address and the academy's server."

English, please, Audre thinks.

"Were you able to identify the perpetrator?" Audre asks.

"Oh sure, that only took a few minutes," Laurie Hummel says. Audre feels like Ms. Hummel is treating their very serious Zip Zap issue like a dress she forgot to pick up at the dry cleaners.

"And...?"

"Someone was able to upload a Tiffin-specific Zip Zap but limit access to posting. This person then hacked into the academy's Wi-Fi in order to access everything that passes through the server. Think browsing history, emails, texts if they were using Wi-Fi rather than cellular data. That's how the sensitive information was accessed. I uncovered three IP addresses. Two of them appear to be privately owned laptops, but one is a desktop computer on campus."

Audre's morning coffee repeats on her. A desktop computer on campus? What does this mean? Audre has a desktop computer and Cordelia Spooner does too, of course. There's one in the kitchen where Chef Haz does his ordering. There used to be computers in the Teddy for students to use, but now everyone has a laptop—either their own or one discreetly provided by the scholarship fund.

"Which computer on campus?" Audre asks.

"It's located in the Edward Tiffin Student Union," Laurie Hummel says. "In the *'Bred Bulletin* office."

Charley is in the middle of English class when her phone buzzes with a text. This is highly unusual: Everyone Charley knows is in class. She fears it's her mother; something must have happened with Joey. (Charley doesn't know if she should wish for this or not.)

Charley sneaks a peek at her phone while Mr. Rivera's attention is on Taylor's response to last night's reading. The text is from Ravenna Rapsicoli: Call me ASAFP.

Charley rolls her eyes. *Call* Ravenna? Charley doesn't call *anyone*. Also, it's the middle of C-period? Ravenna might have a free period, or she might be skipping. It's the first beautiful spring weather day of the year, the wildflowers in the Pasture are starting to bloom (as proven by Dub Austin, who has sneezed two dozen times since class started). Ravenna is a sixth-former and headed to NYU. Maybe she doesn't care about school anymore, but Charley does.

Charley tries to orient herself in the discussion. Mr. Rivera has finally finished with the old white dudes; he's assigned *Coleman Hill* by Kim Coleman Foote. The book is a brilliant novelization of the author's family history from the Great Migration to the 1980s. The voice and perspective are as fresh and welcome as the weather outside. Charley was so excited to discuss the book that she almost didn't sleep last night. (Yes, she is that weirdo.)

Charley's phone buzzes again. Is Ravenna *drunk*? Why does she keep texting? But then Charley hears other people's phones buzzing as well. In fact, if Charley isn't mistaken, Mr. Rivera's phone is buzzing.

Tilly Benbow, who puts "actually doing the reading" in the same category as attending a JV fencing match (in other words, beneath her), brazenly checks her phone and halts class discussion with a gasp.

"They found out who's behind Zip Zap," she says. Her forehead crinkles. "But wait, I've never heard of these people. Grady Tish and Levi Volpere? Do they even *go* here?"

Now it's Charley's turn to gasp. *Grady and Levi are Zip Zap.*

The instant C-period is over, Charley races to the *'Bred Bulletin* office to meet Ravenna, who's dressed like she's going to a celebrity funeral: black Chanel jacket, black palazzo pants.

"I can't believe it," Ravenna says. "Those two little chew toys terrorized the entire school."

Mrs. Spooner's questionable admissions practices, Charley thinks. *Annabelle Tuckerman's senior speech. Tilly Benbow's sexting, Chef Haz's gambling losses, Royce Stringfellow using ChatGPT, Tiffin's ranking under investigation, Taylor Wilson's obsession with Dub, Miss*

Bergeron's disgrace at McGill, Davi's eating disorder, Charley "going down" on East. Grady and Levi, a couple of nobody third-formers, targeted the most visible people in the school.

"I came in here one afternoon while you were at play practice," Charley says. "The two of them were doing something inappropriate on the computer, I could tell. I thought they were looking at porn." But in retrospect, Charley thinks, it's so clear. Levi told them he was a computer whiz. And Grady told them he learned about some gossip app from his little friend at Brownwell-Mather.

"The irony is, they've just given us the best story of the year." Ravenna sits down at the offending computer and opens a new document. "Has a high school student ever won the Pulitzer?"

Charley tries not to roll her eyes.

That night at dinner in the Paddock—she and East have claimed the Booth as their own—Charley leans in and whispers, "It's a relief, right? That Zip Zap is done?"

East says, "I went to that kid Levi's room."

"What?"

"He was packing up his shit," East says.

Right. Charley heard that Levi got kicked out because he was the one who had actually done the hacking. Grady would merely be Honor Boarded.

"Was it sad?" Charley asks. "Was he crying?"

"*Crying?*" East says. "The whole third-form was lined up to give him fist bumps. The kid is a *legend*. I walked in and asked for his number."

Charley can just imagine the third-form boys parting like the Red Sea to let East through, jaws hanging open.

"Why do you want his number?"

"When I get my business up and running," East says, "I'm going to hire him. That kid's got a set, pulling off that kind of disruption."

"I don't want to think about Levi's 'set,'" Charley says. "Especially not while I'm eating a meatball sub."

"Fair enough," East says, pressing his thigh against hers. "But to your point, yes, I'm relieved. With Zip Zap gone, we can open Priorities." He steals a crouton from Charley's Caesar salad. "Next weekend."

Next weekend, Charley thinks, and she pushes her plate away. She knew East was getting close. He had the granite counters installed over spring break, and the furnishings are apparently sitting in some storage unit in Haydensboro. He hasn't invited her down since break because he wants her to be surprised. This is fine; Miss Bergeron has been double-checking Charley's whereabouts in the evenings anyway.

East plans to have his "source" deliver the furnishings while everyone is in Chapel. His source must be Mr. James. Charley has asked but East won't confirm or deny. The less she knows, the better.

She fears she knows too much as it is. Next weekend, she and East may be the ones packing their bags. But there's no turning back now.

Later, when Charley is lying on her bed, reading *Coleman Hill,* there's a knock at her door. Internally, she groans: She wants to keep reading, she has only thirty pages left, and the only person who ever knocks is Miss Bergeron.

But when Charley opens the door, she finds Davi.

"Hey," Davi says.

Charley would be lying if she said she hasn't been imagining this moment. In Charley's fantasies, she shuts the door in Davi's face.

But in real life, Charley parrots back a "hey." Then she waits.

"Can we talk?" Davi asks.

Over Davi's shoulder, Charley sees Olivia H-T loitering in the hallway. Madison J. and Willow Levy have just returned from their lacrosse game and they're regaling whoever is sitting in the common room with how badly they suck. They lost to Northmeadow 12–1.

Charley doesn't speak, but she opens her door wider so Davi can enter, then closes the door behind her, but not before catching Olivia H-T's eye and flipping her off.

Davi fingers a leaf of the parlor palm. "I've missed your plants."

Charley doesn't respond.

Davi takes a breath. "I'm sorry I thought you betrayed my confidence," she says. "You were the only person who knew about me, and I didn't have another explanation. Now I realize those little turds read my email to Dr. Pringle."

"I told you that," Charley says. "But you wouldn't listen."

"It's just...the timing?" Davi exhales. "I think I needed someone to blame."

"You iced me out for"—Charley pauses as if she doesn't know the exact amount of time—"nearly a month, Davi."

"Please forgive me," Davi says. "I've missed you."

Charley has spent twenty-seven middle-of-the-nights preparing for this. "Friendship isn't something you turn on and off like a faucet," she says. "You can't *pause* it like one of your TikTok videos and then expect it to start back up at the press of a button."

"I know," Davi says.

"You gave me no credit," Charley says. "You were judge and jury, you declared me guilty, you turned everyone on the floor against me." Charley waves a hand. "I don't give a shit about anyone else. Olivia is a sycophantic twat."

Davi's eyebrows knit and Charley reads her mind: She wants to look up *sycophantic* in case it appears on the SAT.

"I care about you," Charley says. "Or I did. Because what I learned about you, Davi, is that you are way more than your persona on social media. You have *edges,* which you try to hide, but that's my favorite part of you. You let me see past the hair mask and lip gloss to your humanity."

Davi now has tears running down her face; this has also taken place in Charley's fantasies.

"But after the way you dropped me, then ridiculed me—I know that was your comment on Zip Zap—I reconsidered my opinion of you." Charley gives a sad laugh. "It was so predictable, what you did, making me the scapegoat. When really, I was the only person at this school who has ever told it to you straight." Charley pauses. "Well, I can't speak for Cinnamon."

Davi wipes at her eyes with the back of her hand; her makeup smudges. Although Charley wants to resist, she hands Davi a tissue.

"I was hurting and I wanted you to hurt too," Davi says. "I should have known you wouldn't tell anyone."

"I didn't tell anyone. Not East. Not *anyone*."

"I know," Davi says. "I'm asking for forgiveness. I want to be friends again. I want to hang out."

Charley, of course, wants this too. "My father once told me the greatest gift you can give someone is a second chance."

Davi's expression brightens with a hope that is so...*childlike,* Charley wants to cringe.

"Will you...?" Davi says.

Charley huffs. "There won't be a third chance, Davi."

"Understood."

"Fine," Charley says. "Now get out so I can finish my book, please." Charley accepts a squeeze from Davi and then shoos her from the room. Olivia H-T is right where she was before, pretending to be scrolling on her phone a few yards down the hall. When she looks up, her expression is one of naked longing. Will Olivia H-T be relegated to Davi's number two again?

Yes, Charley thinks, and she blows Olivia H-T a kiss.

25. Priorities

A week later, Chef Haz hides a case of vodka (Tito's, Cîroc, Grey Goose, Finlandia), a case of gin (Hendrick's, Bombay Sapphire, Tanqueray), a case of bourbon, one of rum, and half a case of Casa Dragones tequila along with specialty liqueurs and mixers in the rock garden adjoining the Back Lot. He paid cash at four different liquor stores on the far side of Springfield, and when he unloads the boxes, he wears gloves. It's well past midnight, but Chef has been assured that the boxes will be gone by the time he returns to prep for breakfast service.

Chef climbs back into the cab of his brand-new truck—a Ford F-350 long bed, whose interior smells like hundred-dollar bills and a bottle of Gentleman Jack that he kept for himself—and he speeds off into the night. He was never here.

East sends out a voice memo: *Sunday morning one a.m. join me for the opening of my new speakeasy, Priorities, one floor below the basement of the dorms. Meet at the cellar steps behind Classic North and South. Dress up. If you mention it to anyone, you will find yourself forever banned and worse. You're receiving this message because I think you're worthy. Don't prove me wrong.*

Saturday morning, Charley watches everyone who received the message: Davi, Dub, Taylor, Hakeem, Madison J., Royce, and

Willow. Do they seem different? In Spanish with Señor Perez, Royce winks at Charley and puts his fist to his chest and Charley thinks, *Oh god*. She warned East that Royce would be the weak link, but East assured her that he'd put a lot of thought into whom to invite. East and Royce take Diff EQs together—and yes, Royce is a meme, but he's also super brainy and will lend the group an intellectual air. Madison J. was also a risk—she's a dorm prefect!—but as they were brushing their teeth Friday night, Madison caught Charley's eye in the mirror and somehow Charley knew she was cool with it.

Davi and Charley are now together all the time, but Davi doesn't mention the message at all. Charley worries that it got lost amid all the chatter from Davi's followers. On Saturday evening, as they're walking back from the Teddy (the weekend's entertainment was an open mic night, populated by third- and fourth-formers, and Ravenna Rapsicoli singing "Don't Cry Out Loud," which she dedicated to Levi), Charley says, "So I'll see you..."

"Later," Davi says.

Charley lies in bed, her heart expanding with hope then shriveling with fear. Will they get caught? East fully believes they won't, and Charley has moments when she allows herself a ride on his sleigh of carefree optimism. But then she snaps back to reality. Of course they'll get caught. You don't operate a speakeasy beneath the dorms and not get caught.

The question is: What will happen when they get caught? If Ms. Robinson expels one person, she'll have to expel them all, and this is where East's guest list comes in. Will Ms. Robinson throw out Davi Banerjee? Royce Stringfellow is at the top of their class, Dub and Hakeem are football stars, Madison J. is a prefect, and Taylor's mother, Kathy Wilson, and Willow's father, Ari Levy, sit on the board of directors. And then, of course, there's East, with his cloak of impunity. The only person on the guest list who doesn't have a personal flotation device is Charley.

Great, she thinks.

At twelve thirty, Charley slides out of bed, zips into her dress (a fringed flapper number), brushes out her hair, and applies makeup by the light of her phone. She cracks open her door; the hallway is silent.

This is her last chance to back out. For an instant, Charley imagines herself as an older person—twenty-seven, thirty-nine, forty-six—watching her sixteen-year-old self. She waits for that person to give her a sign. Is she about to ruin her future?

She doesn't care. She goes.

Half an hour later, Charley is in the midst of a dream. They all are.

Priorities is... glamorous. Sleek. Sexy. The spare, utilitarian bomb shelter has been transformed into a Jazz Age jewel box. The centerpiece of the room is an L-shaped bar, the long end a slab of black galaxy granite with five brass barstools topped with spruce-green velvet cushions. The short end is the wet bar with its hammered copper sink, above which are illuminated shelves lined with bottles. In the foreground are a long leather sofa and three suede cup chairs. Between the sofa and chairs is a curvy, mirrored "reflecting pond" coffee table. The Ice Palace chandelier spangles the room with light; a wireless speaker plays Billie Holiday.

East, wearing navy-blue pants, a crisp white shirt open at the collar, and a Gucci belt that Charley has never seen, greets everyone and offers cocktails. There's a pitcher of ice-cold martinis already prepared (just add olives, olive juice, or onions). Hakeem asks for one, then Royce. Dub requests a beer and East frowns. "No beer, man." That's fine, Dub will have tequila with lime and club soda, known as Ranch Water back in Durango.

Charley and Davi each have a Tom Collins served in a tall, slender glass, garnished with one luscious purplish-black Luxardo cherry. When they touch glasses, Davi says, "I can't believe this is happening and we'll have no proof."

That's the best thing, in Charley's opinion: They all handed their phones over to East, who tucked them behind the bar. There will be no pictures, no videos. But Charley knows, once she's finished her first Tom Collins, that she'll never forget this night.

Taylor, Dub, and Hakeem sit three across on the leather sofa like it's old times. Taylor is drinking a lavender-hued cocktail called the Aviation: It's gin mixed with a liqueur called crème de violette, served in a coupe glass. East is handcrafting all the cocktails himself, and what's even crazier is that he renovated this room all by himself, or nearly. He had some townies help him during school breaks, and his mother is apparently a decorator? Taylor didn't even realize East *had* a mother; the only parent anyone talks about is Jesse Eastman.

Being invited here counts as the coolest thing that has ever happened to Taylor, and that's not just the crème de violette talking. Stepping into the room was like entering an alternate reality. Dub stands up to get another Ranch Water, leaving Taylor with Hakeem.

"You look good, Tay," he says.

She's wearing a long silk skirt with her Vejas because she didn't want to make any noise sneaking out. (It's crazy that the rest of the school is fast asleep on the floors above them. It's not real, except it is.)

"You look good too." Hakeem always looks good, but then Taylor reins herself in. "How's Cassie?"

"Not here," he says.

Hmmm, Taylor thinks. She turns to check on Dub and finds him at the bar talking to Madison J. So Taylor recrosses her legs, turning them toward Hakeem.

Davi has been out at bars, cocktail lounges, proper pubs, and of course nightclubs—she has more experience drinking than everyone here combined—but she has never been anywhere this unexpected and... *rarefied* ("distant from the lives and concerns of ordinary people"). For example, Willow Levy is sitting on Royce Stringfellow's lap in one of the cup chairs, and who had *that* on her bingo card? Davi perches on one of the green velvet barstools, finishing her Tom Collins as she listens to Billy Joel singing "Vienna." She dips her hand into the bowl of red-skinned peanuts and says to East, "I had no idea you were capable of something like this."

He grins. "I know," he says. "Nobody did."

The night ends at promptly two forty-five. East flickers the chandelier, collects glasses, and deposits them all in the sink. He returns their phones and everyone grabs their jackets.

Charley kisses East. "This," she says, "was a triumph."

"What did I tell you, Charles?" he says, goosing her. "Be careful getting back. I'm staying to clean up."

Charley wants to stay with him, she wants to make love on the sofa after everyone's gone, but Davi, Taylor, Madison, and Willow are waiting for her to lead them through the tunnel and back to reality.

Nobody can wait to do it again—and so they all return the next Saturday, and the Saturday after that. There are no slipups, no leaks;

Charley can't quite believe how seamless it is. They leave in darkness, they return in darkness. They've always been given Sunday mornings to sleep in, and because they've each had only two or at most three cocktails, no one is messy and their hangovers are easily cured with one of Chef Haz's Monte Cristo sandwiches.

Charley wonders if they should include more people, maybe a few sixth-formers? Ravenna, with her New Yorker sensibility, would *love* Priorities. And what about Teague Baldwin? "I feel bad that they'll graduate without experiencing the best thing about Tiffin," Charley says.

"No," East says. "We have something that works. The group is tight. As soon as we introduce a new variable, we change the equation, and who knows what will happen." He kisses her. "Trust me, Charles."

Charley knows he's right—and doesn't she love how exclusive it is? Doesn't she love that people like Olivia H-T and Tilly Benbow have no idea what's going on directly below them every Saturday night? Charley and the others have created the beloved trope of every campus novel Charley has ever read: the secret society.

Out of the blue, Charley receives a text from Beatrix. What's *new* at Tiffin these days? U being *good*?

Charley tenses. She hasn't heard from Beatrix since spring break. *What's *new*?* Charley thinks. *Am I being *good*?* Are the timing and phrasing of this eerie, or is Charley hypersensitive?

Charley hearts the text, then responds: Being good. Followed by the angel emoji.

She thinks how shocked Beatrix would be to learn this isn't at all true.

Going to Priorities, Taylor thinks, is kind of like conducting a love affair.

And then, suddenly, Taylor *is* conducting a love affair—with Hakeem.

During the nights at Priorities, they claim seats on the sofa. Dub has taken to chatting with Madison J. or Charley; he likes to get into intellectual debates, it's English class 2.0, but Taylor and Hakeem prefer to leave school behind. In the third week, Hakeem pulls Taylor close and holds her hand. Taylor checks to see if Dub is watching, but who is she kidding? He doesn't care. By the end of the night, Hakeem is whispering, *I want you back.*

The following Monday, Hakeem texts Taylor, asking her to Intervis. Taylor types Fuck yes, then deletes it. If she Intervisses with Hakeem, everyone on his floor will know it and word will get back to Cassie Lee, whose world will come crashing down. Part of Taylor would love to crush Cassie's dreams, but Taylor has just been elected next year's Honor Board chair, and she doesn't need the strike against her integrity. She says, How about God's Basement?

Hakeem sends a thumbs-up.

They meet in God's Basement twice and then, because the weather is nice, they spend one night out by Jewel Pond; when Taylor gets back to her dorm she has sand in her underwear. She still doesn't cede her virginity; she's not ready. Hakeem says he understands, he says he respects her, says he's so happy to have her back. He tells her he loves her.

The fact remains that Taylor loves Dub. But for now, she'll enjoy being the beloved.

As relieved as Audre is to have finally eradicated Zip Zap, she feels terrible about expelling Levi Volpere.

The Academy

"He left you with no choice," Cordelia Spooner says. "Besides, I have it on good authority that St. Albans snapped him right up."

The only good thing about Zip Zap was that it distracted Audre from the mess of the *America Today* inquiry—at least until Audre receives an email in her inbox from Mikayla Ekubo, secretary of ISNEC, entitled "America Today Inquiry."

Audre's breath catches and she quickly checks her phone for news of any bribery charges brought against Jesse Eastman on behalf of Tiffin Academy. Nothing. She opens the email.

Dearest Audre, it says.

Blah blah blah...found no evidence of wrongdoing...blah blah blah...interviewed the editor of the Best Boarding Schools list...informed us that they used a substantially different set of metrics this year and these new, nontraditional criteria led to Tiffin's ranking at number two...

On behalf of ISNEC, I offer you heartfelt congratulations. Tiffin was ranked number two, fair and square.

All best...

Beneath Mikayla's signature is a PS: Maybe we can grab a drink in Oak Bluffs this summer. Call me!

Yes! Audre thinks. *At Nancy's!* But then she stops herself. Mikayla Ekubo and Douglas Worth put Audre through this nonsense based solely on envy and bad faith. They contacted the press, throwing Tiffin's reputation into question. Audre will *not* go for a drink with Mikayla; furthermore, she deserves an apology from Worthless.

Audre wonders if any news outlets will pick up the story that Tiffin achieved its number two ranking legitimately, but she suspects the answer is no. The *absence* of corruption and bribery isn't interesting to anyone.

Audre could—and should—share the email with Jesse Eastman and Cordelia. She will in good time, but right now Audre would like to savor the academy's vindication alone. She decides to go for a stroll. It is, as her grandmother would say, one of god's days, offering the kind of spring weather people write poems about. The Japanese cherry blossom trees outside the chapel are blooming; the path below them is carpeted with brilliant pink petals. The wildflowers in the Pasture are worthy of a Monet painting. Mr. James is out and about on his riding mower, leaving the scent of fresh-cut grass in his wake. Audre heads for the athletic fields, where she spies the girls' lacrosse team running drills. Along the fence, Audre notices Madison J. and Willow Levy, heads together, whispering. Audre is captivated by the tableau. This is what a top-tier boarding school is supposed to look like: a balance of hard work and intimate relationships. Audre strides over to the girls.

When Madison J. sees Audre, her eyes widen. "Hey, Ms. Robinson."

Willow Levy spins around. Her expression can only be described as panicked, but Audre must be misreading things. She and Willow have a good relationship.

"Sorry to interrupt, girls," Audre says. "It's such a glorious day, I wanted to get some air."

Madison J. and Willow stare at her, both of them looking like they're about to lose their lunch.

"Is everything okay, girls?"

Yes, yes, they quickly assure her. "We just didn't expect to see you," Madison J. says.

A whistle blows and Willow reinserts her mouth guard. The girls run off, cradling their sticks.

Audre supposes the incident with Levi — he's the only student to be expelled in recent years — has changed the way students view Audre. They're wary of her now.

Audre strolls past the dorms, which are quiet; everyone is at afternoon activities. She considers doubling back to Jewel Pond, but she wants to see the rock garden near the Back Lot; it's bordered by dogwoods, which must be in full bloom.

And they are! Audre is so dazzled by the snowy white blossoms brightening the homely Back Lot that it takes her a moment to notice Chef Haz and East standing together next to a shiny silver pickup.

The pickup, Audre knows, is Chef Haz's new truck. Cordelia had mentioned it, then wondered aloud if Chef had placed a particularly profitable bet. "A truck like that would be difficult to afford on what he makes."

Suddenly, Audre gets the Feeling. There's nothing outwardly *wrong* with Chef and East talking in the Back Lot. East doesn't have an afternoon activity—he's exempt, yet another rule bent on his behalf—and it's not as though she's caught him huffing glue or running a dice game or tagging the campus with graffiti. Audre marvels for a second at what a good year East has had; there were a few vaping infractions from Mr. Ewanick, but nothing more. Audre is tempted to chalk it up to his relationship with Charley Hicks. Or maybe Andrew Eastman is finally growing up.

But something about Chef and East's conversation seems clandestine. They're standing very close together with their heads bent, the same sort of posture Madison J. and Willow were just affecting. Of course, Haz and East know each other from New York City, the Dewberry Club; they might be closer than Audre realized.

Then, suddenly, Chef looks up and sees Audre. He cups his hands around his mouth and says, "I have a surprise for you at dinner tonight!"

Oooh! Audre thinks, and the Feeling instantly vanishes. Strolling the rock garden will have to wait; it's time for Audre to return to the office. After all, the number two boarding school in the country doesn't run itself.

Hilderbrand and Cunningham

Dinner Service, a Celebration of New Orleans!

Tuesday, April 28

STARTER
Blue crab beignets

SALAD BAR
Tonight's addition: creole deviled eggs

SOUP OF THE DAY
Gumbo

ENTRÉES
Cochon de lait po' boys, shrimp and grits, dirty rice (vegan)

DESSERTS
Praline bread pudding, bananas Foster tarts

May

26. Tiffinpalooza

Olivia H-T's favorite day of the school year is the first Sunday in May: Tiffinpalooza. Everyone gathers in the Pasture to listen to live bands. Food trucks line up outside the Paddock, the artsy kids do face painting, and girls rock festival outfits.

At eight o'clock on Sunday morning (it's a little early for a regular Sunday, but this is Tiffinpalooza), Olivia walks into Davi's room to ask her opinion: Should she go with jean shorts and a baby tee or the more elevated look of a long, sky-blue jersey dress with cutouts?

But Davi's room is pitch-black when Olivia enters. Davi rolls over, saying, "What the fuck?" She pulls down her silk eye mask, sees Olivia, and huffs. "What, Olivia?"

Shit, Olivia thinks. She should have waited. Davi is, once again, obsessed with Charley—she has even started eating with Charley and East in the Booth, despite the dozens of times Davi told Olivia that she thinks East is a burnout and a waste of space—but Olivia is praying she'll gain back some of her social capital today. The headlining band is Liquid Butter; Olivia's cousin Roddick is the front man. Davi and Roddick had a moment a couple of months ago during the school musical, and Olivia hopes Davi is still interested in him. (Even if she isn't, she will be once she sees him perform. Who has ever been able to resist a rock star?) It was at Tiffinpalooza the year before when Davi seemed to consider Olivia relevant for the first time—*He's your cousin? Can you introduce me?*—and Olivia would love similar magic to happen today.

"Sorry," Olivia says. She holds out the outfits. "I just wanted your eyes on these looks."

Davi pulls up her shade a few inches, then sinks back into her pillow. "God, I'm exhausted."

"You are?" Olivia says. Olivia had asked Davi to hang out the night before, but Davi had said she wanted to go to bed early.

"Yeah," Davi says. "I woke up in the middle of the night and studied vocab, then had a hard time falling back to sleep."

Olivia knows Davi is obsessed with vocab and all fifth-formers will take the SAT in a week and a half. But when Olivia's eyes adjust to the dimness of the room, she sees Davi's hot-pink Cinq à Sept slip dress in a puddle on the floor. Olivia blinks. Was Davi trying it on for some reason or did she...sneak out?

Davi waves at her desk. "Would you hand me the Advil, please? I have a headache."

Olivia complies. "Are you hungover?"

"Hungover?" Davi says. She seems even more annoyed now. "Can you come back later?"

"I mean, yeah," Olivia says. She'll go with the jean shorts even though she doesn't love how her thighs look in them, but a long dress feels like too much. "So Roddick and the guys are arriving around one..."

Davi replaces her eye mask. "I don't care about Roddick, Olivia. Can you please go?"

At least the weather is perfect, Olivia H-T thinks as she helps Miss Bergeron carry the common room sofa out onto the grass. The stage is all set up and the first band—students from the local high school in Haydensboro—is warming up. Everyone flows out of the dorms and the Teddy; the smell of barbecue smoke from the food trucks is literally mouthwatering.

Olivia and Tilly stand in line at the Moon Palace food truck because egg rolls and fried rice seem "healthier" than ribs and brisket sandwiches. Not that they're overly concerned with wellness; Tilly has a water bottle filled with vodka and she offers Olivia a swig. "Act natural," she says.

Hooooob! Olivia nearly spits the vodka out, it's so nasty. But one swallow on an empty stomach does the trick. Olivia immediately catches a buzz. She throws back another mouthful, then says to Tilly, "I'm pretty sure Davi was hungover this morning."

"That's funny," Tilly says. "Madison J. got in my face earlier and she reeked of last night's tequila."

"Really?" Olivia says. *"Madison?"* That isn't really possible. Madison J. has just been elected next year's Head Prefect. "Well, Davi's pink silk dress was balled up on her floor. Almost like…she wore it out last night?" Olivia realizes how crazy this sounds. But Davi was tired, and maybe hungover; she was probably lying about studying vocab, and the dress was right next to the bed where she would have taken it off before climbing in.

At that second, Davi, Charley, and East appear, all of them moving in slow motion and wearing dark sunglasses. Charley spreads out her Yale blanket in the grass and the three of them collapse. They're joined by Madison J., and then Taylor, Dub, and Hakeem.

Olivia H-T and Tilly technically have the best seats — on the common room sofa, dead center — but now Olivia feels left out.

Tilly whispers, "You know that East keeps a truck on campus, right? In the Back Lot?"

"Yeah?" Olivia says. There are a lot of rumors about East; she's never been sure which ones are true.

"I wonder if those guys are sneaking out and going to the Alibi," Tilly says.

"What's the Alibi?"

"A dive bar in Haydensboro."

Would Davi wear a silk slip dress to a dive bar? Olivia wonders. Maybe if, like Olivia, she had no idea what the Alibi was.

When Olivia sees Willow Levy step out of the dorms, she waves her arms. Willow can sit with them; three people will be slightly less pathetic than two.

But Willow heads for the food trucks. When she returns, she's holding hands with Royce Stringfellow. Olivia blinks. Is this real? She looks at Tilly, who's swilling from the water bottle. Is Tilly okay with this? Royce has been obsessed with her since third-form.

"I already knew," Tilly says. "Someone told me Charley and East set them up."

Sure enough, Willow and Royce head right over to Charley, East, and the others and they plop down.

Olivia lowers her voice. "How did Charley go from being weird to being the center of everything? Is it just East? She's more relevant than even Davi."

Tilly hands Olivia the water bottle. "She's a freak. But don't worry, I'm getting revenge on her."

Olivia takes a third mouth-puckering swallow of vodka. "Tell me more."

Before Tilly can answer, the band rips into "Teenage Dirtbag" with surprising authority and everyone jumps to their feet. Tiffinpalooza has begun.

Honey is back.

Cordelia isn't sure how or why it happened, but Honey has returned to their relationship with a sweetness that has been missing since school started. It might have to do with all the college decisions coming in. Honey cleared the biggest hurdle: Annabelle Tuckerman got into Princeton—and after that, everyone else fell into place. Now that the Class of 2026 is all set, Honey can relax until September.

Honey spreads out her navy-and-white striped ChappyWrap blanket and pats the spot next to her for Cordelia to sit. They're off to one side, away from everyone else, but they still have a decent view. Simone Bergeron weaves through the crowd in yet another inappropriate outfit—a blue silk cami top and tight orange leather miniskirt. (The dress code is suspended during Tiffinpalooza.) Cordelia hopes Simone doesn't come over to them—and her wish is granted. Simone glances at Honey and Cordelia, then veers in the other direction, leaving Cordelia to bask in Honey's undivided attention.

Every once in a while, Honey will reach for Cordelia's hand—and during the final band's rendition of "Brown Eyed Girl," she pulls Cordelia to her feet and they dance. Is anyone watching?

No: The entire school is dancing in the sun—even Audre, even Chef Haz, even Mr. James! Other schools may have their spring fairs and spring flings, but they can't compare to Tiffinpalooza.

As the band launches into their final song of the day, "Mr. Brightside," Honey whispers in Cordelia's ear, "Should I come to your cottage tonight?"

Cordelia is so overcome with happiness she can barely answer, so she just raises her hands over her head and sings along.

In the week following Tiffinpalooza, Olivia can't shake the idea that Tilly is right: Davi and Charley—and maybe even Madison J.—are sneaking out of school and driving to bars in East's truck. Olivia watches Davi obsessively—more obsessively than usual—and notes the people she pulls for chats. It's not only Charley and Madison J. but Willow and Taylor as well.

Then, a piece of gossip rocks the school: Cassie Lee has broken up with Hakeem.

"What?" Olivia says to Tilly. "Are you sure it wasn't the other way around?"

"I asked the same thing. *She* broke up with *him*. Nobody seems to know why."

Olivia H-T can easily find out. She and Cassie Lee take Visual Foundations together. It's the introductory art requirement, but Olivia hasn't had room in her schedule for it until this year. Taking a class with third- and fourth-formers was initially mortifying, but Olivia quickly bonded with Cassie Lee and her little friends. They are properly deferential to Olivia H-T because she's two grades older and she's tight with Davi.

Or she *was* tight, Olivia supposes one might accurately say now.

Olivia sits next to Cassie. "Girl, spill."

Cassie pulls her perspective study from her portfolio and reaches for a graphite pencil from the bin of supplies in the middle of the table. "I was sick of it," she says.

"Of what?" Olivia says. She regards her own perspective study, which looks like it was drawn by a rambunctious three-year-old with one eye closed. She rummages through the bin for the big eraser.

Cassie gazes at Olivia in disbelief. "You can't tell me you haven't noticed. The fifth-formers have some kind of major secret and Hakeem won't tell me what it is."

Olivia nearly responds: *I'm* in the fifth-form. But Cassie obviously knows this and knows Olivia isn't privy to whatever the secret is. "Are you sure you're not imagining things?"

Cassie starts to shade with the flat edge of her pencil. Her perspective study is damn near perfect. "Don't be daft," she says. *Daft,* Olivia notes, is a word stolen straight from Davi. "There's something going on."

It can only be happening on Saturday night, Olivia thinks. The rest of their week is fully accounted for. On Saturday evenings there's always some kind of activity, and this week it's a badminton tournament in the gym. Olivia suspects this is way beneath Davi, but it turns out Davi is going and so are the other girls on the floor. Fine, Olivia will go as well. Shockingly, Charley asks Olivia to be her partner against a couple of fourth-formers. When Charley and Olivia win the match, Davi jumps out of the bleachers to give them both a high five. Charley and Olivia quickly lose the next match to Teague Baldwin and Benj, the third-form offensive lineman, but Olivia doesn't care. She feels herself drawn back into the fold. After badminton, Olivia goes with Charley and Davi to the Grille for milkshakes; they're both so friendly to her that Olivia gets suspicious. Do they know Olivia is on to them?

They all walk back to Classic South. Miss Bergeron is doing a *Bridgerton* binge in the common room. She's ordered petit fours from a bakery in Haydensboro, and some of the girls are making herbal tea in the microwave.

"Join us!" Miss Bergeron cries out. She's always dialed up on Saturday nights, as though she's trying to compensate for how dull Tiffin is on the weekends.

Olivia is tempted. The petit fours look good, though she's just had a Reese's milkshake. Charley declines—she hates Bergeron, as everyone knows, and she never sets foot in the common room. Davi yawns, or fakes a yawn, and says, "Thanks, but I'm going to sleep."

Olivia doesn't have to answer because she is, as ever, invisible. She goes into her room, closes the door, and begins her vigil.

She lies in bed on her phone. She could easily stay up all night scrolling Instagram and TikTok, even her mother's pathetic

Facebook account. Tonight, this bad habit serves her. The *Bridgerton* binge ends, and Olivia H-T hears Miss Bergeron bidding everyone good night. Olivia pops into the bathroom to execute her skin care routine, which revives her. She then goes back to her room and keeps her door cracked until Bergeron calls out, *"Bonne nuit, mes chéries!"* and, one by one, all the lights go out.

Olivia continues to scroll—fashion, makeup, singing pit bulls—until her eyeballs feel like they're bleeding. She closes them for just one second, then jolts awake. She checks her phone: it's one thirty. *Shit!* she thinks. She eases open her door and peers into the dark, quiet hallway.

When she tiptoes down to Davi's room to press her ear against the door, she hears nothing, but what did she expect? She cracks the door and peers in. Davi has room-darkening shades, but even so, Olivia can tell she's not there. She hits the light on her phone. Davi's covers are pulled back; her Roller Rabbit pajamas are on the floor. The room smells freshly of perfume.

Olivia closes the door, then heads to 111 South: Charley's room. Olivia opens the door with no idea of how she'll explain what she's doing...but she doesn't have to. Charley's bed is empty.

Ditto Taylor. Ditto Willow Levy. Ditto Madison J. Madison J., who is Head Prefect next year, is *gone?*

Olivia H-T opens the door to Tilly Benbow's room, fearing everyone on the floor has been included in the sneak-out except her. Or maybe she's having a waking nightmare where all the other girls on her floor have been abducted? But Tilly is in bed, wearing a silk bonnet to protect her precious blond hair, and snoring like the old man in the children's song.

Olivia returns to her room, her whole body buzzing. How should she handle this? she wonders. She has so many choices.

The Academy

It's during their seventh consecutive Saturday night at Priorities when East chimes a spoon against a glass and makes an announcement: This will be the final gathering of the school year.

The girls all groan, except for Charley, who must have been warned this was coming. "We can squeeze in one more time before Prize Day," Willow says.

"We could," East says, "but we won't." He offers no further explanation, nor does he need to: He's the boss. Dub feels as crushed as the girls but he nods along in agreement. In some sense, it's a relief. They're fucking lucky they haven't been busted. Dub could have lost his scholarship, if he was even allowed to stay. His mother would have killed him.

"We'll resume next year as sixth-formers," East says. "For tonight, let's drink up."

Dub doesn't have to be told twice. He sidles up to the bar for another Ranch Water, his third. Hakeem and Cassie Lee had broken up, and Dub knows this means Hakeem and Taylor will get back together eventually. They're on the sofa now, talking.

Dub downs his third drink, then his fourth, and he's not alone: Everyone else is drinking more — and tonight, East pours with a heavy hand.

Royce hoots and everyone turns to see Hakeem and Taylor making out on the sofa. The other girls check for Dub's reaction, but he's careful not to give one. Hakeem and Taylor together are as inevitable as death.

Dub wonders if East will push back last call. He hears Davi say, "Just thirty more minutes, since it's the last time?" But at two forty-five, the lights of the Ice Palace chandelier flicker, the cue for everyone to finish their drinks.

As usual, East stays behind to clean up, but what's unusual is that Royce leaves with the girls. He and Willow are going to join the Harkness Society tonight.

Dub can sense Hakeem wondering if he too should leave with the girls, but Dub nudges him toward the door of the north tunnel. "It's not worth getting caught, man. You're Ivy League bound this time next year."

"So is Royce," Hakeem says.

"Not if he gets Honor Boarded."

This lands. Hakeem turns on the light of his phone, which illuminates their way down the tunnel. It's been a long time since the two of them have been alone like this. Hakeem must be thinking the same thing because, as they climb the stairs up to the cellar, he says, "Dude, if I ask you a question, will you tell me the fucking truth?"

Dub's gut suddenly turns to liquid; he burps up tequila. "Yeah, bruh, of course."

"Did you fuck Taylor? Because she's telling me she's still a virgin. I just find it hard to believe that the two of you didn't..."

"Nah, man," Dub says. "Taylor and I never even kissed."

Hakeem starts laughing; he punches Dub's shoulder, which throws Dub off-balance and nearly launches him down the stairs. Hakeem reaches out to steady him. "Whoa, bro, sorry, but you're kidding me, right?"

"I didn't kiss her, didn't touch her," Dub says. He pushes open the door at the top of the stairs. "I told you, we're friends."

"Dub, stop..."

"I'm serious, Hakeem."

Hakeem shakes his head. "So you just...what? You really never had a thing for her? Really?"

"Really," Dub says, his voice husky. He's almost drunk enough to say, *It isn't Taylor I have a thing for.*

Sunday, it rains. Simone gets an alert that the boys' baseball game against Brownwell-Mather has been postponed and there's nothing else on the schedule. Simone hears some of the girls leaving for brunch at the Paddock, and although she dreams all week about Chef's eggs Benedict with extra hollandaise poured over her hash browns, the dining hall has become a minefield. She has to avoid not only Rhode, but now Honey Vandermeid as well. Honey, who tried to *kiss* Simone in the back of their Uber several weeks ago, then pretended like it was no big deal, and who has proceeded to freeze Simone out as though *Simone* were the one who did something wrong.

It's so *unfair,* Simone thinks. Rhode behaves badly, Honey behaves badly, and Simone pays the price.

With nothing on her docket all day, Simone is free to go to the weight room and start working on her "summer body," or she can write prompts for her students' final papers. But why waste a rainy Sunday being productive?

She rummages through her stash in the closet. Of the twelve bottles she brought back from her parents' house after spring break, only four remain. Well, three and a half. There's half a bottle of decent burgundy, two bottles of fumé blanc, then the prize: a bottle of Billecart-Salmon champagne. Simone's mother loves "Billie"; she never fails to mention that Madame Billecart and Monsieur Salmon were the first married couple to hyphenate their names. (Is this true? Simone has never bothered to check.)

Simone was planning on saving the Billie for a special occasion, by which she supposes she meant Prize Day, though the end of that day requires Simone to do thorough room-cleaning checks, which cannot be accomplished while shit-faced.

It would be better to drink the Billie on a day when Simone has nothing going on. Like today, for example.

The bottle is room temperature and the Billie deserves a proper chilling. Simone sticks the bottle in the freezer compartment of her mini fridge and sets her timer for three hours, which will bring her to two p.m. *A perfectly respectable time to start drinking,* she thinks.

She's at her desk drafting possible essay prompts — it's much easier to work knowing she has champagne waiting — when there's a tentative knock on her door.

"Come in!" Simone calls out, but no one enters.

When Simone cracks open the door, she finds Olivia Hudezech-Tottingknaffer on the other side, looking very grave indeed. Simone ushers Olivia inside, taking a beat, as usual, to read the quote in red in the center of the papered side of the door: *"I think most of humankind would agree, the hard part of high school is the people."* Simone had been tempted to rip the paper down and start fresh because it's such a negative sentiment. Recently, however, she has found herself in complete agreement with it.

"Come sit," Simone says, indicating the stool at the foot of Simone's bed.

"No, I don't...I just..."

"Olivia," Simone says. "What's up?"

Olivia's facial expression is giving *Someone's dead or dying,* or possibly *Plan B failed and I'm pregnant.* "If I tell you something, it's confidential, right?" Olivia H-T says. "As in, you couldn't even say it was me who told you?"

Simone nods; now, she's intrigued. She reminds herself that Olivia H-T is insecure, which causes her to be overly dramatic, and she's a bit of a pick-me girl besides that. "Everything you tell me stays in this room. If it needs to leave this room to ensure someone's safety, your anonymity is assured." There are, of course, exceptions to this rule, but Simone won't go into all that until she hears what Olivia has to say.

"Some of the girls on the floor—Charley, Davi, Willow, Madison J., and Taylor," she says. "They're sneaking out. Last night, and I think maybe every Saturday, they go somewhere. Maybe to the Alibi? In Andrew Eastman's truck?"

At the mention of East's name, Simone tenses. "I'm sorry?" she says. "What makes you think this?"

Olivia H-T's eyes flick toward the door. Simone says, "It's okay, you're doing the right thing. You can tell me."

Olivia describes entering Davi's room a while ago and seeing the silk dress on the floor. She tells Simone about Davi's headache and then, in the days following, the whispering, the unusual groupings. *They're all in on it,* Olivia says. Five girls from their floor. Olivia started checking their rooms, including last night at one thirty. They were all gone. Olivia couldn't explain it, but Tilly thought they were going somewhere in East's truck. The Alibi in Haydensboro.

The Alibi is a trigger. Simone can't believe that Honey turned out to be every bit the predator that Rhode was. Honey was worse because Simone had trusted her.

"You wouldn't wear a silk dress to the Alibi," Simone says. "Plus, they're all underage."

"Davi has a good fake," Olivia says.

Simone thinks about the bartender, Jefferson. There's no way he'd serve a bunch of high school kids. They aren't going to the Alibi. The Wooden Duck? But that doesn't sound right either. They aren't going off campus. *So then,* Simone wonders, *where are they going?*

Suddenly, she knows.

She gives Olivia a hug. "I'll take things from here," she says. "Thank you for letting me know."

Olivia breathes out against Simone's shoulder. "I'm just worried about their safety," she says.

No, she isn't, Simone thinks. *She's jealous, and bitter that she wasn't included. Like any tattletale, she wants to see them go down.*
And oh, they will.

When Olivia H-T leaves, Simone takes a few intentional breaths.

She tucks her essay prompts away and pulls the Billie from the freezer, wrapping her hands around the base. It's not quite cold enough, but no matter. She quietly pops the cork and pours some in the mug she uses for tea. She needs to think.

27. Impunity

After drinking the entire bottle of Billecart-Salmon on an empty stomach, Simone has two choices: vomit or eat something. A smashburger and fries from the Grille sound good. But when Simone leaves Classic South, she turns left instead of right. She stands at the door of Classic North and waves her arms until some little third-former sees her.

Oh fuck, Simone thinks. It's Grady Tish, accomplice to the Zip Zap mastermind. Simone nearly reams him out — how dare he poke his nose into other people's sensitive business! — but he's such a pipsqueak and besides, he's already faced the Honor Board. Simone notices him ogling her chest and she realizes she's still wearing what are essentially her pajamas — a pair of Lululemon shorts and a threadbare white T-shirt. So yeah, her tits are on full display; she should go back to her room and change, but this feels like too much effort. She's on a mission.

"Thank you," she says. "I'm here to see if Mr. Rivera wants to go to the Grille." She breezes past Grady with authority—she's a teacher—but instead of heading down to Rhode's room, she takes the elevator to the sixth floor.

She pauses outside East's door. The hallway is deserted; all the boys are probably holed up, jerking off. Is that what East is doing? She turns the knob and walks in as though she has every right. She's a teacher.

The room is empty. East's laptop is on the bed open to a paused scene of some war movie and his phone is plugged in on the nightstand. Simone sits at East's desk and flips through his differential equations textbook (it might as well be written in hieroglyphics), and then she notices a key in a brass tray lying among paper clips, pens, and a pair of cufflinks that look like martini glasses.

She tucks the key into the tiny zippered pocket at the back of her shorts at the same time that she hears a slapping noise in the hallway. A second later, East walks into the room wearing just a towel and a pair of rubber slides; his dark hair is wet.

"Whoa!" he says. "What are you doing here?"

"I know about your little hideaway," Simone says. "The room at the end of the tunnel. You've been inviting people there. You've been drinking there."

"Speaking of drinking..." East raises his eyebrows at her. "What have *you* been up to this afternoon?"

As he comes closer to her, she puts a hand on his chest, which is still warm and flushed from the shower. He's so beautiful, it's a crime.

East steps back, picks up his phone, and starts typing. "Miss Bergeron," he says. "I'm going to have to ask you to leave."

She has no intention of leaving until she's gotten what she came for. She came to win.

"I know what you're up to. You fixed up a room down there."

He pushes a button on his phone, then sets it down. When he looks up, he seems newly surprised to see her, but this of course is him acting cool. "We can play this out and see which one of us has more power," he says. "Or you can leave now and I'll forget you were ever here."

"I have more power," Simone says. "I'm a teacher at this school and you're a student. I will go to Ms. Robinson and tell her everything and see that you're expelled."

"You'll tell her what? That we kissed? That we fooled around in your classroom? That you brought a bottle of wine up here to drink with me over spring break?"

"That you sneaked into my room back in the fall!" Simone says. "You're the one who set this whole thing between you and me in motion."

East blinks. "But you let it happen. And, like you said, you're a teacher and I'm a student."

Simone glares at him. If he would just take her in his arms, she would let the whole thing go. But he doesn't. Even drunk, she recognizes the disdain, and the pity, on his face.

"We'll have to see what happens, I guess," Simone says. She backs toward the door, willing him to stop her. Willing him to touch her. Does he not notice her breasts?

He sits on the bed, turning his attention to his computer. "Have a good night."

When Simone steps out into the hallway, she bumps smack into Rhode.

"What are you *doing*?" he hisses. He looks at her, then at East's door. "What happened in there?"

Simone sees Royce Stringfellow's head pop out of a doorway down the hall. Simone is drunk, but not too drunk to get herself off the hook. She takes Rhode by the arm and leads him to the back stairs. "I had a student come to me. The kids are sneaking out, they sneaked out last night. They go down to where the tunnel is, remember? There's a room down there where they drink. I was just confronting East about it. He's the ringleader."

Rhode does his mighty best to look Simone in the eye and not let his gaze drift down to her chest. Five minutes earlier, he was at his laptop registering for tutoring websites when his phone buzzed with a text. Rhode was surprised to see it was from Andrew Eastman. Rhode gave all the boys in the dorm his number, but East had never before used it, which made sense — East was on the sixth floor, Roy Ewanick's domain.

Rhode clicked on the alert: Miss Bergeron appeared in my room uninvited and she won't leave. I think she's drunk.

Simone is in East's room, she won't leave, East thinks she's drunk. Rhode wasn't at all surprised.

Now, in the stairwell (which has a wicked echo), Simone is blathering about a room down where the tunnel is. She fumbles with the back of her shorts and produces a key that she — Rhode can't believe this — *stole* from East's room.

"You can't just steal things from the kids' rooms!" Rhode says (forbidden: page 1 of *The Bridle,* no stealing or "borrowing without permission"). "Besides, that's probably the key to his truck."

"Thisssss," Simone says, "is not a truck key. Surely even a city boy like you realizes that."

She's slurring her words, but before Rhode can figure out what to do — text Audre? Does he want to be that guy? — she drags him down six flights of stairs, then outside into the rain.

They make a run for the door to the cellar and descend the steep flight to the brick barrel-ceilinged tunnel. Rhode had hoped never to return, though now that he's here, he gets a vivid flashback: He saw Simone and East together in this tunnel pulling apart after what must have been a kiss. Rhode was too naïve (and optimistic about his own chances with Simone) to have let himself believe it way back during First Dance.

But he is neither naïve nor optimistic anymore.

Rhode turns on the light of his phone so that Simone doesn't stumble and fall on her face. The hallway ends with, yes, a door. When Simone turns the knob, it's locked. She brandishes the key, and the scene then becomes a comedy of errors—first she puts the key in upside down, then she pulls it out and drops it and neither of them can find it. Rhode panics for a second because now his curiosity is piqued. He spies it almost all the way under the door and he says, "Why don't you let me..." but Simone wants to be the one to open the door. This is her discovery.

Finally, the lock releases with a satisfying *thunk* and they both step in. Rhode fumbles against the wall for a light switch, and when he finds it, a chandelier in the middle of the ceiling throws spangles of light across a... *wow*. It's a room unlike any other at Tiffin. There's a Persian rug, a deep leather sofa and suede chairs, a granite-topped bar. Rhode moves farther into the room. The walls are brick, the floor is glossy hardwood. In the back there's a powder room that looks like it belongs in a magazine: light fixtures with fringed red shades, wallpaper printed with sailor's tattoos, a hatbox toilet.

"This is the coolest place I've ever seen," Rhode says. "East masterminded this?"

"It's a drug den," Simone says. "Or a sex club. At the very least, the kids drink down here."

Rhode sees how she might think this; he would love to settle on the sofa with a bourbon himself. Alongside the copper sink he finds a garnet-red cocktail napkin with the word PRIORITIES printed on it in gold. Beneath the counter is a stainless steel drinks fridge, empty. The illuminated shelves above the sink are bare.

"I'm going to tell Audre," Simone says. "I want to see East get kicked out."

Her words are, of course, fueled by passion. Rhode has read both *Anna Karenina* and *Madame Bovary* multiple times; he knows what a woman undone by her desire sounds like. He won't ask Simone straight up, she'll just lie.

Rhode says, "I'm not going to tell anyone that you're drunk or that you confronted East in his room or that you stole his key, okay?"

Simone moves her lips but the sound she makes is unintelligible.

"But I would advise you to think long and hard about how you explain this place to Audre," Rhode says. "It could backfire on you."

"Backfire how?" Simone waves her arms at the chandelier, the copper sink. "Nobody could forgive this."

"There's no alcohol, there are no empty bottles," Rhode says. "You don't have any proof that East or anyone else was drinking down here."

Simone scoffs. "Isn't it obvious?"

"I just don't want you to get hurt." Rhode swallows. The truth is, he cares about Simone even more now that he can see her cracks. "I don't want to see you get in trouble."

"Why would *I* get in trouble?" Simone asks. Her eyes blaze; she's challenging him. "Go on, say what you think."

Rhode crumples the cocktail napkin and stuffs it in his pocket. "I think Andrew Eastman is untouchable."

Simone glares at him, but then a single tear rolls down her face. "I want to see him fry," she says.

Of course you do, Rhode thinks.

28. Alias

Monday morning in the office is hectic for Cordelia Spooner. There are only a few days before the sixth-form graduates and the rest of the school leaves for the summer, and there's a lot to cram in. Today, the entire senior class is having their picture taken on the beach at Jewel Pond, with everyone wearing a shirt from the college they will be attending. While Audre and Honey are overseeing that cat-herding, Cordelia will answer the phones (the sixth-form parents have lots of questions about dress code for Prize Day) as well as run the final information session and campus tour of the year. She hopes nobody shows up. It's too late for this year's applicants, but there are always those dialed-up parents of *next* year's applicants who want to get a jump on things, and Cordelia isn't in the mood for anyone that Type A.

When, at ten o'clock, there is no one signed up, Cordelia breathes a sigh of relief. She'll pop over to Jewel Pond to see if Audre and Honey need any help. (A mini-crisis arose when the Princeton T-shirt that Annabelle Tuckerman ordered didn't arrive in the mail. Her ever-adoring parents came to the rescue, driving all the way from Westfield, New Jersey, with their own vintage Princeton-wear.)

Just as Cordelia is leaving the Manse, a gentleman jogs up the stairs. He's a middle-aged white guy in horn-rimmed sunglasses with a bushy head of Bob Ross hair, which is so unlikely that Cordelia wonders if it's a wig. Oh, how she'd love to ignore him and pretend like nobody's available, but she can't just let a stranger walk through the Manse.

She smiles at him. Is something about this gentleman familiar? No, she would have remembered that hair. He's dressed in khakis and a linen blazer, straight from suburban Dad central casting. He's not wearing a wedding ring, but he could be divorced. Why on earth is he here alone?

"Can I help you?" she asks.

"I was hoping to attend the information session," he says. "And then I'd like a map so I can take a self-guided tour."

"Are you a"—Cordelia checks behind him, but he seems to be alone—"prospective parent?"

"Not exactly," he says. "I have twin nieces who are in the throes of end-of-the-year activities at their middle school. Band concerts, spring sports banquets. So they sent me to check out the school, then report back to the fam. I'm vetting their list." He pulls a notebook out of the breast pocket of his linen jacket. "I promised I'd take notes, and pictures too, of course."

Well, well, Cordelia thinks. This year it's twin nieces; last year it was triplet nephews. This same gentleman, minus all that hair, attended an information session last spring and then asked for a map so he could do a "self-guided tour," and Cordelia had thought, *Are you crazy? I'm not going to let you prowl around camp.* And so she'd insisted he take a tour with...well, with the only student Cordelia could call on at the last minute, one who also happened to be the best tour guide at Tiffin.

The gentleman seems to suspect he's busted because he takes a step backward. But Cordelia doesn't want to scare him away.

"You're the only one here today," she says. "Come inside and we'll chat."

"I don't need any special treatment," he says. "Just a map and..."

"Follow me," Cordelia says.

"I'm Cordelia Spooner," she says as she leads the gentleman up to Audre's private library and closes the door behind them.

"Philip Jennings," he says, shaking her hand.

Cordelia nearly cries out in delight at the alias; she's watched all six seasons of *The Americans.* She can't remember the alias this same gentleman used last year—was it as obvious as Jim Bond? Cordelia does recall that he was bald and wore glasses with black square frames.

"Please have a seat," she says.

Philip Jennings is gazing out the window toward Jewel Pond. The kids are arranging themselves by height. They're laughing, goofing off; Cordelia hears Honey say, "All the Elon kids stand together."

"That's our sixth-form," Cordelia says. "They're having their class picture taken in their college shirts."

"They're good-looking kids," Philip Jennings notes.

Cordelia looks him dead in the eye; she would like to avoid a conversation about the appearance of Tiffin students. "I know who you are."

Philip Jennings tents his fingertips and releases an exhale. "Ahhh, I thought you might."

"And I have questions."

He laughs. "Why did I choose this wig? Or why did I return myself instead of sending a colleague? The answer to the first is my wife picked it out. The answer to the second is we're understaffed."

"Why did you rank us at number two?" Cordelia asks. "We aren't the second-best boarding school in the country and we know it. We don't have a huge endowment like other schools, we don't have a hockey rink, our dorms are outdated. There's no speech or debate team, our head math teacher is well past retirement age, and we don't have a marching band." Cordelia could go on, but she won't.

"The inquiry brought by ISNEC verified our ranking but it never explained why." Cordelia pauses. "There has to be a reason."

Philip Jennings nods, and briefly closes his eyes. "Younger staffers at the magazine thought criteria for our rankings should be less numbers-focused and more subjective. Feelings-forward, if you will. This past year we prioritized, for lack of a better word, the 'vibe' of a school. Was the school a pressure cooker, or a place of joy? Are the students happy? My impressions of Tiffin..."

Cordelia can guess. Philip Jennings drove through the wrought-iron gates, he saw the wildflowers of the Pasture in full bloom, he heard the bells of the chapel chime the hour. He would have been wowed by the Teddy; it's the finest student union anywhere. He might have sat in on Señor Perez discussing *The Shadow of the Wind* with his AP Spanish students or Mr. Chuy teaching the lyrics of Lennon and McCartney. But she's not sure any of that answers the question.

"...were favorable, of course. But the reason I ranked you at number two was, in large part, because of the eloquence and passion of my tour guide."

"Cinnamon Peters," Cordelia whispers.

"Cinnamon Peters," Philip Jennings says. His somber tone of voice lets Cordelia know that he knows. "I'm sorry for your loss."

Cordelia brings her hands to prayer. "What was it about her?"

"I've done a lot of tours at a lot of boarding schools," Philip Jennings says. "But I have never met anyone who loved a school the way that Cinnamon Peters loved Tiffin."

Cordelia mists up. "Tell me more."

"She took me to all the expected spots—the Schoolhouse, the student union, the library. She explained about the Senior Sofa—and during our visit to the chapel, she pointed out the needlepointed kneelers with their equestrian themes. She told me about senior speeches. And then she asked if I would mind stopping by the music room so she could pick up her guitar." Philip clears his throat. "The music room was empty and she asked if I'd like to hear a song. She played that song 'Home,' I'm not sure if you know it, but she changed the lyrics to *I know I'm not alone, because I've made this place my home.*"

Cordelia is happy to find Philip Jennings has a pleasant singing voice.

"When she finished, I applauded and she said, 'I grew up in Wisconsin but it was only when I came to Tiffin that I found my home.'"

Cordelia wipes away her tears. "So that was it, then? Your interaction with Cinnamon Peters was why we were ranked so high?"

"Well, you also sent eight students to the Ivy League last year, your grounds are fastidiously maintained, I love that you have your own beach — that was new since my previous visit. Your student newspaper still comes out in newsprint; I gave extra points for that, being a journalist myself." Philip pauses. "And at the dining hall, I had a roasted turkey sandwich with green apple slaw on homemade focaccia that might count as the best sandwich I've ever eaten in my life."

"If you'd come on wood-fired pizza Friday," Cordelia says, "you might have ranked us number one."

"I wouldn't go that far," Philip Jennings says. "Old Bennington is hard to beat."

But not impossible! Cordelia thinks.

She and Philip Jennings take a moment side by side at the window as, down below, the Class of 2026 cheeses for the camera.

"Such attractive kids, every single one of them," Philip Jennings says. "It's uncanny."

Cordelia takes Philip by the arm. "Let me walk you out," she says.

After Philip leaves — he wants to do a quick walkaround and hit the Paddock for lunch (obviously) — Cordelia hurries to meet Audre, who is walking from Jewel Pond back to the Manse.

"You're never going to guess what just happened," Cordelia says.

"I'm going to have to guess later," Audre says. "Roy Ewanick just called me."

"*Called* you?" Cordelia says. Roy Ewanick owns the last flip phone in America and barely knows how to use it.

"Yes," Audre says. "He wants to meet with me, pronto."

"Is the impossible happening?" Cordelia says. "Has Roy Ewanick finally decided to retire?"

This is Audre's assumption. Roy Ewanick is the last of the old guard. Doc Bellamy retired last year; he and Roy were great friends. Maybe Roy Ewanick found he was too lonely without Doc and was leaving, despite his vow to teach at Tiffin until the day he died.

Roy is already sitting in Audre's office when she arrives, his flip phone on the desk in front of him. When she enters, he stands. Roy has lovely manners that way, and he always wears a coat and tie when he teaches. Today's jacket is brown tweed, which is a bit at odds with the balmy weather.

"Good morning, Roy," Audre says. "To what do I owe the pleasure?" Mentally, Audre is already in hiring mode. She'll reach out to her friend Tamoy Wilbur, who chairs the math department at Spelman College. *Feel free to send me your best prospects... as long as they don't mind living and working in the middle of nowhere.*

Roy opens his phone and slides it across the desk to Audre. "I check my messages only periodically. This one is from young Eastman, sent yesterday afternoon at quarter past five."

Audre reads the message: Miss Bergeron appeared in my room uninvited and she won't leave. I think she's drunk.

Good lord, Audre thinks. Did Simone Bergeron get drunk on her Sunday (against the rules) and then barge into East's room (allowed only in certain circumstances)? She must have had a reason. She's East's history teacher; maybe he owed her an assignment? Maybe she'd requested it via email but hadn't heard back?

"There's another thing," Roy Ewanick says. "A voice memo."

Yes, Audre sees it, though navigating Roy's phone is like trying to read *Beowulf* in Old English. She clicks on Voicememo1 and hears East and Simone talking. *I have more power,* Audre hears Simone say. *I'm a teacher at this school and you're a student. I will go to Ms. Robinson and tell her everything and see that you're expelled.*

You'll tell her what? That we kissed? That we fooled around in your classroom? That you brought a bottle of wine up here and drank it with me over spring break?

That you sneaked into my room back in the fall! Simone says. *You're the one who set this whole thing between you and me in motion.*

But you let it happen. And, like you said, you're a teacher and I'm a student.

Nooooo, Audre thinks. But yes, undeniably yes. She's embarrassed to meet Roy's eyes.

"Do you mind if I forward this voice memo to my own phone?" Audre asks. "I'll need to have it when I speak to Miss Bergeron."

Roy waves a hand. "Do what you must," he says, then he stands with a chuckle. "I don't envy you your job, Audre. Good luck."

When Simone arrives, she's as put together as she was on the day of her final interview the summer before: pencil skirt, blouse, kitten heels, braids wound into a bun. Lipstick. Audre sighs. *If only she'd been this professional all year long.*

"Simone," Audre says.

"He's lying," Simone says.

Does Audre want to ask Simone who she means by "he" and trap her that way? No, Audre will cut to the chase. She pulls out her phone and plays the voice memo.

Simone drops her face into her hands.

"You had a sexual relationship with Andrew Eastman?" Audre asks.

"We never slept together," Simone says. "Back at First Dance when you sent me to look for Charley, I bumped into him. He kissed me that night."

"I'll state the obvious," Audre says. "You should have pushed him away, then reported him immediately."

"He broke into my room after a home football game," Simone says.

"Did he...threaten you, or touch you against your will?" Audre asks. "Did he *force* you?"

Simone waits a moment before answering, and Audre feels like she's teetering on a tightrope. *Please say no,* she thinks.

"No," Simone says.

"If you found him in your room, you should have reported him." She turns off her phone. "What I hear in this voice memo is enough to dismiss you."

"But it was his fault."

Audre leans over her desk. "Do you hear yourself? You're a teacher at this school, Simone. Andrew is a student. The moment any impropriety transpired, you should have come directly to me." She pauses. "You brought alcohol into his room at spring break?" Audre wants to shout, *What is wrong with you?*

"So this is all my fault? East won't get into any trouble? Oh wait, that's right, he's the son of the board president. That's how things roll around here, right? He gets off scot-free even though he opened a *bar* in the basement of the dorms."

"What?" Audre says. She's back on the tightrope. The involvement between East and Simone can be placed squarely on Simone's shoulders: She is the teacher, she is in the position of power. But... a *bar* in the basement of the dorms?

She recalls her thoughts on Move-In Day when she first laid eyes on East: *Don't do anything this year I can't forgive. Please.*

Simone holds up a key. "I'll show you," she says.

397

Simone leads Audre into a part of the school Audre has never been and only vaguely knew existed—the cellar of the dorms. The cellar is Mr. James's domain; it houses the furnace and hot-water heater, all the excess furniture. What Audre doesn't know is that there's a set of stairs that leads down into an honest-to-god brick tunnel. The tunnel dead-ends at a door, which Simone unlocks. She turns on the light.

"*East* did this?" Audre says, spinning around. The space is magnificent. It's elegant and sophisticated. There's no *way* East could have pulled this off, is there? Audre runs her hand over the granite bar. She pulls open the drawers on either side of the sink: empty. The shelves above the sink are empty as well. She pokes her head into the powder room—gah! That wallpaper! Audre tries to imagine East *wallpapering the bathroom;* it's just not possible. And yet someone did all this. The floors and countertops look brand-new; the copper sink gleams.

"It's a bar," Simone says. "He was running a bar."

"I don't see any sign of alcohol," Audre says. "It would be difficult to accuse him of running a bar without any proof he was drinking down here."

Simone checks the trash can under the sink. Empty. "Olivia H-T came to me yesterday and told me some of the girls on her floor sneaked out on Saturday night."

"Why didn't you report that to me right away?" Audre asks. Then she gets it: Simone went to East's room to confront him herself. So many bad decisions.

"Olivia told me she checked the rooms of several girls and their beds were empty. But I promised her anonymity."

Right, Audre thinks. *Because everyone hates a snitch.*

Suddenly, Audre's eyes catch on something poking out from beneath one of the suede cup chairs. She bends down to pick it up. It's a red swizzle stick with the word PRIORITIES printed in gold.

Priorities, Audre thinks. Cute name. She'll keep this room just as it is, she decides then. It'll be perfect for donor events. She imagines everyone's shocked delight when they learn about the new secret hideaway under the dorms. She'll have to change the locks, of course, and install security cameras in the brick hallway, but that's easily done. Audre chuckles to herself: She can't believe East actually added value to the dorms. If anything, she expected him to burn them down.

When they're back aboveground, Audre turns to Simone. "I'm afraid your dismissal is effective immediately. I'd like you to pack up and leave now, please, while the students are in class."

"So I won't be able to say goodbye to the girls?"

"It's better that you don't," Audre says. "You may write to them once you're gone."

"What about my final grades?"

"We'll handle that. Please don't make this any harder than it already is, Simone."

Simone grabs Audre's forearm, and Audre chastises herself for hiring someone so young. What was she thinking? Well, she was thinking she was just shy of desperate — and, to be fair, Simone had shown so much promise.

"There's something else you need to know," Simone says. "One of the other staff members made an unwanted sexual advance toward me."

Audre's heart plummets. Mr. Rivera, of course. *Arrrgh* — Audre should never have let those two go on that date this past fall. Her judgment was lacking this year. Next year she's going to crack down; she'll revise *The Bridle* over the summer.

"Which staff member?" Audre asks. Maybe it wasn't Rhode but rather Mr. James, which would be even worse.

"Honey Vandermeid," Simone says.

29. Tiffin Talks: The Hard Part of High School

Who needs Zip Zap? we think. At the start of finals week, there's so much drama it's like the school musical all over again.

Miss Bergeron gets fired because she "acted inappropriately" with East. Some rumors have them joining the Harkness Society in Miss Bergeron's classroom—third-former Reed Wheeler swears he saw them through the window but didn't want to snitch. The boys on the sixth floor of North confirm that Miss Bergeron went into East's room while East was fresh out of the shower and wearing only a towel.

She was drunk, Royce Stringfellow says. *I heard her in the stairwell afterward with Mr. Rivera. She was shithouse drunk.*

Royce thinks but does not say, *And she knows about Priorities.* He has been waiting to be called in front of the Honor Board, but that hasn't happened yet.

"Have *you* heard anything?" he asks Willow Levy. Willow is a lot more chill about possible repercussions because her father sits on the board of directors.

"All I've heard is that Charley broke up with East," Willow says. Charley isn't the kind of person to scream or throw things, but Willow can confirm that Charley hasn't left her room except to go to class, and that the only person she'll let in is Davi, but Davi won't spill the tea.

Tilly Benbow told Willow that she saw Olivia H-T coming out of Bergeron's room on Sunday afternoon. "She was convinced you all were sneaking out somewhere," Tilly said. "I think that's why she was talking to Miss Bergeron."

"Of course she told," Willow whispers to Madison J. "East should have included her just so she would keep her fucking mouth shut."

"She's dangerous," Madison J. agrees, but as floor prefect, Madison has to be nice to everybody. As such, she's the only person on the first floor still speaking to Olivia.

Cordelia Spooner is extremely glad that "Philip Jennings" left campus before the school became a green-and-gold dumpster fire. Simone Bergeron was getting with Andrew Eastman! This isn't surprising to Cordelia; she called out the provocative way Simone dressed at First Dance. But did anyone listen?

As if this isn't enough... Andrew Eastman has turned an old bomb shelter below the dorms into a speakeasy called Priorities.

Audre takes Cordelia to the bowels of the dorms to see it, and although Cordelia finds the place utterly jaw-dropping, she's surprised when Audre can't answer basic questions. How long has the room looked like this, and which kids were down here enjoying it?

"I don't know and I don't care," Audre says. "It's ours now." She collapses on the leather sofa, pats the space next to her. "Come sit, I have something else to tell you and I very dearly wish the shelves *were* stocked with whiskey."

Something else? Cordelia thinks.

Oh yes: Honey tried to kiss Simone in the back of an Uber on the night of March 28, Ivy Day. Honey and Simone went to the Alibi and had several drinks apiece, including shots of tequila.

Cordelia tries to keep her face from crumbling. Honey canceled their Ivy Day dinner at the Wooden Duck. What excuse had she given? Cordelia can't remember, but Honey certainly didn't mention going to the Alibi with Simone.

Honey tried to kiss Simone on the way home, but Simone rebuffed her.

"Honey admitted to it," Audre says. "She offered to resign; she told me her mother needs her down in Florida. And since her job for this year is essentially over, she's leaving immediately."

When Cordelia returns to her cottage, Honey is waiting on the doorstep. Her spring tan has all but faded; she's the color of chalk. She rushes to Cordelia, wraps her arms around her. She was *so* drunk, she says. She didn't realize what she was doing.

"It was a poor showing," Honey says. "But the whole thing was over before it began."

"Only because Simone pushed you away," Cordelia says coldly. "If she hadn't..."

"It was just a crush," Honey says. "It wasn't real."

Because Simone's romantic interest lay elsewhere, Cordelia thinks. *With Andrew Eastman!*

"So it's true, you're leaving?" Cordelia asks. She must be in shock because her voice betrays no sadness, no anger, though she realizes she should feel both sad and angry. She *knew* Honey was into Simone, so in some sense her mind has already traveled to this place. Looking back, Cordelia realizes that Honey started to pay Cordelia more attention right after this happened.

It was so calculated.

"I want you to come with me," Honey says. "We can both move to Naples. Start fresh. Or take an early retirement. I'll sell my mother's house..."

Right: Honey's mother, Sarabeth, has plenty of money, enough to keep them both in a lifestyle for the rest of their years. But Cordelia can tell that Honey is asking out of desperation. Once they get to Naples, there will be some new distraction, a cute server at The Claw Bar, or one of the nurses at the memory care facility. Cordelia can never trust Honey again.

Besides, Cordelia belongs at Tiffin. There's a way in which (forgive her hubris), Cordelia Spooner *is* Tiffin.

"I'm not going anywhere," she says.

Charley hands her phone over to Davi. "I don't want it."

"There are a hundred and fourteen texts from East on here," Davi says. "Have you read any of them?"

Only the first one: Please let me explain.

Charley doesn't need East to explain because the second she heard—from Tilly Benbow, naturally—that Miss Bergeron had been fired for getting with East, every inexplicable moment from the past year suddenly made sense. East had never liked Charley at all; he was *using* her. He threw pebbles at her window the night of First Dance because he knew she would be in her room, she was new and naïve and weird as fuck—of course she would be his partner in the speakeasy. She would serve as a shield! When East threw the pebbles at her window the second time, the night of the Northmeadow football game, it was so he'd have a way into the building. He'd sneaked into Miss Bergeron's room!

Charley remembers with a sick heart the night she first blew out her hair because she thought East would invite her down to the bomb shelter—but he'd texted to say he was going to see Bergeron for extra help.

That was the night of the Harkness table, Charley is pretty sure.

The only reason she isn't vomiting into her trash can is because Davi is with her, and if Davi can keep her food down, so can Charley.

Charley thinks about how Miss Bergeron's contempt for her started to show. The bullshit room check! Bergeron wanted to bust Charley, she wanted Charley to get thrown out so she could have East to herself.

"I lost my virginity to him," Charley says. She always sensed she wasn't enough for East; she suspected there was someone else he was really scheming—a girl from the city, a fashion model or an influencer. But the threat had been right here at Tiffin. Miss Fucking Bergeron. "How can I stay here?"

"You're not leaving school," Davi says. "That's letting him win."

Charley *could* leave school. She could return to Towson and finish her senior year at Loch Raven; Beatrix would be happy to have Charley back. Charley could claim her year at Tiffin as a one-off, like a year abroad, something to expand her horizons; she would easily graduate as valedictorian. If Charley's mother is correct and Joey is having an affair, they might split and Charley and Fran could bond over their broken hearts.

"Men suck!" Charley cries out. This sounds cheap and glib to her own ears. There are decent men: Her father was one. And guys like Dub Austin, whom Charley had gotten to know better during their nights at Priorities. Dub would never keep a secret like this. With Dub, what you see is what you get; Charley values that about him.

"I think you and East should talk," Davi says. Charley's phone buzzes in her hand. "That's number one fifteen. Oh...he says he'll leave school if you want him to. He says he's not coming back next year if you two aren't together."

Charley is tempted to grab her phone back so she can read the words herself. His contrition is gratifying—but she won't be *won over;* she has self-respect. "He'll probably finish school in Montreal," Charley says. "Where he and Bergeron can feed each other all the *poutine* they want."

"That sounds grubby," Davi says. Charley's phone buzzes again. "One sixteen."

"Can you block him, please?" Charley asks. "And block his email."

"At your service," Davi says as her fingers fly over Charley's screen.

"He won't leave," Charley says. "His father is president of the board."

"You're not leaving either," Davi says. "We only have a few days left. This summer, you can come on holiday with me. We'll fix you up with one of Paolo's friends. Someone older, someone mature."

East is older, Charley thinks. *East is mature. East is everything.* Charley will never find anyone who compares, she just won't. And yet, East is a liar. He and Bergeron were together. The horror of this infiltrates everything—Charley takes no solace from her shelves of books or from the healthy green leaves of her plants or from the vision of herself enjoying a cappuccino and *tramezzini* under the Tuscan sun. She's in agony.

Davi's phone buzzes. "Now he's texting *me*." She reads the message. " 'Did Charley block me?' Yes, Sherlock, she did, take a hint. Chasing is Out."

"I have to study for Spanish and math," Charley says. "But I can't go to the Sink. I can't go to the Teddy or the Paddock. I can't leave this room."

"I'll go to the Paddock and get you some soup and focaccia," Davi says. "I can either stay with you and study or leave you be."

"Stay," Charley says. *How do people survive something like this without a friend like Davi?* she wonders.

The departure of both Simone Bergeron and Honey Vandermeid leaves Classic South without a dorm parent. Audre asks the chaplain, Laura Rae, to take over Honey's floors. Audre will fill in for Simone.

Audre isn't sure what she expects—she hasn't set foot in the dorms since Move-In Day—but she finds the first floor calm and quiet. Most of the girls sign out to go to the Sink or the Teddy to study for finals or write papers. Audre checks in with the girls who are staying in the dorms. Is everybody okay? Does anyone want to talk about the recent events?

Nope. If the girls are to be believed, Simone's abrupt departure was like a stone thrown into Jewel Pond—a disruption, a few ripples, stillness.

Then Audre gets to 111 South. *Poor Charley,* she thinks. When Audre taps on the door, Davi answers with a finger to her lips. Charley is asleep.

Audre mouths, *How is she?*

Davi makes a sad puppy dog face and Audre squeezes her forearm to telegraph: *You're a good friend.* Audre hasn't been able to tell Davi yet about Cinnamon's role in Tiffin's ranking, but she will, she'll tell both Davi and Dub. Audre is grateful this class has another year; she can't imagine Tiffin without them.

Before Audre enters Simone's room, she studies the quotes on the papered door. The most visible quote is front and center, written in red ink. From *Demon Copperhead* (a book that has languished on Audre's nightstand since 2022 because who has time to read?): *"I think most of humankind would agree, the hard part of high school is the people."*

But Audre does *not* agree. Just as Laura Rae was called to serve god, so Audre has been called to serve the students of this school. The kids who surround her every day are in the process of creating their personhood. *Despite all the bumps in the road,* Audre thinks, *it's exhilarating to watch.*

The Academy

Audre wakes up in the middle of the night, unsure of where she is. After a moment of complete befuddlement, it comes to her: the first floor of Classic South, Simone's room. She hears a noise...a *plinking*...that seems to be coming from outside. Audre rises from bed; the last few nights of school are when dorm parents must be on high alert. The kids try to sneak out; the year is coming to an end and they want to be together.

Audre lifts the shade and peers out. At the other end of the building she sees a figure throwing pebbles at the window, the source of the noise. Audre knows she should put on her robe and march outside, but she can see now that the figure is East. He's holding a bouquet of white roses. He is, of course, at Charley's window.

Head of School Douglas Worth is infamous for coming down on his kids hardest in the days before graduation (one of the reasons he's so unpopular) — but Audre has resigned herself to the fact that she's stuck with East until he graduates, this time next year.

She'd called him to her office and informed him that she'd visited Priorities — and she'd enjoyed the discomfort this caused him. She then praised his ingenuity and creativity and told him that the room would be off-limits to students but that she might hold exclusive university functions there in the years to come.

This garnered a lopsided smile. "It's a good space, right?"

"You have wonderful taste, Andrew," she responded. "You're lucky I didn't find any contraband."

"Contraband?" he said, as though he had no idea what she was talking about.

Audre pulled the Priorities swizzle stick out of her pencil holder and waved it at the door. "You're excused."

Now, not even twenty-four hours later, she finds East breaking another rule. But who is Audre to stand in the way of a romantic gesture? She keeps watching as the window opens and Charley pokes her head out.

There they are, Audre thinks. *Tiffin's own Romeo and Juliet.*

They have a conversation through the window; they must be whispering, though East's gestures are theatrical; at one point, he falls to one knee in the grass.

Audre silently cheers when East hands the roses through the opening and Charley accepts them, then shuts the window, leaving East to look after her for a moment before retreating back to Classic North.

Audre drops the shade and returns to bed.

Good for him, she thinks. She hopes he gets her back.

I wasn't using you, I was using her...she caught me in the tunnel during First Dance...I didn't know what else to do. I was with her, yes, a couple of times. I needed to put her in a compromised position so she wouldn't turn me in. It ended after first term. Once you and I were together at the Kringle, I never touched her again. During spring break she came to my room with a bottle of wine. I had to keep my leverage because she saw all the building materials in the back of my truck and I thought she was going to figure it out and put an end to Priorities. I didn't touch her then, I swear to you.

Then she showed up Sunday afternoon, she barged into my room and wouldn't leave and I thought enough is enough, so I texted Ewanick and Rivera and I recorded our conversation.

If you don't take me back, I'll leave Tiffin.

You're the best friend I've ever had.

I don't want to be me without you.

I love you, Charles.

I love you too, Charley thinks, but she'll be damned if she says it back.

When he kneels down, Charley hisses, "Get up off the ground, East." A part of her wants to buy what he's selling: He got with Bergeron because he didn't want to lose Priorities. Priorities was his purpose; he felt about it the way Charley felt about books. Maybe she's an idiot, she's only sixteen, what does she know about men? But the truth is, she doesn't want to be her without him either.

She can't make it too easy for him; she knows that much.

"Leave before I go get Ms. Robinson," she says.

"Will you at least take these?" he asks, holding out the roses. Charley imagines him driving to the florist in Haydensboro—the roses are long-stemmed, swaddled in fancy paper, tied with ribbon—and then choosing white roses over the more obvious red.

White, the color of surrender, of apology.

White, the color of hope.

"Fine," she says. She accepts the roses, closes her window, and drops the shade—though a second later, she peeks out to see East still standing there smiling, and it takes all her resolve not to smile back.

In the final days of school, while we're all talking about East and Miss Bergeron, and East and Charley Hicks breaking up, Annabelle Tuckerman has another question: What happened to Ms. Vandermeid?

"She just...vanished," Annabelle says to her roommate, Ravenna Rapsicoli. "When I texted her, she didn't answer, and my email to her bounced. As editor of the paper, isn't it your professional duty to find out what happened?"

Technically, yes. But the truth is, Ravenna heard a crazy rumor that Ms. Vandermeid had been sexually inappropriate with Miss Bergeron. Ravenna doesn't have the heart to share this with

Annabelle. Annabelle was pretty sure that Ms. Vandermeid and Mrs. Spooner were a couple; she was rooting for that, anyway.

"I think we should focus on the future," Ravenna says. "Annabelle, we're *graduating*."

Annabelle tears up. Yes, she's Princeton-bound...however, she can't bear to think about leaving Tiffin.

She's not alone. All 239 of us (240, if we include Levi Volpere at his family home in Annandale) suspect that we'll look back on our time at Tiffin Academy and tell anyone who asks that these were the best days of our lives.

30. Commencement

Prize Day at Tiffin is all about tradition: The sixth-form boys wear navy blazers with green-and-gold rep ties, the girls wear white dresses and carry lilies of the valley picked from the rock garden by the Back Lot. Chaplain Laura Rae and Audre run the proceedings; Jesse Eastman is overseas for work once again, so Willow Levy's father, Ari, helps to hand out the diplomas. For a speaker, Audre has invited Doc Bellamy—who is not only lucid and pithy, but astonishingly brief. *Retirement agrees with him,* Audre thinks, though at the reception after the ceremony, he says, "I've heard you had some personnel shake-ups. Might you need me back?"

Audre erupts in startled laughter. "We're looking for history, Doc, sorry. And a new college counselor."

"I still have connections at Dartmouth," Doc Bellamy says.

Audre pats Doc's arm, then goes in search of another piece of rosemary shortbread and a second cup of strawberry lemonade. Across the room, Audre sees Chef Haz with East; they have their heads bent down as they talk, and then they shake hands. Audre has been puzzling over how East would have procured alcohol for his so-called bar. He probably has a fake ID, and who knows how strict the package stores in Haydensboro or Capulet Falls are. But something about seeing Haz and East together during her spring walk and then again now puts an idea in Audre's head. When exactly did Haz get his new truck? Should Audre dig in here? Do some investigating?

She should not, she decides. She can live without many people, but Chef Haz isn't one of them.

At the Prize Day ceremony, Charley takes a seat as far away from East as possible, but both times she glances over at him, he's staring at her. The ceremony is followed by high tea in a tent outside the Manse. Charley wants to skip it — she has done nothing about packing and her mother is coming to pick her up in the morning — but because Davi is British, she cannot miss a high tea, and she drags Charley along.

While Davi hits the buffet, Charley wanders among the jubilant sixth-formers and their families until she finds Ravenna Rapsicoli. Ravenna's parents are in attendance, along with the brother who goes to Pomfret; Charley hopes that today, at least, is all about Ravenna.

"Congratulations," Charley says. "Thank you for..."

"One hell of a ride?" Ravenna supplies. "You're going to be editor in chief of the *Bulletin* next year. Don't fuck it up."

"I'll try not to," Charley says, though she's far too addled to think about next year. She can barely handle the next sixty minutes.

Ravenna pulls Charley close. "Remember," she whispers. "Orgasms are always In."

Charley finds Davi over by a display of cheddar tartlets. "I have to pack," she says.

"Okay, we can leave," Davi says. "But we have one stop first."

"Where?"

"The Sink."

Charley sighs. Davi must have fines; she likes to keep library books rather than return them. But when they get to the Sink, Davi bypasses the circulation desk and heads up the stairs. A ceremonial goodbye, maybe, to the third-floor bathroom? Davi hasn't purged in more than two months. Although Charley is feeling very sorry for herself, she's proud of her friend.

People are resilient, she thinks. *They heal.*

When Davi reaches the second-floor landing, she turns the corner.

Charley follows cluelessly... and then she gets it. The Senior Sofa.

Turns out, they aren't the only ones with this idea. Dub Austin is sitting on one arm, Madison J. is on the other arm, and between them are Taylor on Hakeem's lap and Willow Levy on Royce Stringfellow's lap. Davi climbs up to sit on the back, and Charley plops down between Royce and Madison. The sofa isn't particularly comfortable and it definitely has a smell, but Charley feels a sense of pride... and of belonging. She's a sixth-former now, and these are her people. She wonders if everyone else is thinking what she's thinking: *This is just like Priorities, except...*

"Hey."

Charley looks up to see East loping toward them. "Is there room for one more?" His dark hair falls in his eyes, but Charley can feel his gaze on her.

"Course, bro," Hakeem says.

East doesn't move. He's waiting for Charley to answer. Everyone else is waiting for her to answer. She feels Davi's hand, featherlight, on her shoulder.

"Oh, *fine*," she says, giving her most convincing eye roll and shifting over a few inches. "You can sit next to me."

Acknowledgments

From Shelby

Thank you to my support system at St. George's: Mrs. Hyson, Mr. Horn, Mr. Franco, Doc Mat, Dr. Dove, Mongan & Nadeau—I owe you all my utmost gratitude. To my roommates and best friends, Emily and Taylor, I wouldn't have made it without you.

At home on Nantucket, thank you to Maxx, Dawson, Alex, and Dad for making me laugh and keeping me humble. To Sasha and Anna Neumeyer, thank you for giving me the best summer job on the island. To my girls, especially Joan, for your loyal companionship, and Ugis, for being the sister I always wished for and the best friend I could ever imagine. Thank you all for making home such a special place to come back to.

Finally, thank you to my mom. Thank you for this opportunity and for your endless support. You are my rock and my inspiration; I would choose you in every lifetime.

From Elin

The world of boarding school was a mystery to me for nearly fifty years, until, in the fall of 2018, I sent my son Dawson Cunningham to Brewster Academy in Wolfeboro, New Hampshire. Three years later, my daughter, Shelby Cunningham, decided to attend St. George's School in Middletown, Rhode Island, and my experience of being a boarding school parent expanded. Dawson and Shelby had different reasons for attending boarding school, and they both

Acknowledgments

had life-altering experiences. But there were always stories (a few more from St. George's than from Brewster, if I'm being honest), and that got my wheels turning. At some point during the middle of Shelby's "fourth-form" (sophomore) year, I asked if we should write a boarding school book together, and she agreed.

To begin, I could never in a million years have written this novel without Shelby. The world of Tiffin was spun out of her lived experience, even though not a single real person or event is represented. Such is the magic of fiction.

Two nonfiction books I read at the beginning of this journey proved enormously helpful. *Privilege: The Making of an Adolescent Elite at St. Paul's School* by Shamus Rahman Khan was one (St. Paul's was the real-life inspiration for the "senior sofa"). The second was *Admissions: A Memoir of Surviving Boarding School* by Kendra James. This memoir was incredibly elucidating about the experience of a person of color at a school that is predominantly white.

The campus novel has long been a favorite genre of mine, and great debts are owed to Curtis Sittenfeld's *Prep* and John Knowles's *A Separate Peace*. Huge props are due to one of my favorite novels, Meg Mitchell Moore's *The Admissions* (I reimagined Angela's obsession with vocabulary for Davi). I also really loved *I Have Some Questions for You* by Rebecca Makkai, and although it's college rather than boarding school, who can overlook the paragon that is Donna Tartt's *The Secret History*?

I'd like to thank the following people in the St. George's community: Cara Hyson, Dr. Sarah Matarese, the great Chris Horn, and Anthony Franco and Kelly Richards for working their magic in the college admissions office. As for my fellow parents, I wouldn't have made it without Sarah Cannova, Jenny Danielson (none of us would have made it without Jenny), Anne Bunn, Kris Connell, and Debbie Winsor. Big love to Taylor and Emily for taking such good care of

Acknowledgments

my girl. Brava to Kaitlin Lawrence for putting on a brilliant production of *Mean Girls* in 2024! Straight to the pages!

Eugene Grimaldi and Holly McGowan were my experts on all things Montreal and McGill. *Merci beaucoup!* I had a wonderful chat with Krista Peterson; I know our conversations have just begun as I dig into book two.

Thank you to Maria and Tony Sofia and the staff at the Parker House for giving me the inspiration for God's Basement (IYKYK).

Finally, I have to thank my incredible professional team: my literary agents, Michael Carlisle and David Forrer; my Hollywood agents, Jason Richman and Addison Duffy at UTA; and my entertainment attorney, Christine Cuddy.

At Little, Brown, thank you to Danielle Finnegan, Karen Landry, Sabrina Callahan, Chloe Texier-Rose, Marieska Luzada, Sally Kim, and David Shelly. But most of all, all hail the triumphant return of my five-star incomparable genius of an editor, Reagan Arthur. This is one joyous reunion, indeed.

Back home on Nantucket, thank you to my inner circle—you know who you are. Shout-outs to Tim Ehrenberg; Chuck and Margie; Wendy; Wendy; Debbie; Rebecca; my obsession (and Shelby's), Sasha Wren Neumeyer; the rock that is my sister, Heather Thorpe; my ex-husband, Chip, who continues to keep the wheels from falling off the family bus; and my boys, Maxwell, Dawson, and Alex.

Shelby, let's do it again. I love you.

About the Authors

Elin Hilderbrand is a graduate of the Johns Hopkins University and the University of Iowa Writers' Workshop. *The Academy* is her thirty-first novel and the first cowritten with her daughter, Shelby Cunningham. Hilderbrand is a cohost of the podcast *Books, Beach & Beyond* with @TimTalksBooks creator Tim Ehrenberg. She is raising four young adult children and likes to spend her free time at the beach and on her Peloton. She is a grateful eleven-year breast cancer survivor.

Shelby Cunningham was born and raised on Nantucket Island. She's a 2024 graduate of St. George's School in Middletown, Rhode Island, and is presently a student at the University of Miami in Coral Gables, Florida.

RAISING READERS
Books Build Bright Futures

Thank you for reading this book and for being a reader of books in general. As an author, I am so grateful to share being part of a community of readers with you, and I hope you will join me in passing our love of books on to the next generation of readers.

Did you know that reading for enjoyment is the single biggest predictor of a child's future happiness and success?

More than family circumstances, parents' educational background, or income, reading impacts a child's future academic performance, emotional well-being, communication skills, economic security, ambition, and happiness.

Studies show that kids reading for enjoyment in the US is in rapid decline:

- In 2012, 53% of 9-year-olds read almost every day. Just 10 years later, in 2022, the number had fallen to 39%.
- In 2012, 27% of 13-year-olds read for fun daily. By 2023, that number was just 14%.

Together, we can commit to **Raising Readers** and change this trend. How?

- Read to children in your life daily.
- Model reading as a fun activity.
- Reduce screen time.
- Start a family, school, or community book club.
- Visit bookstores and libraries regularly.
- Listen to audiobooks.
- Read the book before you see the movie.
- Encourage your child to read aloud to a pet or stuffed animal.
- Give books as gifts.
- Donate books to families and communities in need.

Books build bright futures, and **Raising Readers** is our shared responsibility.

For more information, visit **JoinRaisingReaders.com**

Sources: National Endowment for the Arts, National Assessment of Educational Progress, WorldBookDay.org, Nielsen BookData's 2023 "Understanding the Children's Book Consumer"